Bugging Out to Nowhere

Paylie Roberts
paylie_roberts@yahoo.com

**This is a fictional story, any resemblance to the real world is strictly coincidental.

1

Table of Contents

Chapter 1

Getting Out

"Babe, we have to hurry"
"I know, I know" I said. As I responded an eerie feeling came over me, we must not have much time left. It is usually me that announces the encouraging "hurry up" words, but this time it was him, and it was almost a whisper.

If Tom says we have to hurry then we are already too late. This is the person that takes his time with everything, for good reason of course. Rushing into something is never right, you have to consider the idea, consider the pros and cons, decide if the cost is worth it, what hassle it will be to return it, and how many uses can you get out of it. Yep, that's Tom, always thinking, always acting slowly and deliberately, never rushing. But not now. Now he says to hurry. The eerie feeling kept getting worse the more I thought about Tom's words. "Babe, really, we have to move." I snapped out of my dread dreaming state and continued to check the list to see what else we need. Things were moving fast, but not fast enough. We were ahead of the curve of most people, but not far enough for safety nor comfort.

Only a year ago we purchased our 'cabin' out in the middle of nowhere. And by that I mean no where. There is maybe four neighbor's within comfortable walking distance at most. A small town, about 500 people, if that. We wanted nowhere. The more we watched the US economy unfold the more productive we became in our preps. We knew that time would eventually run out. The economy as it was, was just being propped up as it slowly crumbled. Kicking the can down the road, that's all it was. Eventually, you run out of road. We knew this time was coming for years. One would think that three years of prepping was plenty of time, but it was not. I sat there staring at my list that we prepared only the night before, and started thinking back to our first practice run. That did not go over well.

Our first practice run was when we first bought the "cabin." There was nothing there yet, empty house on a few acres with mice and rats, some wasps, a well with broken plumbing, no heat source, no running water. But hey, crude shelter is better than nothing. Right after the purchase we decided to make a practice run. Pretend we only have four hours and pack up and go. Only pack things that are essential, and let's not forget the important stuff. First, some water, then tools, blankets, people food, dog food, dish soap, extra clothes, toiletries, the list went on. We stood there dumbfounded staring at the back of the long bed pick up truck wondering why it seemed so big before. Eight hours of packing and we were finally on the road. Tired, exhausted, not in the mood to drive for 5 hours, but the dogs were excited about the next "park" we were taking them to.

We forgot many things, most were minor, but some not so. Hiking boots, yeah, those are good to have out in the middle of nowhere. A shovel, that would have really been good to take care of restroom stuff. A bucket just does not cut it; you have to have somewhere to dump the bucket. Spare sunglasses would have been good, mine broke half way on the trip. We packed shorts because it was in the middle of summer, but really, long pants would have done us well. We thought pillows were not important, but once there, they would have made all the difference. A vacuum may seem like a comfort thing, but there were so many spiders, cobwebs, and bugs, I wished I had brought one. At least we remembered to bring paper and pen, and we made our long laundry list of essential things, and things nice to have. Over the last year, that list of items was slowly brought up.

Sure, we did fine with out these items, and to some, these may seem like common sense. Come on, who forgets hiking boots? Well, I guess when you are in a hurry with a time limit, you don't think about these things as clearly. Regardless, we managed, but after only 3 days, our toilet bucket was full, we ran out of baby wipes to clean ourselves with. We were running low on drinking water, we were miserable from poor sleep, and we wanted to come home, our city home. One of our dogs did not want to come home - she enjoyed the never ending mouse hunt.

All these thoughts kept circling back as we were packing this time. We have prepped a great deal, but no where near enough. What if we encounter an "unofficial" road block? Or two? What if the roads we chose end up being closed off by the National Guard? What if they see our truck full of stuff and confiscate? Yeah, we did not plan enough. It is impossible to predict what will come, we considered it, talked about it, hypothesized, you name it, we discussed it. But no one can really know what will happen. Sure, there is the history of Rome, and how Rome fell. But America is different - we are a lot more technologically advanced. One can only speculate. So we prepared for everything we could imagine, but it was not enough. We did not prepare for what actually happened. Had we been rich rather than normal working class people, we could have prepared for it all ... maybe.

The major highways are all closed. Road blocks set up everywhere. Something about a terrorist attack, homegrown terrorism or something. Truth be told, we did not pay much attention to the mainstream media, it was all controlled hype and no news as far as we were concerned. Perhaps we should have paid a little attention, to at least see what they were up to. But to prep you have to have money, and to make money you have to work, or do something productive. We thought about running a business, but chose to work for others instead. Slowly, each pay day, we were able to add essentials to the "cabin." Things moved so slowly, but we knew in the back of our minds, if it came down to it, we could survive in the cabin as it was, maybe. Each payday we hoped we would have a little extra cash and time, perhaps that is what got us in trouble. We saw the warning signs, but we hoped for more money, more supplies, more time. We pushed it too far.

"Babe, we... have.... to ... go... NOW." I looked at Tom and realized that he is right, we have to go. "Okay okay, but don't yell at me when we get there and we're missing essential things." His responses are always so simple and pragmatic. "We won't get there in one piece unless we leave now." This was our last chance to get anything we may need, so I tried to buy a little more time "fine, but can we just go over this list one more time?" I was surprised at his response, "no, we are out of time, *get in the truck now.*" I stared at Tom briefly, surprised by his response, he has never before questioned my double checking the list after our first run, and now it does not matter? I looked at his dark hair falling over his face today, saw the unshaved scruff on his face, no time for anything this morning.

I let the dogs jump in first in the back seat, then jumped in the passenger seat. I dug out the maps just in case there are road blocks, and got my seat belt on. Tom jumped in the driver seat and put it in drive before he even adjusted his seat. So unlike him. We had taken too long. We knew we had to get on the road as early as permitted in order to get ahead of the "horde." Tom originally wanted to leave in the middle of the night. But once the curfews had been put in place, the risk of getting shot as criminals by the Guard for violating the curfew and travel restrictions had become too great. I thought back again to our first practice run, how long it took us to pack the basics, and we were not even under pressure really. The things we forgot, the things we would have liked, and now the things in the truck. It is different this time: the cabin has running water, it has a wood stove, the rats and mice are hopefully gone, and there is somewhat of a garden already planted in the ground, I guess we could live off the tomatoes, the chicken eggs, and the goat milk. A significant amount of nonperishable food has been stashed away, extra clothes and blankets already there, tools and firearms, and even a futon to sleep on. So really, we would be fine without anything, at least for a while. At least we prepared that much. There were building supplies too. We kept bringing building supplies so that we could fix up the place once time permitted. We are about to have that time we did not have before. Or at least I hoped so, because there is a lot to be done, and there is a great deal of 2 x 4's, plywood, screws, and nails waiting to be put to their proper use.

A curfew has been called for the city. It starts at 7 pm every weekday, and ends at 7 am in the mornings. Those who work different hours were required to change their schedules, or get special permission. Weekends are only allotted for errand shopping and church, so that means curfew runs from 4 pm until 9 am. Anything outside of that time must be approved by your work, physician, or other special circumstances. Today is a Thursday, the cabin is a five hour straight shot drive, and it is only 7am, we should be fine provided we do not run into any trouble, and there is no curfew enforcement in rural areas. We carefully planned our route previously, but not quite for this. Just in case, we packed our bug out bags. Should we have to walk the rest of the way we would have enough to feed us, provided we stick by creeks or rivers, and assuming our bags do not get confiscated with everything else. If we can just get to the cabin, we should be okay. But getting there is half the battle. We waited too long for. One of the reasons we waited was because there are no jobs in the middle of nowhere, and we needed more money to buy more supplies and equipment. The cabin was close enough that we felt safe provided we kept enough fuel on hand to get there. We had most of it planned out. But we did not plan for martial law.

"Babe, is your gun loaded?" No, it is not loaded. "Oh crap" I said. Why not? I hurriedly reached under the seat and grabbed my gun and the accessory bag. What in the world was I thinking? Why did I not load it? Then I said thinking out loud "Tom, I can't load it until after we're on the road, what if we get searched?" Tom thought about it for a minute. It was good to see him think rather than act, it was a sign of normalcy, something not seen the last few days. "If we get searched we're screwed anyway. Our plan *has* to work. Just load it, we'll have to be real good liars if we get stopped." I reached behind the seat, dumped the speed loader into my Smith & Wesson revolver, and placed it under the seat where it was within easy reach but still could not be seen. I'm sure his 45 was already loaded under his seat. I know Tom preferred I used the semi auto over my revolver, but he also knows that I am more comfortable with the revolver than any other gun. He used to poke fun at me that I am not a real feminist because I have a girly gun. I hardly think my revolver is girly when you shoot .357 through it, but in reality, he was partially right. It seemed anyone we met whose wife/girlfriend did not like guns, had never shot a revolver, but once introduced to the revolver, she was hooked, and that is all she wanted to shoot. That was the case with me as well. I agreed that guns were important, but was not fond of them, that was until I shot my first revolver that felt comfortable in my hands. The minute Tom recognized that I liked a particular gun, he tried to convince his buddy to sell it to us, but no way, his buddy's girlfriend loved that gun too, he was not selling it. We spent the next six months searching for an equal gun, and managed to find one for a cash and carry price at a gun show. We were just starting to prep then, and it was my first major purchase towards the coming bad times. The worst part was that I did not know how I was supposed to carry it around with me during the rest of the gun show, as you had to have it shown at all times, but it seemed that letting it be shown only invited others to inquire if it was for sale. I never had so much attention in my life, too bad it was all for my gun. This same gun was now loaded under my seat. I never envisioned that it would be like this, but then I did not know what I was preparing for.

There was one smaller road out of the city that eventually led to the freeway, but bypassed all the traffic jams that you would normally encounter. Surprisingly, it was not a very used road, probably because it was a two lane highway that had a very worn out yellow line, and the speed limit on that road was 25 mph. But it lead straight to the freeway right as you leave the city. Recently more people had discovered it, mostly the gamblers who knew about the Indian casino right outside the city. We figured this was our best shot at avoiding a road block, but as we approached it, we saw the line of traffic already piling up. Guess we were wrong. We pulled up behind the last car, and stopped, then Tom turned off the engine. No need to run it, we knew these stops take a long time. While waiting, I looked through the map, we had to get on the freeway, but the only way was through one of the road blocks. There was just no other way.

Whenever the truck stops, the dogs get excited, they think it is time to get out and explore a new area. I quickly calmed them down, gave them each a rawhide to chew on, that should keep them busy for a few minutes, at least long enough to think and make a rational decision. I told Tom "I think we have to take this route, if there was going to be a clear road somewhere, this would have been it, but obviously there's a road block on this one too, which means we have no other way to get on the freeway but through a road block." We looked on to the traffic of cars, and knew we had to get through this. The cars themselves were an interesting sight. Most were pick up trucks, full of supplies. You could see the blue barrels for water loaded securely, boxes of supplies that people hoped to take with them. The cars too had supplies, though not as organized. One car in particular a few cars in front of us had a blue water barrel strapped to the roof surrounded by boxes. I'm sure their trunk was full too. People made trailers out of what they could. Many people were towing the back end of a pick up truck, even cars were trying to tow them. Guess if you want to take your stuff, you'll load up what you can. I wondered if these cars had a destination, or if they just wanted out of the city.

Earlier this week the economy and the value of the dollar finally collapsed, and the president made an announcement. He said that no one needs to panic, everything was fine. The bank runs were only temporary and had been resolved. The banks were now closed for a bank holiday as "they" were working out a new currency, and everyone would be able to exchange the new currency with the old "dollar for credit," or so we were told. Those of us familiar with other currency crisis like in Argentina knew this was a lie. The president stated that everyone is to keep going to work, the show must go on. Pretend everything is fine, they will have the currency situation worked out, though I am not so sure who "they" are. In the mean time, everyone gets issued a temporary ID card. This ID card provides an allowance for your purchases. He called it a government credit card. Said that we are to use the credits and debits on this card for actual cash transactions, and that for the time being they will be denominated in dollars, at least until the new currency comes out. They even offered portable private transfer machines for those who purchased items via private party. Kind of like ATM machines, you just need both folks to insert their cards and agree to everything. Though the banks have yet to re-open. Funny thing was, they had these cards ready before things collapsed. My job working for the government as a paper pushing "mole" made me privy to some things that were going on. I was not happy about working for the Federal Government, but it did have its advantages. And in this economy, hey, it was a paycheck. These cards were issued to us as employee ID cards 3 months prior. It was a big deal to get these cards. Had to go through a full background check, finger printing, and face recognition pictures. The ID cards also came with RFID chips that could easily be read by a reader, so they issued some kind of metal backing that your card was stuck against to prevent unapproved reading. We were told that once the process was completed, these would be our employee ID cards, but until then, hold on to our other employee ID. Then when the president made his announcement, he stated that the new government employee ID cards will work with the new credit card system, therefore all government employees already have these cards, everyone else is to get one issued to them.

Little did I know that this was to our advantage, as the lines to get the ID cards were long, and everyone still had to go through the identity check. The National Guard and the Army Reserve had activated all their stand bys as per the President. These were the folks that were protecting us, or so the president said. It just does not make sense though. Forcing us to stay in place is for our protection? What about those traveling for work? On vacation? Those who have two places they reside? I had so many questions as did many others, and none of it made sense. And martial law? In America? A curfew? All of this just did not make sense.

It seemed the line of cars was moving rather slowly, and so many were turned around to come back. Tom and I looked at each other every time a car was turned around. We knew what that meant, they do not get to leave the city. That is our only obstacle right now, getting out. We could do it on foot rather easily, but 300+ miles is hardly realistic even on a bicycle. We are prepared for that if we get turned around, but we really hoped we could drive to the cabin. We probably could make it with out the supplies in the back of the truck, but it sure would make things much easier.

Our 'cabin' is really not, we just called it a cabin. It is really an old mobile home on a few acres, though we do not know how much land for sure, the paperwork was off, and we never bothered to get it surveyed. We had better uses for our money, and only one neighbor actually utilizing their land, so there was no dire need for a survey.

We dreamed and talked about a beautiful home with a river running in the back yard, but finances did not afford us such luxury. We pulled every penny from savings, and bought when the first opportunity arose to own outright. It was not easy, it was two years of searching, driving around, looking at places, and finally we got lucky. The previous owners had died and the place was in probate litigation over which relatives were to get ownership. This apparently took a year and a half, and during that time the place got infested with mice, the pipes burst, and the land became over run with weeds. When we looked at the place, we viewed it as a piece of land with a solar powered well, a septic, a sturdy garage/shop, and the old mobile as a structure to provide crude shelter. We also got lucky when the inspection report came back, the inspector made it sound so bad as to no one will want it. Thanks to that report we were able to negotiate the price down a little more, almost to the price of a brand new luxury car, and then it was done. Paid for in full with cash. It was ours. You should have seen how ecstatic we were when we realized there is a seasonal creek behind the cabin. Sure, no river, but still a natural source of water.

Out in the country, things move very slowly. And when you are out in the middle of nowhere, things move even slower. We were so used to city life that when we called the plumber and he casually said next week, we got worried. But there was nothing to worry about. The plumber did everything in one day, as things were not as bad as we thought. The problem was paying for it. At that point, we had no money, and there was only one paycheck coming in. We had to sell a few items, and with gold and silver sky rocketing in price, we were able to sell some of my jewelry, and some of the sterling silverware that we scored at a yard sale.

Once the plumbing was done, the exterminator was next. The comments we heard from our few neighbor's made us laugh. Out in the country, you don't hire no exterminator, nope, the rodents are just part of the house, you are on their territory. We contemplated the thought and considered using metal storage bins to keep all our food in, but then decided that we are just too spoiled to live with rodents, so the exterminator came out, and it is a good thing they did. The wasps we saw were setting up home in our garden shed, and there were some huge fire ants that made home near the mobile as well. You let things like that get out of control, and you will not survive. The exterminator had to come out on several occasions, especially since I insisted on natural methods. I just did not want any poisons on our property, especially with our dogs around.

Once those two things were done, we were able to slow down and slowly started moving supplies up. The house still needed a great deal of work, but we felt that we were running out of time. We moved our stuff up and stayed there as much as we could. We had to store everything in the garage because the mobile itself needed too much work. The floors in manufactured homes from the 80's are made of particle board. Get them a little wet and they needed to be replaced. We brought up enough plywood for the whole house, but time was not on our side, we managed to get the old particle board floor ripped up, and put plywood down. Then the wood stove adventure begin. First, we had to find the one we wanted. We saved up for it, then bought it. But to deliver to our 'cabin' as we called it, it would be an extra delivery charge, and we were already hurting for money. So we delivered it to our city home, and planned on taking it up with our next load of supplies. Well, if you ever tried to move a wood stove, you immediately would know the size and weight keeps you from doing anything practical with it. If it were not for the fact that we owned an enclosed cargo trailer we would have never been able to get that wood stove to our cabin. We got lucky with the trailer, but it was a lesson learned. But that was not the end of it. In order for a mobile to support a heavy wood stove, you need extra reinforcements underneath. With no money, we could not just hire a contractor to fix it in a day, nope. We had

14

to figure out how to do it ourselves. And with the help of a book, and the internet, a little extra money from working overtime, we managed. It took us a week, but we still managed. Once the floor was reinforced, we spent another week laying tile in that area. Then we finally called a professional to install the stove. We may be able to figure out how to do things, but there are some things you just do not do against your better judgment. We decided that having our place burn down due to improper installation was not a good option. So we saved up and hired a professional.

It was about that same time that we had the wood stove installed that Tom managed to find a job an hour away from our cabin. It was a relatively low wage job compared to what we are used to in the city, but it was a job. It was also a way for us to network with our community besides church, and it was a way to pay for some of the repairs. Tom would drive out to the cabin, work for 3 days, then come back to our city home for the rest of the week. Sometimes he would stay up to do more work, but that depended on how much energy he had left to fix the place. There were times that we could do so little, and everything was a priority. Tom concentrated on working the land, he would work the land, pull sage weeds, and plant perennials. We had such a long way to go, but at least we were somewhere.

"Look, they let a car through." Sure enough, the car with the blue water barrel strapped to the roof went through; our plan just might work. At this point we were still quite a ways in the back of the car line. "What if I just drive in the emergency lane and move through without stopping?" Tom asked. My response was quick "don't you think about it, we are fully outnumbered and we won't make it. Our plan will work, don't worry." Indeed our plan had to work, but it is not a full lie. When you have a separate property that you do not want anyone to know about, you have to come up with excuses of why your husband is gone half the week, or sometimes a couple of weeks at a time. You also have to explain where you go every other weekend. And it is not that we wanted to be liars, it is that we knew that once things turned ugly, people would turn to us for help, and frankly, we just do not have the resources to save the world.

Living in the city also means you have nosy neighbors, coupled with the fact that the economy had been bad for a while and crime was becoming more rampant. I liked to pretend that the neighbor's were just looking out for each other. So when the questions came, I started a story of how my mom was sick, and my hubby was up taking care of her. We found a small town on the map that made sense to use for our story, and we stuck to it. No one ever tried to verify my story, and it became a common understanding that my hubby was gone half the time. He had taken some EMT courses, so he was quite familiar with what to do in medical emergencies. He just seemed like the right person for the job, and him being "unemployed" and all, it made sense that he went up. The nosey neighbor's also know that I work for the government, so my pay is not small (well, it is, but they didn't need to know that). So the story stuck, and that is how we managed to fool everyone. This story then moved to my job as I started requesting more Friday's off. I started to tell the same story to my co-workers as to my neighbor's. The sympathy allowed for many three day and four day weekends. What my bosses thought was a trip to see my sick mother, was really a trip to work on the cabin. Truth be told, I had no idea where my mom was. We did not get along very well and parted our ways back in my early teens. I felt slightly bad for using her as an excuse, but frankly, she used me as an excuse plenty of times when I was a child, so really, I learned this from her. It was probably the most valuable lesson she ever taught me.

With several cars still in front of us, I thought about how I am really a dishonest person for making up such a story, and why I would do that. Working in my government job meant working with many veterans, many of which had come back from the war in South West Asia, including Iraq and Afghanistan. Many of these veterans were confused of why they were there, and even more confused of what was going on with them when they had flashbacks, nightmares, and other symptoms of post traumatic stress disorder. Mental conditions are always frowned upon, so no one really ever talked about it.

16

Except for one of my co-workers in particular. It took me a long time to figure him out, and once I did, I knew I had to be careful. As times had become more difficult, the talk of "preppers" was more rampant, and more open, but not in a positive light. This guy in particular would make remarks how if things went down, he would show up at such and such house with his weapon, and take all they've got. At first I hoped he had been kidding, but as time went by, and the more we worked together, the less I thought he was joking. I finally realized he was dead serious. He had no intentions of prepping himself, none at all, though he knew things were turning ugly. I was glad I never made the mistake of sharing our preparedness plans with him, or anyone at my work for that matter, as he had every intention of taking what he wanted from others. It is people like him that we feared would set up road blocks, or break into our home. We had to get out of this city. And we had to make sure that the wrong people would never know where we are going, and since we did not know who the wrong people were, we just did not tell anyone. It seemed safest that way.

It was now our turn to pull up to the guard. Tom started the truck and started to pull forward. The dogs started barking as the guard came up to our vehicle. Tom put it in park and turned off the truck again. I turned around in the back seat and tried to calm the dogs down, they were not having it. I heard the guard say "Identification please." I handed the guard my government employee card with my free hand and explained over the barking dogs "I'm an approved annual leave, I've been approved for two days, we will be coming back tomorrow."

"Where are you headed?" The guard asked with out hesitation. "To Springfield" I replied confidently. The dogs started to calm down but stayed in a prepared for attack position in the back seat. The guard was fully armed and then some. He had a long rifle hanging on his back, his hand was resting on his pistol, and I am sure he had another gun in a shoulder holster somewhere and maybe even one strapped to his leg.

"What business do you have in Springfield?" the guard asked with a stern voice.

"My sick mother is there, we are just heading there to help her take care of some things, drop off supplies, stay the night so as to not be out past curfew, and then we will return tomorrow" I responded.

The guard then looked at Tom "Your ID please." The guard's eyes never leaving either of us, he was good at what he does, no doubt about that. He is a little older than what you would imagine on the commercials for the National guard, probably early 40's, gray hair showing through the dark hair, though hard to see under the helmet. Very properly groomed, shaved, and his uniform was ironed very nice. His features were soft, but he was acting extremely stern, he understood that his expression could be misleading, and made up for it with the tone of his voice.

Tom got out his driver's license and quickly explained "I had an appointment tomorrow for my new government ID, but then her leave got approved and felt we need to get this supply run done for her mom while we can. So I was able to reschedule my ID appointment for next Tuesday." The guard looked him over very carefully, then looked at me. The dogs were down to a soft warning growl in the back seat of the truck, but they had mostly calmed down.

"And your work sir?" asked the guard.

"I am unfortunately unemployed, have been for a couple years, so I do not have any unemployment papers, I'm sorry." Tom said with a saddened tone.

"Tough economy I know. But do you have any proof that you are unemployed. We have strict orders to not allow anyone through if they will be missing work without prior approval. Maybe last year's taxes or something?" the guard suggested.

"No sir, I didn't think to bring our tax paperwork, we can turn around and go get it if that will help." Little did he know that my husband was employed, just "under the radar," and not in the city, but an hour from the cabin. He has been working under the table for the last several months to avoid providing financial support to this corrupt system bent on self destruction. I called it being "on strike," but he preferred to say he was "shrugging" or "gone Galt." That is how the low wage was worth it, it was tax free, and as I said earlier, a great way to network with the small town.

The guard looked at me and stated "I have to call your work to verify, do you have the number?"

"Yes, here it is, I figured you would need it." I handed him a business card that had my supervisor's number on it. At this point I felt a little momentary relief in my surging stress level. I was indeed on approved annual leave, and my work was fully aware of my "sick mother" situation, along with my husband's unemployment status. If he calls, my story checks out. Our plan seemed to be working so far.

He called in some codes on the radio and waved to some other guards as he walked into their office that was really one of those metal storage containers painted green with a window. I wondered if it had a toilet or if there was a port-a-potty somewhere that we could not see. The other guards approached closer but did not draw their weapons, though their hands were all rested and ready. I counted five, though I would not be surprised if there were more. Their uniforms caught my attention, so prim and proper, so neatly pressed, all the ribbons properly displayed, so proud to be an American defending our country, but where they?

It felt like hours. What if they decided to search the truck? What if they found our weapons? We would be detained for sure. I forced myself to calm down and focus on the task at hand. Can not let my anxiety show, or they might get suspicious that something more was going on. I looked in the passenger side view mirror and saw the long line of traffic behind us, it went on forever, it is a good thing we left when we did, or we would be much further back than where we originally started. What seemed like hours was really only a few minutes before the guard came back out. This time the dogs did not start barking as he approached, and his voice was a lot more relaxed. "Look, the roads can be a bit nasty, so be careful. We've had some trouble makers sneak through before we were able to seal off the cities, so you may run into some trouble. I called in your license plate so you should be fine when you get to the next road block which isn't until Springfield. The guards are expecting you there so as long as you use the road block on the main highway then you should be fine. When you return tomorrow make sure you use this road as well since our unit will be here again and can let you back in. Do you have enough fuel to get all the way there?" "Um... yes" I responded.

"Good, because fuel is only allowed to be sold in major cities, so you won't be able to fill up anywhere else. Try to fill up tonight in Springfield if you can. Fuel rationing is coming to help control those not cooperating with the President's orders." Sure I thought, good excuse, but I think it's really because OPEC countries are not accepting US "dollars" for oil any more. I was not about to argue with the guard however, we have to get through.

"Okay, anything else we should know?" I figured I should pump him for as much information as we could get from him, since we did not have time to check the scanner or ham radios before we left.

He hesitated for a moment, then as he adjusted his uniform collar he said "be careful out there, it's getting uglier every day. I'm sure you know that weapons are prohibited outside of homes, but given your situation, I won't ask. One more thing, if you get into trouble, take your ID out of the protective sleeve, and that will signal the chip is readable. Our satellites are able to read them and we'll be able to find you. I know some people don't believe us, but we really are here for your safety." "Huh?" Tom interjected, "I thought RFID chips are only readable over short distances like 50 feet at most?" The guard smirked. "The technology in these new IDs is not your conventional RFID. It was developed under contract for DARPA, uses GPS. It's more advanced than what the public is used to, but based on technology used in logistics. It's recent, so that's probably why you haven't heard about it." He then called "pass cleared" on the radio and waved off the other guards. I was in disbelief, but managed to keep my excitement hidden until we were far enough away. Tom started the truck, put it in drive, and slowly moved passed the barricade. We made it out of the city, and we were fine all the way to Springfield. But we did not need to go all the way to

Springfield. We should be fine on back roads to our destination provided we did not run into any trouble on the way.

Chapter 2

Road Block

The drive seemed desolate without any cars on the roads. But at least the miles were going by quick. Tom and I had done this drive enough times to know the roads, but Tom knew them much better, as he had done the drive many times more than I had. Which is why he was driving now. He studied the roads, which fortunately were mostly barren so you can see well ahead. He told me over the past year that there were a few areas he was concerned about, thus the loaded guns. I have never actually pointed a gun at a real person, let alone shoot someone. I hoped that my mind would not prevent me from being able to do so when I really had to.

We spent the first hour of the drive talking about the chip in my card. "So that's how the guards are convinced to do their job, they really believe they are helping people" Tom stated matter of fact like.

"What good will them knowing where we're at do us if we're being shot at?" I asked.

"Yeah, I had the same question. When seconds count, help is just hours away" Tom replied chuckling just a little.

"Maybe if we run into trouble somewhere, I can dump the card to make it appear I lost it" I suggested.

"I was thinking the same thing" Tom replied.

"You don't think I should hold on to it just in case for something?" I was hesitant as I asked, I knew the answer before Tom answered.

"No, get rid of it. It's a millstone, if not a Trojan horse" Tom's response was firm. He had already made up his mind about the ID card.

I thought about it for a while, and I really could not find a good reason to keep it. If I dumped it somewhere and they read the chip, and it looks like trouble occurred, then that may excuse me missing. Then maybe they will be less likely to look for us, and although my name is not on the cabin paperwork,

Tom's is, and we are married, which does lead to a slight paper trail. Not much of one though, when you buy with cash outright, you do not need to have a social security number. And we made sure that we paid for all the repairs in a manner that was not easily traceable, which was basically cash. I decided that card might actually be a way for me to be found, and I just could not think of any good reason to keep the card. We were never coming back.

The dogs have done this drive many times as well, so they settled in the back and went to sleep as always. I was worried they might not as we normally exercise them before the drive, and today we just did not have the time. Hopefully they will stay calm throughout the rest of the drive. And hopefully we will not run into trouble.

The truck started to slow down, and I knew we must be approaching an area Tom was worried about. Then all of a sudden he hit the brakes and pulled off to the side of the road. "What's wrong?" I asked.

"Look at those rocks, the smaller rocks up there, they've been moved." He was pointing toward a rock formation that went along with a bend in the road, no way to see what is on the other side, or even in the middle, or on top of the rocks, or behind. The bend in the road is nestled right in between bluffs that have been torn up in the center to allow for the road, which resulted in a very unintentional but artistic view as you drove by. The bend itself is about a mile long, with the bluffs following the whole way. It was actually just a rock mountain in the middle of nowhere that they bulldozed through. But now it was an area of concern.

"I've done this drive often enough to memorize the rock formations, this is one of the two major areas I was concerned about" Tom explained.

"You think there's some bad guys hanging out waiting to loot the next poor soul that managed to get out of the city?" I asked sarcastically. I was a bit in disbelief that we would actually encounter looters. Tom's response was clear "I don't think, I know so, those rocks were definitely moved, probably so they could position themselves better". I looked around, outside of the rock formation there is really nothing. There is some barb wire fencing intended to keep cows in. The land is not worked, all natural, so the farmers use a larger amount of acreage for a smaller amount of cows to keep them fed. The cows find feed in more distant areas, but it prevents the farmers from having to have to plant seed and irrigate.

I decided not to question Tom, life as I know it has changed, and I know the risks too well not to take precautions. After looking around, I suggested to Tom "we can cut the wire here, go through the cow field, and make sure we move far enough away from the bend before we turn back on the road so if they tried to shoot we'd be too far for them to make the shot."

"Makes sense. Did we load the wire cutters in the glove box?" Tom asked worriedly.

"Yep, right here. You want me to jump out, cut, jump back in, and then we go?"

"I think so, I'm sure they hear the diesel engine running, so we don't have much time for decisions."

"Okay, hold the dogs back, I'll be quick." As I opened the truck door, he grabbed the two collars, I jumped out, ran in front of the truck, snipped the wires on the left side and pulled them to the side. They wanted to bounce back to their position, so I had to wrap them to the pole and other wires, then hurried and jumped back in the truck. Tom was moving before I had the door shut. "Get your gun, there's someone coming up behind us" Tom stated as he put the truck in four wheel drive and then stepped on the pedal. I grabbed my gun, yelled at the dogs to lay down, and got my seat belt on. The adrenaline kicked in, my mind was racing, this can not be happening, the world can not change this much this quickly. I looked in the passenger side view mirror and watched the white Toyota pick up truck follow us part way, then it slowed down and fell behind "I think we're far enough away, I don't think they're trying to catch up to us" Tom said over the bumpy ride. He drove fast through the field, occasionally missing a cow or two. I rolled down the window to look back, no, they were not following us, but why?

He started to turn the truck heading in the same direction as the road. You could see the rock formation from a

24

distance, but if anyone was on them, you could not see them. He kept driving for a long time as my adrenaline started to calm down. I did not put the gun away. I could not imagine thugs or looters would give up that easily. We are one car out of so few.

"Think we've gone far enough?" Tom asked.

"I don't know, but this ride is really bumpy. Maybe a little further just to be safe?" I looked to the left and noticed I could no longer see the rock formations, so I looked back, and saw the formations very far behind us. Then asked Tom "what if they're on the road waiting for us to get back on? They can drive faster on the road, so they would be well ahead of us." "We're going to have to chance that, we can't stay on cow field forever." Tom replied. "Let's keep going until we can no longer see the rock formations behind us" I suggested. "Fair enough" was Tom's response.

After what felt like forever, especially in a bumpy ride that caused the dogs to get upset, and some serious maneuvering around smaller rocks and holes, he started to turn the truck back towards the road. I knew once we got to the fence I would have to jump out to cut it again. As we got closer, I scouted the road intensely for any signs of cars or people. I saw nothing. He started to slow down the truck as we got closer, he too was looking intently. Nothing. Something just did not seem right. But all we saw was some scattered cows, the road, and the fence posts holding up the wire. We approached slowly then stopped right in front of some wire then turned towards the back to grab the dogs collars again. I jumped out, cut the wires, moved them aside, though a little tougher this time one handed, I was not going to take my chances with out my gun. I quickly jumped back in, the dogs were being awfully good. Perhaps they sensed the tension and decided it is best to keep calm. Tom pulled out onto the road and we were on our way again. The eerie feeling from this morning came back. Something just did not feel right about this. Perhaps it is just the adrenaline pumping. Or perhaps I am realizing that life as I know it, no longer exists.

"This seemed too simple, I don't think they're going to give up that easily" I could hear worry in Tom's voice.

"Maybe they're just waiting for more compliant targets." I tried to be optimistic. Tom was not so optimistic "but with so few cars going through here, I don't think they're going to give up so easily. Keep your eyes out; there's another bend coming, and it's bigger than this one. We have about 40 miles until we get there." At that moment I recalled that we had the radios in the center console, just plain FRS radios, but better than nothing. I dug one out and turned it on, then set it to scan the stations. "Good idea, if there's more bad guys around the bend, they might be using those for communication" Tom said. I thought about digging out the CBs, or the ham radios, but realized they are loaded up in the bed of the truck, so not practical to access right now. So I just turned on one of the FRS radios to scan for conversations. Nothing. Plain silence.

We kept going but my adrenaline did not calm down. If we ran into trouble around that last risky bend, we would definitely run into trouble around the next one, no question about it. We have read and studied enough survival books to know better. When things fall apart in a society, a certain percentage of people inevitably turn into selfish murderers, and you can hope for nothing more. If there is a problem with the next bend, we will not be able to go around it as easily as we did the last one. There are no cows eating sparse pasture, and no flat land to drive around. It is all rock, and the rocks get bigger the closer you get to the bend. The road is the only way to get through, and if these looters are anything like in the books, they will shoot with out thinking twice, and they will shoot quicker if they smell trouble.

Tom kept driving, but slowly while watching the road ahead of us and behind us. Nothing. Just plain silence. No cars, no semi's, not even deer. As many deer as we have seen on these roads, you would expect to see some now, but there were none.

"I think there's a car behind us, not sure, but looks like there might be in the rearview" Tom announced. I grabbed the binoculars out of the center console and attempted to see through the back window. Good thing the dogs were laying down in the back seat. "Yeah, it's a pick up truck, it's coming up pretty fast." I informed Tom.

"I knew they wouldn't give up that easily" he stated. I turned back around and looked at Tom, he was contemplating out loud "If I speed up, we'll get to the next risky bend faster, and we'll have two sets of trouble, one from behind, and one from up front." He is right. I thought briefly if perhaps there might be an advantage to that, but realized that they might be working together, and then we are really in trouble. Tom slowed the truck down and allowed the Toyota truck behind us to approach us. I turned around again with the binoculars. "Unless there are others hiding, it looks like only one person behind the wheel. I think he has a uniform on - might be guard." I sat back down and wondered. Tom asked "you think it's a real guard?" "Not sure."

As the Toyota approached we heard a voice via a bullhorn "Pull over, this is the United States National Guard, you need to pull over." Tom put on his blinker and slowly pulled over. During this time I wedged my gun between the right side of my seat and the door, out of view as the guard would be on Tom's left side, but easy to reach should I need it. Tom hit the switch to lock the doors even though they were already locked, and the dogs got up from their nap hoping that the ride was over. Tom rolled down the window half way and waited for the guard to approach. My mind kept thinking that this can not be right, the guard on our way out of the city implied that there would not be another road block until we hit Springfield. We have stayed on the main route to Springfield so far. Something told me this was not a real guard. "The reason I pulled you over is because you avoided a check point that is recognized by the government. I need evidence that you are allowed to be on the road." His voice was young, the tone was fast and nervous. I quickly responded "I have been approved to travel and was told my license plate was reported. I am sorry we did not pull over, we thought there were looters there." As I was talking I was scanning his uniform. Being a paper pusher for the government gives you interesting knowledge about uniforms, and I have a pretty good idea of what to look for. So far the uniform appeared legitimate, or at least accurate, though an awful lot of ribbons for a soldier so young. He can not be more than early twenties, maybe late twenties if he aged well. He has sandy blonde hair under his hat, and his uniform was not so prim and proper, perhaps out in the middle of nowhere the uniforms are not kept up as nicely, or maybe he is just one of those soldiers who does not like to iron. "These roads are protected by the US Government, and there are no looters. There is another check point around the next bend, make sure you stop there and cooperate. I am too far away for my radio to call in your license, so I am going to have to trust you to stop at the next bend" The guards voice sounded nervous and annoyed, regardless, Tom replied with a "yes sir," and proceeded to ask questions about the road when I realized something. The dogs were restless in the back, so during their talk I turned around slowly, patted one of the dogs, and said "calm down Goober, good boy Goober." Little did the guard know that Tom and I have some key words pre-selected to use in case of emergencies. Our dogs names are Compass and Velcro, not Goober. Calling the dog "goober" meant trouble. Tom caught on immediately.

"Thank you for all the information sir, we appreciate it, but we should get going if we're going to make it before curfew." Tom was trying to end the conversation.

"Alright then, but make sure you stop at the next check point, it's in your best interest" the fake guard repeated.

"Yes sir, we will."

The guard started to walk back to his Toyota as Tom rolled up the window and started the truck, the dogs calmed down and settled back to their sleeping positions. Tom pulled out and hit the road again. "I thought it was suspicious that the guard would have a check point out here in the middle of nowhere. But how do you know he's a fake?" Tom asked.

"One of the ribbons he was wearing, I recognized it, three red bands in the center with green band outliers, it's the Vietnam service medal. Those were only issued to those who served during the Vietnam era, which ended sometime back in 1975. Either that "guard" served before he was born, or he's a fake. Plus the real guard in the city said there's no more check points until we reach Springfield." I explained.

"Damn it, he's setting us up. The next stop has to be a trap. He probably didn't think he could take us on alone, so he's making sure we stop in a trusting manner at the next stop." I could see that Tom was already thinking about the next plan of action. We were silent for a while, then I realized "yeah, and while he had us stopped, he checked out how many of us there are, how many dogs, and what type of supplies we looked to have."

As soon as the "guard's" truck was fully out of view Tom pulled over. "Well, we might as well eat a snack as we think this through." Tom was right, so I reached for the bag between my feet and took out some water and almonds. I handed them to Tom and started talking. "Okay, so the only way to get through that area is to stay on the road. We know for a fact that the road is guarded by organized looters. They probably have guns, and know we are coming. They must be communicating somehow, but not FRS, cause our radios are not picking anything up, or we're not close enough. They may be using HAM or CB radios. They know there are two of us in a truck, and two German shepherd dogs. So the questions is, what are they planning to do when we get there?" Tom contemplated for a while as he chewed on his almonds, periodically he checked the rearview mirror, then said "If we are lucky they will attempt to pull us over, act like a legitimate guard checkpoint, then probably tell us our license plate don't check out, and get us to get out of the truck. Then they'll possibly attempt to "arrest" us, and "confiscate" our stuff, and then shoot us. If we're not lucky they'll just shoot us with high powered rifles from a distance before we have a chance to react." A chill went through my body as Tom said that. As cold as that sounded, I knew we had to think of the worst case scenarios. Bad guys don't play nice, and good guys gone bad due to tough times don't play much better. There is a psychological phenomenon that occurs when most people get into a position of power. A weakness in their mind takes over, like an addict, and they want ever more power. They lose the ability to feel sympathy, kindness, or even tolerance, and they get greedy. No amount of power is enough, they want more. It is the power addiction of megalomaniacs.

"We're going to have to pull over, roll down both windows, talk to them, have our guns hidden but loaded, hopefully buy enough time to see where they are at and how many, and the first sign of a problem, start shooting. Hopefully they aren't too organized" I suggested. I knew that suggestion was not very realistic, but we had to start somewhere.
"That seems logical, but what if they shoot our tires?" Tom's question put us back into silence for a short while. Tom finally answered his own question "they won't, because if they do, they'll have trouble hiding the truck, which is not to their advantage for the next victims. And they'll lose a perfectly good vehicle."
I then added "we don't know how many of them there are, I fear that if we manage to shoot those surrounding the truck, there might be several more up in the rocks shooting down at us. We'll be boxed in, we won't be able to effectively return fire, and they win." My adrenaline was starting to pick up again, and nervousness kicked in. If it were not for the fact that I knew our last encounter was a fake guard, I would not be convinced there was any trouble up ahead.
"Then we'll have to go ahead on foot and surprise them." Tom's mind is made up, I can tell when he has a plan and he likes it.
"I think you're right, that's our best bet. They're expecting a compliant couple in a vehicle." I decided to support his plan, whatever it was.
"And guns are illegal to travel with, so they expect that we may be un-armed." Tom continued.
"Okay, then let's get ready" though I have no idea what his plan is, so I asked "Should we pull out the CB's or the HAM's and see if we get anything?"
"That'll take too long, and they probably already communicated the important stuff."
We got out of the vehicle and using the binoculars looked in all directions to see if anyone else could see us. It seemed safe. We did not see anything that would imply we could be seen, plus we were still several miles from the rock outcroppings. Though you could see more rocks on the flat land were beginning to form.

When Tom first told me he purchased Level III steel plate body armor, I thought he went a little nuts. But really, I was in denial about the reality of how bad things could get during an economic collapse or currency failure. I had really hoped that neither of us would ever have to wear them, but those hopes had now vaporized. And as he pulled them out of the back of the truck, I was thankful that Tom had purchased them, and I was even more thankful that we wore them under our sweatshirts when we went hiking. You would not believe the amount of time it took to get even remotely used to wearing them. We first started wearing them around the house for 15 minutes at a time, then a half hour, then an hour, then hiding them to go hiking, though that's easier said than done. They are quite bulky, and because of my size, the only way to hide it was to wear a bulky coat. It made me look funny, but I did not care, plus we chose hiking areas that were not very popular. I had to be able to wear it for situations such as this.

He helped me put my vest on first. Then he put on his. We put our MOLLE/PALS gun holsters and magazine pouches on and then Tom said "I know you're more comfortable with your revolver, but that only has seven shots and it's not as quickly re-loadable. You need to take the semi-auto." Tom was gentle in his request "I know, I expected you would tell me that, that's why I always practiced with it." He handed me the .45 and two extra loaded magazines. He then placed his in his holster and two extra magazines for him. I took the revolver and put it in another holster. If anything, that's seven extra shots for backup. He then dug around in the back of the truck for the helmets, which were hidden in one of the plastic storage bins so that the guards would not see them. After the helmets were on, he grabbed the FRS radios and handed one to me. "Let's set it on our first frequency, I'll moo if it's time to go to our next frequency." Tom and I had three frequencies picked out on the radio. We always started with the first one, then we gave each other some signal to go to the next one. "If either of us are in danger, and we can't have voices coming in, click the speaking button a few times so some static will come through, so we have to listen carefully." I nodded and clipped my radio to the side of my vest.

Wearing so much metal can get rather uncomfortable real quick, and we still had to decide our strategy of how we were going to handle this. Tom started "I think we need to get a little closer to the rock outcroppings, but not too close, and then pull the truck off to the side of the road as far as we can." I followed up "We should leave the truck running but lock the doors and take the spare keys, this way we can escape quickly if we need to, and the dogs can have AC. We'll give them another rawhide or two to keep them occupied, and hopefully they won't destroy the truck. Then we'll set out on foot." Tom nodded his head, but had to comment "We're about to do the most dangerous thing we've ever done in our lives, and you're worried about the dogs... They should be happy *if we make it back*." I was surprised by his comment, he is right, but the dogs were my kids since I could not have any two legged ones. And frankly, we got them so that they could protect us, this just is not the right situation for their help right now.

"Of course I'm worried about the dogs, aren't you?" I asked while giving Tom a very dirty look.

"Yes. I wish they could help us, but they're not trained for this." Tom ignored my look, then added "what if we don't make it back, they'll be stuck in the truck indefinitely."

"But if we leave them outside, they'll bark and whine as we walk away from them, and give away our location. Plus we would have to tie them to the truck, and it's really hot out right now" I argued.

We got back in the truck and drove for a few more miles, then Tom pulled over and drove off the road quite a ways. The road had become more rocky by now, and the cow fencing had ended a while back. We were able to find a spot where the truck would hide nicely, and you could not easily see it from the road. We both got out of the truck to assess the area, then Tom said "we still have a few miles to go, but we'll have to hoof it on foot." He then grabbed a scoped .308 rifle from the back of the truck, loaded it, and handed it to me, then he grabbed his and did the same. The sight of him in his body armor with the rifle shot up my adrenaline. This is real, this is really happening, I might have no choice but to kill someone today. Even though logically I knew this day may eventually come, I guess I did not fully prepare for it psychologically or emotionally. Just this morning I woke up to the sound of my alarm clock while sleeping in a comfortable bed, ate delicious breakfast, and then we packed. It has only been three hours since we left the city, this was too soon to be happening. My mind was fully in disbelief. Tom dug out four rawhides and gave them to the dogs, turned up the AC, rolled up the windows, locked the truck, and made sure we had spare keys before he shut the door.

The walk was more of a rock hopping adventure, and I thought back to how we got to this point. The idea was to pay enough attention that we would head for the 'cabin' and be long gone before it ever got like this. The vests were just a precaution in case we missed that window, but we were not supposed to miss the window. Things were starting to get bad rather quickly, but we thought we still had more time. We had taken extra trips to the cabin even though finances were tough because we knew that might be our last trip of supplies, and luckily we decided to leave one of the trucks there along with the trailer. I was able to carpool to work, so there was no need for two vehicles in the city. We maxed out our credit cards, and continued to get more supplies, but we thought we had more time. Then all of a sudden, one morning, we wake up, and the roads are blocked, people are panicking, the military is mobilized in US cities and occasionally knocking on doors a la Katrina, and people were getting arrested for asking too many questions. We realized we were still in the city, that we are not at the cabin as planned, and that we waited too long. So here we are, two city kids with rifles donned, marching along rocks. It is surreal, this can not be happening. But it is.

Tom stopped and turned to look at me. I was struggling a bit with all the gear on, the rifle is heavy, and the weight of the hand guns and ammo was not helping, plus the body armor. "I think we should stop here and check out to see how far we are" Tom suggested. I did not argue, I needed a break. Using the scopes on the rifles, we looked around. The bend of rocks was up ahead, but we were still too far to see anything. We continued to move forward, but moved slower and kept hidden behind boulders, and every couple dozen feet, we checked the scopes again. Nothing. But we were getting closer and knew we had to be extra careful, so at this point, we got on the ground, and literally crawled our way through the rocks. If we are going to have a shot at this, we can not be seen. Although my adrenaline was pumping the weight of my armor still caused me to fall a bit behind Tom, but that was probably a good thing. Eventually he stopped, and started to position himself. I slowly crawled to where he was at and realized he found a good spot. They more likely could not see us between all the rocks, but we were close enough to get a descent shot at them, though we will have to do more than one. The rocks would also protect us from any return fire, but they also have to figure out our exact location first.

We positioned ourselves between the rocks, and looked through our scopes. Still nothing. We were close enough now that if someone was there, we could see them. By now, they must be getting suspicious as we should have arrived over an hour ago or longer, so they might be preparing as well. "I think we have to get closer, they might not be watching guard from this direction, or maybe they are further in the bluffs, not so close to the front" Tom's voice sounded normal, as if this was all part of a routine day.

The adrenaline took over any physical limitations I may have felt. I forgot I was carrying so much weight on me, and I no longer felt discomfort. Actually, I no longer felt anything other than the need to survive, the both of us, not just me. We started to crawl a little closer. In an almost whispered voice, Tom said "look, I need you to cover me so I can move in closer, but you have to be a good shot. I need you to hit anyone you might see on the first try." Yeah, easier said than done. In order to practice shooting, you need money, and to get supplies, you need money, to drive back and forth between the cabin and the city, you need money. Everything costs money, which is why we stayed in the city as long as we did, and some things just got put on the back burner. Practicing with the rifles as much as we should have was one of them. I realize now it should not have been. Finally I nodded my head and said "okay, I'll try, but stay out of their view." Tom laid his rifle and extra rifle magazines next to me and stated "this will be quicker than reloading." He grabbed his handgun, and moved forward at a quicker, but still cautious pace. Quicker than reloading? How many shots did he expect me to fire?

I did not like this part. I was left alone and responsible for defense. I looked through my scope from left to right, for any sign of movement. Occasionally I looked behind me. They were hiding behind rocks, and we were hiding behind rocks, brilliant. If there is three, maybe four of them, we have a chance, but if there is 10 or more, we are in trouble unless we are *really* good, and maybe get *a lot of luck*. Can not count on luck now, it has to be skill, has to be skill or else. These people mean serious business and they want us dead, and they want our stuff. We have to focus and do this right. Self defense is not murder. I was about to fall into tears from the pressure, the stress, the reality of the situation. But then I saw Tom crawling through the rocks, and I realized, I have to get it together, he is counting on me, get it together!

I focused on the scope and looked in every direction for a sign of anything, anything at all. There was nothing, were they waiting for us to come to them? Were they crawling behind rocks? The quiet worried me, where is Tom? If I move, I will lose such a great defense shot, if I do not move, Tom might need my help. What to do, what to do? Wish I had played airsoft, or paintball, or something of the sort. I had never been in a situation like this before, and videogames do not count. I really was not sure what the next move was for me. Tom will alert me on the radio if he needs help, for now, the silence is good. It felt like hours, maybe it was hours. I finally saw Tom move up on some rocks and disappear into the bluffs. I listened carefully for anything on the radio, anything at all. Nothing.

I looked through the scope again, nothing, not even a shadow. He should have alerted me or something by now, what if he is in trouble? I have to help Tom. I can not help him if he is in trouble on the street side of the bluffs if I am on the opposite side of the bluffs. And I can not contact him on the radio in case he is hiding, as that might give his position away. I put the rifle down next to his, got out my .45, and slowly crawled forward. Then I turned around – I knew I should at least unload the rifles. If someone by chance finds them, then they will use them against us. I knew Tom will be pissed at me leaving them. But damn it, they would slow me down, I can hardly crawl through the rocks with one, let alone two. I quickly unloaded both rifles and placed the magazines on my vest. I then started to crawl forward again. I need to get to Tom. Though not much faster than a turtle, I crawled as fast as I could, until I got closer to the road. The boulders around the bend are very large and tall, which is why it is a good spot to hang out if you are going to be a looter. I managed to start climbing a little, but realized that I am completely exposed. Though I am pretty sure I saw Tom go this way, I was about to climb down when I noticed a small hole that looks like it will get me through the rocks, or at least I think it will, and I am small enough to fit through. Well, maybe, with all this armor on, I was not so sure. I decided to go for it, and slowly crawled into the hole, I fit, what luck! Now let's just hope it is not the hole of some mountain lion. I crawled through and slowly allowed my head to poke up the hole on the other side. The hole was tight so I was having a little difficulty safely handling the .45 while climbing through. I peeked up, and saw Tom standing over a body. "Tom?" I whispered. He turned around and saw the top of my helmet, then ran over to me to help me out of the hole.

"Looks like someone beat us to it, they're all dead. We still need to look around – *carefully*."

"How many are there? I asked.

"Four, but there's some under the bluff where the road is." I looked around and saw bodies laying on the ground, then Tom added "we need to look around because I don't know what happened here, though we may have run into some luck given the circumstances."

"First, let's get their weapons away from them. I know you say they're dead, but it just doesn't feel right when their guns are next to them" I said as I pointed towards a body closest to me. I was a bit panicked at this point. We started to kick the guns away from the bodies, and performed some quick pokes to make sure no one was faking it and ready to take us. We watched each others back as we did this, but everyone seemed pretty well dead. When you see people die in the movies, it is all very clean and pretty, but that is not true in real life. Looking at these bodies, they did not look peaceful, their eyes were not all closed. They appeared to have been shot mostly in their heads or chests, so it was actually a really disgusting sight. They were all wearing guard uniforms. One of them had half his brains sprawled next to him, then the stench of death hit me, the smell of stale air mixed with blood, and I felt nauseated. It must have been obvious. "Are you okay?" Tom ran towards me. "Yeah, I think I'm okay, I just need to sit down for a moment." As Tom approached, I felt dizzy, then I looked at Tom, and said "I'm just going to sit for a second, I just need to recover for a minute." I sat down on the ground as the adrenaline wore off, and I felt the aches and pains of my body. I felt the heavy weight of the armor on my shoulders, the discomfort of the armor on my breasts, they certainly were not designed for women of any chest size. I looked down to see my hands were so tore up from the climbing that they were bleeding. "Just sit here for a minute, but stay alert, I'm going to look around to see if there's any other good hiding spots, just to make sure there are no others." Tom left me to recover. As I sat there I realized then that we were in some kind of large cave-like area, kind of like a rock tunnel that allowed you to see the road in both directions, but was pretty well covered. There were some of them hiding up here with a couple guys down on the road below. We would have never had a shot had we tried to come in on the road with our truck. But then we would, because someone beat us to it, someone must have come through here and had taken care of the looters for us. I was starting to feel better but decided to stay seated a little longer, just in case. Tom came back slowly "I think that's all of them, I don't see anything else. Are you alright?" "Yeah, I'm fine, I just needed a minute." I slowly got up and continued to feel fine. "How do we get down?" I asked. "The hole you came out of or jump down this boulder to the street, but first, I want to show you something."

He took my hand and pulled me in the direction of the road where the bend was, and from where we were at, you could see three vehicles parked specifically to block the road. Except that one of them was moved just enough to get a vehicle through. "Something tells me that someone already went through here with the same idea in mind that we had. We need to check those bodies and make sure they are not real guard." We went back to the bodies, and searched for wallets and dog tags, that task was not easy. The bodies had gone through rigor mortis and were stiff. I had to keep myself from looking at the faces because they were creeping me out, almost as if they were staring at me, cursing me all to hell. I stopped searching and looked at their uniforms, I had to find a way to make sure they were not real guard. Tom must have picked up my thoughts as he stated "Based on what I see here, I'm 99% sure they are not real guard." After we finished searching the bodies we found several sets of keys and those who had ID on them did not match the name of the dog tags. The few that had a military ID did not match the driver's license, and certainly none of the driver's license pictures matched any of the military ID's, at least from what we could tell, though people do not look the same when they are dead and alive. Then we slowly crawled through the hole to get to the outside of the rock formation and headed towards the road. Nothing there but two dead guys, we checked their wallets which had standard driver licenses. One of them was just a state ID, not even a license. If they were guards, they would have military issue ID at least, and dog tags or something. Outside of the uniforms, there was nothing to identify them as guards. We started to walk up the bend, and even though we saw what is up ahead, we still had our guns drawn just in case. It seemed like a very long walk, but we finally got to the vehicles blocking the road. I know we found more sets of keys than there were cars, making me wonder where the rest of the vehicles are.

We contemplated going up the road a little more, but given we saw mostly what is up ahead, we felt it would be more efficient to go in our truck than on foot. We started to head back slowly, then Tom stopped me "shhh... I think I hear a car." I listened carefully, and thought I heard a hum of some sort, but wasn't quite sure, until I heard the hum disappear, with a door slamming shortly after. Someone was here, but who?

We started to look around, and there were not many places to hide. The only way back was through the road, with the sides of the road blocked by the steep rock of the bluffs. Only the entrance of the bluffs had the cave like opening, everything else was like a tunnel. Tom and I kept looking for concealment, at least until we knew who it was. If it is authorities of any sort, then we knew how this looks. But with no where to hide, I was almost hoping it was another looter that we could just shoot and get out of here.

"I think we should get behind the cars intended for the road block" Tom whispered.

"That's a good idea. I don't see anywhere else that can provide concealment, let alone cover."

We both turned around quickly and headed back to the former road block. We did not know how much time before our unexpected visitor started to move forward, so we hid behind one of the pick ups, but made sure we both still had a view.

"Where are the rifles?" I knew this question was going to come sooner or later. I responded very defensively. "I could not carry them both, it was too much. Don't worry, they are unloaded, so it's unlikely they will be used against us." I could tell from Tom's face that he was not happy, actually, to put it mildly, he was pissed, just as I expected. I continued to defend myself "look, I'm not as strong as you, I'm wearing this vest, plus my guns, plus my gear - it was just not practical okay." It was almost a whispered yell, Tom knew he had asked too much of me.

"Do you know where you left them?" He asked in a controlling calm tone.

"Yes, don't worry, I can find them" I was still on the defensive.

We were kneeled behind one of the trucks wheels, the truck was parked at an angle, and we could slightly make out the road. We did not have much of an option for concealment, so this had to do. We both had our guns drawn with safety off. After what seemed like forever, I heard what I thought was a car door slamming again, but I was not sure until I heard a slight humming sound. Tom and I looked at each other, we knew whoever it is might be coming this way from around the bend.

The hum sound started to get louder, and Tom signaled me to lay down prone. We both did so and continued to have our guns drawn. Such an intense moment. If this person drives on by, then we could run back to our truck once they were out of view. But chances are they saw the two fake dead guards where they stopped first, so they are likely to stop by these parked cars as well. No matter which way I looked at it, this was not good, the intensity of the situation kept increasing as the hum got louder. Then the car stopped not far from where we were at. I tried to see from under the truck what kind of car it was, but I was not in a position to do so.

We were positioned in silence, though I was sure I could hear Tom breathing, or maybe it was me, I don't know. But as soon as I heard the car door open and shut, I stopped breathing. Then I heard the faint foot steps. Who ever it was, they were walking with confidence. As the foot steps were approaching, I started to panic, what if they see us and we do not see them? No, we were positioned pretty well, they could only see us from the ground, and all we saw was their feet. As the steps got closer, I realized it was possibly the pants of a guard uniform. Tom must have recognized it as such as well, as he looked at me, and signaled that he is going to go behind the truck and for me to stay on the side. I nodded as I realized I had not been breathing, and took a long quiet breath of tire scented air. Tom kneeled and very slowly proceeded to move behind the truck, the steps were close enough that the person would not be able to see behind the bed of the truck, or on the side of the truck where I was. I saw Tom disappear behind the bed. As I looked back towards the street I realized that the person was now in front of the truck and would see me any second. I froze with my gun pointed in his direction ready to fire, and as I began to see his approaching body I realized it was the fake guard that pulled us over earlier. At that instant he must have seen me out of the corner of his eye as he jumped back slightly and started to raise up his handgun.

This can not be good, he saw me for sure, I was a sitting duck, well, laying duck is more like it. I contemplated if

I could fit under the truck, but no way, not with everything that I was wearing. I saw his feet still standing in front of the truck, and wondered what he was thinking. I looked under the truck to see if I could determine where Tom was, and saw he was exactly where I was, just on the other side of the truck. I did not know how to signal to him that it was the fake guard, so I tried to at least get the message that the guard saw me. I pointed my finger at his feet and then used my index and middle finger to point towards my eyes, Tom nodded, he understood I thought.

"Look, I don't know what happened here, but I'm sure we can talk this out. Why don't you put your gun down, come out and we can talk about it." The fake guard's voice sounded panicked, but I could tell he was trying to project authority. I did not respond. I looked over at Tom who just put his finger to his mouth and implied for me to shhh. I nodded. "Not responding to me is not the answer, we can work this out, why don't you come on out from behind the truck and drop your weapon." I still did not respond. I looked over at Tom and saw that he was starting to move toward the front of the truck, the guard's feet were positioned in my direction, and then I saw the guards feet start to move toward me. My gun never stopped pointing toward the direction of the front of the truck, and as the guard emerged we both had our guns drawn on each other. The second I saw the gun pointed in my direction I pulled my trigger. Tom must have done so from the other side at the same time. He must have shot twice, I heard three shots, maybe four or five? I don't know, maybe it was just three?

The loud noise of the guns was startling. We have always used ear protection when practicing, but that was not an option here. The loud noise echoed in the rock tunnel. I heard ringing in both my ears immediately. Almost as if in a daze I came to, everything felt like it had been in slow motion for a moment. Self defense is not murder I repeated to myself. I saw the guard try to shoot his gun, though his arm was dropping to the ground as he did so. The sound of his pistol was not as loud, it sounded distant, and I saw the bullet ricochet off the ground in the direction to the left of me. Then the guard fell forward near the front left corner of the truck. I continued to lay in my position with my gun drawn, everything still in slow motion.

"Rache, are you alright?!!" came Tom's panicked voice.

"Yeah, I think so, I'm not sure..."

Tom ran over to me and started looking me over with his EMT eyes. "I don't think I was hit, I saw the bullet hit the ground and bounce that way" I pointed in the direction of the bullet. "Is he dead? Did I kill him?"

"We both did, but he was about to kill you" Tom said reassuringly.

"I know. As soon as I saw the end of that barrel in my direction I just shot" I explained.

"Good thing you did."

"Is he dead for sure?"

"Yeah, I got him in the back of the head, though I'm not sure where you got him."

"I don't know" I said as I started to get up. I was very uncomfortable and had this uncontrollable urge to get out of there.

Tom started to help me up, and we walked the few feet to look at the guard, I had hit him in his right leg, it is a good thing Tom shot him at the same time, as the leg shot would not have stopped him. I would have been killed.

"We need to get out of here, someone else might come and we might not be so lucky." I said panicking.

"I agree, let's take his truck back to our truck, that will make it quicker." Tom had already worked out these details in his head.

"Okay." We looked in the pickup, but the keys were not in the ignition, so the guard must have had them. Tom searched his pants pocket and found the keys.

"Should we check to see if he was a real guard?" I asked as I repeated in my head, self defense is not murder, self defense is not murder.

"I know he wasn't, but if it makes you feel better. Let me see if he has a wallet on him." Tom searched him and found nothing, not even a dog tag.

"Military always carry ID, at least a dog tag, plus he's wearing medals that aren't even appropriate for the uniform" I justified out loud.

"Yeah, he's a fake, let's go." Tom took his gun, put the safety on, then we got in the white Toyota pick up with Tom behind the wheel. When we got back to the start of the bluffs, I asked Tom to pull over so I could find the rifles. I looked painstakingly in the direction of where I might have left the rifles, I found the trail that looked like it might lead to the space we found earlier. I jogged down that trail and after looking around a bit, I found the rifles. I picked them both up and slung them on each shoulder, then headed quickly back to the road. We proceeded to walk over to the other dead fake guards on the street and take their guns, no reason for other potential looters to find them. We decided to leave the ones with the guards on top of the bluffs in an effort to save time. We also found duct tape and rope in the back seat of the Toyota, along with extra ammo. Tom looked at me and said "Since when do Guard carry duct tape and rope as standard issue?" It was more of a statement then a question, then he continued "Anyway, no reason to walk all the way back, let's just take this truck back to our truck." I agreed.

We got back to our truck that was still running. The dogs got excited when they realized it was us. "Think we should keep our gear on?" I asked, hoping he would say no, but instead he said "can't hurt, I know it's uncomfortable, but it could potentially save us – especially since there might still be some looters up ahead. The only concern I can think of is if we come up to a *real* guard check point. Level III body armor might be a bit hard to explain" he chuckled. He is right, yeah, uncomfortable, but it could save our lives, but at least when sitting down the weight is not so bad. "I don't think there will be anymore checkpoints in our direction, we are not passing any major cities." That was my way of reassuring him that no one official should see our vests. We unlocked the truck with the spare key and jumped in before the dogs could jump out. Tom was about to start the engine, then stopped and thought for a minute, then finally said "why don't you walk the dogs and I'll transfer some of our new duct tape and rope to our truck, along with that nice set of ammo for our new guns too. This is a good opportunity for me to refill the truck from the Jerry cans as well – since all that idling left us lower on fuel than we planned for." I nodded, then I grabbed the leashes and got the dogs out. I was disappointed from the weight of the body armor again, the two minutes I sat in the truck was a huge relief. I decided not to go too far from the truck. Once both dogs went number one, I walked back and grabbed their water bowl and filled it up. They must have been thirsty after sitting in an air conditioned truck this whole time. Then I realized how parched I felt. By then Tom had transported everything he thought was useful to our truck, and was almost done refilling. I found the water bottles and handed one to Tom, then we both finished them off as if we had not had water in weeks. We parked the Toyota where we originally parked our Dodge diesel, and went on our way.

We drove towards the bend and approached slowly. Even though we think they were all dismissed - mostly by someone else's hands, we could not be too careful. "We should search those vehicles to see if we can find more evidence that they were real looters and not guards." Tom suggested. "Real guard don't carry rope and duct tape in the back of their truck." I said frustrated.
"Well, in this situation they might." Tom responded.
"I really just want to get out of here" I did not hide my frustration. My mind can only handle so much, and this was already too much.
"I know, but we need to make sure we didn't do anything wrong here!" Tom was frustrated too.
"HE HAD HIS GUN POINTED AT ME!"
"I know, I know, but we still need to be sure."
"HE PULLED THE TRIGGER..." I made myself calm down, "please, can we just get out of here?" I asked in a calm voice.
"I will be quick, and if you help me, it will be even quicker" Tom wasn't giving up, so I reluctantly agreed.

During the search, we found little outside of rope, and extra ammo. The vehicles themselves were not military issue, just an old 1984 blue Camaro, and two white Toyota pickup trucks. If they were real guardsmen, they would have military issue HMMWVs or something. After coming up a little short of evidence that the guys were good guys, and we made sure we had searched everyone, Tom stated "I think we should go back up to the bluffs and get the other guns from the other fake guards, we could use them for barter later on or something." I really wanted to leave, but agreed reluctantly and volunteered to go through the hole to get them. I crawled through again and slowly put my head up the hole. They still looked dead, just as we left them. I collected their guns and checked them for extra ammo, then making sure the safety was on, carefully dropped the guns down the hole, no way I can carry so many weapons and crawl through the hole at the same time. I then dropped the extra magazines and crawled down through, then hurried back to our truck. I really really wanted to get out of here.

"Look over there, it looks like there might be a car there" Tom pointed across the street on the other side of the bluffs. It was hard to make out, but yeah, something was there. We loaded the back of the truck and then agreed to briefly check out the other side of the bluffs. "What if someone is there?" I asked in hopes that Tom would not ask me to go, it worked, as he said "why don't you stay here, I'll go, and if there's trouble I'll radio you." Tom disappeared behind the bluffs while I stood guard. I saw the dogs inside the truck, they were very confused, but they sensed something was wrong, so they just sat and waited.

My mind raced back to the cabin. Yeah, there was a lot of work to do, but at least it was safe, surrounded by a descent small town folk, and away from everyone else. Sure, we have to work hard to be self sufficient, but we did not mind hard work. Before I knew it Tom was back, he must have ran back, and he looked terrible, his face was pale as if he had seen a ghost. "What's wrong?" I asked. He was silent for a minute, then he said, "we weren't the first ones through here, or the second. There's a family of 5 in that car, and they're all dead. I just got close enough to see in, then I turned around and left. They must have been killed before these guys were taken out. Something very strange happened here. We need to get the hell out of here." Tom started to get in the truck, and I followed. Once we were both in the truck, I asked "How would they get a car over the rocks?" "I don't know, I don't want to know. You're right, we really need to go." Tom started the truck, and the eerie feeling from this morning had returned.

As we pulled out I asked "think this is a good place to leave my badge?" Tom thought a second and said "yeah, leave your ID badge. Once we're passed this bend, in less than 20 miles or so, the road splits three ways, and they won't know which way anyone would have gone. Assuming they would even come all the way out here."

"Well, if they do, then they can clean up this mess." I grabbed my badge, took it out of its protective cover, and threw it near one of the parked cars intended as a road block as we were driving away. Right after I did that, I worried that maybe that was a mistake. We may be the ones blamed for this mess. Too late now, what's done is done.

Tom drove carefully through the rest of the bend just in case - even though we had already gone up and down this road a few times. Once the bend cleared, the road and surrounding area was fully visible again. Tom drove as I sat with a .45 on my lap, and the revolver still tucked away in my second holster. Periodically I picked up the binoculars and looked ahead and tried to look behind. The road became desolate again. Once we hit the turn off, we were headed in a completely different direction than we were supposed to, so it was good we left the badge where we did, maybe.

The rocks started to disappear, and grass started to reappear again. Occasionally a cow or two was seen, but for most of the rest of the drive we were both silent, except for the occasional "can you hand me the water" comment. I was wondering if Tom was contemplating what we had just seen. Probably not – he is usually thinking ahead, solving the next set of problems. Then out of the blue Tom asked me, "how many shots did you fire?"

"One, why do you ask?"

"Because I shot two, but I thought I heard more."

"The guard shot one, I saw the bullet ricochet, but I thought I heard more too."

"There might have been someone else there" Tom stated though unsure.

"Why didn't they come after us?" I was puzzled.

"Maybe they didn't have a good shot?" Tom suggested.

"Or maybe it was the person responsible for the first set" I rationalized.

"Something tells me not" Tom's words surprised me.

"Why not?" I asked.

"No reason." Tom's response was not like him, but I decided not to push the issue.

I could not help but think about the events and the dead bodies. For one, the heavy armor was killing me, and I really wanted to rip it off me. I had to sit in an awkward position just to be halfway comfortable, and my shoulder muscles were beyond exhausted. I needed to get my mind on the positive. I started thinking about the cabin and what was awaiting us. So much work ahead of us, so much to get done.

We drove in silence until about 50 miles from our new 'cabin' home - where the only rest stop was in that area. "I think we should stop and clean up a little. I think we can afford it, plus I think I need you to drive for a while."

Tom pulled off to the exit, and as he did, we both watched intently for any cars or signs of trouble. It all looked clear, and all was silent except the sound of the diesel engine. Tom parked then said "You go first, I'll guard the truck while you go." I got out, ran to the restroom, and in the metal mirror saw myself for the first time since this morning. I was a mess, my face was dirty, my hair was disheveled, my hands were covered in blood and dirt. I washed up the best I could and as quickly as I could, but I do not think it made much difference. I then ran back and guarded the truck while Tom went to do the same. When he came back, we let the dogs out and walked them a bit. This was hopefully our last stop before we got to our cabin. We decided to take our gear off. It was real heavy at this point, and we both ached. We knew the roads well enough to know that it is unlikely that we would run into anymore trouble. Taking off the weight felt good. I am not sure I would have been able to drive with all that gear on. Once the gear was off, I felt about a 100 lbs lighter.

As I was about to put the truck in reverse to get out of the parking spot, Tom turned to me from the passenger side and looked at me very seriously and empathetically, and while his words did not surprise me, I did not want to her them. "Rache, you know you can't write about this in your journal right?" I hated to admit it, but Tom was right. I knew it before he said it. "Yeah, I know, I was not planning on it." "Good, because this could be interpreted the wrong way" he said.

"I know" I replied quietly. Tom would never tell me what to write or not write in my journal. He knew that was one of the few things I held dear in my life, being able to write down things that happened. It is something that helped me grow. I would write down a horrible event that occurred, someone said something to me at work, or some rude check out person, or more serious things about life, but then I would look back at it couple weeks later, and realize that my emotions were much higher than they should have been. The only exception was when our old dog died, my emotions never quieted down, they were as strong as ever, and that is when I learned to journal real things.

Tom kept looking at me curiously. I knew he knows I want to journal about it, but I knew I should not, it was too risky. I wanted Tom to stop looking at me, it was intimidating. So I finally said "look, if we get there in one piece, then that will be better than any journaling I could have ever fathomed." Tom looked away content, he knows I would not do it.

The rest of the drive continued to be uneventful, other than the promising green fields ahead of us, the road slowly turned from brown to green and life seemed calm and happy again. But I knew this was not the case. Life would never be the same as we knew it. At least not for a long time, if ever. We still had to make it to the 'cabin', and we still had to make sure we blocked off the roads to our "neighborhood," assuming the folks there had not already done so. One advantage of us being city folk moving out to the country is that the town was very curious about that. Some of them wanted to know why we would do such a "silly" thing. Some of them may have already suspected why. But "everyone knows" that cities are bigger and better. This afforded us the opportunity to talk with the town folk and tell them what has really been going on. We had to be careful so as not to come off as paranoid kooks afraid of the Federal government officials and corrupt corporate executives, but we managed. And we did get a good number of the people to listen. At least they agreed to block the roads at the first sign of trouble, and most of them agreed to try to stock up on emergency supplies. We never asked for anything more.

We even managed to put together a few events that included presentations on things such as canning, first aid, food storage, solar power, and other emergency survival topics. We had small turn outs as some of the town wanted nothing to do with us, but for the most part, I think we communicated well. The church was a good connection, and we were never questioned on why we did not continue to attend, though we were invited back on numerous occasions. I was just hoping that they let us back in the town if they had blocked off the roads already.

The drive continued to get greener and greener, a sight we both enjoyed on every trip, but especially at that moment. My excitement grew as we turned down the street to the town - that was until we approached a large downed tree. The townsfolk must have blocked off the roads already. We pulled up to the tree and slowly got out, after looking at the situation for a while, Tom started "we have another 8 miles to the cabin, we could just walk it and come back with the other truck to transfer the supplies." For some reason that idea did not fare well with me. "Maybe one of us should walk it and the other one stays to guard the truck?" I suggested instead. We both stood there in front of the tree scratching our heads trying to figure this out until we saw a truck off a distance start to get closer. It was one of our neighbors' trucks, he must have been watching out for us. We waited for him to pull up to the other side of the tree, then Roy got out and asked "Need a ride back home?" "That would be great!" We both responded simultaneously. First I crawled over the tree, then Roy lifted Compass over and I helped guide Compass down, then Velcro was next, and Tom after Velcro. We all got into Roy's truck and he took us to our mobile. During the drive, Roy updated us on the tree blocking decision, and what he's heard on the news. Thankfully he did not ask us any questions about our drive up.

As soon as we got there Tom got the other truck out, and said "Leave the dogs here, we'll just transfer all the stuff real quick and be done with it." I put the dogs in the house, and then ran into Tom's truck and off we went. It was dusk now and so we had a limited amount of time to get all our stuff over the tree if we wanted to get it done in daylight. Going around the tree was not much of an option, so we had to make do. They sure picked a big tree to block the road with. As if my muscles were not tired enough from wearing all the gear earlier, now I was using a whole different set of muscles to move stuff over the tree. Fortunately all the big items were already at the cabin, and all the stuff that was left fit nicely in smaller boxes, though not any lighter. We managed to get all the stuff transferred right as we were running out of daylight. We cleaned the truck up and Tom mentioned coming back later to siphon the diesel out since that truck could not get through the road block. But I suggested "It might be useful to have a truck on the other side, we never know when we might need to leave here." He gave me this stern look and said "If we have to leave here, then I don't know where we are going to go."

We drove back silently and then unloaded the truck silently. Exhaustion hit, and we both sat on the futon with a heavy sigh. Tom turned to me and said "welcome to our new life. Welcome to 'nowhere'."

Chapter 3

The 'cabin'

We were woken up by loud banging on our door. We jumped up in realization that we had fallen asleep with our clothes on. We did not even brush our teeth or get under the covers, though probably a good thing considering how dirty and grungy we were. The events of yesterday were exhausting. Our male German shepherd, Compass, was barking at the banging. I grabbed the revolver which is always loaded and headed for the door. "Who is it?" I yelled.

"Rachel, it's Roy, we need to talk." I looked at Tom who had a look of relief when he realized that it was just Roy. I opened the door and let him in. "Rachel, Tom, there is stuff on TV you have to see. When you guys are ready, come to my place, but hurry OK" There was obvious worry in Roy's voice. We never bothered to move up our TV as we never saw a need for a TV at our cabin, and for the most part we really did not like what was on television anyway. TV seemed nothing more than mindless distraction as far as we were concerned. We preferred the internet, and we did have satellite internet. Tom chimed in "just tell us Roy, we will look it up online."

"You won't be able to. All internet use is suspended until further notice." Roy's response was quic.

"The internet has been... 'turned off'!?" I asked.

"Yep, cell phones too. No cell phone use unless it's an emergency or authorized by political officials for work purposes" Roy clarified.

"You are kidding" Tom was in disbelief.

"Nope, I don't kid 'bout stuff like that. I think we ought to have a town meeting" Roy suggested.

"Yes, how soon can we get a meeting together?" Tom asked.

"Noon. Maybe one" was Roy's response.

Tom coordinated, "okay, let's do that, let's all meet at the church at one."

Roy complied "okay, I will spread the word." He paused a moment then said "by the way, I collected eggs while you were gone. I also figured you were tired last night and that you forgot about your chickens. So I locked them up for ya, and I let them out this morning too. And made sure the goats had water. But I imagine you are back now and do not need my help any more?"

"Roy, thanks so much, we really appreciate it" I thanked him. He was right, we did forget. Roy added "even brought you back some eggs so you can have some breakfast. From what I hear on the news, your drive was a bit dangerous." Tom and I looked at each other. I reminded myself that self defense is not murder. Roy must have seen the confused look on our faces because he continued to say "well Rachel, apparently you have been kidnapped by somebody who left a few of their comrades for the vultures. Apparently you took your government card and set off the chip or something, and they came looking for ya, but found a big mess. News said something about how they don't think you'll be found. They said this is exactly why they do not want nobody to leave the cities, said it's dangerous."

"Roy..." I started.

"Ah, don't you worry, we all know you here, we won't tell. We are just sad that a lot of what you warned us about has come true. But hey, we will have that meeting at one, and we'll get it all figured out then" Roy said optimistically. Roy was a good man. He was level headed and was a hard worker, but definitely a "country boy." A Vietnam veteran that was hard of hearing until he found out the VA would pay for his hearing aids if he could convince them his hearing loss was due to his combat in Vietnam. It turned out to be easier than he thought once he knew what to do. The extra money also supplemented his social security so he was able to stock up on quite a bit of supplies, including his medication for his ischemia, which he very carefully ordered a little early every month. No one noticed, and he managed to stock up at least 3 months from refilling early. But that was not all, Roy was smart. He found three different doctors in three different towns, and ended up paying cash for prescriptions from the additional doctors so that no one would ever question what his motives were. So he was set on medication for at least a year. You could tell from looking at his face that he was an honest man, and a hard worker, and old. The wrinkles hid what he may have looked like as a young man, - a rounded face that would be smooth except for the lines of the wrinkles. And he had shrunk in height in his advanced years as well. But that never stopped him; he still did all his own repairs. Though his health prevents him from working as much as he used to, so he makes due with his small income.

Roy handed me the egg basket and then left. I locked the door behind him, then I looked at Tom and said "looks like we got out in the nick of time."

"Yeah, barely" Tom responded though a bit annoyed.

"Can you believe they are using me as an example already?" I tried to change the mood.

"Well, at least no one expects you back at work" Tom decided to be optimistic.

"Yeah, that's a good thing in it is own way" I smiled as I said that, I hated that job.

"Hey, you hated that job" Tom knew exactly what I was thinking.

"That's because I didn't do anything productive" I argued.

"Well that all changes now" Tom had a seriousness in his tone. It does all change now. I will probably never see any of my co-workers, friends, or acquaintances from the city again.

"Yeah, why don't I start with some breakfast." I really just wanted to end the conversation, so I quickly walked to the kitchen with out looking back.

I put the eggs in the fridge then I went to check on the animals first. Compass and our female German shepherd, Velcro, followed me out. They loved herding the animals, and sometimes did it even when I did not want them to. Though that was not the case before we trained them. Previously they wanted to eat the animals, as is in their nature. The initial training was costly, and the continuous training has been extremely time consuming. It was fortunate that Tom was unemployed for a while, and had the time to provide that constant training. That is the only reason the dogs were as obedient and as well behaved as they are now. They certainly did not come that way.

Roy had been a wonderful neighbor, though kind of far away. In trade for eggs and goat milk, he tended to our animals whenever we were not here. He also checked on the sprinklers to make sure nothing was broken in trade for whatever fruits and veggies were ready to be picked from our garden. It was thanks to Roy and our other neighbor Rita that we were able to work and live in the city and not worry about our "cabin." But it was not always like that.

When we first got the place and would come up on weekends, Rita avoided us at all costs. A middle aged woman who loved growing flowers, until she lost her husband to cancer. Once he was gone, she went to church daily and never bothered to grow flowers anymore. She had a greenhouse on her property that she never used, and it happened to border our property line. When we first bought the cabin, we tried on several occasions to meet with her to see why she is not using the greenhouse, but she always avoided us.

Then one weekend when we had rented a tractor, we started removing brush right on the edge of the property line, right where her greenhouse is, and she finally came out to talk to us. That is when we learned of her misfortune with her husband, and realized that she wanted nothing to do with anything except to go to church. We worked out an agreement with her that she could have enough fresh fruits and vegetables from the green house for her own needs, and to sweeten the deal we offered her free range chicken eggs as well. It was an easy deal to make, and it allowed us to de-prioritize a greenhouse on our shopping list. Although we still wanted a greenhouse, or at least hoop houses of our own, Rita's would suffice provided she did not change her mind. So far so good, and it made Rita a bit friendlier and more willing to help us out when we were not at the cabin. So between Rita and Roy, we had enough help to tend to our property, including our goats, and chickens, plus the gardens and fruit trees.

As I was heading out to the animals, I noticed the garden looked amazing, especially considering I was only there on weekends and sometimes only every other weekend; occasionally only once a month, and although Tom was there during the part of the week for work, he had weeks where he worked 14 hour days, leaving no time to work on anything at the cabin. There were times when everything would just get neglected. I was getting distracted with the luscious red tomatoes everywhere, and had to remind myself the animals had to come first. The chickens were already out and scavenging for bugs, and the goats were out in the pasture. Looks like I needed to move them as the grass was a little low where they are at. The next pasture over had tall grass, I would be able to mow it and let it dry for winter feed, then let the goats eat the rest. Maybe I would get to that tonight, as it had not rained in a while so it is safe to mow and store. I checked all the waters though there was no need, as Roy had already taken care of them, and made sure all the fencing was secure. I then ran back inside to grab the milk jugs and proceeded to get some goat milk. That in itself was a steep learning curve. We watched many youtube videos to learn how to do it, and we studied many techniques. But when it came right down to it, what we lacked was experience. It took a great deal of practice along with hands on training from some experienced folks, and some bruises from being kicked a few times. But eventually we learned, and got it down to an art.

After I was done milking, I went inside to put the milk away. Tom had the music blaring and was doing pushups and pull ups. Getting his appetite up I guess, and that was also his way of getting his anger out. I have no idea how he had any energy for exercise after yesterday's events. I snuck quietly to the kitchen and grabbed the harvest basket, then went back out the back door, the dogs following me every step of the way. I was very quiet because I did not want Tom to see me, as he would encourage me to join him, and I was just too exhausted for exercise.

It is amazing how much a garden will grow in a short amount of time. Rita must have been tending to it a lot. I picked some tomatoes, green onions, and bell peppers, then snuck back inside, found some garlic left over from a few weeks ago, and started making omelets. About the time I finished, Tom was done with his work-out and joined me in the kitchen. As we ate our breakfast we talked about the internet and cell phones being "turned off." Why in the world would they do that? How would they do that? And how is that in anyone's best interest? These questions only led us to more paranoia and we decided to stop. It was bad enough that my name was on the news because of my ID badge. We did not need to bring anymore trouble to us by sounding like paranoid lunatics to our local community. After breakfast we decided to clean up and get ready for our town meeting.

Tom volunteered to feed the dogs while I showered first. I walked into the bathroom and saw myself in the mirror, a real mirror this time rather than some piece of reflective metal, and oh my, did I look bad. My hair was tangled and grungy, my face was covered in dirt. One could hardly see the red through the dirt, one would think I was a brunette. My face tone was covered in dirt where you could not see a freckle on me, though I was generally covered with them. My hair which normally would be straightened with a flat iron was showing its natural half curl that I had always despised, but Tom loved. Such silly things to think about. Given the situation I might have no reason to straighten my hair anymore, if anything, it was just a waste of time. At least my hands were clean from doing the morning chores.

My clothes looked awful, and my shirt was ripped, though I did not recall how that happened. I turned on the water in the tub then switched it to shower, undressed and got in. A shower never felt so good. I wanted to stay in forever, but our on demand hot water heater was limited and used a lot of electricity when it was in use. That was one thing we wished we had researched more before we decided to go with one. So I hurriedly washed up and got dressed.

Tom went next and I went back into the kitchen. Despite the huge omelet that I finished, I still felt hungry. It must be the stress I thought. Looking in the fridge, I found nothing appealing, so I must not really be hungry. As I closed the fridge door I heard a soft "woof woof" warning from Compass. I looked out the kitchen window, but could not see anything. There was a time when Compass barked for no reason, but those days were long gone, and it was only when we first started to come up to the cabin. Compass was our neutered long hair German Shepherd who Tom and I thought might be part Golden Retriever; but one never knows what you get when you rescue from the Humane Society. At that time Compass was a little over a year old, and one weekend I came up with just the dogs. They were not used to the cabin, or the cows on all the surrounding ranches, and Compass kept me up the first night because he kept barking at the moo sounds. It was his protective bark, and he probably felt more protective because Tom was not there that weekend. But since then, Compass has been an excellent guard dog, so it is not like Compass to alarm bark unless it was something real. So I grabbed my revolver and started to look out all the windows. I saw nothing. "Woof woof.... grrr... grrrr..." Compass was pointing in the direction of the back door. I walked closer to the door and opened it, and Compass and Velcro, our pure bread spayed German Shepherd, both ran out after something. Then a few seconds later I heard laughter. I recognized the voice immediately; even her laughter had an English accent. It was Rita's voice. I put the gun away and realized we did not let Rita know we were back.

I walked outside to speak with her. She was petting the dogs and telling them what good dogs they were. Her straight hair was nicely organized around her face, she must have recently dyed it as I saw no gray today. Her face was colorful and plump, now that she was getting over the death of her husband, she had been dressing up trying to impress someone. Who, I did not know, but she sure had a lot of make up on today.

As I approached Rita I said "I'm sorry, we should have told you we were back." In her classic British accent she responded, "oh one knew. One saw your truck behind the tree, not where you, one's old bean, left it last time you were here. Did you knoh you're all ovah the tele news?"
 "So I hear, apparently I'm missing."
"And what ah lessohn you aaare teaching."
"Yeah, I like to be made an example of."
"Doh not worry, noh one here will tell. We all knoh you needed to mustah out of there."
"Yeah." I felt exhaustion, as if I had been hit by a bus. Rita's happy energy just felt too much for me at the moment.

"Hope you doh not mind, I thought one would mustah ah few more tomatoes; making some tomatoh sauce."

"Of course not, you practically did this garden yourself."

"Hah hah, I tended to it ah little bit here and there."

"No really, you are always welcome here, we can't eat all of this anyway, and I'm not in the mood for canning today."

"I imagine not. Soh I'll see you at one for the meeting?"

"Yes, we plan to be there."

"Then you should be awaaare, some of the folk doh not fancy you here. They think you're going to bring trouble." Only Rita could deliver bad news with a happy tone of voice.

"Great, just what we need."

"Don't you worry about that bullocks. Everyone that matters fancies you here."

"That is a little reassuring."

"And thanks greatly to yourselves, more than half of this town has teah and crumpets and supplies tucked awah. One think we will be jollyoh through this."

"I hope so, but it sounds like things might get ugly."

"Yes, we will chinwag about it at the meeting, all roysh?"

"See you then."

I went back inside with a sigh of relief, the dogs reluctantly following. The last thing I needed was a stranger snooping on the property. When you are trying to warn an entire small town of what may come, it is hard to keep your preps a secret. There was no doubt that a few of the folk did nothing from our warnings, and now plan to get what they need from us. Tom and I had discussed that a lot, and we made the decision that we were just not going to share. Frankly, driving back and forth is a pain in the rear, and we did it to keep working so we could have more money for more supplies. It was not easy, and as we learned recently, could have cost us our lives. There were a few people who spent their pay checks or retirement checks on junk, and were not even willing to learn about how to garden or raise a chicken. Those people are few in this town, but we knew exactly which ones to avoid.

Tom was walking out of the bedroom fully dressed as he was towel drying his hair, as soon as he saw me he said "I was thinking about it, and I don't think you should go to this meeting Rachel."

"Why not?" I was hurt by his statement.

"Well, I think that because you are all over the news, that maybe some folks here might not be ready to see you yet..." he said cautiously.

"Are you thinking someone might turn me in?" I asked bluntly.

"Yes" his response was just as blunt as my question.

"But if you're here, then they will know I'm here" I argued.

"Not necessarily... I won't say anything, and I'm guessing based on the news, they'll be too respectful to ask" Tom rationalized.

"But Roy and Rita have seen me already, plus who knows who else when we pulled up last night, it was still a little light out" I continued to be on the defensive.

"True, but no reason to shock everyone and have them see you. Until they actually see you, it's just a rumor." Tom winked.

"Well, if you insist... though it's probably a good idea just so someone is here to keep an eye on this place. I have a weird feeling that it's being staked out. Lots of people know we have things, and if the roads are closed that means trucking shipments have stopped. If so, then people will have no way to get things except from us or others."

"Good point, now that makes two reasons you should stay here" Tom stated. I decided not to argue anymore "alrighty then, but make sure you take notes, I want to know everything that's going on."

"Maybe you can go through the house and make a list of what still needs to be done" Tom suggested, to which I gave him a dirty look, like it was not obvious. We did not have any interior wall paneling in the living room, we barely got the plumbing done before we finished replacing the sub-floors and had the wood stove installed. That list will be a long one.

"Sure, I'll look around and see what needs to be done. I will also organize all our food that we brought in last night, and maybe hook up the portable reverse osmosis water filter. But will you please take good notes at the meeting?" I begged.

"Okay. See you shortly then, love you."

"Love you too." The words felt heavy coming out. To think, less than 24 hours ago had we not been careful, that would have been the end of us. Who knows what would have happened had the looters caught us. I realized I did not want to be apart from Tom, but he was right, I should not go to this meeting. I gave him a quick kiss bye, something we always did before parting ways.

He walked out the door and got in the truck to go. The dogs ran to the window and watched as he drove away. While the dogs were distracted, I grabbed a notebook and a pen, and started going through the house to see what needed to be done now.

I decided that I was actually rather relieved that I did not have to go to the meeting. I knew it was important, but frankly, I was tired, the events of the day prior really wiped me out, and I just did not feel like dealing with grumpy old people. I especially did not want to have to answer any questions regarding what happened yesterday, and how my ID badge got loose. No one would ask Tom anything, they respected him too much.

I wandered through the house making notes. We spent the last year bringing up supplies, but very little actual time in fixing things except for the urgent and basics. We were limited on funds, so we had to get creative. I started going to yard sales and picked up folding chairs and TV trays. They made great temporary furniture, and that was all we had in the cabin the first couple times we were here. So I did more yard sale shopping, and I will tell you, sometimes you just score. It was amazing what people will sell. Most of the stuff I would not believe I scored for either really cheap, or free. Our local freecycle Yahoo group was very active, so freebies came up often. I first offered up a bunch of stuff that I decided I no longer needed. Mainly nick-knacks and such, but also things I bought that I realized did not work very well, but were too late to return, such as one of those round dehydrators without a fan. I learned quickly that a fan was almost essential if you want to dehydrate food for long term storage and you can not sit there and babysit it for 16 hours. Once I established my email address as someone who gave away a bunch of stuff, getting people to give me stuff that they posted instead of someone else became a little easier. But that meant stalking the email freecycle list. The same was true with Craigslist. I had to refresh that page every 10 minutes to make sure I did not miss a deal. You would not believe the things that city-people give away. The sink in the cabin spare bathroom we got for free and was practically brand new. We even scored a free bathroom vanity in excellent condition, which came with a sink and a faucet, practically new. The guy that got rid of it said it was too short for him, so he bought a new one. We had to act fast though. The second it posted was the same second I was on the phone getting directions. There was no time to think if we really wanted it. Truth was, if it turned out we did not want it, we just give it away for free to someone else. By the time it took us to get off the phone and get there, the guy told us that he had to remove the ad because he had 5 more phone calls after ours. We just got lucky because we were first.

That was the life of Craigslist and Freecycle. You had to be fast, and you had to be willing to get there now. Tom quickly adjusted to this type of lifestyle with me, if he walked in the office and saw me looking at Mapquest, he would just say "what are we picking up now?"

Yard sale shopping was a whole different story, but about the same. When Compass was only four months old, I would start taking him with me. I wanted him used to other people because I knew that German Shepherds can get too aggressive if not introduced from a young age. Plus I did not know his prior history, so the sooner I socialized him properly the better. Compass went to the dog park regularly, and he went yard sale shopping with me regularly. Little did I know that his big ears would give me a cute puppy discount. I hardly ever paid for a toy for him, and when I found "junk" that others did not know what to do with, I would get that cute puppy discount and only pay a dollar or two. Yard sales were great because people just want to get rid of stuff. I managed to score a great deal of new left over insulation pieces, plywood pieces, paint, tools, shelving, folding chairs, TV trays, blankets (which work great for moving blankets and dog blankets), gardening supplies, planters, fencing, and once I even scored an amazing

61

set of silverware, which was 90% silver. Some people just did not know what their grandparent's stuff was worth, and they would sell it cheap just to get rid of it. I am the person that went around yard sales and low balled the price to get a deal, and since most people just wanted to get rid of it, they agreed. I once got a popular brand stand mixer (worth $300) for $2. The guy had no idea what it was; it was off in a corner with a bunch of other kitchen utensils. I asked him how much for the stand mixer, and he looked at me and asked me what it was. I told him it is a bowl that had a mixer with it and mixes stuff. He said "how about $2?" I did not even try to talk him down, I handed him two bucks, grabbed the mixer and ran. I did not even ask if it worked, the bowl on that alone was worth $30, so if it did not work, I could always sell the bowl. But it turned out to be in perfect condition, just needed a little cleaning.

Probably one of the best scores of all time, though some may disagree, was going to a few different super market bakeries and asking what they do with their food grade buckets. The first was a discouraging moment when we were told that they do not give away buckets because they use them to catch the roof leaks. The second implied that they can not do so, and finally the third was happy to recycle the buckets. They said they will save them all week and to pick them up on Friday before 9 am. They even put them through their dishwasher for us. We went back several Friday's and managed to collect quite the array of 1 gallon, 3 gallon, and 5 gallon buckets. All food grade, all previously had food in them, all clean, and with handles and lids. You can never have enough buckets, and we kept going back until we got the sense that they were annoyed with us, so we stopped. We always talked about going back to get more, and maybe trying a different store, but time was just never on our side.

Then of course our paychecks covered supplies that we either could not find used, or were not willing to get used. By the time that we purchased the cabin a year ago, we had run out of room in our home in the city, the garage was full, and so were the spare bedrooms and our enclosed cargo trailer. When we took the first load up in our trailer, it did not even put a dent in the amount of stuff we had. And yet we continued to pay our "tax" as we called it, every time we went to the store. If we needed toothpaste, we bought two, one for now, one for the future. If we needed shampoo, we bought two. Need chicken? We bought one canned for the future. We did this for three years prior to our cabin purchase - every time our paychecks allowed it. Four years later, here we were.

The living room needed interior walls. We had no choice but to finish the floors if we wanted a wood stove installed. It was such a steep learning curve for us. We had never owned a manufactured home before, and came to find out, most of the building materials for older manufactured homes is specialized, at least until the year 2004. Then the parts became standard. Finding replacement parts was like living in the old days where you had to find a distributor, call them and ask them if they carried something. There were some websites that offered manufactured home supplies, but it was not like you could go on Amazon and click and buy. It was even harder to find reviews on manufactured home products. Not to mention the poor quality of manufactured homes built in the 80's. While the quality of older manufactured homes may have been lacking, the upside was that they offered fast and inexpensive shelter for those needing housing out in the middle of nowhere.

We were amazed that someone came up with the brilliant idea to use particle board as sub flooring. Really? Particle board? It took us many hours of research to figure out what size plywood would be best suited to replace it, and until we replaced it, we walked around carefully as our home had experienced some minor water damage. And let's not forget asbestos. Our home was built around the time that asbestos was being phased out and banned, but we were not sure how ours was built. We carefully took samples from various areas that had linoleum, and sent them in for testing before ripping up the floors, and we patiently waited for the results. We had plan B in mind should there be asbestos, but we were fortunate that there was not any found on the test results. At least we did not have to worry about lead paint, our house was built way after that scenario.

The previous owners seemed to have replaced little bits and pieces of the subfloor, but not with anything standard. It seemed they replaced the problem areas with whatever they had on hand that fit. We finally replaced the particle board with ¾" tongue and groove plywood. Then there was question over what should be used for the flooring. Vinyl was out, as it typically (but not always) contained too many toxic chemicals like formaldehyde which would "off-gas." We may be frugal, but we would not compromise our health. Some people do not care if they breathe in toxic fumes, but we did. Just because we knew the economy was falling apart, that was no reason to compromise our health when we did not have to.

We decided that tile was the way to go, but we were told that putting tile in a manufactured home was "not appropriate." More hours on the internet to research why you can not use tile in a manufactured home. No real answer came out, until we stumbled on a discussion group: you do not want to use tile in a manufactured home because when you go to move it, then it will cause the tile to crack. Okay, got it, do not move the manufactured home and you can use tile provided you used proper sub flooring (at least 3/4" plywood rather than particle board).

The living room took us what felt like forever, and all we did was replace the subfloors with plywood, then backer board, then we put in tile. We also had to fix the underbelly while we were at it. Those supplies took a bit to find. I am sure a contractor could have done the job in a few days, but we did not have that kind of money, so we did it ourselves. We did not even care about the color of the tile, we just found the least expensive tile and went for it. We did not skimp on the mortar though, we researched that to make sure any adhesives we used were non-toxic. It is unbelievable what some of this stuff is made of, no wonder we have such a high cancer rate in the US.

So the main room floor got done, and we hired a contractor to install the wood stove. We paid to have the house re-plumbed with PEX piping so it would be more resistant to freeze damage. We did also get rid of the mice problem. I could have written an entire book based on those experiences alone. The previous owners put a few holes in the walls in an effort to run in cables for the internet and television, but they failed to seal the holes, which was like a huge welcome mat for the mice. Plugging up the holes was not difficult, just needed some wire and tape as a temporary measure, we would do a real job when we replaced the walls. But getting rid of the mice that were already in was the adventure. Let's just say that if you set out mouse traps, make sure your dogs can not reach them, and if you think the dogs can not reach them, you are wrong, because they can. Also, do not be surprised at the natural skills your dog has to catch and eat mice. And if your dog comes down sick shortly after eating a mouse, it probably carried something like coccidia, so be ready for some veterinary bills.

We got to a point where we felt that if the time came, and we had to bug out, we could survive with what was done. Sure, we would be restricted to the living room, one bathroom, and a mostly usable kitchen without a stove, but it was enough should the inevitable happen. Running water, a wood stove, and preferably electricity, is all you need. In the meantime, we continued to work and collect supplies. The garage was full of plywood, 2x4's, paint, sheetrock, spare used wood stove obtained for free (thank you craigslist), miscellaneous wood pieces, and what not. Money was tight, and the price of food kept rising, and the more prices went up, the more I stalked Craigslist and FreeCycle. Sure, used wood is not ideal, but when it is free, it is useful. There were also plenty of people finishing up home projects who had descent size pieces of plywood left over, I snatched those right up. It was not easy, and often times I sat at the computer calculating the cost of fuel versus the cost of the item. It turned into a hobby I guess. And now I was standing in a living room with tiled floors but no interior wallboard, with a ton of building material in the garage that could solve that problem. Maybe it was not all for nothing.

There were times where we asked ourselves if the economy would really collapse. Based on the numbers behind the US economy and government debt, and based on the amount of GDP, and how the dollar continued to be devalued by the Federal Reserve, we knew it was inevitable for the dollar to collapse. Mathematically it was just impossible for things to continue to stay afloat. But at the same time, things did manage to stay afloat, and there were times we really questioned our choice to buy property out in the middle of nowhere. Eventually, we came to the conclusion that if the inevitable did not happen, at least we had a nice little vacation home for those times when we want to get away from it all. Or maybe our place to retire since we owned it out right.

I moved to the other rooms, I knew what I would find. The subflooring was replaced with plywood, and is pretty much ready for tile. My only fear was that we did not have enough materials. We tried to keep track, but having two homes to tend to, it got rather confusing quickly. If we did not have enough, then we were in big trouble, because as we learned, there was no where to get more materials unless we dare head back to a major city. And that was not part of the plan. We knew from the beginning that when things turn bad, governments will only make them worse, and it is best to avoid government, its handouts, and its enforcement agents.

After going through all the rooms, I went out to the pump house. Not much to do there. We practically re-built the pump house structure when we did the floors in the house. It was another priority item. No water, no life, so it had to be fixed. This was also another one of those steep learning curves for us. We had no clue about solar, yet here was this pump house full of solar panels on top of the roof. Did the power to pump water come from the grid? The solar? Were there batteries? The inverter? Combiner box? We had no clue. But, our world before yesterday was marvelous. You could go on the internet and learn almost anything. You could watch videos of any process, idea, whatever. Every time we thought we came up with an ingenious idea, we searched the internet and learned that someone beat us to it. Regardless, the internet was an amazing tool. And now it was gone, or at least temporarily suspended. How sad. At least we purchased books for just such an occasion. Well, not exactly; we thought we might not have power, therefore no internet, we never considered the internet would be suspended. I just hoped we covered every topic with our books. I guess we would find out soon enough. We did also save a lot of files on our lap top, especially on topics that we had a hard time finding books on. So maybe if we are lucky, between the books and the laptop, we covered all our bases.

Nothing in the pump house needs fixing, so off to the garage. Never mind, it is full of stuff, you can barely get around. I made a mental note of some of the supplies we would need immediately, and then I went on to see what the animals needed. All the animals shelters were built thanks to some books and internet sites, and those free materials from generous city donors. The animals seemed content, and the chickens were chasing bugs, everything looked in place. Aah, cold frames, yes, and maybe hoop houses. We needed to finish those if we wanted food every season. We have plenty of windows thanks to craigslist and freecycle, plus the old windows from the house from when the previous owners replaced them with double paned windows. And we had plywood scrap wood to finish the piece, and lots of hinges that we removed off the doors in our city house just last week. Yes, we needed lots of cold frames. But now to decide, what is more important, building more cold frames or putting up interior walls? I know what Tom would say, and I would disagree with him… well… after yesterday… maybe not.

I went back inside the house and wrote up my little report for Tom. It was mostly a list of things to do in what order. I decided to make the walls first as Tom would prefer it that way, and I really did not have the energy to argue. So the list had interior walls first, then cold frames, and then putting down tile if time allowed, though it was commercial vinyl tile (CVT) this time, not ceramic. We found a deal for commercial tile that was (non-toxic) and LEED certified, so we went with the commercial stuff. If we did not get to the tile, then sanding and staining the plywood would have to do. We had no conventional stove, but we had two 5th burners, so we could make do. The only problem is that without a stove, I could not bake, or pressure can easily. But I would find a way to manage. It was not that we were being stupid about the stove, it just sort of worked out that we did not get one in time. The one that came with the house was broken like everything else in here, and we considered buying a brand new one, but price stopped us, especially since we knew we could find a good used one for less, and money was scarce. So we kept looking for one. But every time we found one advertised, the local recycle store had already purchased it, and then tried to re-sell it for triple the price. We did not like this practice, and chose not to buy from them, and kept looking for our own stove. We figured worst case scenario, we would bring up the one from our city home, but when it came time to bug out, we were not able to do it because we did not have the time or the room. Plus we would not have been able to hide it well in the truck, so we may have been questioned a little more on our way out of the city. So we left it behind. I could bake in the wood cook stove, though we would not be running the wood stove in the middle of summer. So no baking for the three months of summer? I think we can survive that way. I could always bake extra and freeze it. Yeah, I think it will work. And I should be able to pressure can on the wood cook stove as well, I will just have to watch the pressure gauge more carefully. The 5th burners would work for canning too, I would just have to be careful about the weight. So all and all, I think it is manageable with out a stove, though it would be nice to have one.

The to do list also included setting up a gray water system for the fruit trees we managed to barely plant last December. That was a close call, we happened to find an advertisement for 25 fruit or nut trees for 400 bucks, what a deal! We jumped on it, but not without much research first. Figuring out what trees would survive in our corner of the world was a chore, but we figured it out, and planted 15 fruit trees and 10 nut trees. We also put protective tree guards against them so that the wild animals do not eat the bark, and talked about setting up a gray water recycling system to water them.

Planting the trees was a challenge in and of itself. We knew that it is best to transplant trees in the middle of winter, that is when they are dormant, and thus the best time to transplant them. We knew things were getting worse everyday, we heard it on the news, we saw it at the grocery store when prices were going up each week. So we decided that although we only sort of had an idea of what we were doing, and we really did not have the time to do it, we researched, purchased, and planted the fruit and nut trees.

The things we learned! The fruit and nut trees require a certain amount of chill hours in order to produce fruit, but fortunately our locale already covered that one, it was cold in the winter. Actually, it was cold much of the year, so the chill hours were not an issue. We then had to decide what fruit and nuts we wanted, and decided to go with walnuts and almonds for nut trees, and plums and cherries for fruit trees. We also decided to get some blueberry bushes and grape vines, as they are also best to plant in winter. All the trees required a certain amount of chill hours, and all the nuts and fruits are healthy, and were something we ate regularly.

The next step was to figure out what kind. That part was not hard other than several hours of research on the internet. We decided to go with varieties that were self pollinating. There were a couple cherry trees we got that are not self pollinating, but we made sure to order the pollinating trees as well. Fortunately, the almonds and the walnut trees we ordered were all self pollinating, as the choices for them were more limited. One other major consideration was whether or not we wanted trees that were grafted on a different root stock. The choices for dwarf and semi-dwarf were many, but we were not sure that was the way to go. After much research we decided that semi-dwarf was the best for us. Not only would that require less space for the trees, but it would also allow the trees to remain shorter, thus easier for harvesting. Lastly, we chose varieties that would require harvesting at different times to stagger our food production, except for those that needed to pollinate each other; those we selected to have the same blossom times.

During our research we learned that you can not plant walnut trees near anything else as their roots release a toxin that prevents anything from growing around them. So we had to find a spot on our property where they would be away from any garden area, or animal area. Once we decided on a spot for the walnut trees, we then figured out where we wanted the rest of the trees. This was not easy, as you have to make sure they are not shaded, get the right amount of sunlight, are protected from wind, etc. We settled on our orchard to be north east of our detached garage, we figured the garage would produce enough of a wind barrier, and there was an area that was just between two large evergreen trees that allowed the sun to be present all day. Plus we removed the branches from the evergreen trees from the bottom up to allow more sunlight through. We removed the branches eight feet high as was recommended to help prevent the spread of fires.

The next step was a difficult one. We had to time the order of the trees, with delivery, and with a schedule that allowed us enough time off work to get the planting done. We almost had it figured out only to realize the week we picked would not work because the trees were not available yet, so we had to rethink our strategy. Most of the trees we were told would be available in the middle of December, however, the walnut trees and our blueberry bushes and grapes, would not be available until the middle of January. So we figured the week between Christmas and New Years would be our first trip, and the end of January would be our second trip.

We put in our order for our 25 trees, 12 blueberry bushes, and 12 grape vines, requested the time off work, then waited for the phone call when the trees were ready. Turned out that all the trees were available in the middle of December, we informed the nursery that we would not be picking up until a week later, which they were fine with. Apparently they just "heel" in the trees until ready. A week later, I drove to pick up the trees and brought them to our city home. We put them in our attached garage figuring it would stay cold enough not to break dormancy, but not freezing to harm the tree roots. We also checked them to make sure the roots had enough sawdust and moisture. The next day, we packed them up in the trailer. We also had two cherry trees in our back yard that were not dwarf or semi-dwarf, but two real cherry trees that we purchased when we first started prepping. We had planted them in a large plastic bins with every intent to move them once we found a property.

We took off for the cabin and arrived to discover that the well pump had frozen. We should have known that would have happened, and we should have taken measures to prevent it. The problem could have been prevented simply by putting a lamp with a 100 watt bulb in the pump house, be we did not realize that until it was too late. But it was our first winter owning a place out in the middle of nowhere, and it was our first time dealing with well water. We immediately placed a space heater in the pump house, but reality was, the motor burnt out, and we had no running water. Fortunately our picky healthy ways forced us to pack a ton of filtered water from our city home, and we had about 40 gallons of filtered water. The intent was to leave some behind at the cabin should we be in a situation where we did not have water. That situation was then.

We unpacked the trailer and placed all the trees on the deck that connected the house. Since the garage was detached, we figured the trees might freeze there, so we chose the enclosed deck. The next morning, we started to dig holes. We took a risk knowing that the ground may be frozen, and you can not plant trees in frozen ground as the ice crystals apparently can damage the roots, or at least that is what we read. Fortunately, only the first couple inches were frozen ground, the rest was fine. So we used a pick axe to break through the first couple inches, then we dug holes with shovels.

That was back breaking work. Tom and I considered ourselves in good shape. We met at a gym, and were always taking our health as a first priority. But with college and work, we ran out of time for the gym, so we both started to slack a bit, only due to lack of time. Digging those holes made us very regretful that we ever slowed down on our strength exercises; we certainly could have used the extra strength. We managed to get 16 trees in the first day before we ran out of daylight. Go figure, best time to transplant the trees was in the middle of winter, during the shortest daylight of the year. Though I am not so sure that any more daylight would have kept us going, by the time we finished those 16 trees, we were exhausted, and with no running water to take a shower with, or to water the trees with.

The next day we were at it again as soon as daylight hit. Nothing like ibuprofen and curcumin to ease the pain, and coffee to get us going. We dug 14 regular sized holes and two larger holes for the adult trees in the plastic bins out of our backyard. We encountered many rocks along the way, some of which were quite large and heavy. We managed to pull them out with the help of a crow bar and sledge hammer, and finished the holes to the right size. We put in the 14 bare root trees, and then struggled to get the two larger trees to their perspective holes. We used a dolly to help us move them, but there were a couple issues. One, they were super heavy, and two, the plastic bins they were in were breaking off due to being out in the sun for three years. The bins breaking off in pieces ended up being a blessing, as that made it easier to take the trees out of their temporary container and put them in the hole. Still, the entire process took every bit of energy and time that we had.

By then, daylight was gone for us again. We sat down in our cabin, ate a ton of food, and drank a good amount of wine to ease the pain. We normally did not drink too much, but we did like red wine, and that day was an exception. We were hurting. It hurt to get out of our folding chairs, it hurt to do anything.

After planting all those trees, I wanted nothing but a hot shower. But even with the pump now thawed, there was still no running water. We figured the motor had burnt out, but we had no money to call someone, nor did we have a phone book to find someone, so we were stuck on YOYO (You're On Your own) time. We managed by heating up water in a tea kettle and pouring it into buckets of water, then using a washcloth we were able to wash up, if you want to call it that.

The next day, Tom drove to the general store in town to see if they had any bottled water. We were in better luck than we thought. While they only had a dozen gallon containers of drinking water, the store owner Bob, did offer us the use of their hose, and said if we collect right at noon, we can get water that is not too cold. We decided that with the dozen gallon bottles, plus what we still had left from what we brought, we were fine for drinking water, but the trees we just planted needed water. So we loaded up all our free bakery buckets with lids into the pick up truck, and Tom drove back to the general store to fill it with water from the hose. We ended up having enough water to water all the trees properly, and even had some left over to add hot water to and take baths.

Go figure, that evening, it rained. We probably would have watered the trees anyway, as we did not want to count on nature during such a crucial time. The following morning we figured we had enough water to drink and wash dishes with to last us only another few days. We planned for a full ten days, but given the water situation, that was just not going to happen. We spent the next couple days doing very small and light things around the cabin, as we were too exhausted and sore to do anything else. And we knew that we would have to do it again in a month to plant the blueberries and grapes. We were fortunately able to come up with enough money to fix the well pump by then.

Fortunately the grapes and blueberries were no where near as much work; their holes did not have to be anywhere near as big. The only thing was to measure out the right amount of acid mix to add to the blueberries, so that their roots could properly develop. We also had to put up the grape trellis, but we just used t-posts with nine gauge galvanized metal wire. About the only snag we ran into was a snowstorm the week they were supposed to be shipped, so the shipping was delayed, and our time off did not correlate, so we temporarily placed them in potted containers, kept in the garage as to prevent breaking dormancy, then transplanted once the weather allowed for travel and we were able to take the time off. Though on the second planting trip we once again we ran into water issues, as the sediment from our well water had settled in our new PEX plumbing, resulting in clogged faucets. We were fortunate to have one working bathroom, but the rest of the house was plugged up. Once again we were with out hot water, but at least we had running water this time. And at least this time we were not as dirty from the planting shrubs, unlike the trees, and we were able to water them using buckets. Having at least cold running water allowed us to stay longer as we did not run out of drinking water as quickly.

For a while we were not sure if we did it right, and if our labor would pay off. We knew we would not find out until spring. When we started to see leaves on the trees, we were ecstatic, our hard work was not for nothing. We expected that there will be some delicious fruit once the trees were mature enough to produce fruit. Our two adult cherry trees should produce this year, they did produce a little last year, and that was while they were still in their containers. So we hoped for greater production this year. The grafted semi-dwarfs should produce by the following year, we hoped.

I looked at the sun, probably 3pm. I had lost track of time reminiscing. Wow, the meeting must be intense. Tom will be hungry when he comes home, I thought that maybe I should prepare something for us. I went out to the garden and found some vegetables that I could steam. I looked at the chicken coop and thought about slaughtering a chicken. There were more than enough of them, but I just did not have the energy, so canned chicken it would be. Bread baking is exhausting, plus I did not want to start the wood stove, it was too hot, so that was out. But I did dig up some rice and threw that in the crock pot. Then I threw the canned chicken and the veggies in the crock pot as well. If it gets over cooked, so be it, I did not have the energy to cook a real meal.

I sat on the futon and I looked at my list. We needed to work the land. There was so much of it that it was a never ending project. But now we were going to need all that land. If we were going to grow food to sustain us, we would be using all the land we could, not to mention that we need to save seed for next year's planting as well. It seemed everything on the list had significant importance. But frankly there was only two of us, so we had to prioritize what was most important. I knew what Tom would say, so I left the walls as top of the list. Setting up a hidden retreat with a cache out in the woods? Let's move that higher up on the list. The more I look at the list and the more I think about the previous days events, the more I realize how often Tom was right, and how much I hoped he was wrong about the future. But given how things had played out so far, I think that was unlikely. I was just glad I never argued about the items he invested in. And I was glad he thought in that direction. Oh how could I forget! The solar panels. I did not have to go to the garage to see how many we had, that was already figured out. We should have just enough if we are extra careful about our electricity usage.

The solar panels were not easy for us to budget, and was a little dishonest. We could not afford both the solar panels and batteries along with an inverter, so we invested in a system for our city home. We could not find a place that would include the batteries, everyone wanted to hook us up to the grid so that we could make money from the power company by selling the excess power back to them, though that was not really much. We went ahead and financed the solar system and had it installed in our city home, though not on the roof, but separately next to our building. We also insisted on a system that could run on a generator should city power go out. We had to purchase our own generator, but we found a nice diesel one on Craigslist for $800. The solar system turned out to be okay as our electric bill was reduced to almost nothing, and we used the money that we would have paid for our electric bill to pay the monthly payments on the panels. Then we purchased a battery a month as a "survival tax" as we called it, making sure to use a battery charger and keep the batteries charged regularly. Then we put the inverter on a credit card. We knew we overpaid for the panels themselves, but it was the only way we could figure to get it financed. We never made money from the power company as we used too much power, but at least we did not really have a power bill. Once we accumulated enough batteries and had the inverter, we disconnected the solar panels from our city house and took them up to the cabin. When the nosy city neighbors asked what we were doing, we told them we could not afford the solar system as we thought we could, and thus were returning it. We then carefully stashed the panels and batteries in our cabin garage, and swallowed the cost of having an electric bill in our city home again, along with monthly payments of the overpriced panels. Plus the extra time to charge the batteries regularly to keep them from going bad. We had not had the time to hook up the panels at the cabin yet, but now we would have the time. But we were going to need help. Those panels are fragile and not easy to maneuver.

Simultaneously the dogs ran to the living room window tails wagging. Tom must be pulling in. I walked over to the window, and sure enough, he was pulling in to the gravel driveway. I stood and watched as he got closer. He did not look happy. As I was watching him my attention was caught by the body armor that was thrown into a corner. There was something odd about it. I walked over to look at it and realized that one of us had been shot. I picked up the vest and started to inspect it, looking it over I was startled by Tom's voice "I meant to tell you about that, but I didn't want to worry you." Tom caught me by surprise, I was so mesmerized by the fact that one of us got shot, that I did not hear him walk in.

"Who got you?" I asked him.

"I don't know, but it was only a 9mm" he said reassuringly, as if being shot by a smaller caliber made it okay.

"Did you not feel it?"

"Of course I felt it, but it was more like getting hit by a paintball gun at close range without armor than anything, and now I have a huge bruise and it's sore, I think the shot came from far away" his response was strange, does he not realize he could have been killed?

"Were you ever going to tell me about it?" I was a little annoyed by his nonchalant attitude.

"I don't know, I was still thinking about how to tell you. I think it happened during our standoff with the fake guard" Tom said defensively.

"Is that why you asked me yesterday how many shots I fired?" I realized his question yesterday made sense now.

"Yeah, I heard more shots than I was able to count" he replied.

"So someone else was there?" it was more of a statement then question.

"Had to have been" Tom replied.

"Whose side were they on if they shot you? Must have been one of the looters?" I was trying to make sense of the situation.

"It doesn't matter, we're both safe and sound. Let me tell you about the meeting. Turns out the government wants all small town folk to evacuate to large cities if they have somewhere to stay, or to relief camps if not."

"What? They are forcing people to leave? And what are relief camps?" I had so many questions, Tom did a good job of changing the topic. I put the armor back down and sat down to listen to Tom.

"Not forcing them, yet. But that's coming. And I don't yet know exactly what a relief camp is. According to the news, it is a place where shelter, food, and water are provided to anyone that needs it."

"Wait, I don't understand, how are they getting people to leave?"

"Any city with a population less than 50,000 people will have all supplies cut off. They are encouraging residents to leave their homes and go to relief camps. They are arranging transportation for anyone that wants it" Tom explained,

"Are you serious?" I was baffled.

"They also apparently announced that any farmer who is willing to sell their livestock to the Federal Government will be credited a descent sum on their cards" Tom said while rolling his eye. Yeah, like you can trust a government that declares martial law on it's own people.

"I don't understand, the government wants small towns to disperse into large cities or relief camps?" I wished I had gone to the meeting as Tom was terrible at relaying the news.

"Yep" Tom replied.

"But why? This town is mostly self sufficient. This town has the resources to provide for it's people - it just takes a little work. I'm sure there are other towns that are self sufficient too" I was in disbelief.

"Not according to the government" Tom replied calmly.

"So… what are the residents saying?" I decided to move on with the conversation.

"Well, they are conflicted. Some are leaving, some are staying, some are still undecided. Many of them are dependent on life saving medications, so they are leaving for that reason alone."

"Are the important ones staying?" This was not to imply that not everyone is important, but in all honestly, some folks just were not willing to do anything to prepare.

"For the most part, though Roy is dependent on his social security check, and that no longer exists."

"So Roy's leaving?"

"No, he's not, I reassured him that eggs and goat milk will

continue to be available to him for all his help this last year, but some others are leaving. The problem is that it's supposedly not a choice. They are saying that everyone from small towns is required to evacuate."

"Whaaaaat?" I asked, none of this was making any sense.

"Yeah, that's just it. Supposedly no one has a choice. There was a big argument about it today, and we decided that we will move the tree blocking the road on the East entrance, and let people leave as they choose. But by sundown tomorrow, we are moving the tree back and re-blocking the road. Also, a decision was made that anyone that chooses to leave, is not welcome back." Tom explained, though I could tell he was not happy with that last decision.

"How will we manage that?" I asked.

Tom responded quickly "we'll have armed volunteers manning guard duty at the road block trees, on both the east and west side, six hour shifts to divide up the day."

"Did you volunteer?" I hoped he would answer no to my question.

"Actually, volunteer was the wrong word. Every person over the age of 18 that resides between the road block trees will have a shift, with the exception of those that have physical limitations that would prevent them from effectively performing guard duty."

"Well, that is probably a good idea, but how often will you have to do shifts?" I was really hoping for an answer that would not take Tom away very often.

"I don't know yet. We haven't figured those details out yet. But, let's see, 24 hours in a day, divide by six, that is four shifts at two people per tree, with one tree at each of the road, that makes two trees, so four people per shift, that is 16 people per day. There is what... 350? 450 people over 18 here?" Tom was more thinking out loud than asking.

"Well, how many are leaving?" I had to point out that there will be less soon.

"Oh, good point. Probably around 100 or so. So let's say there are 300 people left, divide by 16 people, that is a shift twice a month, I can handle that." Tom seemed satisfied with his quick math.

"Only two people per tree?" I wanted to make sure.
"It might increase to three or four, it depends on how things are going I guess. Still that would make it a shift a week, still doable." Tom was confident in his answers.
"Provided they don't sign us up on the same shift, someone needs to watch the house."
Tom replied very sternly "oh no, you are NOT doing it, no one can know you're here, that's too dangerous."
"But if I don't, and folks find out that I'm here, they will be upset that I did'nt do my share." I argued.
"We'll cross that bridge when we get there. For the time being, as far as I'm concerned, you are not NOT here." I could tell from Tom's voice that he was serious, there is no arguing with him right now. I was upset by this, I need to do my part. People will be amgry when they find out I am here and have not done my part. I can see it now, they will punish me by forcing me to make up all the shifts I missed. I know these small town folk, they are relentless when they want their way.
"Fine, but are you really going to turn people away when they return?" I don't know why I questioned Tom's abilities, but for some reason I did. Tom replied quickly and with out any consideration, "yes."

I stared at Tom. I was dumbfounded. Why is all this happening? Why are we being forced to evacuate our homes when we are self sufficient? Why are townspeople being forced to leave? It does not make sense. And we are not going to let people back if they wish to come back to their homes? "So now what?" I asked. Tom looked at me, I knew his response, he did not have to say it, and he did not. I grabbed the list I made and handed it to him as I started to recite the list off memory.
"First, we get the walls done. The sand bags are in the garage and based on what I saw, I think we have more than enough. If anything, we can do three quarters of the house, and skip the areas that are least likely to be hit. After the walls, we will finish the floors for our safety rather than for any other reasons. We should be okay on supplies for that as well. After the floors are done, we should have enough plywood that we can build an emergency shelter out in our bug out spot that we considered before. I can start putting together supplies for a cache to take

out there and bury. Once that is done, then we can start working on things like cold frames, and improving this place, but it sounds like we might not get that far."

"No, we might not, but we can at least try. You think we have enough supplies?" Tom was always worried about having enough.

"Yes, from the looks of it. I didn't measure with a tape measure or anything, but did a pretty good visual with some math. I think we can manage" I tried to sound confident in my response.

"Then we need to get started, we have no time to waste." Tom sounded serious, but tired.

"Are you hungry?" I asked him.

"I don't have time to make anything" he was trying to convince himself more than me.

"But it's already done, just need to scoop it up and put it in your bowl" I said smiling.

"Did I mention I love you?" he said smiling back.

"A few times, but I don't tire of hearing it." I smiled again and filled a bowl of my homemade thrown together stew. He ate voraciously, I am not even sure he tasted it. After our late lunch, Tom and I went to the garage, and started to fill the sandbags with sand.

The walls were a huge debate for a long time. Yet another problem with manufactured homes built in the 80's. The wall space was limited, so one could only install so much insulation. With the walls being so thin, Tom argued that if we were attacked, the bullets will go right through like cardboard, and we had to do something. While manufactured homes offered an inexpensive and quick route to shelter in the countryside, and under normal use would probably hold up, they were not exactly built robustly enough to withstand challenges like bullets or explosives. Money of course was always an issue, as it had been the last three years. Then one day, Tom stumbled upon some ballistic research, apparently bullets get stopped pretty well by sand. So he made the decision that we will get some sand, fill up some sand bags, and put that between the walls. Only high enough to protect us while ducking down, and above that we would do regular insulation. After all, heat rises. A crazy idea if you asked me, but, now as I was scooping up sand into sand bags, I realize that maybe not so crazy, especially after yesterday.

After we donned our full gear of leather gloves, goggles, and knee pads, we started to work. One may have looked at us and thought this was overkill. But frankly, we talked about this a lot before things fell apart, we knew that once things fell apart, small injuries could turn serious, and doctor's may not be easy to find, and even if you find a doctor, antibiotics or other medication will be another challenge. We made a unanimous decision that we should always use protective gear, but once things got bad, our protective gear would be maximized. Better safe than sorry. We spent the money to purchase quality protective gear that actually worked. And we made sure we had at least three sets of everything if not more. As the old saying goes, one is none, two is one. We figured that since we needed two for us, we should at least have a third for backup.

It felt like forever, but we managed to get a good amount of bags together. Then Tom went to grab a wheel barrow. We threw in a bunch of sacks, and Tom took them to the house, then returned with the empty barrow. In the meantime, I found the insulation for the top half of the walls, and the drywall. I moved both of these to the front of the garage. Then when Tom returned, I threw more bags into the wheel barrow and said "I think it's good we are clearing out some of this stuff, I think that when the tree road block is moved tomorrow, we should move the other truck and put it in the garage, just in case they are looking for it." Tom stopped and looked at the other truck, then after a couple of minutes he said "Yeah, I think that's a good idea. Good thing this garage is good sized. Let's make it our goal tonight to clear enough space, we will move stuff into the living room if we have to." He then picked up the wheel barrow and pushed it across the gravel on his way to the house.

I was tired and hurting again, but we had so much work ahead of us. That is the reality of how long it takes to get stuff done. In your mind, you think you can get it done in a day or so. But when you are actually doing it, especially if it is for the first time, then it takes much longer than that, and you find yourself running out of time, and energy. I had made a mental note earlier of all the supplies we will need in the house, and I started moving them forward. Tom came back with the garden cart instead this time, and started loading up drywall and plywood on to the cart. We kept moving stuff into the house, and kept refilling sacks of sand. We did not realize it, but we had a lot of stuff. Tom finally came back and said "there's no more room until we get the other rooms done, so that's all we can move for now. But I think we can make the truck fit now." I looked around, and yeah, he was right, we can make it fit. We re-organized some of the stuff and moved it to the attic shelving in the garage, and then locked the garage and went back to the house. This time I was starving, and finished off my Crockpot specialty stew. If it was not overcooked earlier, it was definitely overcooked now.

After I finished my stew, I looked at our completed interior wall, not bad, though the other three walls were still without interior drywall. When we first tore down the interior wall panels in the living room, I imagined that we would find some treasure, some gold stashed away like they did during the depression when gold was illegal to own. Reality was, this house was built in a factory and in the 80's, so hardly a realistic idea. As the walls came down, one by one, no treasure was found, unless you consider a mouse skeleton a treasure. After we brought down the four living room walls, we decided not to do any other walls, as we learned that the interior walls apparently help to maintain the structure of a manufactured home. We figured we would be okay since the living room was centered in the house, and if the interior walls did indeed help, being with out them in the center should be safe.

I realized how late it was and mentioned to Tom "I need to tend to the animals, it's getting dusk." Tom nodded as I went out to the garden. The chickens had already put themselves away in their coop, so all I had to do was lock the door. I figured I should collect eggs too. I went back inside for the harvest basket then set out for egg collection. The dogs knew what to do. They herded the goats back to their enclosure, not that they had to do so, the goats knew the routine. I locked up the animals and made sure everything was secure should a coyote or a raccoon or something come to visit, then headed back in and put the eggs in the fridge. I was super tired, but at least things felt partially normal. It was just another weekend at the cabin, except that it was not. It was not a weekend, and we were here for good, I hoped.

Tom had taken a break to heat up some canned soup and stated "we should also make a list of how much food we have stored."

"We have that already" I replied quickly.

"But we need to figure out how long it will last" he clarified.

"That will depend on how much harvesting we get done" I replied as if it was obvious.

"Let's see how much we have should we not get any harvest" he further clarified.

"That's an odd request, but okay, we can go over the list tonight." I then heated up a can of soup in the microwave as well, and finished it off before I knew it. Hard work sure makes you hungry. As soon as Tom was done he headed straight to the living room and started placing sand bags in the walls. I went to help him, but mostly just watched. Such an unusual way to do things, but hey, if it prevents a bullet from entering my head, I will take it. We managed to finish the wall facing the front before we gave up for the night. That kind of physical labor is more exhausting than one might think. Working in an office and going to the gym three times a week is not the same as re-building a home.

I found the list of stored food. Some might call me crazy, but I had the food well organized. It is all in buckets or bins and each one had a label to identify it. I had three different lists. One list by expiration date, one list by item in alphabetical order, and one list by bucket or bin number. I figured I would be able to find what I needed based on those three lists. I have learned however that expiration dates mean nothing. Some food spoiled sooner, and some food well after. We only bought what we ate, and we learned quickly the importance of rotating stock. It turned into another hobby. Every four months I would pull anything close to its expiration date or anything that had a tendency to spoil early. Then that food would get placed in our "food rotation cabinet." And as we pulled stuff out to eat, we added it to the grocery list to replace with the next shopping trip.

We looked over the list, and added up the number of cans of chicken and salmon. Enough for the two of us for a year. We seemed to have way too much rice, but that was okay. The canned soups were a good six months for both of us, and the canned veggies were less, but at least 3 months worth non-stop. We also had about a 3 month supply of freeze dried packs of food, and two buckets each of wheat, rice, and beans. Plus about a month worth of MRE's. I went overboard on the pasta, but that was a comfort food for me. I realized I had at least a year for myself. I was presuming Tom does not eat any, but he hated pasta. We also have about a year's worth of tomato sauce (in glass, not cans due to the BPA), but that was good, because I learned a long time ago from a FerFAL book that tomato sauce makes everything taste better. Though some marines will argue that it's Tabasco sauce that makes everything taste better. So it is a good thing we both like tomato and hot sauce.

We also recently started switching from canned soup to dry beans instead. We realized that with canned food, we were storing water, and that takes up a lot space, so if we ate a can of split pea soup, we replaced it with a bag of dry split peas. Lentil soup, bag of dry lentils, black bean soup, bag of black beans, and so on. We also realized this was a less expensive way to store more food. The cost of a bag of organic dry split peas was about $4, made in a crock pot, would make about four full jars of soup. The cost of one can of organic split pea soup was about $3, so for a dollar more, we would have four jars of soup, which were bigger than the cans. So really a huge savings. The disadvantage was that once cooked, you had to eat it within a few days, but with Tom's appetite, that was not usually a problem.

We had plenty of sugar and honey, though we used that rarely except in bread baking and to sweeten our hot tea, so we did not need much to begin with. Instead of storing milk, we decided to store whey and casein protein powder, and found that you can substitute that in any recipe that calls for milk. We had 12 tubs of whey protein powder, and 12 tubs of casein protein powder, which is almost a year's worth for the both of us. We also had a great deal of salt, sea salt, iodized salt, canning and pickling salt, and livestock salt. I think we should be okay on salt. We also had comfort foods: chocolate, green tea, and at least two years worth of the essential coffee. Tom loved his instant coffee. Not likely to grow our own coffee unless we moved to some tropical location, and that was not likely to happen.

After Tom and I looked over the list, we were both satisfied. We have enough food for a year, plus a garden and animals. We just have to have a huge garden this year, and lots of cold frames, so that we can have enough food to store for next year.

"Alright, so tomorrow, we finish the walls in the living room" Tom said.

"Yes, but we need to take a break and move the truck as soon as the road is clear" I reminded Tom.

"Oh yeah, I'm so tired I forgot. So yeah, I'll take care of that first thing tomorrow, then we'll move the truck, then finish the walls in here." Tom was preparing for tomorrow.

"Then we will do walls in the other rooms" I continued the list.

"Then the cold frames" Tom suggested.

"What about the bug out location?" I asked confused.

"Let's get the cold frames done first, then the bug out location." I was surprised by Tom's decision, but I was not about to argue.

"Once all that is done, then we can paint the walls and finish putting down the commercial tile in the other rooms" Tom added.

"What about the solar?" I asked confused again.

"We will need help with that. Not my specialty, and those panels are fragile, plus we still have to figure out the right location for them. Hopefully the grid will stay up long enough for us to get the panels installed" Tom said.

"We should be able to get Roy to help us" I suggested.

"Yeah… not sure I want anyone else to know about them just yet" Tom said quietly, then he continued "okay, so after the house is done, we'll get the solar done, unless the grid gets shut off, then we'll move that up the list."

"Then we are done?" I asked, though it was a stupid question, I knew better.

"Not really, but yeah, with the hard stuff, then we hit the land" Tom answered.

"It's getting cooler, we might be limited to cold frames" I stated.

"Then it's a good thing they are higher up on the priority list" Tom responded.

The dogs got excited and ran to the door before we heard the knock knock knock. It was Roy, we could tell from the knock. Tom unlocked the front door for him and let him in. Roy looked around and said "looks like you got some work done today. Wow, look at this place, just a couple more walls and it will look like a real home." Roy's comment was singed with a bit of country ribbing.

"Thanks Roy" Tom responded with a hint of sarcasm.

"So hey, just came to tell you that we figured out who is leaving tomorrow, and it's mostly just the folks who didn't believe you and didn't prepare" Roy stated happily.

"Are you leaving?" Tom asked.

"Well, I thought about it. But, I figure I am better off with people I know. Plus I have some things stashed away, so I don't want to go to no camp. And if my kids show up, I need to be here for them" Roy answered very seriously.

Tom quickly responded "probably a wise decision."

"Well, Tom and Rachel, nothing new on the news, same old story. Supplies are being rationed, your best bet is to go to a camp, the government is here to help you. Blah, blah, blah" Roy's tone had a bit of sarcasm and annoyance combined.

"Right, cause the politicians always cared about us peons *soo* much" Tom scowled.

"Well, it wasn't so bad, at least while I was getting my social security check. But I guess all good things must come to an end" Roy said in a slightly defensive manner.

Tom just continued "yeah. Fiat currencies may grow on trees, but real money does not."

"Alright, well, I'm glad to see you two settled. It's going to be nice having you here full time. Think I'll still be able to get some milk and eggs from ya?" we were surprised by Roy's question. I chimed in quickly to help break the awkwardness "of course Roy. You and Rita both can get as much as you can eat, you two have helped us out tremendously while we were working. We would not have as much if it were not for you two. So don't worry, we will not shoot if we see either of you out in the pasture or the garden."

"*Oh good*" he chuckled in uneasy relief, then added "though you should know, John Smith is considering giving up some of his cattle for the government, and going off to the camps."

"Are you serious? He has it made here. Everyone goes to him for meat and milk, and for hay!" I did not realize it, but I was almost yelling.

"Yeah, guess he didn't prepare much" Roy said in a quiet tone.

"But he can barter with others!" I was still yelling.

"Yeah, we told him that, but he's not so sure anyone else would have anything to barter. Plus he called that government phone line, and they told him they would set him up real good for his cows" Roy explained.

"Yeah, but for how long, and what happens when they slaughter all his cows? Government bureaucrats don't know anything about ranching. They'll turn every cow into food and there won't be any for next year!" Now Tom was almost yelling.

"Excuse me?" I said.

"You're not exactly your typical government bureaucrat, honey." Tom consoled.

Roy continued "don't know what to tell you. But John is not sure yet, maybe someone needs to do some *convincing* with him... a... little...?"

"So you're saying I should head over there and talk to him?" Tom figured things out rather quickly.

"You know Tom, that's a good idea, glad you thought of it" Roy winked at me and smiled.

"Fine, I will head over there now" Tom said in an annoyed tone.

"Maybe bring him a bottle of wine too" I suggested.

"Fine, you want to go too Roy?" Tom asked.

"Sure, why don't you just ride with me?" Roy's tone revealed that he planned this whole conversation. Then he added "we should also stop by the church, Charles should have our guard shift schedules ready there for us. The way things are going turned out to be four people per tree, so they figure everyone will do a shift per week. For now, I heard that we'll have a set schedule, so that we're doing a shift at the same time every week. I also heard a rumor that they put the younger folk on the graveyard shift" Roy said carefully, but Tom did not respond. Perhaps he did not realize that he is considered younger here.

Tom grabbed a bottle of John's favorite Meritage wine and they both left the house and got in Roy's truck. John likes wine, and will talk to you over wine any time. I hoped this went well for them, because John helped to make this town self sufficient. Though he was a somewhat compliant type of person, especially by country standards. It would be a shame to see him give up his huge ranch, and to give up all his cattle. He provided work for people here, and he produced food. It would certainly make things harder if he left. I hoped Tom could convince him to stay. I grabbed another bottle of wine and ran out to the truck. They had not left yet, they were still talking. I handed the bottle to Tom who just smiled; he must have been thinking the same thing.

Chapter 4

Housework and Surprise Guests

Tom did not get back until well after midnight. I was tired but decided to stay up so I would know what was going on. It was easy to stay up, as there was so much to do around the house. I managed to get the kitchen cleaned up. It is amazing how much dust will accumulate when you are not around for two weeks at a time. Tom of course never saw the dust. I used to think his vision was bad, but then just decided that he willingly did not see the dust. It is almost as if he was in denial about it.

When he walked in, I immediately asked him "well?"

"John is staying" Tom replied happily.

"Yaaay" I said replied with enthusiasm while clapping my hands.

"Yeah, it would have been rough otherwise" Tom stated.

"Sooooo... what's the catch?" I know there would be one, so might as well find out what it was.

"His son has to stay too" Tom said with out much emotion.

"I figured" I said out loud.

"Yeah, well, every town needs a town drunk, even in hard times I guess" Tom has not quite rationalized it in his head yet. He and Jake have never had a pleasant encounter.

"I'm not too worried about Jake, at least John is able feed his son" I tried to reassure Tom.

"Well... he won't be... John told him to work or get out" Tom said looking at me, as if to say, 'how are you going to see the positive in this one huh?'

"When did this happen?" I asked surprised.

"About a month ago. So Jake started renting the Jones's house since they moved to the city, and now it seems they won't be coming back, so he's living there rent free, how convenient huh?" his tone started to show his feelings about the situation. He must have held back during the meeting with John.

"Hope he stocked up on booze for himself" I said half jokingly as I didn't really know how else to respond. But Tom took me

seriously and said "you know he did not! Anyway, John said that he'll stick around as long as his kid is fine, but if Jake gets harmed, then he's turning the cows to the government and going to go live the good life the government promised him."
"Does he really believe that?" I asked.
"Roy thinks so, but I don't know, regardless, I was not about to call his bluff if he is indeed bluffing."
"Well, at least he's staying for now, we need his cattle to help feed this town." This was at least half way good news I thought to myself.

The next morning Tom moved the truck that we used for our last drive up here into the garage. It took quite a bit of rearranging of supplies and equipment before it would actually fit, but we managed. We also managed to finish the walls in the living room, but that was it for that day. We did not know where the day went actually, all we did was re-organize some stuff in the garage, move a truck, and put up a couple walls, which included some sand bag filling.

The next few days we did get the walls in the rest of the house finished. Actually I don't really know how long it took. Time just sort of lost track of itself, and without internet or television, we did not even know what day it was, except when Tom had to get up at 2 am once a week for his shift. Our cell phones were useless, but he was at least able to set an alarm using the cell phone to remind him of his shift, the cell phones still kept the date and time current, or at least we believed it to be current. Regardless, I got out a notebook and started to keep track of days for myself.

Needless to say, all the work was slow going. We moved all the tile supplies from the garage to the house, but decided to get the cold frames done next. The cold frames did not take as long as we thought, and we managed to get 18 really good sized cold frames put together. We then placed them on the south facing grade behind the house, and filled them with dirt mixed with compost from the chickens and the goats. We decided to wait a week, then we would start planting for the fall. After we got the cold frames done, we finished tiling the house. That was tricky, as we had to move everything into the living room where the floors where finished, so that we could work on the other rooms, and then we had to rearrange things as we put them back.

We avoided talking to the town folk as we still did not want to answer any questions regarding our trip up here. Tom said that his weekly shift was with Vince, and Vince knew I was here. He did not know the other two people very well, but they split up on the other side of the road, and did not interact much. So we just worked on the house and land and did not leave our property. It felt good to have it finished. It was almost like a new house, at least on the inside. It is just too bad we did not really have any real furniture, but that was okay. We filled the two rooms up with our food buckets, and used our storage bins as chairs and tables along with the camping chairs and TV trays. That seemed to work just fine. Maybe not stylish or particularly comfortable, but practical. During this time, we also decided on how we were going to build our bug out shelter, and what supplies to put there. I dug out my super sturdy (read expensive) storage bin that I found at a hardware store after reading a recommendation on a survival email list, and we filled it with a couple of spare guns we got from day one, lots of ammo, two weeks worth of freeze dried and MRE food for two, a fire starter kit, water filter, and two sets of clothing for each of us. We then loaded the truck in the garage with plywood, 2x4s, nails, sandbags filled with sand, and some exterior paint, and some other supplies, then headed out to our location.

The bug out location was higher up on the mountain. We staked it out a few months ago and checked in on it occasionally. It seemed like a good spot. Good view of everything, and hidden. It is on BLM land, so it did not really belong to anyone. We drove our truck there this time, unloaded the plywood, and jimmy rigged a shelter. Not exactly jimmy rigged - we had some instructions printed out on building these yurt-like structures, so we followed the instructions with the exception that we doubled up on the walls so that we could put the sand bags in between them. We considered making the structure out of cement, but decided to go with the materials we had. Plus if we had to move it for some reason, it would be possible to do so. We put hinges on and used one panel as a door, just a cut out piece of plywood really. We put latches for padlocks on both the inside and outside of the door, so that we could lock it from the outside when we're not there, and lock ourselves in when we are. Ten feet away, we dug a large hole and buried our sturdy cache bin of supplies. Tom tried to cover it as best he could to make it look inconspicuous. Then inside the structure, we left two cots we scored at a yard sale a long time ago, and threw in our heavy duty -15 degree Fahrenheit sleeping bags, and pillows. Then we decided that we should bring up spare warm clothes, and at least one pot for cooking, plus the mini wood stove for which we traded our extra mountain bikes. We also decided after much debate to bring up our Katadyn water filter. It was a fairly expensive item, and we only had one, although we have a reverse osmosis system for the house, and a Berkey filter as well. We then painted the structure a forest green color with some tan and charcoal grey accents to try to match the background, and left. We did it all so quickly, it almost did not feel real.

I think a month went by, or four shifts for Tom, by the time we were done with all this, though I was not sure, I certainly did not do a good job keeping track on the calendar. It was hard to keep up with time when you are out in the middle of nowhere working 16 hour days. But we were all done, finally. Okay, not all done, but a good portion of it. The house was fully livable, and we could keep the warmth from the wood stove in. The cold frames were planted, and the garden was still going strong from the summer. The animals were happy and content. The building supplies were no longer stacked up against the garage wall, they were now part of the building. I was surprised to see how much building material we had left over, but I figured that was a good thing.

We finally decided to celebrate our hard work, so we opened up a special bottle of Zinfandel wine we had been saving. With the current situation we normally did not drink at all because we could be faced with an emergency situation at any time. We would have to be ready to act, and did not want our ability to respond be compromised due to drinking too much. However, we thought it would be okay to occasionally have a glass of wine in certain circumstances, such as celebration or to alleviate extreme stress, as long as we were very careful not to drink so much that it would incapacitate us.

It was early afternoon, and the weather outside was starting to get chilly. We still had the solar left to install, but there was no way could we do that with just the two of us. Plus we were exhausted. It felt like each day we got less and less done. We were still getting things done, it just took longer each day.

"Now what?" I asked Tom.

"We still have to hook up the solar. I'm surprised we still have power" Tom replied.

"Yeah, me too. They usually notify me of my bill via email, not sure how they are going to do it now since the internet is still down, and we don't have mail service here" I was more thinking out loud than anything.

"Minor details, we knew we would eventually have to supply our own electricity" Tom said confidently.

"Yeah, but I expected the power to be turned off by now" I really was surprised it was still going.

"Me too. Well this is good, now we can concentrate on setting up the solar with out feeling like we have to rush, though we will need some help" Tom added.

"Do you have anyone in mind?" I asked.

"Maybe. You know, we need to keep up with the gardening and the animals" now Tom was thinking out loud.

"It would be nice if we could just be left alone like this huh?" ah, yeah, it would be nice.

"Yeah, not gonna happen" Tom said quickly.

"I know. I'm surprised we haven't had any of our neighbors knocking on our door yet" I stated.

"Well, they might have. We may have just been so busy, we may not have heard" Tom said as he looked at me.

"Well, a lot of people prepared, so maybe everyone is okay" I hoped.

"Don't count on it." As if saying something jinxed it, there was a knock on the door. It was Roy's knock.

"Hey Roy, what brings you here?" Tom asked as he opened the door.

"You guys were right" Roy said.

"Yeah, what else is new?" Tom said jokingly.

"No, I'm serious; people are dying in the so-called "relief" camps!" Roy sounded upset.

"What do you mean? I asked.

"Yeah, remember Samantha and Terry? They left for the camps, but they came back" Roy said quickly.

"I thought we were not letting people back in?" I was confused.

"Come on now, you know better than that" Roy said firmly.

"So what happened?" Tom asked.

"Well, apparently when they left, they were treated exceptionally well by the military. That was until they were checked in, badge'd, finger printed, "processed in" as they called it. Then they were thrown into what was more or less a prison. They had to sleep on the ground, no blankets, hardly any food" Roy explained.

"That bad?" as if I had to ask, I knew better.

"They were told it was temporary, until they had room in the real camps, but they didn't believe it at that point" Roy continued.

"So, they just let them leave?" Tom asked quizzically.

"No, they didn't, that's the problem, it was like a prison. They found out that they were going to be moved to the real camp, but that they separated the men and women, even if married, regardless of age"

"Then how did they get out?" I asked.

"Well, they got loaded up on the same school bus for transport to the permanent camp, and during the ride, all the, ahem, "refugees" started to riot. The driver was not paying attention to the road very well, and he was going way too fast around a curve, and the top heavy school bus tipped over on its side. I guess some people died, but Terry and Sam made it, though Terry ended up with a broken hand or wrist or something. Anyway, all the prisoners then broke through the broken windows or the vent on the ceiling of the bus and got out that way" Roy finished.

"Wow, and they hiked it all the way back here?" I asked.

"Yep, they walked all the way from outside of Springfield" Roy confirmed.

"That's over 100 miles!" Tom exclaimed.

"Yeah, can you believe it? Terry's hand is healing poorly, but he can use it somewhat, and the two of them were looking pretty bad when they got here. Said they followed creeks and ate wild berries" Roy's tone was of excitement.

"Do they have anything stashed away?" Tom asked.

"About that, so when they came back, their house had been broken into and emptied, they have nothing" Roy said with a sad tone. Tom and I looked at each other. We do not believe in hand outs, but Samantha and Terry are a nice, honest, older couple, and they mean well. They just made a bad decision.

"Tell you what, why don't you tell them they can come by here and we will feed them. Maybe we can even find some work for them to do around here to help us for the winter. And we can do some food bartering or something" said Tom.

"I knew you'd be kind, I'll tell them right away!" Roy exclaimed with joy. With that, Roy let himself out the door.

After Roy left I looked at Tom and questioned him "I thought we were not going to share with those who did not prepare?" Tom looked back at me and smiled, after a minute of thought, he responded with a rationale. "I look at it this way. They have just been through hell, and they have seen how the government likes to "help" people. They will be the last ones to back down now, which means that if we need help against getting forcefully relocated, they will be the first ones to pick up a weapon and help shoot." There was a certain logic in Tom's idea, but I was a little concerned over the fact that Sam and Terry were in there mid or late 50s, and I wondered how much their age might slow down their ability to help around here.

While waiting for the couple to arrive, I turned on the crock pot and threw in more of my specialty stew, rice with chicken and veggies. The veggies were fresh from the garden, but the rice was from storage and so was the chicken. The hens outside had quite the large number of chicks this year, but we had not had time to slaughter the males yet. I guessed we might have some help now. Though I was glad that we got the house done without anyone seeing what we really did to it. No one needed to know about our "creative construction."

A couple hours later Roy returned with Samantha and Terry. They looked awful. Not only had they lost a ton of weight in one month, but they were bruised up and looked like a bus hit them, well, I guess in a way, a bus did hit them, or they hit the inside of a bus. And Terry's hand, wow, that did not look good. As soon as Tom saw Terry's hand he pulled him aside and started examining it, asking him questions about it. He came to the conclusion that it had been broken and was healing incorrectly. We certainly did not have the means to re-break it and treat it properly. Terry was just going to have to live with it, at least for the time being. At least it was not his dominant hand.

The crock pot had a while to go, so I made some omelets for the time being. Terry and Samantha were most grateful. We sat in the camping chairs and used storage bins as tables. The couple did not seem to mind. Tom and I decided that after what they had been through, they could probably use a glass of wine as well. Over dinner we decided to find out what we could.

Once everyone looked comfortable, I started with the first question, "so tell us, now that you are safe and sound, do you think you were really going to go to a better camp?" Terry was first to reply "no, of course not, it was all a lie. I doubt FEMA has the means to provide much "relief" to very many people, even if they intended to do so. And I don't think that was actually their intent anyway. We actually figured it out as soon as they started to process us in when they took our essential supplies away from us. But it was too late, there was no way out at that point."

"So they really starved you?" I kept asking. This time Samantha replied "it was horrible, everything was rationed, and people fought over moldy bread! We mainly kept to ourselves, and talked about escaping. We knew if they transported us to the next camp we would be done for, so we talked about how we would escape".

"Did you plan the bus riots?" Tom asked.

"No, that was someone else. We thought that would be too dangerous, but we did not think of anything better either. So when the opportunity arose, we went for it" Sam replied again.

"We're glad you two made it back, it's rough out there" I said. "Yeah, actually, knowing that you two had made it back that first day really kept us going. We knew that the town would be in good hands with people like you around. We just wish we had listened before having to have to experience all this" Terry was apologetic in his response.

"Yeah, well, it's not like we were foretelling happy futures here" Tom consoled.

"Yeah, all the more reason to have listened to you" Sam interjected.

There was a brief silence between us all. Sam and Terry both appeared tiny and frail sitting in front of us. It is amazing what a month of near starvation will do to you. Sam, appeared even more fragile than before her experience with relief camps. A petite and short graceful woman, with dark hair that used to be trimmed short, but now longer made her look older. The silver running through her hair made her age even more, but she was hardly in her late 50's. Her skin pale, with a smile that told you everything was going to be alright, no matter what. It was obvious what Terry saw in her. And Terry, normally short and stocky, now short and thin, with his sandy straight hair that could use a haircut, and his deformed hand, looked frail too except for his straight posture that gave him an heir of having control. Then Sam started, now her with the apologetic tone "we actually did have some supplies stashed away, we just thought that we would be better off with the government. They have been sending us checks for so long, we figured they would keep up their end of the bargain."

"Yeah, I know - you don't have to explain yourself" I quickly responded.

"We thought all along that if anything seemed fishy we would turn around" said Terry.

"Really, you don't have to explain yourselves" Tom replied.

"Well, we do, because now our house has been robbed and we have no supplies left. They even took our shower heads" Sam's voice sounded as if she was surprised by something so inane. "Is your house livable?" I asked.

"Not really, but we can make it livable, maybe" Terry replied.

"We have some building supplies if that will help" Tom offered.

"Yes, that would really help, we need to cover up the broken window at least" Terry explained.

"Okay, we can help with that. I will even drive it over for you and help you nail it in" Tom offered.

"That would be great, but I don't know how we can repay you" Terry said quietly.

"Well, we could use some help around here" I quickly replied.

"Oh, I can help, and if it's something I don't know how to do, I can learn" Sam was enthusiastic.

"Okay, it's a done deal, when do you want us to start?" Terry was eager as well.

"Tomorrow morning would be perfect, now let me get you home so that we can fix that window." Tom got up and grabbed the truck keys, then we walked over to the garage, and threw some plywood and some hammers and nails into the truck. We locked up the house, with the dogs inside. We thought about giving them a rawhide to chew on, but decided against it, we did not want the dogs distracted if someone tried to break in. We then drove the couple home. It was nice to finally have some company after all this time, but it was a huge realization of the times going on right now. People being thrown into "relief" camps and starved? Really? In America? By agents for the US government? Had Tom not been warning me of the signs of a totalitarian government for the last four years, I never would have been able to fathom what was happening right now. Times are scary for sure. I only wish I had begun to prepare sooner. I feared our preps of the last three to four years would not be enough.

During the drive, Terry told us more information about what was going on. We had been so busy working away at the house that we had not listened to the short wave radio, or to our Ham radios, or even tried the internet. Terry had told us that fuel is being rationed, apparently one gallon per person per day, and only if authorized to use to get to work and back. Helicopters and drones police the major cities day and night due the crime and riot problems, and also the major highways due to the looting that has been going on. And curfew is still in effect, with much stricter hours. All government entitlement benefits have been stopped, and no one has received anything, including any types of credit on their government cards after registering. Only those who have been working have been getting paid, and that did not matter much anyway because supplies were scarce. What supplies were available had become very expensive due to the loss of value of the dollar. That was, at least until the Federal price controls went into effect, and they started using the new digital "currency cards." Soon after those went into effect people started to panic and riot due to shortages of food, fuel, and medications. There had also been a threat to cut off power to small towns that did not comply with the relocation "request." But according to both Terry and Sam, they would rather live out in the woods and fend off coyotes and bears than go back to a so called "relief" camp. At least out in the woods they would have their freedom, and much less risk of abuse by "internment /resettlement specialists."

After we covered their window with plywood, we looked through the house to see if anything else needed fixing. The shower heads were indeed stolen, but Terry and Sam were not too concerned. They were just happy to be home. I then realized that I had forgotten the crock pot so I said "by the way, I have dinner in the crock pot, so why don't you come by tonight if you are hungry, and we can chat a little more. Then it's all work starting tomorrow."

We left Terry and Sam, and drove back to our place. We did not talk much, there really was not anything to say. We knew these times were coming, but now these times were here. The inevitable had finally become the immediate. It was a whole different world we were living in.

When we got back to our cabin, there was a TV in front of our door. I looked at Tom and said "must have been Roy, he really thinks we need to be aware of what's going on in the world." Tom responded "well, considering the internet is probably still not available, why not, at least we can try to keep up with what's going on, or what they want us to think is going on." We pulled up, unlocked the door, and brought the TV inside. We plugged it in, and realized that we needed some kind of antenna. Out in the middle of nowhere you needed satellite for either internet or television. We had internet satellite, but that was not what we needed to be able to use the TV. So we were scratching our heads, when we realized Roy had walked in. "I hooked up my spare satellite dish for you. You guys really need to know what's going on out there. It ain't pretty."

"Wow, thanks, but we don't know how..." I was cut off.

"Oh, let me just take care of it" said Roy. He walked fully in, went to the back porch and

pulled in coax cable from the satellite dish that he must have installed while we were gone. The TV was still not working, so he went out to the dish and made some adjustments. Roy was very resourceful, but I wasn't sure he knew what he was doing. He then came back in, pressed some buttons, and wow, we had television.

"Okay then, now you don't need me to tell you what's going on anymore" Roy stated with a smirk on his face.

"Thanks Roy, we appreciate it... you know, we haven't seen you around for milk or eggs. You doing okay?" I asked.

"Yeah, I did some organizing, and moved all my supplies to one location. I figured I should move my valuables to one place, and now that I hear Sam and Terry got robbed, I'm glad I did. I also checked inventory on what I have, and fixed up a few things around the house, so just been busy. But if you have some extra, I would certainly take some milk and eggs off your hands." That was Roy's way of saying he needed more.

"Not a problem. We're going to be making cheese in the next few days as well, so make sure you come back for that" I stated clearly.

"I will, and now that I'm thinking of it, I need to get some firewood split before they turn off my power, so if you need some split as well, let me know" Roy offered.

"We appreciate it, but we actually split five cords when we moved here. Well, we didn't split it, we paid extra to have it split. Regardless, we should be oaky on wood for the winter" Tom responded.

"Okay, then I will see you in a few." Roy was about to leave, so I quickly walked over to the refrigerator and collected a couple dozen eggs and a gallon of goat milk. Then I decided to give him two gallons of milk, as the fridge was running out of room. Each of our goats produces about 2 and a half quarts of milk, sometimes three quarts a day, and sometimes keeping up with it is hard. I got out a crate and put the two jugs of milk and the eggs in it. Then I walked it over to Roy's truck and put it in the passenger seat after Tom opened the door for me. Roy looked a bit exhausted, perhaps the reality of what is going on was taking a toll on him as well.

"You sure you're alright Roy?" I asked.

"Yeah, just been busy. It's weird not having money. Not that it matters, the general store has been picked clean, so there's really no way to get supplies anyway" Roy replied.

"You just look tired" Tom observed.

"Well, you know, I'm wondering if I stocked up on enough supplies now. Probably not" Roy said with some concern in his voice.

"Well, we're here if you need anything, and don't be afraid to ask either, you've done more than your share of helping us in the last year, it's the least we can do" I said.

"Yeah, but you need your supplies too. Plus Sam and Terry will be using some of what you've got as well" Roy wasn't convinced.

"Don't worry Roy, we'll make sure that if we can help you, we will" Tom clarified.

"Thanks... you know, I haven't been able to get a hold of my kids since all this happened."

"At all?" I asked.

"Their land line hasn't been working for some reason, and normally I would just drive to see them. But given the road restrictions, and fuel rationing, I've been worried that I would get stuck and relocated to a camp... but I expected them to be here by now." Roy's kids lived in Springfield because that is where the work is, well... was. Roy told us that he made them promise that they would come to his place should something strange happen. Apparently they had not shown up as he expected. I looked at Tom and said "maybe we can dig out our ham radios already, and see if we can get any info that way."

"Good idea Rache." Tom then looked at Roy and said reassuringly "we'll see if we can get in touch with someone with a ham in Springfield and see if we can find out anything." "Really, that would be great. Mind if I come by tonight?" Roy asked.
"Not at all, we'll make extra dinner, Terry and Sam will be here too" I said.
"See you tonight then" said Roy, and with that, Tom shut the passenger door and Roy drove away.

Tom and I figured that during the type of emergency we had been expecting there was a significant risk that most conventional communication systems could go down. Cell phones, land line phones, and even the internet all required significant maintenance of network infrastructure to remain operational and reliable. As a result, we figured communication technology that was self contained and did not rely on external infrastructure to work might end up being our main sources of information and communication should those traditional systems go down. The types of communication we came up with were CB radios, short wave radios, FRS radios, and ham radios.

CB radios had a lot more local traffic so were good for communicating with people nearby. But CBs were relatively limited in range and frequency options. Shortwave radios had wider frequency options and a greater reception range, but most people could only receive broadcasts, not transmit. We found FRS radios good for communication around our property, or if we got separated while hiking or hunting. But FRS radios were too limited in both range and frequency options for most applications. That left ham radios as the best choice for exchanging information with other radio operators over significant distances, since ham radios were capable of both transmitting and receiving over much greater distances. It was also common for ham radio operators to set up "repeater networks," which functioned as relays for the ham radio signals, but the radios did not depend on them. Those repeater networks were frequently maintained by individuals, ham clubs, volunteers, and emergency services personnel for their own use. So ironically there was a better chance they would

102

remain working than the commercial communication infrastructure. Ham equipment was also relatively simple and robust, and therefore easier to maintain. So Tom and I invested in some quality ham radios and short wave radios. We also got our ham radio licenses, and practiced with the radios so we were experienced with how to use them. As we learned later on, once the economic collapse hit, no one really paid attention to licensing anyway. Regardless, our goal was to be able to keep up with, and keep in touch with the outside world. We may have relocated to "nowhere", but we didn't want to be blind sided by events from the outside world if we could help it.

I told Tom that something did not feel right about the situation with Roy's kids, they should have been here a long time ago, but there was not much we could do. We went back inside and turned on the television to see what was going on in the world. It was strange seeing the news anchor lady. Clearly she was new and inexperienced. She had a tremendous amount of make up on, and she looked to be happy and well fed. As she reported the news it was clear she was reading it, and had no emotions to what she was saying. Actually, I was sure that she had no clue what she was talking about, she just said what she was reading in a very monotone voice and smiled after every sentence.

The news only talked about the shortage of supplies, and how relief camps will save you if you live in a small town. "Go now, go quickly, you will be taken care of." The news also talked about the "resolution" of the bank runs, and a new currency coming out soon, but for now, people were to use their "credits ." It almost felt like these "credits" were the new currency, they just did not call it that yet. Supposedly the government had placed price controls on everything to keep prices from skyrocketing, and it was supposedly working great. And although fuel was rationed, there was enough for everyone that was working, just no "frivolous travel" or "joyriding" was permitted. After an hour, we had enough and turned off the television. Tom went to tend to the animals while I emptied the crock pot to make another batch. I placed the current batch in a glass bowl and covered it with aluminum foil. It should stay warm until everyone got here. I put the new batch on high, and then organized the living room to accommodate five people.

When Tom came back from tending to the animals, we went through the house to find the bin that had the ham radios. We could not find it at first, but then we remembered that we did not have the hams in a bin, they were in a small metal trash can in case of an EMP. Perhaps, a little paranoid, but given the sun had been producing unusually high activity, we figured it couldn't hurt. We unpacked the hams and set up the base station. We turned them on and searched for a frequency that was active. The dogs got excited and we thought that Sam and Terry had arrived already. We got up to look out the window, and saw a quad pull up. Tom guessed "it's probably Vince." We watched as he got closer, and realized he had his kids with him.

We left the dogs inside and walked out to meet Vince Adler. He pulled up and jumped off his quad. He was a brawny looking man, with dark brown hair, brown eyes, and a strong jaw line. He must have been on his way to go hunting, as he was wearing his camo cargo pants with a forest green fleece jacket. Or maybe he was coming back from hunting. His kids were the best behaved kids in town. They unfortunately had lost their mother to a drunk driver in Springfield. Karina was her name, I never had the opportunity to meet her. Vince was devastated from what I was told; his kids were only six and seven at the time. They were now twelve and thirteen, Vincent Adler Jr., and his younger sister Kasha Adler were sitting on the quad behind their father. Vincent Jr. looked nothing like his father with his lustrous blonde hair and hazel eyes that matched his sisters. One would wonder if Vincent was Vincent Jr.'s father, but put them next to each other and the features no doubt matched. Kasha I was told was a spitting image of her mother, and apparently was a better shot than her older brother.

Tom approached Vince and shook his hand, and said "good to see you. What brings you by Vince? Looks like you're coming back from a hunting trip?" Vincent's voice was deep that matched his features "I just thought I would stop by. I don't get to see you unless we're pulling guard duty, and I haven't seen Rachel since you two bugged out here." He then

104

turned to me, nodded, and said "nice to see you Rachel. I wasn't sure if you were really here." I smiled in response. Tom replied "just getting caught up on things here, since we're here full time now, and just prepping a little here and there. Though we haven't had time to get out hunting yet if that's what you're asking." Vince was the one that invited Tom to go hunting when we first got the cabin, and he usually did not come by unless he wanted Tom to go with. Tom was only mildly interested in hunting, but figured it was a good skill to develop. So Tom would join Vince and his kids, and one day, they got a Bobcat. Tom couldn't believe that a good hide could go for as much as $1,200. Tom was all about hunting after that. Vince responded to Tom and said "yeah, figured you'd be too busy, but thought I'd check anyway. If you feel up to it sometime, you know where to find me." "That I do" said Tom. With that, Vince got back in his quad, turned it on, and waived, with the kids following a wave by.

We went back inside, and went back to the Ham radio, which told a different story than the news did earlier. The people were rioting, cities were burning, crime was out of control, martial law was in place in the major cities but was not very effective. Police had begun using deadly force, the ones that showed up anyway. The jails were overflowing and could not serve food. Store shelves were usually empty. Water was often contaminated as treatment facility staff only sporadically showed up for work, if at all. And the relief camps, that news was the worst of all. It sounded all too close to concentration camps or prisons. The difference was that those who required medicine were being left to die as there was precious little medicine to spare, and it was too valuable to "waste" on "relief" camp inmates. Those that could work, were being forced to work to death, literally. Security at the camps was out of control as the guards, often contracted foreigners, did what they pleased. People were dying, every day, *in America*. We lost track of time and the dogs snapped us out of our daze when they barked. We heard a truck pull up and tried to look out the window, but it was dark. Where did the time go?

I turned on the outside light and realized that it was Roy. He pulled up and got out, and apparently he brought

Terry and Sam with him. After the dogs did their sniffing and security, they let them pass through to the house. I quickly ran to the kitchen to check on the stew, and it was plenty done. I realized though that the older stew had gotten cold. I got out a huge bowl and mixed the cold stew with the hot stew, then placed the warm stew in individual bowls, and brought them out with spoons. No one hesitated; everyone sat down quickly and devoured every bite. We all sat in silence as we ate, after we finished, Tom volunteered to put the animals away, and when he returned, we started talking.

We started talking about the relief camps because of what we saw on TV versus what we heard on the ham radios. Terry made a comment that he could not believe that the US National Guard would behave the way that they did toward Americans. He could not believe that these were American raised people, even though he experienced it first hand. Tom brought up the Stanford prison experiment and explained what the experiment showed, that basically when people are put in a position of power, they lose sight of who they are and act according to their position of power. And also the fear that was involved for refusing to obey orders as the Milgram experiments showed. It had all been psychologically experimentally documented, and we were not really surprised that this occurred, and that it would only get worse. Tom also pointed out that some of the camp guards were not National Guard, they were employees of hired military contractor corporations. That also implied that some of those contractor guards were likely not American citizens doing this to Americans, but foreigners.

We noticed that Roy was getting antsy, and we knew that he wanted to try to contact his kids via the hams. As if reading each other's minds, Tom and I looked at each other and then quickly changed topics as we turned to the hams. We gave a quick synopsis of what we heard already, and explained we might not be able to get in touch with Springfield. With that said, we scooted over the bin that the ham base station was set up on, turned it on, adjusted the volume, and started searching frequencies.

After what felt like forever, we finally got in touch with someone in Springfield. Things were worse than we thought. People are confined to their homes, although city water was only available during certain hours. The new smart meters that were installed by the electric company controlled when someone was allowed to use power, and if they had not paid their bill, they were shut off. Except that few had work except for government employees, so most people were without power. People had been running out of medication, and despite the fact that extra police had been set up at pharmacies, most had been robbed with nothing left. Prescription drugs were now only available on the black market, and only during certain times of day. Trying to get them was dangerous, both due to crime and due to never knowing what you were actually getting.

We tried to see if we could find someone that lived near the neighborhood where Roy's kids lived, but we had no luck. However Roy's discouraging face told us he wanted us to keep trying. So we did. While Tom stayed on the radio with the rest of the world, I quickly picked up the dishes and washed them, then set them to dry. Although Tom put the animals away, I went ahead and checked on them, and made sure everything was locked. After I came back in, Samantha had approached me quietly and said "I don't think we're going to find his kids." I nodded in agreement, and we both stood there staring with sad faces.

Finally, I said "Roy, Tom and I will keep the radio on all night and day, and the second we hear something, we'll let you know. I know this is hard for you, but it might take some time to find them." Roy reluctantly agreed, and then looking at Terry and Sam stated "well, I better get you two home, and Tom and Rachel, thank you, and I'll check back with you tomorrow."

After they left, Tom and I looked at each other sadly. We knew this was hard on Roy, and we also knew that his kids probably took off for the camps. They were fully unprepared for these events and were completely convinced by the mainstream media propaganda that the "government" had the best interests of the people in mind. They certainly never believed their dad when he warned them to prepare. We left the hams on, but went about our nightly routine.

The next morning, Roy brought the couple down and we all had breakfast as we listened to the hams for any new news. Tom again tried to find anyone who might have information on Roy's kids. We had no luck. While Tom and Roy were tuned to the radio, Terry, Sam and I all went out to the chicken house to figure out what we would be doing with the chickens. We decided that we should slaughter about 25 chickens this week, and another 25 next week. That would leave about another 25, 23 hens and two cocks. That would reduce us by almost two thirds, but that would be plenty for eggs and new chickens. I showed the couple where we had set up a sink with a separate hose, explained that the chickens with the black zip ties on their right leg where the young roosters, or at least we thought they were roosters, though you could not really tell very easily. I then told them I needed to boil water for the feather removal. I left the couple to tend to the chicken catching so that they can be placed in an enclosure until their fate, and went inside to lock up the dogs so that they do not "help," and also to boil water.

I put the pot on for boiling water, and got out another pan that I filled with ice cubes to place the chicken meat in. While I was at it, I plugged in and warmed up the dehydrator, and dug out the canning supplies. I wasn't sure how I was going to make this happen on two 5th burners, and then decided we would just make chicken jerky. It would be much easier to use one process for preservation. Maybe next week I would use the canner.

I got the ingredients together to make the marinade for the chicken, mixed it, and put it in the fridge. By then the water was boiling so I went out to the shed to get a bucket which I then filled with hot water. By the time I got back to Terry and Sam, they had already taken care of 10 of the chickens. I was surprised; apparently they had done this before. While holding the dead chicken by the feet, I then dunked the chicken bodies in the hot water and removed their feathers, and then Sam cut off their feet. By the time we de-feathered those first 10, Terry was done with the other 10 chickens, and proceeded to remove the guts out of the first 10. The first few were a bit tricky, but then he figured out a routine and it was going pretty fast. Sam would rinse them and slice them into jerky slices and then place the strips into the ice pan.

After the pan was full, I took it inside and placed the strips in the marinade, and returned the pan outside to give to Sam again. Somehow without much direction, this process was going rather smoothly; with the exception of how much meat was really in 25 chickens. I left Sam and Terry to finish, and took the marinated meat and placed it in a shallow dishpan to marinate overnight. I had to do some creative maneuvering around the fridge as I had no room. I finally gave up, took all the milk out, and decided that we would start making cheese today too. That was until I realized how late it was, and no, we would not have time, or would we? Screw it, I took all the milk out and was able to fit all the marinating chicken in, including the next batch that Sam had brought in. I gave her back the empty ice pan, and she went back out to finish the rest of the chicken, while I fumbled with making more room in the fridge. Then I gave up, and decided to take the first batch and put it in the dehydrator with out marinating it over night.

I filled up ten trays of chicken jerky and started the timer on the dehydrator. Then I had room for the rest of the chicken in the fridge. As long as the power stayed on it sure would have helped to have more refrigerators than the one full size and one mini-fridge we had. I had to get more marinade ready as I underestimated the amount that I would need. So I made another batch, put it in another shallow glass baking pan, and when Sam brought the rest of the chicken strips in, I put it in the marinade, covered it, and placed it in the fridge.

Terry then filled the iced pan with the left over pieces of meat that were not suitable for jerky, and I placed those pieces in a pot to boil, then contemplated giving the bones to the dogs, but decided against it. Instead, I threw the bones in the chest freezer in the garage so that I could use them for chicken stock as needed.

It was dark by the time we were done with the chickens, though we worked very well together. We were all sitting down recovering from the laborious task. Terry broke the silence, "It sure isn't like going to the store and buying your chicken ready to go in the oven." I laughed then responded "that's true, I learned that a long time ago when we first started to practice being independent. It was not easy either, there were plenty of times I just wanted to give up and go to the store instead."

We were all still sitting and resting when Tom added, "yeah, I remember when we first got this place and I attempted to pull weeds just in the back of the house, I grabbed a machete and attempted to cut the grasses down, but they were so tall and so thick, that by the time I got a few square feet done, the machete blade had dulled, and I was too tired to keep going. That's when I started telling Rachel we needed a tractor." Tom looked at me and I added with amusement "but it's been good exercise, look how good you look." Tom's smile turned into a dirty look and he said "I would rather lift weights than weeds." We all laughed.

Then Terry asked, "with all the land cleared, won't it be easier now to keep it up?" Tom and I looked at each other, we knew this was not the case, after a few seconds, Tom answered for me "no, not even close, we have to spread composted chicken manure on the garden beds, we have to pull weeds, plant seeds, and water. Plus the harvesting itself can be time consuming and tedious. If we had to clear the land and garden, we would be overwhelmed." We all sat in silence for a few minutes in realization of what it takes to be self sufficient, then Tom got the ham radios out and turned them on.

Fortunately making cheese is a simple process that does not require much work. I managed to get the milk up to temperature on the 5th burner, then added the ingredients, and let it cool. Tom and Roy were still at the radio – they must not have left. I imagined there was no news to be heard. I walked over slowly and asked "Roy, would you be able to help us with some heavy work around here tomorrow?"

"Sure, I'd love to, especially if you keep trying on these hams" he said.

"Of course we will" Tom responded with out hesitation.

"What kind of work you need done?" Roy asked.

Tom and I hesitated, but then decided it would not make a difference at this point and said "we have some solar panels we need to put up. We're afraid that they're going to turn off the power any day, and we need to establish an alternative."
"You got solar panels?" Roy asked clearly surprised.
"Yes, we have some, but they are fragile, and they have to go in a specific location" Tom responded.
"Yeah, I'll be here bright and early tomorrow to help" Roy said.
"Great, the five of us should be able to manage the project" I added.

After a little more planning discussion, I served boiled chicken with rice and some vegetables from the garden, and then Roy took the couple home and left. I was glad no one was complaining that I kept serving the same thing over and over. But really, we did not want to start using our stored goods any more than we had to, and all we had was chicken, vegetables from the garden, and rice from storage. We also had the goat milk and chicken eggs, but that too we offered daily. Maybe tomorrow I would make pasta with the chicken, and rice too so that Tom can eat the rice, since he hated pasta.

The very next day, at the first sign of daylight, Roy was back with the couple for an omelet breakfast, and our tedious job of setting up the solar panels. I checked on the jerky and set the timer for a little longer, it did not seem quite ready yet. Then we all sat down and discussed how we would make this work. After we had a plan, we went to the garage, and removed the blankets that were covering the carefully placed solar panels. We had very carefully stacked them in a corner with blankets in between them. We slowly, moved the panels out to the area where we would set them up. These were large and fragile panels, and we had to be carful with them. Terry struggled with his broken hand, but Sam made up for it. It was a lot of meticulous work, but we finally got them all moved. Once they were moved, we arranged them how we wanted them, and then tightened down the mounting frame structure we had constructed for them. That's part what made this so difficult, was the mounting frame. There was no way we could install them on the roof, mainly because the roof of the mobile would not be able to handle the weight. We already had to fix the roof in a few areas because the manufactured homes in the 80's were designed poorly, which could result in leaks. We had repaired the roof so that there was an overhang now, which resolved much of that problem. Anyway, that roof could never handle the weight of solar panels, and that was the whole point of making them independent off the roof.

We started to hook up the cables to the combiner box, the charge controller, the inverter, and then the batteries. The batteries we kept on our enclosed "mud room" or porch that was an add on to the mobile in case they released hydrogen gas. Not ideal, but it worked. We ran the wires through conduit piping, and when were ready, we each grabbed a shovel and buried the conduit as much as was practical. Then came the scary part: disconnecting from the grid, and switching over. This would either work or not work.

I went inside the house, turned everything off, and flipped the main panel breaker. By then the dehydrator was finished, and the jerky looked done, so I left it in the dehydrator until I was ready to deal with it. Fortunately Terry had some prior experience working for a power company, and Tom had some prior experience working for a solar installation company. We turned off the main switch at the pole, and disconnected the city lines. We then connected the inverter/controller to the main power box of the house and after much debate about the wiring configuration, flipped the switch. Nothing blew up, no sparks or smoke appeared, nothing seemed to happen. Tom checked the inverter and it appeared to be working. However, assuming there were no problems, it would take a while for the batteries to become fully charged, so we needed to be careful of how much power we used.
"Guess I should have cooked up some dinner before we switched huh?" I said jokingly.
"I'm sure you can run a burner, it won't hurt anything" Tom was quick to reply.
I decided to run nothing, and instead, served fresh chicken jerky with salad. And in celebration, decided to open a bottle of wine.

"What are we celebrating?" Sam asked.

"Friendships and self sufficiency" I said as I raised my glass for a toast.

We all toasted, and drank wine and talked happily - until Roy looked at the hams, and we knew he wanted us to get back on them.

Nothing, no luck with contacting Roy's kids.

Our routine for the next few weeks was for the three to come by, help with whatever, and we fed them. It turned into a routine where we watch the news on TV solely for the purpose of finding out what the world is being told by the "official media," and then we listen to the hams to find out the truth.

The garden was just about harvested, though the seedlings were appearing in the cold frames. With two 5th burners we managed to can most of the garden tomatoes. I feared that this would be a waste of efforts, but I was extra careful. I risked ruining the 5th burners with the extra weight of canning, but so far the added weight had not been a problem.

We did settle for tomato sauce instead of tomatoes. We canned the next batch of chicken, though we dehydrated most of the rest of the fruits and vegetables from the garden. We made cheese from the goat milk using a recipe I found online a long time ago, and supplies I purchased before the crash. We also canned some of the goat milk. We did not really have to go into our food storage too much, other than for rice, and multivitamins for nutritional insurance. We felt that since we had an abundance of rice, we should supplement our meals with it as a calorie enhancer, since we did not know when transportation of goods would recover. We figured it was best to save what we could. We were very careful on our power usage, but we had to use certain things like the dehydrator. Regardless, we managed pretty well. The weather was definitely starting to turn colder, and we started to appreciate our wood burning cook stove more and more.

Chapter 5

Self Sufficient

Time started to slow down as there was less and less to do as autumn set in. The weather was definitely getting colder as fall had too quickly arrived. The last project to be built was a root cellar to keep our onions, carrots and sweet potatoes in over the winter, to possibly replant some of them next spring for seed. Roy and the couple actually suggested the root cellar, and I happened to have a book about it in our collection of reference books, so we started on the project and after carefully selecting a location, digging the place, and laying some cement, we finished within a few days.

We picked out an array of jars of tomato sauce and dehydrated food kept in jars, along with rice, and our spare older water filter, and we gave it to the couple for their home. We also picked out the nicest cheeses we made, along with eggs and goat milk, and gave it to Roy and the couple. We also offered our miniature fridge to the couple, but they declined, along with declining the cheese and milk. They said they would just walk over here when they need some. We offered them the use of our bikes, but they declined that as well. The couple and Roy went on their way, with the agreement that they would come by to help with the fall gardening and other work on a regular basis. Tom and I were looking forward to having time to ourselves again, though we definitely appreciated the help.

After they left, we played Frisbee with the dogs and went on to have a little dog time and "us" time. Velcro loved her Frisbee, and Compass loved to be chased, so Compass would steal the Frisbee so that Velcro would chase after him. It was such a nice break from everything, that it almost did not feel real. To think that only a few months before, our lives were in such danger, and to think that outside of our little acreage there were people suffering in relief camps, or even their homes because they have no food, no clean water, no medicine. Heck, there are not even doctors available unless you find them on the black market or in your neighborhood. What had this world come to?

After Velcro started to look tired from the running, we decided to go inside and watch TV to see if there was anything relevant going on. Things had slowed down for us immensely, thanks to the help we received. There was no way we would have gotten as much done as we did without the help. We came back in and decided that wine was in order, so that just the two of us could relax and maybe have a little fun, just the two of us kind of fun. Things were difficult enough. Working 16 hour days was exhausting, though the days were getting shorter. And with the shorter days, we wanted to be inside more often. It was getting dusk, so Tom decided to lock up the animals before it got too dark. Being out in the back country, you do not take your chances with a major source of your food against coyotes, or cougars/mountain lions, or even a little skunk.

I went back inside and decided to prepare dinner, something special tonight. We had been working hard, and really needed a treat. I opened a bottle of wine and poured two glasses, then I looked through the fridge. I found fresh spinach and kale, along with some broccoli and cabbage. I decided to sauté some vegetables. I looked for carrots, but we must have moved them all to the root cellar. I will have Tom fetch some when he comes back in I thought. I grabbed our sauté pan and poured a little water, then added olive oil and some salt, then I added the broccoli, cabbage, bell peppers and garlic. None of it looked like what you find at the grocery store, but we were quite satisfied with what we did get out of the garden. Tom was taking a while, so I decided to go to the root cellar myself. I grabbed the key and a flashlight and went out to the cellar.

Once inside the cellar I realized that not only carrots but onions sound good too, so I picked out a couple of those. I looked around for a little bit. I had never used a root cellar before, but I had read about them, and how to use them. The book we had on how to construct them also had some information on how to best benefit from them. I hoped it worked, because I know dehydrating and canning works, but to be able to save these for fresh vegetables through the winter and for seed would be nice.

As I walked out I heard Tom's and Rita's voices, so I went to see what was going on. We had not seen Rita with the exception of the day after we got here, and although we thought it was unlikely, we actually wondered if she went to the camps. Plus her dog was gone as well, and so was her truck. As I approached, Rita saw me and ran to me to give me a hug, she was full of excitement.

"Rita, we haven't seen you since we've been back!" I said with excitement.

"Well, as one was telling Tom, one has bin engaged with Chaaarles. We have made ah lot of plans, and have splashed out the last month living togethah, and decided that we aaare going to mustah maaarried."

"Official? You are getting married?"

"Yes, we aaare, isn't it exshahting?"

"Yeah, but so soon?"

"Oh, we've bin eyeing each uhthah for donkey's yeaaars noh, fie neithah of us was brave enough to approach the uhthah one. Well, with one's husband passing, that was difficult enough, and with his positiohn in the church, he didn't feel it was roysh. But when things fell apaaart in the rest of the world, we decided that time might not be ohn our side, and if you, one's old bean, love someone, you, should seay soh!"

"Wow, congratulations!" I exclaimed.

"Soh, we're debating which home we're going to move intoh noh. One has the woohd stove, but his hice has more land with the orchaaard, and well, we haven't figured it out yet."

"Wow, Rita, this is all very exciting, when is the wedding?"

"Well, that will have to wait, we might elope to spaaare ourselves the hassle."

"Well congratulations, I don't know what else to say, other than we're very happy for you" I said with much excitement. It was good to hear good news for a change.

"I'm ecstatic, you have noh ideah, but came down to pick up ah few things, and one need to head beck, but saw Tom out soh wanted to let you knoh that I was aalright."

"Thanks for telling us, we were starting to worry a little. We thought maybe you ran off to the camps" I said. She laughed with her English accent and said "ne'ah!" as she ran off.

116

Tom and I returned inside and Tom started to feed the dogs as I started to peel the carrots and onion skins into the compost.

"Wow, I don't think we have ever seen Rita so happy" Tom started.

"No, I've never seen her smile for more than two seconds." I replied.

"Well, I guess this is good for her" Tom continued.

"Yeah, and given how she has devoted herself to the church, it only makes sense that she hook up with the preacher" We both chuckled.

"Yeah, that's funny, I didn't think of that" Tom said happily.

"It works out though, they both have preps, and now they can pool their resources together" I said.

"Yeah, except the church always helps people, so as long as Charles is not asking for hand outs from us..." Tom gave me a look, I know what he meant.

"I don't think he will. But if he does, we'll just put more people to work" I said quickly.

"We're already feeding two extra mouths, well, three for now. Anyway, while we've been successful with our harvest, we might not be again" Tom was very serious.

"I know, but having help increases our chances of success" I argued.

"We need to find a male goat soon, because we need more goats" Tom was being very matter of fact, he gets to the point, and quickly. We previously avoided male goats because if you keep a male goat in the vicinity of a female, their milk gets a very strong odor that we did not like. We always figured we would just borrow a male goat, but there were not many goats in this area.

"That may prove to be a bit difficult, but we'll work on it" I said optimistically.

"People have got to be running out of stuff, maybe we can set up a weekly barter session after church or something."

"That's a good idea, let's talk it over with Terry and Sam next time we see them" I said.

I proceeded to add the carrots and onions to the pan, and Tom went to turn on the television. As I turned on the heat of the 5th burner on medium, I only vaguely listened to the TV, until I heard my name. What? Did they just say my name on TV?

"Rachel, you need to come watch this!" Tom yelled. I dropped the stirring spoon and ran to the TV. I could not believe my ears or my eyes, my picture was plastered on the television!

As stated, if you see Rachel Roberts please call 911 right away. Rachel Roberts is believed to be armed and dangerous. As stated earlier, what we thought was an ambush on Rachel Roberts turns out was really an ambush by Rachel Roberts and an accomplice. An eye witness who hid nearby and watched the scene unfold has come forward to tell the truth. The eye witness reports that Rachel Roberts and her accomplice, who is suspected to be her husband Thomas Roberts, who goes by Tom, attacked a group of innocent travelers who were stranded due to a broken vehicle. The eye witness reports that both Rachel and her accomplice attacked in cold blood, for no reason, and later stole supplies from the victims. And finally, dropped her ID badge to make it look like she was in trouble. Again, if you see Rachel Roberts, she is considered armed and dangerous, and needs to be reported immediately. Please do not try to apprehend her or her accomplice yourself, as she is considered armed and dangerous.

Tom and I were staring at the TV with our jaws wide open. We could not believe what we were hearing. Tom finally broke the silence.

"We missed someone? Damn it, he probably got paid off for lying like that."

"They were not innocent, they were going to kill us! And we only actually killed one ourselves!" I started to repeat my calming mantra to myself, self defense is not murder, self defense is not murder. The events of that night came rushing into my head, and I felt light headed.

"Rachel, sit down, you need to relax." Tom pushed me into a camping chair and then went to the kitchen. He poured a glass of water, and while there stirred the food that I was cooking, turned the burner on low, and came back with the glass of water.

"Calm down Rachel. You and I both know this is a lie."

"They were wearing stolen guard uniforms, they were not real guard, we checked their IDs against their dog tags, they did not even have military IDs!" I was rationalizing to myself outloud.

"Rachel, breathe... here.... have some water." I could not believe what I had just seen on television. My picture was plastered all over the area. I am apparently an armed and dangerous individual who kills in cold blood?

"NOOOOOO, this... can.... not... be... happening, this... can... not... be... happening" I was at a state of panic.

"Rachel, you have to calm down, let's talk about this" Tom was trying hard to soothe me.

"Tom, I am a wanted murderer, someone is going to turn me in! It's just a matter of time!"

"No they are not. Most of the town does not know you're here, and the people that do, know better than that."

"But not every person that lives in this town is an honest person. Someone is bound to turn me in" I argued.

"Rache, come on, calm down." Tom had switched to a soothing voice. I realized that I was overreacting. I could not let such an insignificant lie get to me, except that it was not insignificant, it was huge, I was wanted for MURDER!!!

Tom went to the kitchen to stir the veggies, and apparently decided they were done, as he turned off the burner and split the veggies into two bowls. He grabbed two forks, brought the veggies to me, and placed both bowls on a storage container in front of me. Then he went back to the kitchen and grabbed the two glasses of wine and brought them back as well.

I knew I had to calm down, so I accepted my glass of wine and sipped slowly as I took in long breaths of air to help me relax. This can not be happening. Self defense is not murder, self defense is not murder, self defense is not murder.

"Tom, they didn't post your picture, just stated your name, and they even got your last name wrong" I was asking more than stating.

"That's because I was never in the system like you. Notice the photo they used was from your badge?" I had to think about it for a second, and realized he made sense, "oh, you're right, I didn't even think about that."

"I was never in the system, and they probably didn't check your records enough to see that you never took my last name" Tom reassured me. That helped me calm down, it was a lie, otherwise they would get the info right. I did not take Tom's last name because I felt that men and women are equal, and I strongly disagree with the idea that a woman should take a man's last name, as if she were his property. So I kept my maiden name.

"Look, they have a picture of you and your name, and most of the people here don't even know that you have a different last name" Tom was still using a soothing voice.

"That's true" I thought. When people assumed that I had Tom's last name, I just did not argue it, it was not worth it, I let them assume that. The people of this town made the assumption that I was Rachel Wagner, not Rachel Roberts, because most of the people in the town met Tom first. We are legally married, so it did not really matter, and we never set up a mail box or received mail here, so no one ever saw the names on the mail. "Still, the picture, and my first name, everyone will know" I thought out loud.

"Yeah, but everyone will be confused and not so sure" Tom said optimistically.

The news came back on after several commercials about the president making certain announcements. There were no longer any real commercials. It was just clips of promises the President was making. The news announced a few other "wanted murderers" and I wondered if their story was anything like mine, and if they were hiding out somewhere on some acreage as well, or if they were not as lucky.

The official lights off campaign begins this Saturday morning. All small towns who have refused to cooperate will have power shut off. The people residing in these small towns have not paid their power bill, and have been allowed to continue receiving electricity in an effort to give them time to pack up their belongings and make appropriate plans to move to either bigger cities or to go to relief camps. However, due to lack of compliance, and lack of payment, their power will be shut off. Power will be turned on once daily for one hour from 6pm until 7pm so that these people can receive updates via the news on television. However, it is strongly recommended that they leave the small towns immediately. It is unknown at this time how long the daily hour of electricity will be available. All landline telephone service is suspended as well, including 911 services for any city with a population under 50,000 people.

We knew this day was coming: no currency, no power. But that meant that some folks will be with out heat. Terry and Sam have an electric furnace, and they will not make it through the winter without power and heat. As if reading my mind, Tom turned to me and said "we might have some long term company." I just nodded. I was still in shock over the earlier bit of news. I had to try to concentrate on the present. We had turned ourselves off the grid only a couple weeks earlier, or was it days? I could not even remember how long it has been. But the solar panels were working well. There were a couple times when power was reduced, but we learned quickly what could and could not be run together. At least the well pump had it's own separate off grid solar system, so we did not have to worry about running water.

Tom decided to turn off the television and turn on the ham and find out the real news. But this time, all we heard was the frustration of the people who were not fully prepared. We had been intently listening for instances of gangs banding together and heading our way, but fortunately we had not heard of such news – at least not yet. There were many looters out there, but mostly in the cities. We did not hear too much about that outside of the cities – at least not yet. We were sure this would change, and thus the importance of keeping up with the ham operators.

I finally calmed down enough to enjoy my sautéed vegetables and wine. Though I did lose the idea of Tom and I together alone. Instead, we listened to the ham for any sign of useful news, and played with the dogs as they ran down the hallway to catch their ball. Roy had all but given up on the idea of contacting his kids through the hams. After hearing what was going on in the cities, he decided not to chance driving in, especially since he was from a small town, and had an ID with an address that gave that away. He told us that if he had any idea of where his kids were, and if he knew they needed help, he would go. But he would not even begin to know where to look for them now. Regardless, Tom did try every evening to try find out Roy's kids' whereabouts, even when Roy was not around.

"I think we should call it a night" Tom said.

"I agree, but I'm not sure that I'll be able to sleep" I replied.

"Have some chamomile tea, that might help you relax" Tom suggested.

I got up and put the tea kettle on the 5th burner, then found the jar that had the chamomile tea bags, got some honey, and stared at the tea kettle as I waited for it to warm up. How could they do this? Why would they do this? What does it matter if I am missing? Why do they care if I am in jail or not? They know I did not murder those people, so why are they doing this? Are they doing the same thing to all the other names they mentioned on news? Tom startled me as he came up behind and began to rub my shoulders, he knew I was stressed out. I turned around to give him a hug, and held him tightly until the tea kettle whistled. I poured the hot water over the tea bag and honey, and went to sit down with my cup of tea.

"Tom, what are we going to do?" I asked.

"We're going to keep doing what we've been doing" was his simple reply.

"But what if someone turns me in?" I pushed on, it was not that simple to me.

"Then we'll cross that bridge when we get there" Tom said matter of fact like.

"Maybe we should take up more stuff to our bug out location?" I suggested.

"That's a good idea, we still need to take up additional clothes, plus we should check on it to make sure no one has taken over the spot. We have quite a few nice things up there."

"Okay, let's do so in the morning" I said as I felt a little relief. Though not much.

The next morning bright and early I prepared a full plastic storage bin of stuff I thought might be useful in our bug out location. Mostly warm clothes and socks, but a solar shower as well, a heavy duty pot, and a miniature camping wood cook stove. Shortly after Tom got up and had his morning instant coffee, we loaded up some of the smaller pieces of firewood, along with the bin I prepared, and we headed out to our bug out location.

When we got there, everything still looked in tact, the lock looked untouched, and the area 10 feet away were our cache was buried looked untouched as well. We unlocked the lock and had a little trouble opening the door as the paint dried over the hinges, but after a little elbow grease, we got it to open. Nothing inside but a few spiders and our cots and sleeping bags exactly as we left them. We unloaded the bin along with the other items we brought, and tried to leave, but the dogs did not want to as they thought it was a perfect den. After much persuasion, we finally convinced them that the truck was more appealing, we locked the yurt structure back up and went back home.

Upon arriving, we saw that Terry and Sam had been waiting for us. As we pulled up Tom yelled out the window "hope you weren't waiting long!" Terry's response seemed casual, almost non-chalant, "No, not at all, we just got here." We parked the truck and got out. I tried to hurry, as I felt bad for making them wait. Once I was out of the truck I said "come on in, are you hungry?" I was expecting a huge yes, but guess they ate already as Sam responded "no, we ate breakfast at our place already. Do you need help with anything today." I was struggling to get myself organized, I did not expect them so early, but I guess we did invite them. Fortunately Tom chimed in, "well, if you can make the news go away, that would help." They looked confused, and we remembered that they do not have a TV. So I quickly added very sarcastically "apparently I am wanted for murder, so be careful, because I am cold blooded, and you may want to call the authorities ASAP."

They both just laughed and looked at me. Then Sam said "really, do not let that get to you, we know better, we are the ones that lived in those wonderful "relief" camps remember?" For some reason, that made me feel a whole lot better, something about the fact that not everyone believed the official so-called "news" offered me an amazing amount of relief. Tom must have seen me relax because he put his hand on my shoulder, kissed me on the cheek and quietly said "see, I told you it would be fine."

We went inside and sat down in our usual camping chairs around the storage bins used as coffee tables. Tom and I looked at each other at the same time realizing that they had not heard about the power outages coming, so we turned on the TV. Terry and Sam looked puzzled as they know we do not usually watch TV that often. Tom realized their confusion and quickly explained "there is some news you might want to know about." The first news we heard was irrelevant to anything of interest to us. When the news about me being a murderer came on, I did not have an anxiety attack about it this time, it actually did not even look real. I could tell that it was fake, and I felt immune to the topic at that point. It may have helped that Sam and Terry were chuckling the whole time, and kept turning to me and saying things like "oh, that's a good one, yeah, we're scared of you Rachel," and "At least you look good in the photo of you they are using."

After my 45 seconds of fame ended, the "commercials" of the President promising things came on, and that was comical all in itself. *"New currency coming soon..., turn in your farm animals..., we will reward you well..., the relief camps are there to help you."* Samantha spit out her water in laughter when she heard that part. "'Relief" camps? That's what they are calling them now, RELIEF camps? They are concentration camps, that's what they are." The next bit of news was a repeat of last night's lights out campaign, just what we wanted them to hear. After it was over, Tom asked them "is your heat dependent on electricity?"

"Yep, it is" Terry replied.

"Do you know what you are going to do?" Tom asked.

"Guess we will start a bon fire in our kitchen during the cold nights" Terry responded. I wanted to believe he was being sarcastic, but something told me he was not fully.

"Or you can move in here" Tom broke the charade.

There was silence for a long time. Terry and Sam were not the type to take hand outs, at least not from friends, only from a government scheme they had paid into. But, this area was at a somewhat high elevation and it did have cold winters. When choosing the area, Tom and I determined that the elevation was tolerable, and we could still grow food with the assistance of greenhouses or hoop houses and cold frames. We needed the cold for the fruit trees anyway because they need a certain amount of chill hours. We knew there was a risk of moving to this area, but we also saw its advantages. Cold weather meant less people to bother you because they would likely head in more southern warmer directions.

"Do you have room?" Sam finally asked.

"Well our house is small, but we do have a spare bedroom and bathroom. We will have to work out the shower situation because we have limited hot water with our PV powered water heater, especially in the winter. But we can figure out a way to make do" Tom explained.

"We would work you know" Terry said quickly.

"We don't doubt that in any way" Tom reassured.

"Then we would love to take you up on your offer, and thank you" Sam seemed content.

"Great, then it's a done deal. Rache and I will clear out the spare bedroom and bathroom for you. Now, changing topics, what do you think about a weekly barter session at the church?" Tom asked.

"Oh, that would be a wonderful idea - people are bound to need things" Sam replied.

"Maybe we can spread the word?" Tom hinted.

"We'll get on it right away, let you know what comes of it" Terry promised.

"Great, and we're okay for today; we don't really need any help with anything. So if you want to go home and pack your stuff, go ahead" Tom suggested.

"You know, our house is pretty bare, but we still have some windows, and I noticed you built cold frames out of windows just like ours. What if we took out the windows and brought them here to build more cold frames?" Terry asked.

"Wow, that's a great idea, but are you sure you want to tear apart your house like that?" Tom asked, I could tell he was uncomfortable with the idea.

"Our house is really empty and sad, and doesn't feel like home anymore. And we are moving in here, so we might as well make use of the materials that are still left up there. Plus if we don'ttake them and move out, someone else will probably steal them" Terry pointed out.

"Fair enough. If that is what you wish to do, we won't stop you" was Tom's reaction.

"Great, can we borrow your help then? We're not skilled at taking windows out" Terry asked.

"Of course I'll help. Rache, do you mind staying here and tending to the animals?"

"Not at all, have fun pulling windows" I said with a bit of sarcasm. I was glad to not have been volunteered. I think I can get used to this hiding out thing, no one expects you to do anything you don't want to.

With that, they left, and I was left alone with the dogs and animals. Things had become pretty routine, except that it was getting very cold at night. We had not been running our electric furnace because there was no way the solar batteries could handle it. But it was definitely time to start using the wood stove. I went outside to the shed and started to bring in firewood, making sure to brush off any spiders I saw. I did not want to bring any of those inside with me. The dogs followed me around every step, and sometimes even got in front of me trying to trip me. Once I brought in enough wood, I figured I should start the fire. Given the cold nights, we would probably be keeping one going regularly. This also meant I did not have to rely on the 5th burners for cooking because I could just use the wood stove. It was a wood cook stove after all. With the shorter days creeping up on us, any solar power we could save could mean a huge difference in how much lighting we would have after dark.

After I got the fire going, I went into the spare bedroom and started to move boxes and bins out. Might as well make them feel at home I thought. I did not even know what was in some of those boxes, though I tried to mark everything when I packed it. After going through what was written, I decided to keep some of the boxes for the couple, it was just filled with fabric, but they might find it useful, and there were some fleece fabric pieces in there as well. I also found a bin full of clothes that we bought at a thrift store one year. They were having a black Friday sale where every item was 50% off of the already thrifty prices, so we bought a ton of clothes, regardless if it fit or not. We figured we might need it one day, if not for us, maybe someone else, or for barter.

After I moved the boxes out, I made a path from the master bedroom to the spare bedroom, and then went to move the futon mattress we slept on out of the way. I grabbed the mattress underneath and dragged it to the spare bedroom. I had not realized it, but all the physical labor we have been doing has made me stronger. I hardly struggled with the mattress, though I still struggled a little, especially since the dogs were insistent on killing me by running under my feet constantly.

We only had one futon frame, but we had two futon mattresses, which we normally stacked on top of each other. I figured I could donate one of them, and they could just leave it on the floor. After I positioned the mattress I organized two of the plastic storage bins as end tables, and found a lamp for them as well. Once I made it look sort of like a bedroom, I went into the bins and pulled out a bunch of fabric pieces. I figured some could be used as pillows, and I found fleece pieces that could be used as blankets for them as well. I knew they had been sleeping on the floor of their place after the robbery. They never complained, and I considered offering them the spare futon before, but just never got around to it. Plus, I did not want to make them feel uncomfortable. But since they were coming here, I would not feel right sleeping on two mattresses when they had none.

Shortly after I finished, the dogs ran to the window. Compass did his quiet warning bark. I ran over to the window and peeked out, it was Rita, so I opened the door before she could even knock, and let her in.

"Hi Rita, have you eloped yet?"

"Noh, not yet, but soohhn, I came down to let you knoh that with the powah outages coming, chaaarles and I aaare moving intoh my place for the woohd stove. But we don't have any more gas in our trucks, we've actually bin riding bikes to mustah aaaround."

"Oh, you know, we don't have any gas stored because we have diesel trucks. But you know what, when Tom gets back, I'm sure he'll be happy to help you move with our truck" I regret it saying it as soon as I did. I know better than to volunteer Tom for projects.

"Rairlairh? Oh, that would be jolly sticks" Rita was super enthiusiastic.

"Yeah, he'll be back shortly, Terry and Sam are moving in with us for the wood stove as well, so he's at their place getting their things" I explained.

"Didn't they get robbed while they were gone?" Rita seemed a little confused.

"Yeah, but they accumulated a few things since returning, and I think they might be taking the windows to make more cold frames" I quickly added.

"Is that what this world is coming to?" Rita had a little sarcasm to her voice.

"Yeah, I guess. Have you not seen the news?" I asked, hoping to find out what she thought of me being a murderer.

"We have, but we refuse to be unhappy. Life is toohh short" she replied.

"Well, that is a great attitude Rita" I was a bit relieved.

"Yeah, I splashed out enough days being unhappy" Rita continued.

"So I guess we will be real neighbor's this time" I said jokingly.

"Yeah, you, one's old bean, won't be gone 28 out of 31 days" there was definite sarcasm in Rita's voice.

"Come on, it was 27 out of 31!" We both laughed about it.

"Great, can you have Tom come by when he gets beck? I need to mustah one's place ready for Chaaarles's things" Rita asked.

"No problem, do you think you'll have a lot to move? We could hook up the trailer if that helps" I suggested. I was trying to make Tom's life easier by making him do less trips. "Rairlairh, that would be spiffing. 'Eaaars, we're going to move everything in his hice, and you knoh what, I have ah distinct fancy of your ideah" Rita said as she walked out.

After Rita left, I went back to the spare bedroom and looked in. It almost looked like a bedroom, I was quite happy with it. I then went to the kitchen and grabbed some beef jerky out of a jar, picked up my cheese making book, and sat down to read a little bit before Tom got back. I didn't really read anything though. I was enjoying the quiet, if you want to call cows mooing and rooster's crowing quiet, but to me it was. Even though I know that the city people were struggling badly, it was so peaceful here. Peaceful, even with the two dogs begging in front of me waiting for me to throw them a treat of jerky – even though I never did.

It was scary for me the first few nights here alone. The dogs kept barking at the sound of the mooing cows, the house kept making strange noises, the dogs also barked at the coyote sounds coming from the forest up the road. I guess the dogs were a bit frightened as well. It sure made it easy to be aware of what was going on at all times, without too much work. But at the same time, when you are used to the hum of the city, and you are not familiar with so much silence, it can be a bit eerie at first.

Weekends away from the city were tough, especially if I went without Tom. I had always been comfortable being by myself, but this was a major factor that I had not been prepared for. The cabin was lonely out in the middle of nowhere. There was no TV (not that we watched that garbage much anyway), no neighbors nearby, not much of anything. Just me and the dogs, and sometimes just me. I would speak to the dogs as if they were human. I longed for my husband to be with me. Little things such as him not picking up the phone when I called resulted in worry, followed by devastation hitting. It was one of those strange things that made me understand the meaning of loneliness. It was a realization of how much Tom meant to me, and how much I wanted him in my life.

But in reality, for the two of us to always be together was not always possible, and often not practical. When Tom finished school and was looking for work, the job search was slow at first. Actually, it was impossible at first. Send in 50 resumes and not one call back. Nothing. And his resume was a good one, college degree, various experience, EMT, etc. The economy was bad, and unemployment was much higher than reported. My co-workers would ask me about his job search, and I would tell them the truth. So they would suggest he apply for a government job like mine. I had to remind them that I only got my job because I was a veteran, and he was not. I guess that's the President's idea of stimulating the economy: force places to hire a certain group, give them a preference to give them a head start on getting a job, and then hand out bonuses for hiring veterans. That's one way to convince the public that the military is the way to go: bribe them. The government would sure take care of you afterwards - at least before the economy and the US Dollar fell apart, the government often did take care of certain groups of people. I had something ridiculous like 30 vacation and 20 sick days a year. I never used them all, perhaps I should have. I also had a nice retirement package, not that it meant anything now, because there was no economy to pay for it. But those who actually got to use theirs, they were well set. So Tom found a private sector "under the table" job, or as he called it, a "true free market" job. As a result, we had to be apart quite a bit the last year. But you do what you have to do to survive, and that was what we had to do.

I spent many weekends alone, and after I got used to the noises like the dogs did, I felt comfortable, peaceful, happy. I was even happier on the weekends that Tom joined me, but of course that was not as often as I liked. I often wondered if he felt the same way on days that he was here without me. He certainly never talked about it.

When we first bought this place, we were in for a surprise. Rural life was not what we thought it would be, and neither were the people. Actually, our first few experiences were not so positive. Rita avoided us at first, and the first time that Tom went to the transfer station to dump a bunch of junk that was left at this place, some guy went off on him criticizing religion. Tom was very discouraged. That was until he found out that the guy was not from here; he drove all the way from Springfield hoping he wouldn't have to pay dump fees, and was ticked off when he found out he did.

Looking at this town on a map, we thought it had a lot going for it. Lots of rivers and creeks for water, lots of trees for timber, elevation at 3300 feet, an acceptable growing season, lots of farmland, ranchers and cattle, a modest size city not too far for supplies, etc. And guns seemed to outnumber people. We thought that if an EMP went off, this town would not be too badly affected. Other than possibly fuel shortages, the main way the people here would find out about something like that would be on the evening news.

We figured that people here would work towards getting back to normal quickly. No supply trucks, that's okay, who could make what? The reality was, once we got to know a lot of our "neighbor's," we realized that even out here in the boonies they were to some degree dependant on hand outs from the government. They were dependent on their television, and even more so on supply trucks bringing in supplies from distant locations. It seemed that in the current world, very few people were able to escape dependence on long and fragile supply chains across regions or even across borders. Sure, the people out in rural "nowhere" may not spend as much or be *as* dependent. But they still had fancy cell phones with instant internet like everyone else. We were still the odd ones out, advocating for local production and as much self sufficiency and self reliance as possible as a means to buffer some of the harm that would occur as a result of the inevitable disruption of those long fragile supply chains. But either we did not move far enough out into the country, or there was no such self reliant place anymore.

But with time, once the community got to know us, they softened up, and they accepted us. We learned quickly that the general store is the way to find what you need. Whether it's a little help with work around your place, or just to learn about the neighbor's, you go to the general store to ask. There was also a trading post. We stopped by there on several occasions,

131

and even traded our spare bicycles for a camping mini wood stove once. This mini wood stove was now in our bug out location.

I sat there staring at the pages of my cheese making book, I could not comprehend what I was reading. I realized that exhaustion had hit. Living out in the country was draining on the body in two ways: 1, you have a lot more physical work. 2, the comforts of regulated temperature and warm showers are not as reliable. One does not realize the energy that the lack of these comforts can consume. What would normally take me 8 hours often took me 8 days to complete, and that was just the beginning.

When we first got the place, it needed serious cleaning. Bleached the mouse droppings once the mice were gone, actually, bleached everything. I was a maid at one time, I have cleaned a 2200 sq. ft. home from top to bottom in 8 hours before. But this was different - this had mice, rat droppings, and squirrels. Just deep cleaning one bathroom alone took a whole day. And the job was disgusting. We kept finding dead critters everywhere. Our biggest surprise was what may have been a chipmunk, though we're not really sure, in the exhaust above the stove. It did not help that during this time the furnace was still broken and that we had yet to install a wood stove. I thought I could tolerate a cold shower while the hot water heater was out, but I was wrong. I barely got my head washed before I gave up and decided that being greasy and dirty was better than taking a shower with water the temperature that came up from the well. To say that our adventure was discouraging at first, was an understatement. But that was what we could afford, and we had to make do.

Then Tom wanted horses. He had this crazy idea in his head that we would just get some horses and have non-motorized transportation. It took me a while, but I finally convinced him about the amount of work it takes to keep a horse healthy, and the many health problems they can encounter, such as colic. We eventually stuck with goats, and chickens. Even that was not easy.

Believe it or not, milking a goat was hard work. So was collecting chicken eggs, locking up the animals at night, and changing their water. It all added up. It may seem simple to someone inexperienced, but it really was a lot of work. You also couldn't just up and skip a day if you were tired. The animals had needs, and if you ignored those needs, your animals could potentially die. If you ignored locking them up, you could guarantee that a coyote or cougar/mountain lion would find them, or even a ground squirrel would find its way to the chicken feed. Out in the country, you were on their territory, and you had to learn to do it right. There was no calling in sick, there were no vacation days, there was only do it so that it gets done. And that was just the animals. You still had to tend to your wood stove, split wood, store it, rotate your food stock, irrigate your gardens and orchard, pull weeds,and do whatever it is you do to produce value, even if it is just barter.

We had been going non-stop for the last year, with the last few months more intense due to the amount of work that was needed. And here I was, staring at pages written for a 12 year old, and I could not comprehend a word. I had never before, felt such exhaustion.

I would have fallen asleep trying to read if it were not for the dogs running to the window in excitement. Tom was back, and he was driving super slow. I saw the windows stacked up in the back of the pick up. That's why he was driving slowly, to make sure they were safe. Once the truck stopped I let the dogs out to greet him and Terry and Sam. I walked out slowly. It was the first time that I felt such exhaustion since we had been here, and I felt it over my whole body.

Tom jumped out and pointed to the garage. I ignored my body aches and ran back inside the house to grab the keys, and then ran to the garage, the dogs running happily behind me. I unlocked the locks and lifted the door. By then, Tom and Terry had unloaded the first window and carried it in. I jumped in the truck to get the next window started, and Sam followed my lead. We picked up the next window and then carefully removed it off the bed of the pick up truck. Then I jumped off the truck and carried the window in with Sam. By then Tom and Terry were at the next window. Terry's hand had fully healed by this point. It was only somewhat usable, but he managed.

There were 14 windows in total, and we got them all moved to the garage even though the dogs tried to trip us a few times. Then Tom locked up the garage and we went in the house. Terry and Sam looked exhausted. Perhaps my exhaustion made me see what they felt. Regardless, they looked tired, with wrinkles taking over their faces. They both sat down on some bins with a sigh of relief, and while I was afraid to ask, I had to.

"Are you sad about your house?" It was Sam that replied this time, usually Terry did the talking.

"A little, but we know that either we took them, or someone else loots them."

"I'm sorry, this has got to be hard" I tried to be consoling.

"Nothing is as hard as escaping those so called 'relief' camps" Terry quickly pointed out.

"Oh yeah, I forgot you went through that, I guess this is better than there" I replied, though still feeling guilty about their home.

"We would rather fight a grizzly bear than go back to that place" Sam added.

"Fair enough. So hey, I got your room ready, would you like to see?" I wanted to change the topic even though I started it.

"Sure."

"Follow me." We had never before given a tour of the house, because there was not much to see. But this time, I felt they may appreciate it.

"You're probably familiar with the guest bathroom as this is the one everyone uses. And here's your room, kind of small, but it's yours."

"Wow, it has a bed? Where did the bed come from?" Sam asked.

"It's just a futon mattress, and we happened to have two. Two is one and one is none, after all. No need for us to keep sleeping on both, so enjoy. And the bins have fabric in them, plus this bin has some clothes we picked up at thrift stores back in the day. I don't know if they'll fit, but you can help yourselves. I found some fleece and military surplus wool blankets too. I couldn't find pillows, and I don't think we have any extras, but I rolled up a bunch of fabric, so that should work." I pointed at bins as I walked around the room showing them where to find stuff.

"Wow, you did too much, it was unnecessary" Sam seemed overwhelmed.

"It was actually really simple, so I hope you are happy with it" I replied.

"I think we'll be fine" Terry stated.

"Great, I need to go add wood to the fire, so I'll let you get settled" I said as I walked out of the room.

I felt good as I was walking away. I know they were good people, and being robbed while you were out battling with the government because they lied to you was an awful experience. I really didn't do that much for them: gave them a mattress, not even, a futon, some sheets and blankets, and some storage bins and a lamp. That's really nothing. Most people on "food stamps" had more than they did, at least back in the day when food stamps existed. But I still felt great, because I was able to do something nice for them when they didn't ask for it. And they had certainly helped us a lot with the work around the homestead. I wondered though how they would react if they found out the walls were filled with sand bags and not insulation. What a weird thought to have go through my head.

Tom had disappeared to wash up while I was showing the couple their room. He came out of the master bedroom drying his hands with a towel. "There's an emergency meeting tomorrow at 9 am at the church, they want to make sure everyone will have a way to stay warm without power" Tom stated.

"Oh, then I should probably tell you, I volunteered you to use our truck and trailer to move Charles's things to Rita's place." Tom thought about it for a moment, I could tell he wanted to be mad for volunteering him, but he could not, because he knew that we needed to be a community. "Can you do it?" he finally asked after a minute of thought.

"You want me to tow the eighteen foot cargo trailer?" I asked surprised.

"Sure, it's just a few miles" his response was not convincing.

"Okay, but you can't be mad if I accidently wreck something" I said in a strict tone.

"Okay, you win, I'll help them. Did Rita say when?" Tom sounded defeated, though I did not try very hard. He must be tired too.

"She said that she's getting the house ready, so she might want to talk to you now" I answered.

"Fine, but I need to eat first" he replied.

I could tell he was not happy with the situation, but he did not say anything else. Instead, he went to the kitchen, ate a bunch of food, then took off for Rita's place. I saw him take the truck and hook it up to the trailer. He must have been mad, because he usually asks for my help to guide the trailer hitch, but not this time. He insisted on doing it himself, and then he took off.

Chapter 6

Basic Necessities, and the Comforts of City Life

The dogs woke me up bright and early. I reluctantly crawled out of bed, dragged on my slippers, and walked to the door to let them out. I could not believe it was light out, how late had I slept? It seemed the whole house was still asleep, so unusual. We are usually up before the sun. Perhaps the exhaustion finally hit everyone hard. With the morning haziness starting to burn off I realized the temperature in the house had a biting chill. I quietly opened the door to let the dogs out, and I left it ajar so they could get back in. I hurried to the wood stove to add wood. Maybe I slept so late to stay warm under the covers? The wood stove had burned out completely over night. Usually a large slow burning log will last through the night but apparently not last night. We all must have slept through the stove and house going cold.

The dogs snuck back in one by one, and I knew they wanted their breakfast. Once I saw both were in, I shut the door and got their bowls ready. I went to the mouse proof storage bin to scoop their food. It was a metal trash can really, nothing attractive, but it fit 250 lbs of their dry food at a time, and we had two back ups filled with an additional 250 lbs each in the garage. Once the dogs were happily eating, I checked on the fire again. It didn't seem to want to start, so I added more paper grocery bags. Over the last three years, when I was asked if I want paper or plastic, I happily said paper. Once the groceries were unloaded, I folded the paper grocery bags and placed them into another paper sack, and saved them for fire starter. As I added more paper to the fire and used the lighter to re-light it, I saw it flickering, I thought it might work this time.

I snuck to the hallway to get my boots on. I learned a long time ago when I volunteered to feed cows with hay over the winter at a "teaching" ranch, that you take your boots and coveralls off at the same time. This way you don't have to take the coveralls over your dirty boots. The heavy duty coveralls that I bought to help volunteer, were now being used on my own homestead land. The boot tops were covered by the coveralls, and I had placed a plastic bag on top to prevent spiders from crawling in. I removed the plastic bag and I put my feet in through the crumpled down coverall legs. I lifted the coveralls over me and snapped the straps into place. I tied my boots on top to prevent water from getting in, then got on my coat and hat and went out to let the animals out and refill their waters. If Tom were awake I'm sure he would tell me to take a weapon with me, "just in case." I normally did, but this morning I just wanted to get this over with.

It was a lot chillier than I thought. At least I was dressed for the occasion, though my toes might get a little cold. I quickly tended to all the animals, let the chickens out, filled up their water, let the goats out and refilled their water as well. We had also considered getting ducks, because we read that the ducks could live in the same coop as the chickens overnight. But with so many chickens and only one large coop, we never got around to it. We also decided against ducks because we lived in an area that had a large population of wild ducks and geese. Tom figured that he could always go hunting for them if we chose to do so. I partially disagreed with him on that point, as I was not so sure the animal populations would be as robust as he thought after the financial collapse.

But I went along with it. We knew we needed to build another coop so that we could separate the chickens into two separate flocks. We also needed more fencing. The fencing we had was minimal to keep the animals in. We really wanted to fence the whole property. Although we managed to collect a ton of fencing and posts and other supplies, we did not get enough to fence the whole property. So we built the animal fencing to keep the goats and chickens from wandering off, and left it at that until we could get more fencing. We continued to collect freebies, but no where near enough. We knew that not having the whole property fenced compromised our property security, so fencing the perimeter was something that was still on the "to do" list. Anyway, here I was, staring at our fence work. It was kind of funny looking because the gauge and type of fencing did not quite match all the way around the goat area. We used what we had, and now the place looked like a quilted fence. I did not mind really, as long as it worked. As a bonus we decided that since it looked so horrible that we would be less of a target for criminals. In a time when there is little law and order, and crime was common, one of the best camouflages you can have is to look poor.

As I was headed back in, I was struck by the beautiful sunrise. We had been so busy that the idea of sitting down to watch a sunset or sunrise never occurred to us. The norm was usually something along the lines of 'we have 30 minutes of daylight left, we need to hurry to get this done.' This place was very beautiful. The plot was a typical five acre rectangular plot, where the house sat on the top third line portion. It was mostly flat land though there were some rolling hills toward the top that made the plot look smaller than it was. At the bottom of the plot ran the seasonal creek that we discovered. We actually learned when we were looking for a property that there used to be water there based on looking at decades old maps filed with the state. We just figured it had dried up; though that turned out not to be the case.

The rolling hills faced south, which was the only reason we considered a property with any type of hills. We later came to realize that it was actually very advantageous to have a home on a hill. The well pump was just uphill of the house, which allowed for easy gravity flow of the water from the pump tank to the house. The only expense was the pump actually pumping the water out of the ground. The covered sun deck that came with the house faced south as well, the previous owners clearly knew what they were doing. Just behind the house was the area we designated for the chickens, and further south was the septic system, and the leech field that the septic system would empty into. That is where decided to plant only chicken feed, and the grass pasture for the goats. This was the one plot we would not rotate, as the scientific literature strongly suggested it was not safe to use night soil as a form of fertilizer for human food.

Southeast of the chickens was our first garden area. Tom had cleared most of that land by hand before we got the goats; though it would have been easier to have them do it for us. He wanted a tractor, but it just was not in the budget. So little by little, he cleared it by hand until we rented a tractor. We burned the brush as weather permitted. South of the first garden plot was where we put the goat housing, and south of the goat housing was the second garden plot. We wanted to keep the plots far enough away from each other to prevent unwanted cross pollination when it came to saving seeds for vegetables of the same families, such as broccoli and spinach. We also wanted to make sure the gardens were far enough away from the septic field in case of over flow. We later realized that with the grass and chicken forage, we did not have to worry much about that, as those plants took up nutrients quickly.

Just north of the house a little to the east was the free standing garage, and we put garden plots to the east and north of the garage for more shade tolerant plants. The cherry and plum orchard, grapes, blueberries and strawberries were settled southwest, slightly downhill from the house. This allowed us to run pipes to them from the house and utilize a gray water system for irrigation. South of the orchard we had another garden plot. We kept some shade trees just west of the house to reduce the summer afternoon heat. At the southwest corner of the property line is where we buried our trash. At the top of the property line northwest of the house we had planted some walnut trees, figuring they were far enough away from any garden plot. Unknown to many, walnut tree roots release toxins into the surrounding soil that prevent other plants from growing nearby. We also planted fast growing blackberries along the north fence line that met the road. We figured the thorns would help to act as a deterrent to trespassers, and if some hungry looters took the berries then that was not a big deal to us. We figured it was better to use those as a "sacrificial deterrent" rather than have something more important stolen from deeper in our property.

Because of the rolling hills, you could barely see the house driving up. When we first bought the place, I would drive to the general store in town, then be so mesmerized by the beauty of the area on my way back that I kept missing our driveway, partly because of the native foliage surrounding the entrance. I would realize it eventually, then turn around and miss it again. I eventually learned to recognize the area and knew the driveway was coming up. The animal housing was well hidden by the hills as well, which made it nice when we did not want to deal with the county building inspector or the property tax assessor. They were terrible to work with and it seemed they would come in from Springfield just to stir up bureaucratic problems for bureaucracy sake, or try to parasitize ever more "fees." Tom had filed paperwork to declare the home a homestead and we figured we would use that as protection should they find out about the additional building structures. According to our research, a "homestead" is exempt from such permits, at least in our county.

There were some native trees on the property, which we did not want to cut down, so we worked around them considering shade for the animals and gardens. Because we went with semi-dwarf fruit trees, they looked very small in comparison to the pines and conifer native trees that were already on the property. All and all we managed to fit most everything we wanted on the land, but could have used more land. We could have used more forest land to provide firewood. We talked about buying adjoining land but money never allowed it. So we had to source our firewood from nearby National Forest or BLM land.

In addition, the plot immediately next to ours was undeveloped and still full of brush. We had considered clearing it now since the owners were not around, and we did not want that weed seed to move back over to our land. On the other side of our property was Rita's place, which her husband built from scratch before he died. About the only difference from Rita's plot and ours was that she had the greenhouse that they fit on one of the flat areas between the rolling hills, and she did not have any animal housing.

I was mesmerized by the sunrise. It was then I realized that I had not seen or heard any planes since the economy crashed. We had heard that helicopters and drones were being used for guard patrols, but we had not seen any out here in nowhere. It was almost as if everything stopped. We had heard on the ham radios that in the city very few people were using cars anymore, since fuel, which was supposedly rationed, was really not available. Those who did have fuel had it siphoned out of their cars when they were not looking. It was surreal to realize that here I was on this small plot of land, reasonably comfortable, while the rest of the world around me was miserable and hungry. I was thankful that Tom had convinced me to start prepping years before. And even though we did not have a lot, we were better off than most, who had put their trust in government, and paper assets.

After a moment I realized I had been doing nothing but staring at the land as the sun was coming up, and the morning chill started to bother me. It seemed to get colder first thing in the morning just after day break than it did overnight, so I snuck back inside. I will milk the goats later when it is warmer I thought to myself. I undressed my outside winter gear and was back in my pajamas. As I was washing my hands, I noticed the wood stove was going strong, so I decided to heat up some water for instant coffee.

It was strange that Tom was still asleep, but then I slept in late as well. I am sure the cold had something to do with it. Plus, I did not know how late he got in. I was already asleep before he got back. As the tea kettle started to steam, I made a cup of instant coffee, added some goat milk and some stevia, then sat down in front of the wood cook stove to enjoy the morning brew. Perhaps the smell of coffee got everyone's attention as all of sudden the master bedroom door and the guest bedroom doors opened simultaneously and everyone came out.

"Good morning everyone, water in the tea kettle is hot, though it's still a bit chilly in here" I said trying to be inviting to our new guests.

"Nothing like a good hot cup of coffee to wake you up" Terry commented.

"Yep, help yourself" I mumbled. I pointed in the direction of the cabinet that held the instant coffee and the coffee cups. "Hot water is on the stove, the milk is in the fridge."

Everyone headed for coffee first, and we all sat there sipping away, blankly staring at the wood stove. Tom stood up and started heading toward the TV "mind if I turn on the TV, I need to know what's going on before the emergency meeting."

"Good idea" Sam agreed.

Tom turned on the television only to discover that there was now a reward for my capture. Not sure why I would be worth a reward, but whatever, there was a reward for the others as well. I had become immune to my picture on TV. There was actually nothing new on television. Power is to be turned off tomorrow morning for all the small towns as planned.

"Rache, you're not going to the meeting, you know that right?" Tom stated as he was looking at me.

"Yes, Tom, I'm well aware that I need to be hidden away so that no one that doesn't need to know I'm here knows" my response did not hide my annoyance.

"And we need someone to watch the place" Tom added.

"Yep, that would be me" I said happily. I actually did not mind being excused from all the town meetings. It was time to myself, which has become more rare, and it was time not listening to old people bicker about petty things. Tom did not want to talk about last night, so he must be over it. Though I did not hear him come in, they must have been moving Charles' stuff real late.

"Are you going to bring up the barter idea?" I finally asked.

"If the opportunity presents itself" Tom replied.

"Good, cause we need to borrow a male goat, and we could use more fencing" I added. Everyone knew what was on our wish list, but I felt a reminder might be good.

After we warmed up, we discussed the shower situation. We decided that we would each shower every other day in the evenings, after the PV system has had sunlight all day for the batteries. Plus it worked out better to shower and go to bed clean rather than dirty because we would not have to wash the sheets or our pajamas as often. Of course, there is a possibility we would not have enough battery power if there was little sun. In that case we would have to take baths by heating up water on the wood stove, and we would of course skip showers if we did no manual labor at all.

Then the discussion of the septic system came up. Most homes out in the country have septic systems. Since they can eventually fill up, we made sure to get our septic tank pumped empty and inspected, to buy us the most time before we had any trouble with it. We also made sure to buy toilet paper that was septic safe, and then researched how to take care of a septic system. Tom and I had long lived by rule of only flushing when brown, and not when yellow. We actually started this practice in the city to make sure that we were already accustomed to doing so, though it was a hard habit to break. I ended up putting notes all over the bathroom to remind us. At 3 gallons of water per flush, that's a lot of water that could be saved.

The couple was more than agreeable to only flush when brown, and since they had their own bathroom for the two of them, it wasn't really anything that we considered gross or unsanitary. Tom and I used our bathroom, and they used theirs. We also had a system of saving some of our water from the kitchen, mostly water from rinsing vegetables, and the excess water from our reverse osmosis water purification system.

As things were right now, we had a water recycling system that was a little time consuming, as you had to babysit the bucket under the left side of the sink that was set up to collect the "waste" water. Once full, you had to replace it with another bucket. We had three buckets set up for this, and once all were full, you had to stop what you were doing and put lids on the buckets, and carry them out the back door. Once outside, we used our garden cart to put the buckets on, and then we had a system where you would walk down the hill while pulling the cart, and water either the trees or the berry bushes. It was certainly a tedious system, but it saved our septic from gallons and gallons of re-usable water that would otherwise be wasted. It also saved our well pump from pulling up more water than necessary. None of us liked the bucket system, especially now that it was getting colder and the plants would not need as much water, but we did not have the plumbing materials to finish a true gray water system. That was the intent, to hook up the left side of the kitchen sink for a gray water system that would automatically go down the hill behind our house to possibly a barrel, or maybe even dig a trench along where we wanted the water to go. This meant we had to make sure we did not use soap on the left side of the sink. We also saved the excess re-usable soapy water in three gallon buckets, which was used to flush the toilets.

After explaining this process to the Terry and Sam, Terry smiled, and suggested "how about we pull some of the plumbing from our old place so we can finish the system? It will be much easier and safer than hauling buckets of water. We'll still use buckets for the flushing, but at least we'll be able to send water to the orchard without hauling buckets, and it will save time on babysitting the system."

"Terry, you already took your windows out, are you not planning on returning to your home when things get better?" Tom asked.

"If I don't take it, someone else well. And that's also assuming that things *do* get better. Tom, let's stop by the place after the meeting, though I'll need some tools." Terry stated,

Tom obliged "we don't have any plumbing specific tools, but we have an array of standard hand tools. We can probably find something we can use among all that" Tom looked a little worried. It is true, our tools were limited, and plumbing tools were never made a priority.

"I'm sure I will be able to find what I need. I know a good bit about plumbing, so I'm sure I can figure it out, but I'll need a little help of course. With my hand the way it is, I'm not sure I'll be able to turn more than one wrench very well" Terry sounded confident.

"I can help with that, no problem" Tom seemed relieved.

Terry offered to make omelets for breakfast, and I didn't argue. He did make some mean omelets, so it was probably a bad idea as they were much better than what I ever made. Which means I would want him to make breakfast more often. Maybe it was the exhaustion talking, and everything tasted good because my body needed sustenance. Shortly after, everyone crawled in Tom's truck but me, and went off to the emergency meeting.

I had learned to enjoy these moments alone. It was a time for peacefulness, and a time to assess the situation. Here we were, living full time at our "cabin." We now had full time guests. So far we had only had to dip into a small amount of our stored food supply, though that would change with winter almost here. We were super busy making cheese, dehydrating food, etc. I am falsely wanted for alleged "murder" across the country so I have to hide, and the dogs are constantly trying to (metaphorically) kill me by getting under my feet. I really did enjoy these moments.

I got dressed and decided to do the dishes first. They were already soaking in a dishpan of hot soapy water, so all they needed was a quick scrub and rinse, then to be put on the drying rack. We had decided to only use the dishwasher for sterilization of things like jars for canning, as the dishwasher uses large amounts of water, and we could not recycle that water the way the plumbing was set up now. After the dishes were done, I filled up the three gallon buckets with the dishwater for toilet flushing. I went outside to tend to the animals again, see if anyone needed a water refill, food refill, collect eggs, and do some milking. However, one of the goats we decided to stop milking so that she could be bred for her young when the time comes. I checked all the fences, looked for evidence of trouble makers or predatory wild animals. The daily chores: nothing new. Though it was different doing it alone, I really enjoyed it.

I did have moments of being city sick. It was only the comforts I missed, not the city itself. I missed being able to get fully prepared food without notice when needed. And I missed shopping for supplies, or even Craigslist and Freecycle and yard sales. Those were such a huge part of my life the last three years that I had grown accustomed to having those "hobbies." I missed the internet, as that was also such a huge part of my daily life. Email to communicate with friends, Google to search for whatever topic I wanted to know about, define a word I do not understand, find out what was really going on in the world that was not mentioned on the five o'clock news. Sure, we still had books, but I had to dig them out, and it was just not the same. I actually kind of wished that we had gotten a nice set of encyclopedias when everyone was giving them away for free. But for some reason, we did not. So we had subject specific books, and our college textbooks, but those were just not the same as Google and the internet. So I missed all that.

On the other hand, I did not miss the useless news on the internet, or the advertising. It had gotten to a point of ridiculousness: you go to click for something, and a huge window pops up with no way to close it. It was annoying more than anything. I certainly was not going to make a purchasing decision for the product based on advertising like that. Actually, it made me less likely to buy the product, but marketers did not seem to understand that. So I did not miss the advertising, and I did not miss the million and one spam emails in my email. I suppose there is a positive side to everything.

I missed my friends. Tom and I had only a few close friends, and very few knew about our preps. It was not that we did not want to tell them, but we were warned early on that you can not invite just anyone if you really want to survive. Since Tom and I did not have extended family that we would even call as such, we felt that we could invite certain friends and they would be our family. We ignored the first warnings and included one friend in our preps. It was one of my best friends at the time, and frankly, at first she was all about it. She saw how things were falling apart. But her husband was not interested, and neither were her parents, or her sister. She was kind of alone in her thoughts. So she could not prepare. If she tried, her husband would eat all the extra food, or sell the extra supplies and equipment on craigslist - he did not think they needed any of it. So after two years of planning with her, right before we found our cabin, I asked her, "what will you do when things fall apart?" She looked at me surprised, then with the most honest answer she could give, she said "go to your house of course." I realized right then and there that she would count on me to support her. So I asked if she would bring her husband, her sister, etc. "Of course" was the answer to everything. Somehow in her mind, she figured I would not be able to shut the door on her, which meant I would not shut the door on her family either.

You can prepare all you want, but unless a person was wealthy, there was no way someone could feed that many mouths, unless they all contributed by working hard – and possibly not even then. I talked it over with Tom and we agreed that she alone could stay with us at our city house, because she was a hard worker. But if she brought family, we could not allow them to stay. As a result of learning from that experience, we never told her about the cabin. Actually, we hardly told anyone about the cabin as we knew it would be detrimental - especially if anyone found out where it was. We included that friend in my "sick mother" story. That was not an easy decision, as I cared for her greatly, but it was one of survival. And that was the decision we made with our other friends who were in the same scenario. Many of our friends were "all talk and no walk," meaning they thought the idea of preparing was a good one, but took little action to actually prepare. We had considered a nice couple that we knew, as they were on the same page as us, or so we thought. But when trying to prep, they were always busy having a good time at some party or another. When we inquired about prepping, they made the remark that there is plenty of time, and life is no fun if all you are doing is prepping. When we asked what kind of water filtration system they had, they replied that they had not selected one yet. Tom and I discussed that couple carefully. At that time, we had four different methods of water filtration available to us, and they had none. We made the painful decision that they too were out. They would only destroy us by consuming all our preps, and partying it out to the end.

　　As it turned out, there were only two friends we told about our cabin, both of which were far ahead of us in getting prepared. Both of them already had different places planned out. So as it was, we invited no one that we knew, not for any other reason than our survival. However, I did plan that if or when my best friend was to happen to show up at our house in the city, there was a nice care package left for her. I knew she would show up at our city house when things fell apart, and we knew that we had to leave before she showed up. Thus Tom's added urgency the day we were bugging out. I did not know if she ever got her care package, or if she even showed up at our city house. I was hoping that she did, and that it was enough to keep her and her husband safe for a couple months. Or else who ever looted the place, got a nice care package for themselves.

Since I was spending so much time reflecting in my solitude anyway, I decided that I ought to be writing some of my thoughts in my journal. So I got it out and started writing.

As my fingers were getting cold from inactivity I tried to warm them up with my now cold cup of coffee, and I realized that I also missed the simple ways to get heat. You used to be able to just push a button, set a setting, and the temperature was exactly how you wanted it. Sure, you had to pay a bill each month, but that was hardly going out to the wood pile and stoking a fire, or chopping or bringing in wood. And I had it easy, our wood was already split. We will not be so lucky next winter. I thought to myself how we probably wouldn't be able to have it delivered if people didn't have fuel for their vehicles. This line of thinking made me realize how most people have grown up with certain comforts, and frankly, have never had to survive without them outside of possibly a camping trip here and there.

On a different line of thought, I went to college so that I could earn a degree and get a better paying job, but with that education came the requirement that I take certain courses to get that degree. I took some courses that I found useful towards surviving out in the country. But most of the other courses that were required toward my degree were all fairly useless; they have served me no purpose. Instead, I wish I had taken a plumbing class, a diesel mechanic class, a solar power class, a gardening class - something other than what I did take. If I had the opportunity to do things over again, I would learn from my mistake and put that college time to better use. Perhaps if someone was in medical school, that may be different. But useless degrees that require students to take useless classes were probably a thing of the past at this point. College may altogether be a thing of the past at this point.

There were many things I would change if I could do it all over again. And some things I would not change at all. I guess until you know what exactly will take place, it's hard to make those kinds of decisions. In hind sight, I would not have

149

dropped my ID card had I known that it would result in me being wanted for murder. But, what's done is done, and I did the best that I could with the knowledge that I had of that time.

I didn't realize but my empty cup of coffee had gotten very cold in my hands, and it was time to put another log in the wood cook stove. Ah, the comforts of heat by the press of a button are gone. I walked to the wood stove and added another log. It lit up quickly without arguing this time. Afterward, I went out the back door, and pulled the garden cart, without the water buckets this time, over to the wood pile, and selected more wood to bring back into the house.

Terry and Samantha seemed to be adjusting well. We tried not to take advantage of them even though they depended on us. We certainly did not want to upset them, and we wanted them to feel welcome. They were certainly not lazy; they did at least their share of work around here, if not more. If things keep going well then we should have enough food for all of us to get us through the winter, and with their help, we should have a successful harvest in the summer.

I brought in enough wood for the next couple of days, and then wondered if I had enough time to bake bread. We did not normally eat a lot of bread, but with the winter cold coming in, hot bread with melted butter sounded comforting. I decided to wash my hands and get started, as it took several hours to make bread from scratch. Since I had never used our "baker's" wood cook stove for such a purpose, I figured it might be a good learning experience.

I picked out a nice size bowl and weighed out flour, salt, yeast, and honey. I then added a little olive oil and decided that I do not have the strength or energy to knead it by hand today. For some reason I still felt exhausted even though we had not been working as hard physically. So I dug out my $2 "yard sale special" stand mixer and plugged it in. I wondered if it would take too much battery power. I decided to go around the house and make sure anything unnecessary was unplugged, and everything already was. Then I went to turn on the stand mixer. It ran fine, so I let it knead the bread for six minutes. I transferred it to a bowl and put a kitchen towel over it, and let it sit for the next two hours. It was a little cool in the house as we were only heating with the wood stove at this point, so it probably would need a little longer rising time than usual.

I got the stand mixer and measuring utensils washed just as the crew was coming back. The dogs got excited and ran to the window with their tails wagging. As soon as they walked in I inquired "how did it go?"

Tom sarcastically remarked "it's good to see you too. Anyway, better than expected. It seems a lot of people will be moving in with each other based on where there is heat."
"That's good I guess," I said without realizing I was thinking out loud.
Terry added "yeah, but there's concern about looting of the empty homes, and no one really came up with a good solution for that."
Sam further clarified "yeah, not sure what you can do about it. The Sheriff and most of his deputies left after the Feds directed people to leave small towns for the bigger cities. And the deputies that stayed are too busy taking care of their own families to try to enforce any laws. So it's not like we have a police force available any more. And most of the rest us are already exhausted and just getting by surviving."
Tom continued, "some people are leaving, because they don't want to bunk with others, and they didn't believe Sam or Terry about what they went through at the camps. They're convinced things have gotten better."
"Yeah, I'm sure it has, the TV said so." My tone was dripping with sarcasm.
"There will be changes in guard shifts due to some of the folks choosing to leave. So we won't have the same schedules, and we might be pulling extras" Sam informed me. Then Tom added, "yeah, we won't get to pull guard duty with those we prefer anymore, so we'll be doing different shifts, and separated from those that we're used to working with." I could tell Tom was disappointed, he liked pulling guard duty with Vince.
Terry changed the topic, "we got the piping, so we have enough to get the gray water system done."

"What about the barter day?" I asked.

Tom quickly answered "oh yeah, that will be happening every Sunday at noon, right after church, at the church." I immediately shot back, "good, because we need to add rennet to the list, we've used up more than half already making cheese. I underestimated how quickly this stuff goes."

"Have we figured out what we'll barter in exchange?" Tom inquired.

I thought about this while they were gone, and I had an answer ready. "I was thinking some of our bulk rice, and some of our cheeses, since the cheeses do not store all that great, and we can only eat so much."

"But most will be with out refrigeration" Sam pointed out.

I countered, "true, but that just means they'll have to enjoy them sooner. We do have some extra canned milk, and some extra canned tomato sauce we could barter as well."

"Then it's a done deal, we'll head down on Sunday" Tom sounded satisfied.

"But we might want to walk. Most folks are out of fuel, and we might not want to advertise our stored diesel reserves, especially since we might need them at some point" Tom warned.

"You could ride our bikes instead of walking, though we only have two left, so two of you could ride. I'm grounded to the house still I'm sure" I added.

Tom agreed, "yeah, some people were asking about you, but I just didn't respond. I ignored them all together actually. I figured it was best that way."

"They'll figure it out soon enough" I fretted.

Sam changed the topic this time, "I was thinking we could work on some more cold frames before it gets too cold. Is there still time to plant anything?"

It was probably better for me to get my mind onto something else so I gladly responded, "well, it is kind of late in the season, but we can try. We have enough seed. Actually, I can use seed that I saved myself that I'm not sure about. That way we will not be using up our stash of survival seeds."

Tom jumped in "then let's do that, we can start today. We brought some wood from Terry and Sam's house as well. Terry figured that if we were going to take the plumbing, we may as well take the some of the wood too.

Terry seemed eager to end the talking and get to work, "alright then, let me get started with the window measurements."

We ended up putting together only one cold frame due to getting interrupted by Rita and Charles. But we did cut the wood for a few of the other cold frames. Unfortunately we ran out of hinges. That meant that it would not be as easy to lift them to let them vent if it got too hot, because we would have to fully take off the glass covers. So we decided to add hinges to the list of things to look for at the barter days.

Rita and Charles had come by to check in and let us know that they were doing fine. They had stocked up on water, but may be asking us for water if they run out, as they were not blessed with a solar powered well. We agreed to share water, and explained our recycling process. We offered some of our extra buckets, which they gladly accepted. In return, they offered us a few pieces of furniture since they had combined homes. We declined initially, and told them that the buckets were no big deal. We had plenty, but they insisted. They gave us a nice kitchen table with four chairs, a coffee table, a couple of night stands, and a couch to sit on instead of folding chairs. They also gave us a couple of floor lamps. They said they would not need them since they have no power. We insisted they take some of our candles in return, which they also gladly accepted. They decided to keep the extra bed in case they had guests. It was a strange barter moment, but I suppose this is what things had come to. We were very thankful for the furniture, and it was a pleasant sight in our home. We shared some of our canned milk and chicken, and some eggs as well. They told us that between the two of them, they had plenty of food, and plenty of fire wood, it was the water they were worried about. After that Rita and Charles headed off back to Rita's place.

A short while later, the dogs jumped out of their spots and started barking at the back door, I looked out the window and saw Rita was running towards the house in frenzy. I rushed to the door to see what the problem was, and as I unlocked it

Rita was already in front of it, the dogs stopped barking when they recognized it was Rita. In a panicked tone she yelled "Rachel, It's Chaarles... I need help!" She grabbed my hand and pulled me toward her house. I followed her running. She did not say what was wrong; I did not think she knew what was wrong, she just kept running towards her house with me following.

We stopped in front of her back door, Charles was laying on the ground his face swollen, I looked at his hands which he was holding to his throat and saw they were swollen too. "Charles, can you breathe?" I asked. All I got was a slight shake of his head "no" with some wheezing. I looked at Rita and said quickly "be right back" and I ran back to my house. As I got in the back door Tom looked confused when he saw me, I immediately said "Charles is going into anaphylactic shock, he must be having an allergic reaction. We need the epi pens." Tom did not think twice, he rushed to our bins that had our medical supplies and dug out an epi pen. He was about to get up then decided to grab a second one. I ran back to Rita's place with Tom following me. I was out of breath the by the time we got there. Tom saw Charles who was starting to turn a pale color, but instead of sticking him with the epi, he was looking at it.

"What's wrong?" I asked him impatiently. He quietly asked "what date is it?" I was surprised by his question, and said "I think it's September 25th or 26th, but I am not sure, is there a problem?" Tom looked like he was deep in thought, then said "this epi expires this month, I'm not sure if it's safe to use. Most expired medications are okay to use expired, but not epi; it could seriously harm him. I can't tell from looking at it." I looked at Charles and said "I think he's dead without it too, we have to do something." Tom was hesitating, I knew he knew it was a huge risk, but so was not administering it. Then Tom broke open the epi and just squeezed out the contents. Then he said "it doesn't look discolored, so it should be okay. This second one has the same expiration date." As soon as Tom finished talking, Rita, who looked totally panicked, said "I'm not losing another, no!" She grabbed the epi pen from Tom, pulled off the top and stuck Charles with it in the right thigh.

The results were almost immediate. Charles' wheezing decreased significantly, and I could tell he was starting to be able to breathe. After a while the swelling started to reduce off of his hands. Tom had him continue to lay there for a while longer. After what felt like forever, Tom asked Charles "How are you feeling, getting better?" Charles replied, "Yes, much. That was terrible." Then Tom asked "do you know what you are allergic to?" Charles lifted his arm and tried to turn it so that Tom could see the back side of his upper arm, and said "bee stings." Tom smiled, then said "I need to get some equipment, I'll be right back." Then took off for the house.

After a while he came back with a stethoscope and started to listen to Charles's heart and lungs. Then he asked "do you know if you have any heart problems?" Charles shook his head no, then Tom continued the examination. When he was done, he said "we have a few more epi pins we can spare. Make sure you carry them with you. Just know that they are at expiration, so it's always a risk. And you have to wear long sleeved shirts from now, no matter how hot it is. It's just too risky." Charles nodded. He was looking a lot better now, almost back to normal. Rita ran to hug Tom and I, and thanked us for the epi pens, and reassured us that Charles would not leave the house with out a long sleeve shirt on ever again. He was also banned from all gardening, though he tried to argue that suggestion. Tom and I walked back home in silence. Medical supplies is something we had very little of, and fortunately have had to use very little. But we knew that that will change soon enough.

That night we cozied up in front of the wood cook stove eating dinner with burnt bread. I guess a wood cook stove is not ideal, but at least I tried. Maybe I just needed a little practice? When I first started to learn to bake bread, I certainly had many failures, the dough would not rise, the flavor was off, but never burnt bread. Perhaps this was just another learning curve? We began discussing how we could further conserve resources. We talked about the compost pile and how handy that is considering we do not have a way to dispose of our garbage. Fortunately much of our food stores were in jars rather than cans. We originally started with canned goods but considered the trash situation about a year and a half ago. So we found brands that offered what we needed in jars rather than cans. Plus we did not like the health implications of the BPA found in most cans.

We also switched from storing canned soups, to storing dry lentils, split peas, beans, etc. that we bought in bulk, and stored in glass jars. As we rotated stock we switched over. We still had canned chicken and salmon, but there was nothing we could do about that. We also had plastic packaging that the rice came in. As a result of our planning, our trash was minimal, but it was starting to pile up, and we had no place to take it. We realized that there was a burn barrel from the previous owners, so we could burn the paper at least. Maybe the plastic? No, not a good idea – toxic emissions. We agreed to burn the paper and start separating plastic from the cans, and setting up recycling bins. We would store it outside, but make sure to rinse it well so as not to attract animals. There was not much else we could do, at least we could not think of anything else for the time being. Maybe we could start hauling it up the road to the old transfer station? We would have to hook up a cart to a bicycle instead of using a truck, so we that we did not advertise too much that we still had diesel fuel. There was no longer any trash service there, but at least it would not be on our property any more. Then I figured that would not work, as the transfer station was probably already full.

With four of us living at the cabin, hot showers turned out to be an issue. So we had to change our method of showering. Basically get in, turn on the water to get wet, turn off the water, soap up completely, then rinse, and you are done. Baths were an option, but really more of a pain than we liked. So we just put up with super short showers. We also skipped showers on days that we did not get dirty outside. Sometimes we just washed up with a washcloth soaked in hot water.

The official lights off campaign came and went without much notice by us, with the exception that Tom, Sam and Terry had increased shifts at the tree road blocks. The permanent power outage to the town did cause some people to leave, and fewer people meant the rest had to pull more guard duty shifts. Interestingly enough, even though we had power, there was nothing on television during the 23 hours that the power was turned off. During that one hour of electricity, there was "news" as some referred to it, but it was nothing but propaganda about how the government was "fixing" all the problems and to convince people that we should be grateful for the "option" to go to the relief camps. The news never talked about the starving or sick people living in them, or any other negative issues. We decided to switch to the ham radios almost full time. We found no use in wasting our power on television. I thought to myself that it was nice not to have to see the long list of wanted fugitives, including Terry, Sam, and myself.

The hams had different stories to tell. A network of liberty minded activists had formed, and they were working with ham operators to spread the truth about the reality of what was going on in the camps. These activists had been observing the camps from a distance to gather information about them. Apparently there had not yet been any attempts to rescue the people that had been "resettled" to the camps, however there were rumors that some where going to try to do so. It was also unclear if all the people in the camps wanted to be "rescued," since they had nothing, nowhere to go, and must have been terribly desperate to voluntarily endure the conditions at the camps. Not only were the camp guards rationing food tightly, but there was little heat, or even descent clothing to keep people warm. Those who brought warm coats had them confiscated. People were dying from cold and from malnutrition. And to make matters worse, some kind of flu virus was spreading around, and everyone was getting very ill, camp guards included.

Tom and I had anticipated that an economic collapse would precipitate the spread of dangerous infectious diseases due to reduced sanitation, cramped quarters, and shortages of medication and supplies. This was another reason for us stocking plenty of medical supplies, and for wanting to get out to middle of nowhere. The fewer people one was exposed to, the less likely one would become ill. And with supply lines cut off from the rest of the world, it was less likely that any kind of infectious disease would find its way to our little town. But exposure at barter days was still a slight concern, and eventually someone would find a way to bring in supplies from the outside.

The hams further told horrible stories. People were committing suicide in record numbers, whether it was in the so called "relief" camps or in their homes. Sometimes bodies were not found for weeks, as emergency services were very limited, or nonexistent. Funeral homes were overloaded with the dead, and resorted to cremating them all out of necessity, regardless of the families' wishes. There were just not enough caskets, or time, or space, or workers, to bury everyone. Only very rich people were able to have their family members buried properly, and then only on occasion. There was a rumor, though no one was able to confirm it, that those who died in the relief camps were taken to dumps and incinerated. No one could really confirm this though.

Looting was at an extreme high, as people had become desperate. There were also rabid animals running amuck. When the budgets got shut off, animal shelters euthanized all their remaining animals, and shut their doors due to lack of staff, lack of veterinary care, and lack of food for the animals. Once those doors shut, the loose animals got out of control, and people were getting bit by rabid animals.

Perhaps it was not as bad as it sounded, but given our peaceful life at our "cabin," near a small town far away from everything, it sounded awful to us, and we were thankful that we managed as well as we did.

During times of ideal ham weather conditions, Tom was able to communicate with American ham operators in foreign countries who had left the US in anticipation of the economic collapse. However, it seemed that the US dollar, Euro, fiat currency collapse had an impact on many places throughout the world, and not just the US and Europe.

Although other countries did not have problems with things like "relief" camps or martial law, they had their own sets of problems. With reduced medical services in central and South America, severe infectious diseases had spread greatly to near pandemic proportions. Many European countries were suffering from near famine conditions due to large scale infestations of farm land. Without modern technology supplied via complex economies and lengthy supply chains to help keep nature in check, these types of problems were getting much worse than they had been in quite some time.

We never heard of any of this on the news, it was all from ham radio communication. I am sure we would have heard about this on the internet as well, if it had still been accessible to us, but our service was still down. However, we did hear from some of the ham operators that various hacker groups in several locales had been able to set up ad hoc wireless networks and darknets that bypassed the big telecom backbones, routers and switches that were controlled under Federal Government's national emergency directive. Tom was eager to learn more, but it was hard to find out much about this via the hams out in the country. Much of the computer networking talk bored me to death, so I was glad Tom was interested in handling it. Though he always made sure I understood the important parts.

While the cities were ravaged with crime and fires, we enjoyed our peace out on our homestead while we could. We knew, or at least strongly suspected, it would not last forever. We figured that eventually the gangs and the looters would make their way out to rural "nowhere" as well. Along that line of thinking, Tom decided that we needed to maintain our shooting skills, and we took a couple trips out with Sam and Terry to do some practicing. We were very careful with our ammo usage, as we knew it was unlikely we would be able to replenish what we used. Tom also planned to keep an eye out for additional fencing when he went to barter days so that we could improve our security around our homestead. However, we learned that fencing was one of the items that people seemed reluctant to give up for barter.

Barter day turned out to be somewhat of a disappointment. People seemed like they did not have anything worthwhile to barter, or if they did, then they were saving it for themselves. Finding a male goat was more difficult than we thought it would be. We continued asking around for one, but we had no luck. We were able to find some door hinges for the cold frames, but not too many, and at a higher cost than we liked. Clothes were easier to find, but warm clothes were a bit of a different story. Fortunately Sam and Terry were able to set themselves up with a couple weeks worth of clothes. We did score a nice sewing table that I could put my sewing machine on, and Tom used a cart to get it back to our home. Tom said he saw other furniture, but we were not really willing to trade any of our supplies for furniture, at least not yet. We were able to find rennet from John, but he would only take wine as payment, so we reluctantly agreed. Alcohol was not something we stocked too much of, we only had four or five cases of wine, and only a few bottles of hard liquor, which was strictly for medical emergency use only. It probably would have been a good idea for us to learn how to distill alcohol, but we had so many other things to learn first, and so much other equipment to get before we could afford a still.

We also wanted to keep bees for honey, and for pollination, but that was another thing we did not quite get around to. However we had the books and supplies to possibly figure it out if we could find some honey bees. Biodiesel was another specialty that we had prioritized getting the equipment for, but we did not have a sufficient source of vegetable oil, used or otherwise to run our trucks exclusively on. Other limiting factors were the amount of methanol and lye that we had stored. Both are required to make biodiesel. We had enough of each to make several batches of biodiesel as an emergency fuel source, but not enough to make it indefinitely. Plus it would work better if we installed some type of heat source in the garage to make the chemical reaction work, and that would mean either draining our PV powered batteries more with a space heater, or using a wood stove in the garage. The biodiesel chemical reaction just did not work very well at cold or even moderate temperatures. We also had concerns about the safety of making bio-diesel where there was a flame nearby, such as a wood stove. We also still had to come up with a way to dispose of the waste water from the process.

With winter here, we had much less daylight now, and we used more electricity. We had stashed quite a few candles in our reserve, but really did not want to use them unless we had to. So we all agreed to use less power. We also discussed food options, as the chickens had, as normal, reduced their egg production. Tom liked to joke that chickens must be solar powered since their rate of egg production was tied to the amount of daylight they had. We had quite a few eggs saved up from the summer, since we properly rotated the eggs as we collected them. But we figured half way through January we would be down to a few eggs a day from our chickens, and if one went broody then we ought to let her hatch the eggs instead. We also had limited chicken food, we grew our own, and stored everything we could. Fortunately, the chickens loved our left overs. We may have stopped milking one of our goats too soon, but we expected to find a male goat by now. At least the cold hearty greens in the cold frames were looking marvelous, and they were edible. We were able to harvest enough for a nice salad for each of us each day. We did plant more as we picked, but cold hearty greens do not grow as fast in the winter as they do in the warmer times.

As far as dog food, we had about half left, and figured that we would have enough to get us through until spring – perhaps longer if we supplemented the dogs with our scraps. By then there should be enough chickens to get both us and them through for a while. But not long enough. We should have had a pregnant goat by now so that we could have meat and additional milk later. But two goats was not enough, especially when we did not have a male. We failed greatly in this aspect. At least we still had a decent amount of milk, therefore we had enough cheese and yogurt. Hopefully we would find a male goat soon.

Roy stopped by a couple of times. However, due to running out of gas, he was restricted to a bicycle, and given his health condition, he did not ride it very well. He too was pretty well set on his food preps and firewood. He had a year round creek at his place, so he was not worried about water either. He also had plenty of medication for his heart, and mentioned that with all the physical labor he had to do, and the fact that he had to walk everywhere, he felt that he was feeling better and even reduced his medication. He even made a joke about the situation, "Who knew that eating healthy combined with exercise will make you feel better!"

Things were pretty routine for the next couple of weeks. We continued to attend uneventful barter days, we carefully planned how much we ate to make sure we had the appropriate amount of calories for on our activity levels. We would bring in fire wood, tend to the animals, tend to the cold frames, recycle water, and so on. Things almost seemed too quiet, except when the hams were turned on, and we heard about the chaos in the cities. I worried that sooner or later, that chaos will find its way out here. I hoped it was later.

Although I did not want to admit it, we were running low on supplies. We ate the chickens that we slaughtered, including the chicken broth from the bones. Our rice was half gone, the cold frames were not producing as much. We had milk from our one goat, but we let the other go dry, and the chickens' egg production had reduced. We reduced our egg intake to one hard boiled egg each a day, making sure to return the shell to the compost so that we had healthy soil come spring.

Although we did not talk about it, we knew that rations were running low. We started to cut down on the amount we ate. We had enough to last us through spring, and some for next winter if we had a good harvest. We would not have been so short on supplies if it was just Tom and I; we probably would have had enough food stored away for about a year and a half. But we were not going to throw Sam and Terry to the coyotes –literally- after all they had done. And things were still so chaotic in most of the non-rural areas that we feared we would have to live like this for several years, and we were just not prepared for that. We did not have all the skills we needed, nor did we have the resources for that long a time period. Next winter might just be a tough one to get through, presuming nothing else went wrong before then.

To make matters worse, boredom hit. We were all in our folding chairs following our morning routine. Things had been so routine it had become very monotonous. We all felt it. We tried to do different things in the evenings, such as reading books or playing board games to break up the monotony, but that only helped a little. One of the problems was that I stocked up on reference and useful books, and not entertainment books. Back in the day when I was doing all my yard sale shopping, I saw many books for sale at yard sales for 50 cents each, but I only picked out books that I felt were useful or in some way relevant. Now I realize I should have picked up some books for enjoyment. I also wish I had picked up more board games, or maybe even some jigsaw puzzles, or even crossroad puzzles. Something more than what we had.

The work itself was long, tedious, and boring. Since we were always saving on electricity, it was rare that we would play music, plus when we did, none of the contemporary music we had seem to fit the scene. It seemed that most of our music was from... the old world. We did have some classical music CDs, and Sam and Terry danced occasionally. Tom and I never got into the slow dancing, so we just let Terry and Sam enjoy themselves.

I also wish we had stashed away more dog toys, as the dogs seemed to be getting bored with what they had too. Though Velcro still loved his Frisbee, the Frisbee was starting to fall apart with all the tug of war the dogs did when playing.

About the only entertainment we had was the so called news, which we laughed at most of the time, and the ham radios. Though the radios were not entertainment as I would call it, but rather a serious reality check of how good we have it, even if we were bored out of our minds.

Chapter 7

Trouble Locally
"Always a Calm Before the Storm."

They were back from barter days much earlier than usual, and as they opened the front door I realized that something bad had happened.

"What happened? Who hit you?" I asked impatiently. Tom had an obvious swelling under his left eye that was already turning purple. Tom was quick to respond "It's nothing, don't worry, there was just a little disagreement at barter days." He gave me a hug in trying to reassure me. "But what happened?" I asked.

"Remember Mrs. Minnick?" Tom asked. I had to think about it for a few seconds, then it came to me "yes, that sweet old lady who lives by herself behind the community center right?" I asked. "Yes" Tom replied, then continued "she was at barter days, had her own spot set up, and was just minding her own business trying to barter her knit scarves and hats. When Bob, you know, the general store owner, came up to her and started yelling at her, telling her that she was unfair, and overcharged for her scarves when she was selling them through him, and that she was practically giving them away for free now, but not to him, and still over charging him."

I was surprised to hear that and stated to Tom "Mrs. Minnick would never rip off anyone; she would not even know how to." Terry cut in, "that's exactly it, she would not, that's why Tom and I stepped in to help her, but our mediation was not effective." Then Sam added "that's only because Bob would not listen, he did not let anyone get in a word, he was just yelling ridiculous irrational things, and it was causing quite a scene."

"So who hit first?" I asked, hoping Tom did not say it was him. But as he was about to respond, I saw the answer in his face before he said it "well, I had to do something, so I punched him. He was yelling at an innocent old lady over stupid scarves! And they are her scarves. She made them, so she can do with them as she pleases!" Tom was getting angry, and there was no reason to keep the anger going. So I took in a deep breath and said in a forced clam voice "I understand, I'm not blaming you, I just wanted to know what happened."

Tom started to calm down and continued his story. "Well, after I hit him, he naturally hit me back. But after he got me, a huge crowd of men came in and separated us..." Tom contemplated if he was going to say more, then decided to do so. "We were not the only ones fighting. After the event calmed down with Mrs. Minnick, we heard another argument break out at the other end of the church lot. These two buffoons were arguing over whose 'fault' it was that all this happened. One screamed that it was the democrats' fault, another that it was the republicans' fault, and they just went on and on. We stayed away from that argument, because it was a completely absurd argument." Tom's adrenaline must have still been lingering because he started to rant. "They should realize that the two party political 'system' is just a duopoly of two corrupt, controlled groups of puppet whores, with little substantial difference... And the causes responsible for this economic and social disaster are numerous, including fifty years of bad fiscal policy by corrupt politicians bought off by elitist special interests, coupled with one hundred years of bad monetary policy by Ponzi-esque central bankers, coupled with a culture that has descended into entitlement decadence, not unlike Rome! But I guess that is the simpleton thought process of people who get all their information from the main stream media. Regardless, they ended up getting into a fist fight too, though they got a few more punches in before they were separated."

Sam added "it was decided that today was not a good day for barter, and barter days was shut down early. There was a rumor that if more fights occur, they will ban barter days altogether, but I'm sure it was just a rumor."

Then Terry added "we walked Mrs. Minnick home and reassured her that we will be picking her up next week and hanging out near by her area so that she can barter her scarves and hats safely. She was most thankful, but never did understand why Bob had accused her of cheating him."

I took another deep breath and said "well, with food being so scarce, and with no fuel to run machinery, everyone is a bit overworked, stressed, and possibly malnourished. I'm surprised it has taken this long for people to start losing it. That is so kind of you to walk with Mrs. Minnick every week, but is she not out of your way?"

"No." Tom said firmly, clearly she was, but he felt it was more important to make sure she was safe. She was a widow and had been for many years. The community had always looked out for her by doing things like chopping her wood for her, and purchasing her sweaters even if they thought they were hideous. Some people even joked around that she has to be color blind to create the 'styles' that she does. Though with the cold weather and no outside resources, people were not so picky about the colors of their sweaters and scarves. Regardless, I can not imagine her running a dishonest business. She probably was willing to lower her barter prices because she too needs things.

Tom walked to the bathroom to look at his shiner I presume, and the three of us just stared at each other for a while. Then Terry said "you know Rachel, if he had not taken the first punch, I would have. You should have seen it, Bob was behaving like an aggressive chimpanzee and someone needed to do something."

"I understand, I'm not mad that he did so, I was mainly concerned that he would be banned from barter days, but it sounds like that's not the case, so everything is fine." I smiled as I finished. I did not really think everything was fine. The people of this town had never experienced such hardships, or at least most of them had not. Maybe a few that were old enough to remember the great depression. And this was probably only the beginning of what was to come. Sam interrupted my thought process when she announced "I need to go pull my guard duty, I'll be taking your bike Rachel."

After Sam left, Terry went to his room, and I went to seek out Tom. He was taking care of his shiner, and clearly was still upset. I felt the need to reassure him that I was not mad at him. "Tom?" I asked softly. He turned around from the mirror and said "what?" in a very stern tone of voice. I made myself breathe in deep and said "I'm not mad at you for fighting, I just wanted to know what happened, it's not everyday you come home with a black eye."

Tom thought for a few minutes before responding, then finally said "clearly people did not prepare for what we were warning them for. You'd think that someone who owns a general store would have more resources than most to stock up on goods, and yet, he seems to be one of the least prepared. Rachel, this is only the start of what's to come." Tom did not have to tell me, he was preaching to the quire. "I know" was my response. I then gave him a hug and then headed to the kitchen to make lunch.

We were all settled in the living room contemplating chores when the dogs got excited, we saw that Sam was riding the bike back from guard duty. Though when she walked in, we saw that she looked distraught. We all noticed something was not right, and Terry started "You okay Sam? You don't look so good." Sam nodded her head yes and slowly said "I had to turn someone away at the gate, I felt terrible. I felt so terrible that I almost caved, but I had help out there, so I didn't." I have not had to do guard duty myself, so I did not even consider the idea of having to have to turn someone away. Terry asked "what about it made you feel so bad?"
"Well, it was a dad and his two kids. I don't know where the mom was, and I didn't ask, but I could only imagine. And, well... it was obvious, they barely made it out of the city, they had been on foot for several days, they were skinny, dirty, clearly hungry, and probably thirsty too." Sam paused for a moment then kept going "they were surprised when I came out from hiding, pointing a rifle at them, and I could tell the kids were scared. The kids couldn't have been more than just seven and nine years old. Their dad gave me a sad look and told me that he had plenty of guns pointed at him already, and that he was just trying to find a place to settle. He tried to reason with me and told me he was willing to work, and that his kids could work. And oh, I felt terrible." Sam finished, almost in tears.

I was a little confused, probably because I had not had to do guard duty, so I asked "why are we turning away people willing to work? Is there no way to allow them in? We have empty houses, and if they want to work their own land..." Terry cut me off, probably in defense of Sam, as she was feeling bad enough already "because there are too many of them, we don't have room for every straggler that comes through here, and at the same time, we can't trust strangers. We just don't know where they came from or what they are capable of. Too many sociopaths and criminals out there, even if they look innocent, they might not be. If we start letting people in, word will get out and everyone will be headed here."

Sam then picked up her story "the worst part was that I kept saying no, the rules state we can't let anyone in or through, and I started to tell him where the roads headed and which way his chances may improve, where there was a creek and such. Then he asked me if I would at least... take... his kids if not him." Right then Sam burst into tears and through her tears she said "what kind of person tries to give their kids away?" Between sobs she added "clearly he just wanted what's best for them, and was willing to give them up so they might have a chance." Terry hugged Sam and tried to console her, but she kept crying.

I felt chills run through my body, the reality of the situation hit me. There were hungry people out there looking for help, and we refused to help them. But Terry was right, if we started letting people in, we would have more people here than this little town could handle. And the people of this town were already stretched thin enough on supplies. We were all barely getting by as it was. It seemed the timing for my question was poor, as it only upset Sam more. I thought about how I could fix it, but the damage was already done. I decided instead to heat up water in the tea kettle, and offer Sam some chamomile tea with honey instead, which she took graciously.

On a cold day in January, Tom and I finally decided to discuss the food situation with Sam and Terry. They knew it, but it needed to be discussed. We certainly had not prepared to feed an additional two people. Although they were earning their keep, we were just not prepared for such a situation. During my morning coffee I brought out our list of food supplies, which mostly consisted of crossed out items we had already used up. Quite a bit of room opened up too as we were able to stack the empty plastic food bins inside each other.

I decided to share the situation, "we have enough to get through this winter, but we need to get a head start on spring if we are going to make it past the end of April."

Sam replied "that's better news than we expected really."

I did not feel as confident "yeah, we weren't as prepared as we could have been."

Sam tried to consul my regret "you have no idea how much we appreciate your help, with out you, we would have either starved or frozen to death."

Tom decided to chime in "well, you certainly do your share around here."

Sam kept replying "we just don't want to take advantage..."

"You haven't been, don't worry" I quickly responded. I wanted to make sure they did not feel they were a burden, thus why I avoided this conversation for so long.

Terry, always being bottom line practical asked, "so what can we do to help?"

I had a list in my head all ready for such a question "we have the covered deck, so we can use that as a sun room to start seedlings, along with the additional cold frames we built. It stays above freezing out there most months, so we can get a pretty good head start. I just don't want to bring in the soil from the outside, or we could have quite the infestation."

"Do you have store bought soil stashed away somewhere?" Sam asked.

"No, we don't. But if we can get our hands on an old stove at barter days, then we can sterilize our own soil.

"I'm sure we can find an electric stove, hardly anyone uses them anymore, except those with solar." Terry pointed out.

"It doesn't have to be pretty, we will be putting dirt in it after all. Just something that works" I clarified.

"Okay, but we need to figure out what we can barter for it" Tom stated. Looking at me, he knew I had kept an inventory list of all our supplies, and what we might have available for barter.

"I have this box of candles and lighters, someone is bound to want light." I suggested.

"That could work" Sam replied with a sound of hope in her voice.

I was more thinking out loud brainstorming than speaking with the intent to suggest a specific solution already. "I know we still have some jars of food, but I think we need them. We also have a ton of almonds and walnuts that we have stored, but again, I think we'll be using them."

"I don't think there's a question about that" Tom stated matter of fact like.

I responded "once we can get the soil sterilized, then we can get started with the seedlings on the deck. We don't have to sterilize the soil in the cold frames. That mini fridge out on the deck has all the seeds, there's quite a bit, so we should be alright on seed at least."

Terry cut in "okay, then we'll look for an electric stove today. What else can we do with the food situation... besides eat less?"

"I'm not really sure, but I think we need to start substituting nuts for some of our meats. We have a lot of almonds and walnuts as mentioned. We can add them to our salads or even our rice." I paused for a minute, then went on "see if you can find out from John what it will take to get a cow from him, but you guys have already said he has been pretty stingy, and will only barter for other food, ammo, or booze... Why don't we try to find out how many bottles of wine it would take for a cow." Sam and Terry did not question it, maybe they did not notice that I implied we had alcohol stashed away somewhere. Terry replied "I know he's been difficult to barter with, but I hear he does share with his workers very fairly. So maybe we can get him to employ us for a short while." Wow, that is a good idea, but would he do it? I was not so sure, and said "you can try, but I imagine everyone has offered their service already?" Terry was not convinced either and said "well, we'll see how today goes." Terry went to grab a hiking backpack that he used every week to wear on his back as they rode the bikes to the church for barter days, or at least rode their bikes to Mrs. Minnick's house, then walked from there. He loaded up the candles and lighters. He then looked at Tom and Sam who were already getting their packs on, and then they proceeded to check their guns before taking off.

Things were getting violent even out here in the middle of nowhere, and we had long ago made it standard practice not to leave the house without a loaded gun. Plus the house had plenty of ready rifles and shotguns should anyone try to loot or break in. I never went outside without a sidearm anymore, even when just collecting eggs I carried one. This was not a time to take risks. And given our healthy looking stove pipe with constant smoke coming out, we were bound to be a target. It's not like the chickens are quiet; no, they do their thing, and they make a good bit of noise, especially the roosters.

I was looking forward to some time alone again as was the Sunday routine. But I also knew the animals needed their water re-filled, and possibly their hay and feed restocked, as it was freezing throughout the day this time of year. I also needed to clean the coop, and possibly flip the compost again, or at least add some hot water to it. Plus I wanted to go over my seed inventory to see what it was that we had, and possibly pick out the oldest seeds for planting. Germination would be reduced, but they've been refrigerated this whole time, so it shouldn't have reduced by too much.

I watched the three get on their bikes and leave. Thank goodness they found another bike at barter days. There seemed to be an abundance of them apparently, though none of them working. The one that Tom found needed a new tire, but we had planned for that, so it was an easy fix.

All alone again, I grabbed the Frisbee to play with the four legged kids. They too had a routine, which included a short bit of Frisbee time each day. Velcro and Compass were playing their game of chasing one after the other when all of a sudden Compass stopped, he dropped the Frisbee as his ears perked up. Then before I knew it he was running in the direction of the garage with his warning bark, Velcro followed Compass and I followed Velcro. The dogs were much faster than I was and by the time I caught up with them, Compass had cornered someone against the side door of the garage. I heard cussing coming out of someone and hurried to see who it was. I

171

didn't even realize it, but I had my gun drawn and was ready to shoot by the time I got there.

"Well, if it isn't Rachel, Rachel Roberts who is a cold blooded murderer. And look at that, she's pointing a gun at me and her puppy is growling like he might bite me or something." I looked at the slender body in front of me, Jake's hair had gotten long, his blond curls looked tangled and matted. I doubted he had showered recently. His face looked young as ever, though his eyes looked sunken in, clearly he had not been eating well, probably because he had been drinking his meals. "What are you doing on my property Jake?" I yelled.

"What are you doing here, you should be in jail" was Jake's response.

"Everyone knows the news is a lie. I didn't kill anyone, though I might just pick up the hobby now" I said while attempting to stay calm. Compass was still in his attack position growling away, I was not about to release him. I did not trust Jake, and although his dad would leave if something happened to him, I was not going to risk my life for the rest of the town.

"Oh, come on Rachel, the news mentioned they're offering quite a reward for you now" this must have been Jake's way of trying to reason with me.

"Yeah, it's called a concentration camp. I'm sure you could get into one with out turning anyone in" I replied quickly, still trying to give the impression that I am calm, though I was not.

"So you admit you're guilty?" said Jake

"Look Jake, you're trespassing on my property, and I have every right to shoot you if you don't leave. So, you get one chance to leave, I recommend you take it" I was at a loss, I did not know what to do to make him leave. I certainly did not want to shoot him.

"But I came to get some supplies, I know you have some food in there, you won't mind if I just take a little to get me through now do you?" Jake's motive was coming out.

"Yes I mind, because we don't even have enough for us as it is. So what makes you think I'm going to share? Plus you have your dad who has plenty of meat from his cattle" there was clear irritation in my response.

"Oh you know my dad, trying to teach me a lesson. I'd rather get it from you. And if you don't share, then I'm going to turn you in, it's that simple" was Jake's response.

"You won't be turning anyone in Jake. You know better, It will only hurt you too" I was trying to reason with him.

"No it won't, I'll get quite the reward, the news said so" I could tell he was trying to convince me he would turn me in, but I know he would not, I just wanted him off my property. I was getting angry, and my adrenaline was pumping hard. There was nothing stopping me from shooting him, except that I was not a murderer, and I did not know how I would dispose of the body.

"LEAVE!" I wish I had some command for Compass to just attack, but we never did that kind of training. He will protect me, he will attack in self defense, but not unless he is fully threatened, which was not the case right now.

"Rachel, I'm sure we can make some kind of a deal" Jake's tone of voice changed to a pleading tone.

"What do you mean a deal?" I realized that he was holding a set of bolt cutters in his right hand - he had every intention of breaking into our garage and stealing from us. Although he would not have gotten much except for some building supplies, and some soaps and shampoos. All our food and wine was in the house.

"Well, if you share, I won't turn you in" he said, I felt like we were going in circles.

"How about if you leave, I won't shoot you" I replied.

"Come on Rachel, I think we both know that you don't want to shoot me, and my dad might just get mad enough that he would leave town" now he was pleading.

"It's not like I'm getting anything from him anyway" I argued.

"But all the people working for him depend on his generosity" his reply still had a pleading tone to it.

"Sounds like you do too. Look Jake, I want you off my property" I cocked my gun as I said that, I needed him to know I was serious.

"Me too" came Tom's voice, as he came up from the side of the garage also pointing his .45 at Jake. "Get off our property now" Tom repeated.

"But Rachel and I were just making a deal. Come on Tom, harboring a fugitive?" Jake seemed awfully calm for the situation, he was either intoxicated or he'd gone mad. He had two people pointing guns at him yet he remained calm.

"We're not making any deals Jake. We wouldn't trust you to uphold your end of any deal anyway. You need to leave" Tom said sternly.

But Jake persisted, "Rachel, come on, you know if I leave I'll just call the authorities so I can get my reward. I think we can work out a better deal than that."

Tom reiterated "no deals, go before we shoot you."

Jake then leaned against the garage door and slid down to a sitting position. Compass didn't flinch and continued to growl at him, as Velcro was running between Tom and I making sure we were okay. Once Jake was sitting and leaning against the door he said in a very different, almost humble tone "look, I have no heat where I'm staying, it's freezing, I have no food, I don't even have water."

"How is that our problem?" I asked.

"It's not, but maybe we can work out a deal." Jake was almost begging at this point.

Tom started to sound like a broken record. "We said no deals, leave our property."

"I know you can't shoot me because my dad loves me in some weird way. But look, if you let me stay with you, then I can stay warm, and maybe even help you with stuff."

"You are NOT welcome to stay with us!" I yelled.

Jake continued as if he hadn't heard me. "Maybe I can stay in your garage, do you have a wood stove in there?"

Somehow Tom was able to remain calm. "No, no deals, go. If you don't leave on your own now, I will drag you off. And if you resist, we will shoot you."

"Okay, but if I go, I have no choice but to call and turn you in" Jake threatened.

Tom called Jake's bluff, "then do so, and do so quickly."

"Look, I don't want to turn you in, I just need a warm place to stay. My dad won't let me back in, and I just need someplace to stay. I can stay in your garage, I'll stay out of your way."

Jake sounded pathetic at this point, I almost felt sorry for him. I lowered my gun and told Compass to back off. Compass came to me and sat right in front of me, never letting his eyes off of Jake. I then realized that Sam and Terry had positioned themselves on separate ends of the garage and had been watching this whole incident with their guns drawn as well. "Tell you what Jake, why don't you come back in a few hours. We'll discuss this, and see what we come up with, maybe we can figure something out." I could tell that Tom wasn't happy about what I had just said, and I was not really either. But we had to diffuse the situation somehow, and we had to do something that did not resort to killing him. Though I doubt his dad would know if he was missing, but still, that was a great risk to take.

No one said anything for a long time, and Jake started to get up. I had to calm Compass down so that he didn't resume his attack posture. We all started to back up so that Jake could leave. "Fine, I will come back before sunset. I hope you have something figured out." He started to walk up our gravel driveway when he realized that Sam and Terry were here too. "Two more fugitives? Wow, this is great, I imagine that when I come back in a few hours you will be ready with a good deal for me, because I know I would be handsomely rewarded by the government for all three of you." We all refrained from saying anything, we just wanted him gone. He took his time walking on the driveway, and once he was up on the road, we realized he had a bicycle. He got on it and left. We all quietly went inside and immediately sat down to discuss the situation.

Tom insisted, "no, he can't stay here, we need to get rid of him, we should have just shot him and called it self defense."
I didn't find Tom's comment helpful, and made it clear with my response, "well, we didn't shoot him, but he'll be back. So if you're volunteering, go ahead."
Tom seemed to not notice my sarcasm, as his aggravated tone continued. "If we're lucky he'll withdraw into DT's and we won't have to worry about him."
Terry tried to inject some calm reasoning into the discussion, "no one is going to shoot anyone, clearly he's desperate, so maybe we can work out a deal."

Tom was adamantly opposed to that idea. "I'm not making deals with the town drunk! He's totally untrustworthy, not to mention lazy."

Terry tried again, "Tom, I know you and Rachel don't know him, but he's actually not a bad kid. It's just that he's spoiled, and well, there's hope for him. He's never harmed anyone."

"He had bolt cutters, he was going to steal from us" Tom refuted as if this was a competitive debate.

Terry tried to justify Jake's actions. "It's desperate times, people do desperate things, and it's freezing outside. The Jones' place where Jake was staying had electric heat as well."

Tom wasn't having it, "we don't have room for him here."

Terry suggested "well, you have that backup wood stove in the garage, it just needs to be installed, and he can stay there."

Tom gasped, "are you serious?"

Sam nervously finally decided to say something, "well, he would turn us in otherwise."

"I thought Terry said he's not a bad guy?" Tom questioned.

Terry clarified, "I didn't say he was wise, he just doesn't know any better, or what else to do."

"I have no idea how to install the stove piping" Tom protested.

"I do; I've done it before. Sam and I will do it, so you won't have to" Terry reassured.

"And what about all our supplies in there?" Tom asked.

"You'll just have to move them inside the house" Terry answered matter-of-factly.

"And what are we going to feed him?" Tom asked, as if he had just checkmated Terry.

That brought on silence, as we all knew that food was scarce. But Sam, always a clever one, thought for a moment, then responded "we won't, he can ask his dad for food."

Tom and I looked at each other. This was not part of the plan. We couldn't afford another mouth to feed, especially one that would steal from us. We continued to sit there, stunned, as Terry and Sam went to start working on the garage. Terry's hand had healed well enough to almost be practically usable. We saw through the living room window that they went into the garage, and got the ladder moved to install the piping. I did not know how he was going to cut a hole in a metal roof, but it was not my problem as far as I was concerned. Tom and I just kept looking at each other. Then finally we sighed and Tom said, "well, might as well get our supplies out of the garage."

We reluctantly walked to the garage and did a visual inventory. It contained mostly soap, toilet paper, paper towels, diesel fuel, a variety of tools, equipment and what not. We brought most of the household items in, but left the tools, equipment and fuel in the garage. With so many less food bins, we had more room inside for it all. I then looked at Tom and asked "you think we should hide the booze in the crawl space?" Tom knew what I meant. When we were installing the flooring, we added an access point under the dryer. First, we cut the belly and glued on a zippered piece that we found on the internet. We also left that area without insulation for access purposes. Then instead of putting down a whole piece of plywood, we cut out a square, glued the tiles to it, put some hinges on the square piece, and we had a door to the crawl space. We placed this under where the dryer went, and it was impossible to tell that such access existed. The access to the crawl space was also sealed off on the outside, and locked, so it was not possible to get in that way unless the lock was opened or cut from the outside. We installed that "under the dryer" access point just in case, though we weren't sure what we would use it for.

While Sam and Terry were working away in the garage, Tom and I collected all our wine and hard liquor. Our wine was already in glass bottles in wine boxes, so that was easy, and we used an empty wine box to store the hard liquor bottles as well. We moved the dryer out, then lifted the plywood/tile door, and unzipped the belly. Tom went down to the crawl space first, and I handed him the first box. He put it under the house, and asked for a plastic trash bag to cover it up. I ran to the kitchen to find some, and gave him one to cover it up. Then we decided we should put the boxes inside the plastic trash bags instead, and tied a knot on each one. The wine boxes were small enough, so they fit nicely. We hid all of the alcohol under the house in the crawl space, except for one box of wine. We figured we should leave one out for use, and it would also deter Jake from searching for any others if he thought he found them all. Tom then came back up, we zipped the belly shut, replaced the access door, and moved the dryer back in place. We then moved the other wine box into the kitchen, and proceeded to see if Terry and Sam needed any help.

"We knew you would come around, I think this will be good for us," Terry beamed.

"We don't really want to talk about it" I deferred.

Terry was respectful, "understood, but since you're here, we have a slight problem, maybe you can help."

"What's the problem?" I asked.

Terry explained "well, we are about 6 inches short on stove piping. The only thing I can think of is if maybe you have some cement or something we can place under the wood stove to raise it up."

"Will cinder blocks work?" Tom asked.

"Yes, that would be perfect" came Terry's response.

"We'll get some" Tom grunted. Tom and I went to the garden, and collected four cinder blocks. We placed them on a cart and brought them back to the garage. Terry had already finished cutting the hole in the garage roof, and the pipe was ready to be put in. We placed the cinder blocks and then argued a bit about how to lift the wood stove up on to them. That old thing had to weigh at least 400 lbs if not more. We finally agreed that we should use a ramp, and move it up slowly with the help of a dolly. Once the wood stove was on top of the cinder blocks, Terry was able to install the piping. Then it was done.

"What should we do for a bed for him?" Sam inquired.

"What? He can bring his own on a bicycle." I was ticked, I walked away and went back to the house. Jake would be back any minute. Why we had tolerated the idea to help him was beyond me. Tom had followed me in. "Rache, it's alright, we'll figure it out. Let me tell you about barter day today. We found an electric stove, we just need to go pick it up. We're actually getting it from Charles. I'm going to head over to his house shortly to go get it. He didn't even want the candles, he just wanted some of our soil for his and Rita's garden, and a refill on their water barrels."

"That's good news, do you want me to go with you? It would be nice to get out for a change."

"Well, I think someone should stay here to watch the place."

"Right, a prisoner in my own home" I scowled quietly.

"Well, with Jake and all..." Tom tried to reassure me, but I cut him off "yeah yeah, I know!" I took a deep breath. "Was John at barter days? Any luck on a cow?" I asked changing the subject.

"No, he wasn't there" Tom replied sadly.

"Maybe you can swing by his place, maybe even tell him that his son is crashing in our garage and using up our firewood" I suggested.

"You know, that's a good idea, maybe I will" Tom responded with a little enthusiasm.

Terry and Sam had returned, they were finished with the wood stove installation. Part of me hoped they did it wrong so that Jake would burn down with the garage. But then I thought, no, I don't wish that, that was a nice garage.

"We only suggested the bed because the concrete floor would be hard to sleep on, and... well... it's cold" Sam explained.

"Fine, we can place some empty bins side by side and put some blankets on them, we don't have another futon we can spare, and I'm not giving him mine, nor are you giving him yours" My words were very firm.

Sam seemed grateful, though I wasn't sure why. "Fair enough, you think the bins will work?"

"Why not?" I said, "They're sturdy, and side by side he won't be putting weight on just one. And if we put a piece of plywood on top of them, then some blankets, that should keep the bins from separating or moving."

"Okay, but let us take care of it" Sam insisted.

"Fine." They could tell I was still ticked. It was not their fault, I knew that. But I loathed the situation. If I wanted a mooch I would have invited our city friends. At least I could trust them, and I enjoyed their company. Tom looked at me, then said "Rache, why don't you open a bottle of wine, and relax. After all, it might be our last one." I smiled, why not, Jake would probably steal and drink the rest anyway. "How about after you get the stove, since I don't want you drinking and driving."

"Oh yeah, I forgot, let me get Terry to help" said Tom as he started to head out the front door.

Tom went to the garage, spoke with Terry, grabbed the dolly and loaded it in the back of the pick up. Then they both took off. I went to talk with Sam, she looked exhausted. "You alright?" I asked.

"You know, I like this situation as much as you do. We've been to the so called 'relief camps,' I doubt we would get lucky twice and be able to get away again. I just *can't* go back to those camps, or anything like them." Sam pleaded.

"I know" I said.

"Plus they already have us listed as fugitives - you've seen the news. So I doubt they would treat us kindly, probably put us in solitary confinement or something – if we were lucky enough not to be killed. Shutting up Jake may be the only way…" Sam continued to plead.

I interrupted, "we'll figure it out, we'll let Jake stay in the garage, we'll throw him some scraps, and he won't turn us in. We can make this work." I was still angry, but my consoling came on naturally; I couldn't help it, and it also helped me calm down as well. I felt like Sam needed some time to herself, so I went out to collect the garden cart, and started filling it with wood for the wood stove in the garage. I picked out the bigger pieces that might not fit into our smaller wood cook stove. After the cart was full, I rolled it to the garage and unloaded it near the newly installed woodstove.

Afterward, I went to clear a space for the new stove just outside the back door of the house, where it would still be covered by the deck roof. That way it wouldn't get wet, but it would still be outside. Sterilizing soil stinks like rotting manure, and it was gross. I went to the garage to find the correct extension cord. We only had the correct 240V outlet type in the kitchen where the old stove had been. We would have to share that outlet, and since we did not currently have a stove on the inside, we would just use that one for the stove on the outside. How ironic I thought, we have a stove for soil, but not for food.

By then Tom and Terry were back and unloading the stove. Tom mentioned that John was busy working, and said he would stop by later when he ran out of daylight. Tom did not get a chance to tell him what he wanted to talk about though. I showed Tom where the stove was to be placed. Then Terry and Tom unloaded the stove from the back of the pick up, and rolled it around to the back of the house.

Terry inquired "that sure is a nice stove, you sure you want to ruin it with soil Rachel?"

Tom responded before I had a chance, "well, we need one for that more than we need one inside."

But I corrected him, "not really true. We need one for canning and prepping food, the wood cook stove just doesn't cut it for that."

"Well, you've only burned a few things" Tom tried to be optimistic.

But I was trying to be practical, "yeah, but I almost destroyed my canner, we can't afford those kinds of losses."

"I thought you just needed some practice" Tom tried again.

"Well, I'm sure with time I'll get better" I said. "But I still hate risking our tools. If I damage our canner pressure gauge, then we can't can food" I explained.

"What about that antique canner you bought, have you tried using that one?" Tom asked.

"That one will work," I explained. "But I never had an opportunity to get the gauge tested, so I don't know if it's accurate. I can still use it for water canning, just not pressure canning. But most everything requires pressure canning to be safe" I said.

Terry suggested "why don't we leave the stove here and think about it. Maybe we can find another stove since we didn't really have to give up anything for this one."

"That's a good idea" I thought.

We put the stove in place, and then went inside to eat. We got the list of stored food out and found the walnuts, then went to the cold frames to pick out whatever greenery was ready. We rinsed the greens, poured some walnuts over it, and added some crumbled cheese, then served four plates out. As I was serving up the plates I saw out the kitchen window a bicycle turn onto our driveway. Jake must have come back already. Compass went ballistic with his barking. I waited for Jake to get off his bike before I took Compass outside.

"Jake, I need to properly introduce you to our dog so he won't attack you. So you need to just stand there as we approach, don't approach us, okay?"

"Okay" was his reply.

I reassured Compass that it was okay, and walked with him slowly toward Jake. When we were a couple feet away, Compass wasn't so sure as he started growling a little, but I kept on reassuring him.

"I need to shake your hand" I said to Jake as I held out my hand as Compass was watching intently, Jake slowly put his hand up to shake mine. I kept reassuring Compass that it was okay.

"Let's walk together and talk so that Compass gets used to you being around" I expained to Jake.

"Okay, so I take it I'm alright to use your garage?" he asked.

"Yes, Terry installed the wood stove for you, so just think of that when you're thinking about calling the authorities" I replied with a clearly unhappy tone.

"You know I won't call. I just need someplace to stay, and I was surprised to see you here - most everyone thinks your dead" his explanation was not helping the situation.

"I prefer it that way, so don't go spreading the word okay?" I stated more than asked.

"I won't" he said quietly. We headed toward the garage as Compass was starting to calm down. Compass saw that Jake was no longer a threat to me, though he was not as friendly to him as he was to Terry and Sam.

"Wow, you weren't kidding, you did install the wood stove" Jake's voice had surprise in it.

"Terry did" I said coldly.

"And you brought in wood! Wow, you don't know how great this is. I have been freezing every single night, and I just couldn't take it anymore" he explained as if I cared.

"Isn't your booze keeping you warm?" I asked with irritation.

"Actually, I haven't had a drink since the roads were blocked off. There's been no way to get any, and no one seems to be willing to share. So I've been forced to go sober" Jake's response surprised me.

"So how does it feel?" I was pleasantly surprised, this could be a good thing.

"Well, I don't really like drinking, I just can't help myself. And now that it's impossible to get, I do without. I prefer it that way anyway" Jake smiled as he answered.

"Well, you just need to learn some self control" I said.

"That's what my dad says, but it's easier said than done" he replied.

"Look, here's your space. We moved out most everything we could, but you still have to live with some building materials, tools, and diesel fuel. If you run out of wood, there's the wood pile" I pointed in the direction of where we had the wood stored. "I'll also bring you some water so you have something to drink. I don't know what to tell you about food, we have very little as it is."

"I'm fine with your left over's" he suggested.

"We don't really have any left over's, but I'll try to come up with something" I responded.

With that I left Jake by himself in the garage and went back inside the house to eat my salad. All four plates were still on the counter untouched. All four of us just stared at them and then I reluctantly grabbed a 5th plate and started to take some salad off my plate to put on the 5th plate. Then I made sure everyone understood, "if we feed him, we can't afford to increase what we take out of storage, so we're going to have to reduce what we eat ourselves. You do not have to share with him just because I'm choosing to do so."

No one said anything, then Sam took her plate and put some of her salad on Jake's plate as well. Terry contemplated for a while, then did the same. I could tell that Tom was ticked again, and as he grabbed his plate, he grabbed a fork and went to sit down to eat. Clearly he was not willing to share his portion.

I asked Sam to please get the garden cart so that we could move some filtered water to the garage. I then found an older water bottle and filled it with filtered water. I grabbed the 5th plate and proceeded to go to the garage with Sam and the cart of water. I didn't say a word to him when I handed it to him. But after he said thank you to me, I said "you can thank me by building yourself on outhouse. There are plenty of building materials out by the shed that you can use, and there's a shovel to dig a hole. I expect you'll find a spot on the property that's far away from everything, and if I catch you taking a whiz somewhere that's not in an outhouse, I can assure you that you'll need medical attention when I'm done with you."

"Yes ma'am, I'll get right on that first thing tomorrow." I heard a little laughter or sarcasm in his tone. If he thought that was funny, he had no idea what he was in for.

It was getting dusk, so I asked Sam to help me with the animals. We locked up everyone, then went back inside to wash up and eat our salads. I was hungry by that time. Compass was fully calmed down, though I did not like the idea that he would not warn me anymore about Jake. Oh well, what was done was done, I thought.

Shortly after Sam and I finished our salads, I was relaxing by the wood cook stove. I had my notebook in hand and I was making a list of everything we needed to work on, when we heard a knock on the door. Tom asked who it was, and it was Jake. Tom opened the door, Jake was returning his empty plate, and one of the empty water bottles.

"May I use your restroom? I will start building an outhouse tomorrow, but have nowhere to go tonight." Tom laughed and let him in.

"You can use the guest bathroom, but if it's just number one, don't flush, we're conserving water." Tom answered.

"Is it okay I wash my hands afterwards?" Jake asked.

"Yes, of course, we're not cruel, we just don't like the situation that you forced us into" I responded.

Jake rushed into the bathroom. We just sat as we waited the whole time, we heard him whiz, then we heard him wash his hands, then he came out.

"Thank you. Would it possible to get a candle or two? And if you have any instructions on building an outhouse, I could read up on that as well." Jake was being very polite, there was no reason to be mean, and we could sure use an outhouse just in case, so why not put him to work, as he seemed willing. I got up to go to the master bedroom, and looked through the books in there. I grabbed one candle and a lighter, and a flashlight. "The closest thing I could find was a book on building animal shelters. it should give you some ideas, and here's some light for you" I said as I handed the supplies to Jake.

"Thank you." Jake took everything and went back to the garage. It was already dark out, so Jake used the flashlight to see his way, then he disappeared behind the door of the garage.

Tom was about to shut the door when Compass started growling and barking again. "Now what?" Tom asked as Compass tried to run out, but Tom stopped him when he realized that someone was arriving on a horse. "I think John is here, or someone else who owns horses" Tom said. We had to wait for John to get off his horse before we could introduce Compass. We repeated the steps that we took with Jake, except that Compass was not so sure about the horse. We had to drag him inside by the collar. I think Compass may have been confused as to why there was an animal out and not in it's pen after dark.

We invited John in and offered up a folding camping chair. I then went to the kitchen and opened up a bottle of merlot. I grabbed five glasses and brought it all out. I poured everyone an equal amount emptying the bottle. I then decided to see what we had for cheese in the refrigerator, and brought out a little for everyone to have a couple bites with their wine. It's rare that we had guests, and I felt the need to be a good hostess – especially in the case of John.

"Rachel? I thought you were dead!" John exclaimed in shock. It was strange talking to John after pointing a gun at his son earlier in the day. They looked just like each other, except John a couple decades older, cleaner, and much more wise.

"Yeah, I like to keep people thinking that way" I specified to him.

"But why?" John asked.

I explained, "didn't you notice, I'm wanted by the authorities." John caught himself, "Oh that, yeah, I wasn't sure if that was you at first, but after they flashed that picture up so many times..."

I growled, "yes, I'm aware, if you don't mind, I'd like to remain a secret."

John finally got the hint, "sure, sure, I can manage that. So tell me Tom, what made you come all the way out to my place to see me?"

Tom did not waste time and got to the point of the meeting, "well, we need some things, and thought perhaps we could barter a bit. We also have a bit of a 'situation' that maybe you can help us resolve."

"What is it you need? Food?" John reached for his glass of wine, he must have been asked for food a lot.

"Well, actually, -- Rachel, let me see that list you have there" Tom said looking at me as I handed Tom the list, Tom briefly looked at it.

Tom continued, "we need a male goat, just to borrow, to breed with our female. We also could use a cow, but we're not sure we have enough to barter for a cow."

John was puzzled "what do you need a cow for?"

"Umm... to eat" Tom explained.

"You mean you want a slaughtered and butchered cow, you don't have the means here to do so yourself do you?" John prodded.

"Well, it would be tough, but with five of us, we could manage" Tom admitted.

John was not having it, "well, I'm not helping, so four of you."

Tom corrected, "no, five of us."

"Who else is staying here with you?" John asked.

"Jake" Tom announced.

John was surprised. "My son Jake? Really, you were that kind? Where is he?"

"Not exactly. We didn't have a choice. He threatened to turn us in to the authorities. He's in the garage if you want to see him" I explained.

John was not happy with my explanation. "That little shit, really? Well, I taught him better than that. No, I don't want him to know I'm here."

"Doesn't matter, what's done is done, except that with an extra mouth to feed we're low on food" I hinted.

"I see." John sipped on his wine as we all sat in silence. The ball was in John's court now.

I snuck a piece of cheese off the plate and savored it in my mouth, followed by the merlot. It was such a pleasurable taste, I had closed my eyes to enjoy it.

After what felt like a long silence, John finally responded.

"Tell you what, how much wine have you got left?"

Tom answered, "just one case minus the bottle we took out for tonight."

John was interested, "what kind of wine you got in there?"

"Well, there's three bottles of your favorite meritage, and the rest is a mix of Italian and Spanish reds" Tom answered as he pointed in the direction of where the opened box of wine was sitting. John got up to look at it. He picked up each wine one by one and read it, read the back of it, and said "mmm" with each one.

"Tell you what, I can get you a male goat, but you'll have to keep it" John offered.

Tom agreed eagerly "that's not a problem. We have plenty of pasture, shrubs, and hay for the goats to eat."

John was satisfied. "Then it's a deal. I'll be back tomorrow, and I'll pick up this case of wine tomorrow as well. I don't have a good way to take it back with me tonight. Though I might just take this bottle of meritage here as down payment."

With that, he picked out one of the bottles and put it in his inside coat pocket. He started to head towards the door, but realized he had not finished his glass of wine, so he sat back down.

"What else do you need? That's right, some steaks?" John asked.

Tom answered "yes, we could definitely use some food around here. We're running low, but we don't have the usual items that we know you request in trade. I mean we have ammo, but we need it for security, and we just traded you the last of our wine for a goat."

John reluctantly responded "yes, well, you are feeding an extra mouth, and I don't really want him to know that I'm helping him. He has so much he needs to learn. You know, I wasn't really going to leave to go to the camps, and no way would I give up my animals to some government bureaucrats. Our cattle ranch has been part of our family business since the 1850's. My parents left it to me, and well, Jake is all I have, so I have to leave it to him. But he's just not ready to appreciate what he'll be getting... I know that the folks in this town don't appreciate his behavior. And as you know, I too like my wine, but I learned to have self control. If Jake could just learn to have self discipline, and some morals, then he would be fine running the family business. He's got the brains, and obviously the cunning."

We all remained silent as John told his story. He had never really opened up to any of us before, so we weren't about to spoil the moment. He continued "I want to thank you for letting him stay here, and whatever your deal is with him, just keep it up. Don't do him any favors, let him learn the hard way. This might just be what he needs."

"So you're saying you want us to keep letting him stay in our garage as he uses our fire wood and eats our food?" Tom was getting angry, he had never been one to provide hand outs, especially since Jake had a family he could turn to for help.

"No, what I'm saying is that you do whatever it was you were going to do with him. I'm assuming you weren't going to burn him down with the garage or anything like that. And make him work for what he gets, if anything. You certainly do not have to feed him. He's a grown boy, he can take care of himself."

Tom was still not satisfied "and if he steals from us? Which technically he is already doing by forcing us to help him?"

I looked at Tom, and I gave him "the look." He needed to calm down. No one liked this situation, but there was no reason to antagonize John. Ticking off John would not help our situation. Tom read my warnings, and stopped talking.

John brushed it off and got back on topic. "Why don't I get that goat delivered to you tomorrow. I'll be here in the afternoon. And hey, let me ask you, if I did deliver a slaughtered cow, you got working fridges or freezers to put it into?"

I chimed in quickly before Tom's anger showed again "well, I would probably make jerky out of most of it since we have a top quality dehydrator. Not sure if I can can it since we are short an electric stove. But I might try on the wood cook stove.

And yes, we have a working freezer that we can use as temporary storage until we preserve the meat otherwise."

John looked into our kitchen "what happened to your stove?"

I explained, "the one that came with the house was broken, and a fire danger, so we recycled it, and we just never got around to replacing it at an affordable price. We meant to, but it just didn't happen before things fell apart. We're hoping to find a descent one at barter days."

"So you know how to make jerky, and you know how to can meat?" John verified.

"Yes" I replied forcefully.

"Dry pack?" John asked.

"Yes, that's the best way" I answered.

"I see." John pondered for a minute, then asked, "pressure can, not water can right?"

"Yes, of course, don't need any botulism" I commented, almost sarcastically.

John abruptly changed gears "what kind of dehydrator you got?"

I responded in the same rapid fire, fact reporting tone that John had been asking his questions. "It's that big metal box you see in the kitchen."

"Stainless?" he asked.

"Yes, and it's not up for trade." I responded quickly and with a deadly serious tone.

"No no, I was just curious if you had the right means to preserve a whole cow."

"All but the stove, and the wood cook stove can work if we're careful."

With that, John finished off his glass of wine, grabbed a piece of cheese, then put on his coat, and opened the door to the outside, without saying another word. He put on his cowboy hat, then offered a goodbye gesture, turned on his flashlight, and got on his horse. Then he was gone.

It was late, Sam had volunteered to clean up the dishes. Tom and I retired to our master bedroom and cleaned up for the night. I heard Terry add wood to the fire. It was a tough day today, with quite a few unexpected events. I crawled into bed waiting for Tom as he washed up for the night. When he came out of the bathroom, he said "I need to let the pups out one last time for potty, and I want to double check all the doors. You took care of the animals right?"

"Yes, Sam and I locked them up and poured the water into the compost so it doesn't freeze in their waterers."

"Thanks." He walked to the kitchen, and let the dogs out the back door. I heard him check the front door, and then the dogs came back in. He locked the back door, then came into the bedroom with the rifle and shotgun that were near the back door. I knew why he brought them in. No reason to give Jake a weapon should he succeed in breaking in. Tom double checked our handguns to make sure they were loaded, then turned off the light. He crawled into bed while the pups make themselves comfortable on the floor around the bed.

Tom admitted, "I don't feel tired, actually, I feel pretty wired, stressed."

I concurred "me too. It's because Jake is in the garage and we don't know what he's up to."

Tom was frustrated. "Why does everyone say he's not a bad guy? He threatened our safety."

I tried to diffuse the tension a little. "John says he wouldn't actually have done it. Maybe Jake's just cold, hungry and pathetically desperate."

"Don't tell me you're on his side too" Tom snapped.

I tried to use logic, which usually worked with Tom. "I'm not, but we need a male goat, so we need to live with the situation."

Tom relinquished, "I know, but I hate the fact that we're relying on someone else."

Again I tried to reason with him "me too, but it was impossible for us to get ready otherwise. We're barely surviving our first winter as it is. Imagine if we'd spent all our money on additional animals instead of preps."

"Animals are preps" he quipped.

"They're not solar, and they're only food during certain times of the year. Without a dehydrator, or canner, we can't store that food, we had to do what we had to do" I said.

"I know" Tom finally conceded.

We both laid awake for a while, I was not sure how long really. But eventually, somehow I fell asleep. Tom must have too, because we were both woken up by the dogs needing to go outside. It was still dark out, but that did not mean anything anymore, the days were much shorter.

Chapter 8

A Cold Hard Winter

We reluctantly crawled out of bed. The tiles on the floor were cold with the exception of the spots where the dogs been sleeping. I turned on a flashlight to see where I was going, and went to use the bathroom. I washed my hands then snuck out to the living room to add fire to the wood stove. Sam and Terry had already beat me to it.

"Did you sleep okay?" Terry asked.

"Not really" I admitted.

"You were worried too?" Sam asked, rhetorically.

"Yeah." I answered her anyway.

"We are too. But so far so good, one night down" Sam's voice had optimism in it.

"We'll see if he starts building that outhouse" I reminded.

"Yeah, guess we'll see" Terry agreed.

I walked over to the tea kettle. I could tell the water was hot because it was still steaming. I poured myself a cup of hot water, added the instant coffee, and some stevia. I quit using milk in an effort to save it, I did not really need milk in my coffee anyway, and I was getting used to coffee with out it.

Tom joined us with the dogs in front of the fire, and we all sat there, sleep deficient, sipping our hot coffee. We started eating oatmeal from storage for breakfast every other day in an effort to cut back on the number of eggs we ate. Plus we tried to save the eggs for days when we had hard work to do. The chickens' egg production would start picking up soon, as the days should start getting longer, little by little, though it did not feel like it yet. It was much colder here in January than November or December. Still, the chickens should go through their molting soon and they should start laying more eggs again. So we really only had a couple months to get through. If we did get a male goat, it would be just in time for the end of the breeding season. This meant that we could get one of our does impregnated. That would definitely help, as we could use her milk once the little one was weaned. If we were lucky, maybe both female goats would breed. We were already getting much less milk as our one producing goat was drying up. Maybe things would be alright. We also had help to plant seed, so we should be able to get some summer wheat, and even chicken feed planted – in addition to our regular spring and summer gardens.

I was staring out the window watching it get lighter with the time passing and I did not even realize that Terry took off to tend to the animals this morning. Sam and Terry were always trying to beat us to the chores, though we did not ask them to nor expect it. But sometimes we really appreciated it. Today was one of those mornings that I just did not feel like doing anything. So I sat there sipping my coffee as the morning went by.

"Rache, are you alright, I'm worried about you" Tom said with a soft, concerned tone. I snapped out of my daze and looked at Tom. He appeared to have aged over night, maybe it was the lack of sleep.

"I'm fine, just tired. You look tired too" I replied.

"Yeah, I didn't sleep very well, who knows what Jake is up to" Tom got straight to the point.

"He told me he hadn't been drinking since alcohol hasn't been readily available" I tried to find some positive in the situation.

"Did he say he wasn't going to drink if it was available?" Tom got straight to the point again.

"No, he implied that he doesn't have the self control that his dad expects of him" I was repeating what Jake had told me.

"Well, he better figure it out soon, or it's going to get him in a world of trouble" Tom's voice was serious.

"Only if he finds alcohol readily available" I reminded.

"Yeah, he'll probably set up a still in our garage without telling us" Tom joked and we both laughed.

Still laughing I said "if that's the case, then he better share."

The morning daylight bloomed quickly. Sam and Terry returned looking frozen. I added another log to the fire and asked about the animals. "You don't have to beat us to the chores, but since you did, do the animals look okay?"

Terry obliged, "yep, all in place, everyone is fed and happy, though we hardly got any milk today."

Tom pointed out, "well, if we do get that male goat, then we need to stop milking completely anyway so the other doe can maintain her nutrients for her young. We'll have to make due with our canned milk, and then the whey and casein protein powder we have stored away."

"That's alright," Sam said happily, "we can make do without milk, it'll be exciting when they have young."

"Or a lot of work" I commented. "I'll hope for exciting. Let's hope the breed is a docile one too. Though I'm not about to be picky when just finding a male goat has been a challenge."

"Well, once he has done his job, we can eat him if he's being too stubborn" Tom suggested.

I wasn't so sure that was a good idea. "Yeah, I was thinking about that, and I'm not sure I want to get rid of him so quickly. Maybe once we know what the kids are, or if we find out where there are goats around here that we can use for the future."

"True, good point" Tom agreed.

"And, if it's an older goat, as in more than a year, then the meat is really tough - not really ideal to eat anyway" I added.

"But still meat right?" Terry wondered.

"Yeah, still meat" I answered.

"We're not picky" Sam pointed out.

Tom changed directions "Since we're on the topic of meat production, we might want to try to barter for a breeding pair or two of meat rabbits. Rabbits require little care other than refilling their food and water in the rabbit hutches, and making sure we separate them out into additional hutches as they breed. Rabbits grow and breed quickly, so they could provide us with a good source of meat. We have the rabbit hutches, cages and equipment for them, we just need the animals. I know Vince was breeding rabbits for a while so I can check with him to see if he still has them, and what he might be willing to barter for some."

"I can't eat a bunny, they're too cute" Sam admitted.

"Ah, 'Easter Bunny Syndrome'" Tom commented.

"If you're hungry enough you will, and the meat is delicious" I tried to reassure Sam, but okay, so that was a lie, as I had not yet eaten any rabbit meat. So I did not truly know if the meat tasted good, but I had heard from Vince that it does.

Tom tried to explain to Sam, "meat rabbits are low maintenance, grow and reproduce quickly, are cold tolerant, and unlike large animals are easy to butcher. They are also *quiet*, unlike chickens and goats. So we thought they would make good meat animals, we just never got around to actually raising them before things fell apart."

"And their waste makes good fertilizer" I added.

Terry tried to change the topic, probably to make Sam more comfortable. "Speaking of fertilizer, did you want us to start on sterilizing the soil now that we have an oven?" I thought about Terry's question for a while, then thought out load "well, that's a nice stove, and we could use one for canning, so I'm still debating... Let's hold off. We have a couple weeks before we have to get started. Plus we could set up an area where we can use glass to cook the soil, so we could make do without an oven for that. It's just easier to use an oven and you're not dependent on the sun" I finished.

Tom stood up as if getting ready to start the day, then asked "Where are the rabbit cages?"

"There are three in the garage, and the hutch has a set up for a heat lamp" I told him.

"Where would you prefer to keep the cute bunnies if I can get some?" he asked with a little joking in his voice.

"I think on the East side of the house on the deck will work. That will offer the rabbits more protection from the wind. If we had hoop houses, we could have put them in there, as that would really offer protection from the elements, and help to warm the plants in the hoop houses at the same time." After I finished, I thought if we had enough materials to build a hoop house. I did not think so, but we can use Rita's greenhouse, they could warm up the plants in there.

The rest of us were still lazily, and perhaps carelessly, sitting around until we heard a hammering type sound in the distance. We all scrambled to get dressed and grab our weapons to go outside and see if we could figure out what the noise was. Once outside, off on the lower corner of the property, we saw Jake hammering some pieces of wood together. We all walked down to see if it was real, and if he was really trying to build an out house. When we got down there, we saw he had already laid out all the wood pieces, had the hammer, measuring tape, a saw and a shovel.

"Good morning." Jake's voice was full of confidence.

"It *is* a good morning Jake," I agreed. "I see you are working bright and early."

"I have to pee real bad," he joked.

"Come on Jake, you can use the house bathroom one last time," Tom offered, chuckling.

Tom and Jake walked toward the house as the three of us stood there staring at the project.

"Think we should help him?" Terry asked.

"It might go quicker," I thought out loud.

"And he'll stop using our bathroom inside," Sam pointed out.

"He picked a good spot you know," Terry assessed.

"Yeah he did. This is where I was thinking an outhouse should go," I agreed.

"We can't be too nice to him you know, so I'm not going to help. But if you two want to, go ahead," I said.

"I think we'll stay to help, we don't really like him using our bathroom," Terry explained.

We all laughed, and I started to head back to the house. Velcro had dug out her Frisbee and was following me around, so I decided to play Frisbee with her. Tom approached me in the middle of the game.

"I was thinking about it," Tom said, "and I think we should use that stove inside. It will do us much more good there, we can sterilize soil using the sun and a glass box."

"I tend to agree with you," I replied. "That is a nice stove, it would be a shame to see it get used for soil, and I'm tired of eating burnt food."

"And I don't want to see our food preserving equipment get destroyed" he added.

"Me neither." Velcro was getting tired of fetching the frisbee, so I asked Tom "Do you want me to help you move it inside?"

"Yeah, I was thinking we should do that" he replied.

I followed Tom to the stove at the back of the house, and then Tom went to the garage to get a hand truck. Jake, Sam and Terry were all working away on the outhouse, though they were scratching their heads a lot. Tom came back with the hand truck and I helped him load the stove on to the hand truck, then up the small step that led to the hallway of the house, then into the kitchen. It fit in the designated stove spot, though barely. We had to do a little bit of maneuvering to get it to slide in, making sure we plugged it in first.

It was nice having a stove again. Not having one certainly made things challenging. We should have made it a higher priority, but it was just one of those things that did not come up very often, or at least not for the price range we were looking for. We learned our lesson; we should have spent the extra couple hundred dollars and not waited. I turned it on to make sure it worked, and sure enough, the burners heated up rather quickly, and so did the oven. I looked at Tom with a happy face, and then unplugged the two 5th burners and put them in a cupboard. That allowed for a little more space on the counter too.

"I just need to clean it a bit, I'll get to it before the evening is over" I explained to Tom.

"Looks clean to me" Tom replied.

"That's right, I forgot, you are dust blind" I said letting my annoyance be heard.

The dogs ran to the front door in excitement, and we looked out the kitchen window. John was back, riding his horse again, but this time pulling some kind of cart behind him. We rushed outside to greet him and to find out if he brought a male goat. The dogs were super excited too, and as we got closer we realized that we needed to put the dogs inside. Not only was there a nice looking male goat, but also some beef, though still mostly in cow shape, sort of. Regardless, that was way too much meat for the dogs to be tempted with, so I quickly grabbed their collars and dragged them inside. It was almost too late, as they already smelled the beef. I'm sure it smelled better than their stale kibble.

After putting the dogs in the house I hurried back in excitement. Not only was there a nice looking male goat, and the meat, but also an older stove. I realized I would not want that stove inside, but it would work great for sterilizing soil.

And I would not feel bad putting soil into that one. There was also a metal container that looked like it might be designed to hold milk, but I was not sure.

"Hi John. Do you know what breed of goat that is?" I asked as we got close enough to John.

"Saanen. What breed do you have?" John was very efficient with his words, as always.

"LaMancha. Those two should be okay to breed together" I figured.

"Lamancha's? Aren't those the ones with short ears?" John asked with some uncertainty.

"Yep, looks like they froze off" came Tom's reply.

"They should be fine with the Saanen then, should work out for you" John said.

"That's a big goat" I said out loud as soon as I was close enough to realize it's size.

"Yep, about 180 lbs, weighed him before I brought him over. But before you do anything with him, you might want to put the meat away, I realize it's like a freezer out here, but you don't really want it exposed to the elements much longer" John suggested.

"Let me lock up the dogs, and clean off a butcher cart" I said quickly.

I ran to the house and convinced the dogs to go in the master bedroom. I gave them rawhides and closed the doors. I hurried back. Tom and I, with John helping, tried to pick up the carcass and carry it, but with no success. The carcass was like 500 lbs or more. I decided we needed a cart. It just so happened that we bought a hunting cart meant for elk a long time ago when it was on sale for $50 at a sporting goods store. We never actually used it, but I was pretty sure it was in the garage.

"Sorry I didn't have time to finish butchering it up for you, but figured you could manage the rest" John stated, almost apologetically.

"We can. Let me just go get the hunting cart we have, that should work nicely to move it." I left to go to the garage and looked around for the cart for a while, I knew we had one. After a few minutes I found it, with a bunch of stuff stacked on it. I moved all the boxes and wheeled the cart out to the carcass. We managed to slide the carcass over to the cart, and then Tom wheeled it into the house.

"Rachel, do we have any meat paper?" Tom asked.

"Yes, let me go get it" I walked over to the kitchen closet. The meat paper was still in a huge roll that we got at Costco. I grabbed it, and unrolled it onto the coffee table. Then I helped Tom and John move the carcass from the cart to the coffee table. We struggled a bit, but were mostly able to slide it, not really lift it, but close enough. Good thing we had a sturdy metal and wood coffee table I thought to myself, thank you Rita and Charles.

"Yeah, we got it from here, thanks. You already did more than enough" Tom thanked John, I could tell he was in disbelief, and did not want to take advantage of John.

"Well, I kept all the innards, though I did bring you some more rennet so you can make me some more cheese" John said smiling.

"Well, we're low on milk, so I don't think we'll be making cheese for a while" I said sadly.

"No you're not. I brought you some cow milk; it's on the cart as well. Might want to transfer it to something else since I need my container back before I leave" John answered happily. I could tell he enjoyed this part, he must like making people happy. "Tom, do you mind butchering and putting the meat in the refrigerator and I'll tend to the milk?" I asked.

"Sure, you sure you can handle the milk?" he asked in return, he must have been worried about the weight of the containers.

"Yes, I've got the milk. If you can cut the meat into smaller pieces that can fit in the fridge, that would really help" I answered.

"Got it," Tom's tone of voice had happy in it.

"I'll help him, I just need a good butcher knife" John offered.

"Tom, you know where the butcher kit is right?" I asked Tom, hoping he would say yes, as I did not recall where I saw it last.

"Yep, I'm on top of it, let me just wash my hands first" Tom answered.

"By the way, the carcass is cured, I had it hanging in my cooler for the last two weeks, so it should be tender" John was too kind.

"You can't eat a freshly slaughtered cow?" I asked.

"Sure you can, but the meat is tough, you have to cure it while refrigerating for a couple weeks before the tissues break down and makes the meat more palatable. That should make it easier to butcher as well. I would have done it, but I had a busy morning, had quite a few meat deliveries this morning. And I had to pick up the goat" John explained.

With that, I left the two to slice up the meat, and went to the garage to find some empty glass water jugs. We used to have them all filled with filtered water at one point, and planned to do so again. However, there had not been enough sunlight to keep the pump house batteries running for as long as we wanted. And in winter, we did not have as much to water with the waste water. So we agreed to fill up the jugs again in spring as our water needs increased, and daylight for the PV powered pump house increased. When I walked into the garage I was surprised that Jake had touched nothing except for his bed. He seemed to have his own sleeping bag and pillow. He had also allowed the fire in the wood stove to burn out, which would conserve wood. That was unlike the rest of our household who kept our fire going even during the day. Perhaps Jake did not mean harm after all. Then I realized that I should not base my opinion on one sober evening. I quickly grabbed a few empty glass jugs, and went to the cart with the huge goat on it.

I looked over the milk jug that the milk was in. It looked like an antique metal container, about four feet tall, with a handle. It made me think of an old fashioned commercial milk jug. Then realized that John had stated his ranch was started in the 1850's. Perhaps this jug had been sitting around for that long, or maybe they never stopped using it. Regardless, I can see why he would want it back. Looks like I would have to unscrew the top and pour, I did not see any other way. This meant I needed a funnel. I went back inside the house to find a funnel. Tom and John were cutting away and joking around about Jake and the outhouse. John seemed quite happy, and so did Tom actually. Perhaps this situation was not too bad after all? I walked to the kitchen ignoring the boys and found a descent size funnel, one we used for our portable reverse osmosis system when filling our glass jugs with filtered water. I then went back to the cart outside and set up the first glass jug, put in the funnel, unscrewed the huge milk container, and gently leaned it over to pour the milk into the first glass container. It filled up quickly. I put the lid on the first glass container, and started on the second. I did not hurry too much, it was about 37 degrees outside, so I did not feel like the milk was going to spoil quickly or anything, I was more concerned about spilling it, and possibly wasting milk.

The goat kept looking at me with curiosity, though he seemed sweet. I knew a little about the breed, but not too much. If I recalled correctly, Saanen are a docile breed, so v should not have much of a problem with him. I finished pouring the milk and filled 10 of our one gallon jugs. Wo' thought, ten gallons of milk and a male goat, plus an old stove, and a side of beef. John either wanted his kid to l or he really liked that wine. Or both. We still had a dil where to put the milk. We had to do something with ; meat was going to take up all the space in the refrig(least until we could process it into jerky or can it. (refrigerator was big, but not that big. That was a v beef John brought us, and it was going to fill the the freezer, and the extra freezer in the garage. ' used up all the excess chicken broth and bone: figured our best bet was to leave the milk out glass jugs, so it should be safe from animals raccoons know how to unscrew screw tops not much choice I thought. I picked up tw carried them toward the front door. I lin(porch next to the front door.

Root cellar! That was the answ jugs to the root cellar, I thought to m' in there so that I could just put the n inside to grab the root cellar keys a you going to put all that milk?" "In the root cellar" I responded. ' we'll use it up quickly. We'll n make cheese" I added.

seem
Tom
in this
Our tw
that I o
Grantec
still, this
the wate
nose. He
untied hir
behind me
outhouse p
"Looks like
Terry asked
"Yeah, he's
smaller anyw
"Seems docile
"He is. I name

"Good idea. Think it's cool enough in the root cellar?" Tom asked.

"Should be, and it's only temporary" I clarified.

I grabbed the keys and headed to the root cellar. Truth is, I forgot about it completely, almost intentionally. I walked in and saw that our onions and carrots were just as we left them. We were hoping to replant them in the spring to get seed, although we would probably eat a few as well. We had not been getting much out of here, but perhaps we should, I wondered. I moved the milk to the shelves two jugs at a time, then locked the root cellar. I walked back to the cart, and then contemplated moving the goat. Might as well introduce him to our two LaManchas I thought. Since it was just two goats plus one goat, I thought they should be fine with the introductions. I ntied the big white goat and urged him to follow me. He emed sweet, and happy to oblige. He was huge, all white, d looked healthy. Back in the old days I would have an imal checked out by a vet before integrating it with my flock. there were few vets in the area, and even fewer supplies the vets could use to do any kind of testing.

I walked him over slowly toward our two goats. He still ed so sweet, I decided to name him Marshmallow. I knew, told me over and over that we did not name our meat. But case I just could not help myself. I really liked this goat. o unnamed female LaMancha's did not seem to notice pened the gate, and brought in a friend to join their herd. they were a bit far away from where the gate was, but was their area. I walked Marshmallow over to where was, and placed my hand in the water then wetted his seemed to figure it out and drink some water. I then h and walked out of the pasture, locking the gate . Sam and Terry decided to take a break from the roject and came to meet Marshmallow.

a fine goat, though he's huge. Different breed?"

a Sannen apparently. But females are generally ay, so it's expected" I explained.

," Sam commented.

d him Marshmallow."

202

"What are the other two named?" Sam wondered.

"Oh, Tom said no naming our food, but I couldn't help myself. He's just so sweet and all white. How's the outhouse project?" I asked.

"It's going, but Jake seems a bit weak. We don't think he's been getting much food" Terry assessed.

"Well, don't tell him, but his dad brought over a nice carcass. We're having steaks tonight, and we'll share with Jake, so he'll be able to get some nourishment" I said happily.

"Wow, steaks!?" Terry exclaimed.

"Yep, small pieces of course. Tom and John are cutting them up right now as we speak, and trying to find space in the refrigerator and freezers" it was hard to contain my excitement.

"Sounds like we'll be doing some canning and beef jerky making" Sam thought out loud, there was excitement in her voice as well.

"Yep, starting tonight" I promised.

"Well, we would like to help Jake finish the outhouse, but it sounds like you need help as well," Terry observed.

"Don't worry about us. Once the meat is in the refrigerator and freezer, we're fine for a couple of days, plus I have a stove now, so I can start working on the canning" I replied.

"Alright," said Sam. "But if you decide you need help, let us know right away, you are priority over Jake."

"I will. Think I can leave the goats by themselves?" I worried.

"Well, we can watch them as we're working on the outhouse," Terry offered.

"Oh, that would be great actually, do you mind?" I said with a sigh of relief.

"No, not at all, go tend to your stuff," Terry said nonchalantly, and shooed me away.

With that I left, and walked into the house through the back door. Tom and John had quite a bit of meat cut up. I washed my hands and grabbed a box of gallon ziplock bags, and walked over to the cut up carcass. I heard the dogs scratching at the bedroom door, but this was no time to let them out. I started placing pieces of meat in the ziplocks, and walked them to the refrigerator. I thought about the root cellar, but decided that meat was just too risky. After I managed to bag up all the meat that was cut up already, I began making marinade for the jerky, and started the dehydrator to get it to temperature. I had to check my recipe book first to make sure I was doing it right, and had the right temperature set.

John interrupted my thought process "you know, you've got roughly about 300 lbs of good cuts here, plus another 100 lbs of the not so good cuts, then fat and such. Give Jake the chuck, he doesn't need filet mignon you know."

We all chuckled.

"And I figured you don't want things like the tongue, so I took all that out before I brought it, plus I have other uses for all the innards. In case you didn't know, nothing goes to waste, not even the hoofs" John expained.

"What do you do with all that stuff?" Tom inquired.

"Oh, you'd be surprised how many people love cow tongue" John explained. "And the hoofs, well, I made buttons out of those, and the bones are great for gelatin or beef stock. You'd be surprised what you can make out of a cow" John loved his job.

I quickly calculated the amount of meat he just brought us. Out of the 500 lb carcass, we should get 400 lbs of actual meat. 400 lbs of meat will feed the five of us for a year if we were careful. That meant the dogs could get in on this too. Wow, that was a lot of meat, and where the heck were we going to put it all? Time to start making something out of it I thought. I got out a large sauté pan and put the steak pieces in there, including the chuck as suggested by John. I chopped up some garlic, added some spices, a little olive oil, then put the sauté pan on the wood cook stove, grabbed a spatula, and told Tom he was in charge.

Tom and John had finished cutting the meat into smaller pieces, which I finished placing in plastic ziplocks. I filled the freezer, and the refrigerator, and still had a ton of meat left over. I took the rest of the zip locks full of meat and put them in a dish pan, then walked them over to the freezer in the garage. If Jake saw it,… oh well, it's not like we were not going to share it with him. I returned for the next batch and saw that John was washing his hands in the kitchen, which meant Tom must have been in the bathroom washing his. I filled up the next tub with ziplocks full of meat, and walked back to the garage. I put them in the freezer and came back. What was left on the counter I started to slice and place in Zip locks that had marinade in it. This is what I did with the rest of the meat. I checked the temperature of the dehydrator, it was ready. I placed the first set of marinated strips on the racks, and shut the door of the dehydrator. That batch was marinated for too short of a time, but that was okay, it would still work. I put the other marinating batches in the refrigerator to marinate over night. Though I had to cram them in the fridge, we were definitely full.

I then started to get the pressure canner out, but realized I did not have any jars sterilized. I picked out several boxes of jars out of the kitchen closet and then to save time put them in the dishwasher and set it to sterilize. I then got the canning equipment ready, and got out my canning book. Tom and John set out to move the older stove to the spot where we had the newer stove previously. I realized the paper and mess were still on the table. Nice of the boys to leave me a mess. I picked it up carefully, and poured the excess blood into the dogs' bowls; that would be a nice treat for them. The dogs were done with their rawhides and were going crazy in the bedroom. I folded the paper and put it in a plastic trash bag, but did not know what else to do with it. It's not like we could take our trash to the dump. I decided that we should bury it, but in the mean time, it will go in plastic trash bags.

I let the dogs out and they immediately ran to their bowls. Then I washed my hands and returned to the kitchen to cut up meat to put in the jars. In my experience, hot packing was the best, so I cut them into 1 inch squares and got them ready to place in the hot sterilized jars. I also put some water into the canner and turned the heat on the stove. It was so nice having an electric stove again.

Tom and John came back in, and Tom went to give John the box of wine.

"John, that's what, a year's worth of meat for the five of us?" Tom asked.

"Well, you got your two dogs there" John was being smart.

"Plus the stove and the milk?" Tom pointed out. I could tell

Tom was confused by the generosity, no way was all that worth one case of wine.

"Well, I'm getting some cheese out of the milk aren't I?" John reminded.

"Yes, of course, but we need to know how much we owe you, or what we owe you" Tom replied.

"Let's just put it this way. Get my son to straighten up, don't let him fool you, he's good at that. But get him to grow up a little, or a lot. And maybe send me some eggs and chicken come spring when you have extra, and we'll call it even" John suggested.

"Deal" Tom said, he was not going to let that opportunity pass him by.

With that, they shook hands.

"By the way, where did you find the goat, and how old is it?" Tom wondered.

"Tom, I'm glad you asked. There is this very nice couple with 6 children, who built a place from scratch out in the middle of nowhere. They have quite a few goats and chickens, completely off grid. They kind of remind me of you, except that you have four legged children, and only two of them. Anyway, they had been inquiring about some beef from me, so I traded them some for that goat. They were more than happy, and it seems that you too are happy. That goat is about 9 months old, so if you eat him by March, the meat should still be tender" John's reply sounded rehearsed.

"Wow, another couple completely off grid like us? Where are they?" I asked excited.

"That, I can't tell you, as they don't want anyone to know where they're located. And they're not completely like you, they're much more self sufficient and independent" was John's reply, not so rehearsed this time.

"Fair enough" Tom accepted.

John took his box of wine, went outside, put it on the empty cart, got on his horse, and left. I did not even notice the day had disappeared, but it was getting dusk out. Not good. I needed power for the stove and dehydrator, so we would have to use candles for light tonight. I did not want to risk running the batteries too low overnight. I went through the house and turned off every light, and even unplugged everything just to be on the safe side. I then added more wood to the wood stove, and lit two candles. Sam and Terry had walked in at this point.

"Are we out of power?" Terry asked.

"No, trying to save it for the dehydrator. Maybe we can keep the fire going longer so it's warmer in here and the dehydrator doesn't have to work as hard" I suggested.

"Okay, not a problem, do you need help with any of it?" Sam offered.

"Nope, I have it under control. Speaking of which though, I think my jars are done sterilizing." I headed back to the kitchen. Since there was still a bit of daylight left, I did not bring a candle with me. I turned off the dishwasher - no reason to waste electricity to dry the jars. I picked out five jars with lids and screw tops, and proceeded to add the meat cubes into the jars. The water in the canner was boiling, so everything was set. I filled the jars with raw meat cubes, put on the top lid, and lightly screwed on the screw tops. I then used jar holders to put the jars in the canner, poured in a little vinegar to keep the canner from absorbing a meat smell, placed a lid on it, and sealed it. Next I turned the heat up higher on the burner. Tom had our dinner steaks done long ago, and had put them in the oven to keep them warm, along with the left over rice that I removed from the fridge to make room for the steaks. The rice must have been warm by now, and the steaks were more than done. So I turned off the oven at that point as I figured we would be eating soon.

I dug out five plates and silverware sets, and served up five equal portions. Well, almost equal. One was not quite the same cut of meat, but much better than nothing I guess. Tom took that plate to the garage, along with a can of green beans, a can opener, and a small cooking pot. Terry and Sam took their plates and went to sit down in the living room. I had to watch the canner, so I could not leave the kitchen. I stood there eating my steak. Wow, I never thought steak could taste so good. Tom came back and joined me in the kitchen. He brought a candle so we could see what we were doing. About that time, the canner started to steam, so I turned the heat down slightly, then set the timer for 10 minutes, which was how long it needed to steam before I could put the weighted gauge down. We all finished our food in silence except for the hum of the dehydrator and the wisp of the pressure canner, and we were all done when the timer went off. I put the weighted gauge on the canner and watched the pressure build up as I lowered the heat, then I was satisfied. I set the timer for 90 minutes and went to the living room to join everyone else.

I was exhausted, somehow my lazy day turned into a super busy day, but it was so productive. We still had so much work ahead of us. We had to process the milk and cheese within a few days if we did not want it to spoil, and we had soil to sterilize, seeds to plant, and possibly more goat housing to build.

"How did the goats do, are they okay?" I worried.

"Yeah, they stayed away from each other, the two put themselves away, but we had to coerce Marshmallow to go into his stall" Sam explained.

"Marshmallow?" Uh oh, Tom was not happy about this.

"Yes, Marshmallow" I said. "Nothing wrong with eating marshmallows right?" We all laughed.

"I thought we agreed about not naming our food" Tom pressed.

"But Marshmallow is a food" I joked. We all laughed again.

"Mind if we light a couple more candles, it's kind of dark in here" Terry asked.

"Yes, of course, not a problem." I stood up to grab the lighter and lit three more candles.

"How's the outhouse coming along?" I wondered.

"Well, the hole is dug, though nothing to sit on yet. But Jake can just stand and aim, and hopefully he'll figure out the seat situation by tomorrow" Terry explained.

"What if we took a five gallon bucket, put a seat on it, and cut out a hole in the bottom?" Tom suggested.

"That would work. Are you willing to give up a bucket?" Terry asked.

"We just got a year's worth of meat, yeah, I'm willing to give up a bucket" Tom replied.

"What?" Terry and Sam both gasped in awe.

"Yep, we'll be doing lots of canning and dehydrating over the next few days. Oh, and we also got 10 gallons of cow milk, so we'll be busy making cheese and yogurt as well" I instructed.

"Where did it all come from?" Sam wondered.

"Well, John of course. Guess he's secretly taking care of his kid" I said.

"So we're not running out of food?" Terry reiterated.

"Not this year, unless we get more unexpected guests, as the pattern seems to be" Tom grumbled.

"That's wonderful!" Sam exclaimed.

"Yes it is, but we're going to be busy, and we need lots of power to run the canner and the dehydrator. So our electricity usage has to be minimal" I cautioned.

"Not a problem" Terry replied.

We chatted a while longer about the meat, and why Jake got the chuck, and our plans for preserving the milk and meat. By that time the timer went off and I turned off the heat completely from the stove, then moved the canner over to another burner. I went back to the table and suggested that we all play a board game as a diversion to help maintain our sanity. There was not much else we could do in the dark. Tom went to the living room closet and picked out *Risk*. We all started to play, with the occasional interruption of tending to the canner to open the lid once the pressure reduced enough, and then to unload the jars onto a towel so that they could cool over night. We laughed at our game skills and listened to the jars popping as they were sealing with the cooling process. We did not hear from Jake the rest of the night, though I expected him to return the plate at least.

The next morning we were up bright and early. We all got much better sleep this time as our situation seemed to have improved over night. This time Tom tended to the animals, plus he wanted to see how Marshmallow was doing after his first night here. Sam volunteered to cook up scrambled eggs with onions, and I tended to the jars of canned meat. Basically, I just put them away, and started preparing to make another batch as soon as we had sunlight to charge up the solar batteries. The batteries seemed to have lasted all night with the dehydrator, but we did keep the house extra warm last night. Sam passed out plates of eggs, and took a plate with a cup of coffee to Jake. She brought back last night's extra dishes and asked if Jake could have more water. Of course he could, jeez, we were not cruel.

We spent the next four days making yogurt, cheese, beef jerky, and canned meat. It felt good to get all the meat in the refrigerator taken care of. All we had left was the stuff in the freezers, but we figured that was for our everyday use as it was fine in the freezer over the long term. We did also manage to use up all the milk, though we ate a lot of yogurt. We canned half the milk so that we could store it long term. We wanted to finish the meat before we worked on the milk. Between the goat milk that we previously canned, and the cow milk that we just canned, we had about 40 jars of condensed milk. Not bad, not bad at all. Thank you John.

Sam made it her job to make sure that Jake got fed, and she was the one that offered him the bucket for the outhouse, though he had to cut the hole himself. Amazingly, Jake did finish the outhouse, and never asked to use our bathroom again. He did ask for more candles, and more water, but other than that, he stayed away. I wanted to ask him to help out with the chores since we were feeding him, but, we got so much food from his dad that I did not feel it was right. And with spring slowly approaching, we would be using less firewood soon. Maybe I would make him chop firewood for next season – that sounded fair.

The process to sterilize the soil was as smelly as expected, and we often lost our appetites. Regardless, we managed to get enough soil to fill 50 large plastic planters. We placed them on our enclosed deck, and started to plant seeds. We did quite a few per planter as we expected to transplant in just a couple of months. We also added composted soil to the cold frames outside that were not in use, and started planting seed there as well. Our only issue at this point was water. Although the days were getting longer, the pump house required a lot of energy to pump the water, and there were not enough hours of daylight to run the pump house as much as we needed it to. Perhaps the problem was the relatively smaller capacity of batteries that were in the pump house.

Our water recycling system became essential, and not a drop went wasted. We could only water first thing in the morning to make sure that the plants would not freeze over night. But the days were getting warm enough during the day that we even had to keep the cold frames open for a few hours at a time. It was all very exciting to see the plants grow. We were kind of getting sick of steak. The chickens were increasing their egg production too, which was excellent. Though we never did figure out a way to preserve eggs in a way where they still tasted good, we did offer John several dozen, along with the cheese we made, when we saw him again.

With the sunlight hours increasing, our ham radio usage was increasing as well, and the news out in the cities was not good, not good at all. Most everyone had figured out that the "relief" camps were a deception, and that people were better off staying away form them. So now if a guard thought you needed "help," whether you needed it or not, the guard would arrest you and force you to go to a camp – "for your own good" of course. The story was that guard took anyone they felt like taking, and then would loot that person's home. We were told that the cities smelled of death, urine, feces, and who knows what else. The descriptions were nauseating. No trash services, no funeral services, no refrigeration for most, electricity was intermittent. Gangs were everywhere; that was really how people were surviving. People were banding together and stealing using violence. If any city folks had solar power or greenhouses, the gangs would try to steal them. And if they could not take them, they would throw rocks at the panels to break them, or at greenhouses to destroy them. Unless you joined a gang, or at least shared your food supplies, you were not safe – and even then you were not safe. Even those working for government and military were becoming scared of the gangs, as the gang population outnumbered the military. If you wore a uniform, you were at high risk of getting attacked and/or murdered. Although martial law was in place, there were few police to enforce it. Actually, the only ones still on duty to enforce any law and order was the military. But even they were somewhat intimidated by the gangs – due to the gangs' large numbers. It got to the point where any group of people walking together that appeared to be gang like was immediately shot. This became a sort of catch 22, as one did not walk alone in the city for safety reasons, but walking with a group was just as dangerous. Food was dropped from airplanes, but clean water was scarce, and medicine was non-existent. The food itself was often expired, which was a risk itself. It was estimated that at least a third, and possibly half of the population had died due to starvation, cold, murder, infectious disease, lack of life saving medication and medical care, or mental illness resulting in suicide. Though those numbers were a guess.

So far most small towns that were far from large cities had been spared from the worst of it, but the small towns that were close to big cities had been hit just as hard. It was only a matter of time before the gangs started heading out to the more distant rural towns - presuming they had a way to travel due to the fuel shortages. The cities were running out of food, water, and other supplies, so there were precious few scraps to fight over. If the gang members were going to continue surviving, they would have to find new sources for those essentials. The gangs were also getting bigger and stronger, and many of them stopped at nothing. If we thought the situation we ran into on our drive up here was ugly, then we were in for a shock. People eating people; that was what it had come down to in some places. No mercy, no God, you would not think some of those gang members were human any longer. Desperation had driven people to the most ruthless and deplorable of human behaviors.

Listening to the hams was a time for reality check, and it was scary. Once the gangs started moving to more distant small towns, it would get ugly, even out in the middle of "nowhere." Throughout the winter was probably not a good time for the gangs to try to venture out to distant and unknown locations. There were no snow plows out clearing the roads, so many roads had become impassable. Travel conditions had become poor in general as there were many stranded and abandoned cars on the roads, and many car accidents and much road debris that had not been cleared.

But with spring and warmer weather on the way, we figured that the gangs would start venturing further out into the rural areas in search of essential supplies.

The television news of course, was all positive, all happy, no mention of death, no mention of people starving, nor people getting sick. No, it was all happy. The president will fix everything soon. Somewhere in there was supposedly an election or something. So we had a new "President." But I did not recall hearing about an option to vote. Not that I would have at this point anyway. But somehow we had a new person in charge, though it was all the same promises. Nothing was changing, only getting worse. The more things changed, the more they stayed the same I thought. We just continued on our daily routine of food preservation and growing a small farm.

One Sunday morning, Tom and Sam were getting ready. Tom was checking his pistol as if anticipating problems today. Terry was out on guard duty and would miss barter days this week. Then Tom reminded me "we'll be back a little late, we have cute bunnies to pick up on our way back home." Sam gave Tom a dirty look. We finally convinced her that we should raise bunnies, but we will not make her slaughter them, and she can choose to eat the meat or not. They had a pet carrier with a rooster and two chickens tucked away, then they donned their packs and took off.

"Any problems this week?" I asked. Tom was quick to answer, "not directly, but things are not good." I was confused, Tom must have seen my confusion as he explained "people are very much on edge, they are overworked, cranky, and many of them commented to me about how I should have warned them about that too." I was even more confused. "What do you mean?" I asked. Tom took a deep breath and said "apparently, because we were warning people about the coming economic collapse, it was also our job to warn people that living a self sufficient life style is a lot of hard work."

I thought about what Tom was saying, then asked "are you saying that people here think it was our job to teach them about the realities of life?" Tom nodded his head and said "apparently." I looked at Sam still confused, and she clarified what Tom was saying "there were many folk who came to Tom angrily, almost as if they were blaming him for the collapse... blaming the messenger kind of thing. I think people are just run down. This situation has taken a toll on everyone. There were also more fights that broke out, and a lot of people voluntarily left early. I think they were afraid they would get targeted since they had things to barter, so they packed up and left." Then Tom added "Even Mrs. Minnick asked if it would be a problem if she left early. But she said it was because she had not had a sale all day. At least the people in our town haven't resorted to resolving their fights with firearms yet, like they've started doing in the cities."

"Is that true?" I asked. Tom and Terry both nodded yes, then Terry said "it seems like everything has come to a stand still. No one is doing much, and no one wants to barter. It seems like everyone is just waiting for the next person to make a move" Tom explained further.

"Wow" I said, and proceeded to sit down on a folding chair. I knew things would get tense, but I was hoping this town would keep it together better. I can not imagine what it would have been like if most people here had been caught unprepared. I noticed Tom was still holding the carrier, and suggested "you might want to drop off the bunnies in the hutch before the dogs notice them" though I was surprised they had not already. Tom nodded and walked out the back door, and returned shortly. I was disinterested in the bunnies because I was overwhelmed with what I just heard. We have been so comfortable thanks to John and our preps, that I have not really considered how badly this town was affected as well.

The dogs got excited again, Terry must be back. We all got up to walk outside to greet him, the dogs ran out first of course. Terry looked upset, and I realized that he had some bruises and cuts on his face. Sam realized it at the same time and ran to him asking "what happened?!"
"I'm fine, I'm fine, don't worry. I had guard duty with Bob, and he just seemed pissed off about everything" Terry answered trying to reassure Sam.
"hold that thought" said Sam as she ran inside to grab a first aid kit. Tom and I got Terry to come inside and to sit down, as

Sam started to wet cotton pads with povidone iodine solution. As she did that, she said "continue, what happened."

Terry seemed highly irritated and annoyed, and finally said "nothing happened, Bob's an ass. He was irritated at everything, and everything was everyone else's fault. He just kept complaining and complaining. He was not paying attention to the road, and he kept referring to me as a mooch because I live here, and he just went on and on. I kept ignoring him, but that seemed to only make him worse. Finally, I just got sick of it, so I went after him, and next thing I know, we were fighting. Then he got a knife out, so I backed off, and went to reach for my gun, but realized it had fallen out of my holster or something while fighting. Then Bob came at me with the knife again."

We were all staring at Terry in awe as Sam was tending to his face. Then she realized he had cuts on his arms, so she rolled up his first sleeve and started cleaning those as well. Terry continued, "thankfully Vince grabbed my gun and shot it in the air, and that got Bob to stop. Though Bob tried to go after Vince after that, but Vince pointed the gun at Bob and told him to stand down." Terry took a deep breath then continued "Elizabeth, who was also there, was freaked out by the whole situation. And when she saw Bob and Vince have a stand off, she just started screaming at the top of her lungs, mainly at Bob, but at Vince too, to knock it off, we're supposed to be neighbors, and so on."

Sam was now rolling up Terry's other sleeve and said "then what happened?" Terry took another deep breath and said "well, Bob turned from Vince back to me, and I still didn't have a gun, and then I don't know what happened. Elizabeth kept screaming, Vince kept telling Bob to back off, and Bob just kept glaring at me like I was some bad guy on the scene or something. Finally, Vince fired another shot in the air, and told Bob to go home and calm down, and told him he doesn't want to see him at guard duty ever again. He kept pointing my gun at him. Bob called his bluff and lunged at me again with the knife, that's how he got this arm." Terry pointed to a gash on his right arm that Sam was cleaning, and then continued "but then Elizabeth shot her rifle pretty darn close to us. Vince jumped on top of Bob, and started to punch him, and then next thing I know, it was over, and Bob was heading home." Terry had begun to calm down, though you could tell that he was traumatized by the event.

We are all supposed to work together, not against each other. But, the reality of high stress, combined with extensive physical labor and fatigue, and possibly low blood sugar or dehydration, will get to you. I always imagined that with so much work to be done, everyone would be too exhausted to fight, but apparently this was not the case. From what I heard, more people were cranky than anything, therefore more willing to act irrationally. This was not good, something had to change or it was only going to escalate out of control.

Chapter 9

Trouble From Government

"Did something happen? Did you pull two shifts? Where were you?" I asked Tom, I had been worried for the last four hours. He had returned home much later than he should have from one of his road block shifts, and I did not know where he had been. He looked awful, so I assumed he must have pulled two roadblock shifts.

"Yeah, I did. Bob never showed up to relieve me, so I ended up doing a double. Vince and I are going to go to his place and check on him. He usually shows up from what I hear. But given the last altercation, he might have taken Vince seriously when he told him he never wanted to see him at another shift again. I was also told that most shifts that are missed are due to something serious, an illness or death." Roadblock duty had turned into a way to check on people and make sure they were okay. Tom's voice was flat as he continued. "I have a bad feeling about this. I know that Bob has been having issues with everyone, and there was that fight with Terry, but we've all been tolerating each other despite our differences. It's not like Bob to just leave someone hanging; despite his outbursts, he means well."

I watched Tom for a second, and then asked "do you want me to go with you?" Tom's response was quick. "No! He might not like people trespassing, so I think it'll be better if it's just me and Vince. We already discussed it. Vince will stay out of view, at least until I give him the go ahead." With that, Tom went to the kitchen and opened the crock pot. It was a common routine around here. You did not look in the fridge. Instead, you looked in the crock pot to see what dehydrated foods were being turned into soup. He got out a bowl and a spoon, then scooped up a full helping and ate quickly. After that he got his day pack together, checked his handgun before he put it in his holster, slung his rifle over his shoulder, gave me a kiss and left.

"What should we work on next?" asked Terry.
"Well, I don't know" I said. "Let me read the list of things to

get done and give me your input.

"Okay, we're ready" Sam announced as she joined us.

I looked over my carefully drawn up list, and began. "Let the goats pasture out on the plot of land next to our property, outside of the fence. That will require someone to watch them all day to make sure they are safe and don't wonder off. We'll have to do that every day until the pasture we just reseeded has recovered. We need an additional goat building since we'll be having two kids soon. We need a second chicken coop already, and a second fenced off chicken area. There are at least 10 hens that are sitting on six to eight eggs each. We need to pull or wash the bugs off the crops since we have no lady bugs or lace wings to release, nor even any bug spray. Not that we really want to use chemical sprays if possible. We need to keep planting seeds, including wheat, grass pasture, and chicken forage food. And we need to start cutting and splitting fire wood as well, since we will not be able to have it delivered this year. We need to separate the bunnies, so I'll get those cages ready. We also need to meet with Rita and Charles and refill their water barrels. They are bound to be running low by now. We have increased watering needs too. We still have to cover up the cold frames in the evening, as we are still having frosts some evenings."

Terry added "we also have increased guard shifts. We have less people in this town than we did before winter," implying that some people did not survive the winter.

We all sat silently for a minute, contemplating that reality check. Some folks just did not have the right preps, or enough preps, to make it through the winter here without outside support. Jake broke us out of our silence. He had been attending our daily morning meetings since he had asked to help around the property. We did not argue with him, as he had stayed out of trouble, and he did help. Tom missed our meeting as he was out with Vince checking on Bob, plus he must be exhausted pulling a double shift over night. Jake interrupted my thought process "I suppose I should start volunteering with the guard shifts too. I can take up double shifts since I have some making up to do."

Terry was supportive of that idea and said "well then you should come down to the town meeting later today and volunteer" he said.

"I was planning on it" Jake replied.

When Tom came back later that day, I could tell by the way he was walking that something was wrong. I opened the door to let the dogs out to greet him and also went out to see if he was okay. "Did you find Bob? Is he okay?" I asked carefully.

"Yes and no" was Tom's reply. I could tell he was thinking, possibly trying to figure out how to put the words just right. We walked toward the house together, and as we walked in the front door with Compass and Velcro right behind us, Tom finally started explaining. "Bob committed suicide. He left a note." I waited for more, but Tom was not volunteering any more, so I prodded. "What did the note say?" I was surprised by my lack of emotions, almost as if I had expected it. Bob used to run the general store, so everyone came to him for supplies. Since the economic crash, there were no supplies coming in, so his store has basically been empty. Without a good barter system, he had not been able to maintain any kind of inventory, as people mostly bartered directly.

Because his store was his only source of income, he was completely without everything. However, Terry once mentioned he heard a rumor that when the roads were blocked off, Bob emptied out his store for himself, and kept all the supplies while claiming that he had sold out. We all agreed that if that is what he really did, then we did not blame him one bit. Those supplies belonged to him, and any of us would have probably done the same.

Tom finally started talking again. "Bob basically said that he was alone, he had nothing, he had been a burden on us all, that he ran out of supplies a long time ago, and that there was nothing left to live for if it meant living that way." I was silent. I did not know how to respond. Fortunately Tom continued, "Vince and I stopped by the church to tell Charles, since he's been keeping track of everyone. Charles told us that to his knowledge Bob had no family that could collect his things. So it's up for grabs once he's cremated; unless someone volunteers to dig a grave." That had been the way things had gone recently. Something had to be done with the dead bodies, but no one wanted to dig graves for free, and there was no one around willing to pay to do so. So the only people that got to be buried were those who had family that could afford to hire someone, which meant paying them with food, or that could dig the grave themselves. Anyone who did not get buried was managed by being cremated on their property. It seemed cold and harsh at first, but the reality was what it was. It took a lot of calories to bury a body, calories that most people could not spare. And dead bodies had to be disposed of in some sanitary way, or else disease would spread. When resources are limited, people will use methods that are right for the situation. As far as looting of homes of the deceased, that was a problem at first. But once Charles took over, he made sure to notify family first if there was any in contact, which usually there was not. Then he would notify the neighbor's, to give them the first opportunity to take what they needed. He figured the neighbor's would be the most likely to have been friends, and it would be easier for them to move things they wanted. However, in most situations, there was little left to take. Charles also asked for help from the family or neighbors to move the body to a safe location to burn.

"There was nothing in his house you know." Tom surprised me with his comment. I looked at him questioningly, and he continued. "He bartered off everything he had. There was nothing in his house. No furniture, nothing. He had a cup, a plate, a few pieces of silverware and a cooking pot. But he had no food. He had a wood stove, but no wood. He had some blankets on the floor for a bed, and a few sets of clothes. But that was pretty much it. I think that's how most people are living now a days, those still alive." With that, Tom went to the master bedroom as I followed. Then he said "I need a few minute alone. I'm just going to take a shower if there's hot water, then I need to get some sleep." I nodded yes, and left the room and went outside to tend to the animals. It was not often that something would get to Tom like that, but this did. Reality must be sinking in hard for him too.

January and February were cold months here. But in February, despite the cold, we welcomed the longer days. March was still too early to plant seedlings at such a high elevation. But between the cold frames and the 'sun room' as we referred to our enclosed deck, we had the space to start enough seedlings for bountiful summer crops. It was time and daylight that we were low on. Six of the cold frames had wonderful leafy greens growing. We had planted kale, arugula, broccoli, spinach, leeks, maché and carrots. These were greens that were supposed to be cold hearty, and the carrots as a root crop should also do well. We planted those a bit late in the season (October instead of August), but they still germinated, and had been tiny up until now. Now they were all somewhat bigger, except for the maché, which was growing phenomenally. We ate a lot of maché. We would not really know the outcome of the carrots for a couple of months.

With spring approaching, time was against us. There was a great deal of work to be done to get prepared, and little time to do it. I do not know how Tom and I ever thought we could handle all of this ourselves. We were thankful for the help, even Jake's help.

Sam looked at me and asked "why didn't we use Rita's greenhouse this winter?"
I explained, "well, we need to talk to her about it, and start using it now. The problem was that we're not in the right agricultural zone to grow veggies all winter in an unheated greenhouse. And her greenhouse requires electricity for the heater. We couldn't spare the electricity to keep a large, full size green house heated all winter. So really, her greenhouse wouldn't have been that helpful. We would have been better off using basic hoop houses, since they're not designed to be heated, and their smaller size helps to keep any warmth closer to the plants than a large, unheated greenhouse would."
Terry looked confused and stated "I thought greenhouses got enough sun in the winter to keep things warm overnight."
"Well, in zone 5 or 6 and below, a layer of glass is just not enough protection through the cold winters." I explained. "In the colder zones it would require multiple layers to keep

221

enough heat in."

"So what's the point then?" Terry asked.

"Well, first of all, like I said, many greenhouses are designed to be heated in winter. And under the current circumstances that's just not possible. However, the more important point is that although we couldn't use it the last two months, we can use it *now* to get a head start on quite a few seedlings for transplant later. You can also use the greenhouse for our cold hearty crops that we grew in the cold frames. We just didn't get around to it this last winter, we had so much else to do, and some of our cold frames still went empty. But with the extra help, we can mange now" I explained.

"Maybe we can recruit Rita and Charles to help?" Sam asked.

"Maybe," I answered. "We'll talk with them when we get them their water" I answered.

Today, for whatever reason, I felt annoyed. I felt like everyone was counting on me for answers, and everyone was questioning me about our actions. Somehow I was in charge of the gardening, and I had to tell everyone what to do. I did not like that responsibility. If things did not work out, then it would all fall upon me. I felt I needed to pass some of the burden on to everyone else.

"Tell you what, I have some books that have extremely useful information. While you are at the town meeting, I'll go through them and figure out which one each person should read."

"With all the work, we do not really have time for reading" Tom complained. I think he really just preferred asking me, but I did not have all the answers and I did not want to be the go to person.

I responded rudely "and I do not really have time to explain everything, so make time." I rushed off to the bathroom to clean up. I don't know what my problem was; maybe I was craving my time alone today.

Everyone took off for the meeting. Barter days kind of morphed into barter days plus town meeting, plus church. It made it easier on people to only have to leave home once a week for a shorter period of time. As bicycles were breaking, more people were walking, some people had to walk 15 miles to get to the meeting. Thus the reason for moving the meeting to noon, that way people could still walk in daylight. Although things had remained calm in our little town, except for a few stragglers that got rejected at the road blockades, we knew things in the outside world were changing, and changing fast.

I went out to check on the goats, both does were pregnant, and Marshmallow seemed to be happy. We got lucky with the pregnancies. After checking some books, it was actually passed their breeding season, but it still worked out. We figured the Does got pregnant sometime in late January or early February, so their kids should be ready in late June or early July. So we had a few more months before that excitement began. We also figured that if Marshmallow was nine months old at end of January, then we should eat him soon, at least before March was over. Once he was more than a year old, the meat was just not as tasty, and not as tender. I think John also suggested we eat him in March. We still had plenty of beef filling up our cupboards and freezers. But given the circumstances we could never have too much meat – if it was properly stored. I needed to add Marshmallow to the list of things to get done. That was not going to be an easy project.

Chicks take 21 days to hatch, and the chickens started sitting on eggs only a few days ago. So by the end of this month we should have some baby chicks running around. That meant by April, our egg production should improve as well, as we were not going to have as many chickens sitting on eggs and not producing. I kind of wish we had an incubator so we could get more baby chickens, but we never did manage to get one, so we are dependent on mama hens. At least they were doing their job. Our bunnies were reproducing too, but that was a project that Tom and Terry took on. I was with Sam on that one, I too thought they were cute.

Altogether, things should be okay on the meat side, we just needed to make sure that we had enough vegetables, fruit, and hopefully some nuts.

The trees should produce something this year. I decided to go check on them and see if buds are forming yet for the leaves. It was a beautiful March day, I enjoyed the peacefulness, I just hoped it would last. It was a short walk to the trees, and down hill. They seem to be doing very well. I needed to check my notebook to see when I should remove the tree guards. They appear to have worked well to keep the wild bunnies off of the trees. Unlike previous years, we did not see any deer this year, but that could be due to the increased hunting for food. Tom and I had agreed that we would not count on being able to hunt food, but that we would not give up on it either. Anything we got from hunting would be considered a bonus. We figured we should primarily store our food instead, as the increased numbers of hunters would decrease the wild game population. Considering that we did not see any deer at all since we got up here full time, something told me that the deer population had been greatly reduced, if not annihilated.

I inspected each tree, and the tree guards used to keep animals from eating the bark, and everything looked fine. The almond trees were painted white with the least toxic paint we could find as per the transplanting instructions, but we still put a tree guard on them just in case. We figured we could never be too safe, especially since we were going to be dependent on that food. There were indeed buds on the trees, so that was good news. If they flowered, we might get some almonds this year. We might also get some plums and cherries, I thought to myself. I then walked over to the walnut trees. They were planted in a separate area because they produce a toxin in the soil that prevents the soil from being used to grow other things nearby, and we did not want any of the animals near them either for that reason. I walked over to the walnut trees, the walnut trees looked intact as well. I then walked back inside to find my orchard book, and read about tree guards. The dogs seemed disappointed that I did not throw their Frisbee.

Let's see, ventilation, yep, check, no worries, there. Growth? I didn't see any trees grow into the guard, so that should be fine. Oh, here we go, maintenance... oh, okay, I don't have to do anything provided the trees have not outgrown them. Well, that resolves that issue. I got up to put the book away, and as I walked by the back door, I saw Rita and Charles coming up to the house. I placed the book on the counter and opened the door to meet them. Compass and Velcro jumped on the opportunity to run outside and greeted Rita and Charles with excitement before I even got out the door.

"What brings you two over to this side?" I asked.

"Well, we wanted to chinwag about watah" Rita explained.

"Yes, we figured you needed some. We were going to come by and get your barrels so we can start filling them up" I told her.

"Oh, thanking yourselves greatly soh much, we hairlairh appreciate it. We figured if you didn't have enough solaaar powah, we could take ah trip to Roy's creek."

"Oh, that's a long walk. No, we'll happily filter some water for your drinking needs, and fill up your other water as well. Just bring the water barrels over and we'll get started today" I stated.

"Oh, thanking yourselves greatly!" Rita said in her typically excited tone.

"You know, we wanted to ask, do you have plans for your greenhouse this year?" I finally got around to asking about the greenhouse.

"Well, we actually wanted to chinwag with you about that as well. You knoh, one has limited seeds, soh the entire greenhouse will prolly not be useful to us, but maybe we can wok togethah, exchange some labor and seeds, and we could shaaare the teah and crumpets?" Rita was pondering what to do.

"That could work, but how many are we looking to share with? We already have 5 people here" I mentioned. Charles looked at me, and quickly responded "The church has made it clear that there is no extra food, so people have been sharing at church, but that is it. I know you haven't attended, and I don't need to know why. But everyone knows that the church can only offer a shelter, and even that is limited."

"I'm sorry Charles, I didn't mean to imply that you would just give our food away. We have just been a tad stressed around here with the food situation and all." I did not tell them about the cow or the milk, and I think everyone always reported less than they really had, it was really a survival thing I guess.

"Don't you worry about it Rachel. If you remember from when you used to attend church, I always stressed the need for people to have emergency supplies on hand, and from what I gather, a lot of people listened" Charles consoled.

"Thank you again, and I'm sorry for my implication. So yes, we need to get started with planting. I had just set aside a bunch of seeds, you know. Let me go inside and grab some, and I'll give them to you to get started. We can just make it a shared greenhouse, and we'll transplant the starts on to our own land, and go from there. With seven people tending to it, we should have more than enough. Just give me a minute, let me go get those seeds." I quickly ran inside and grabbed a large zip lock bag out of the kitchen drawer. Then I went to the mini refrigerator and picked out the bag of seeds I had picked out earlier to start planting with. I took out a third of the packets, making sure to include variety, and placed them in the large zip lock. Then I went back outside and handed them to Rita.

"Woh, there's fancy 30 packets of seeds in here!"

"Yes there is, and they are all heirloom and organic. I spent quite a bit of money on my seed collection. Now, they are a couple years old, so I don't expect high germination rate. But we will be saving our own seed this year, so that will set us up for next year" I explained.

"You got it! Doh you have an aaareah designated for seed plants?" asked Rita.

"Not yet, I still need to work out those details. But I plan to" this a question in my mind as well.

"Guess we will figure that out when the time comes" Charles added.

"Hey, you know, we could use some help with our goat. We are going to be turning him into meat in the next few days. If you would like to help, we would happily provide some canned goat meat for you, or maybe I could make goat jerky? Hmm... I don't know if that's practical, but I will look it up" I finished.

"Oh, you found ah male hoohf trottah?" Rita asked excited.

"Yes, and both our does are pregnant, so we should have milk again starting in three or four months, depending on how much the little ones drink, but should still be plenty for all of us" my voice had excitement in it.

"That's spiffing news, and we wouldn't mind some fresh meat, we would love to be of assistance!!" Rita exclaimed.

"Great, why don't you bring over your water barrels, and we'll figure out the butchering details then" I suggested.

"Great, see you shortly." Rita and Charles took their seeds and headed back to their place.

I walked back inside. I felt that we really should not share our goat meat, or chevon meat. But in reality, we had so much beef still, that we could certainly spare it, and we were going to need help with the butchering. I had never done a goat before, but I think that Terry mentioned he hunted a few times, and Tom has been hunting, so they should know about this. I then picked up the tree book off the counter, put it back on the bookshelf in our bedroom, and dug out books about goats and butchering, and started to read it to see if I could learn anything useful.

The dogs got excited and ran to the living room window. I must have gotten lost in my reading as some time had gone by. I wanted to check on the blueberry bushes before everyone came back, so I quickly ran out the back door and walked to where we had planted them. We planted them last mid January, and added acid mix to the soil since they like acidic soil. We read that was the way to establish their roots. Then that spring we pinched off any flowers as recommended to help root establishment. So this year we should have some blueberries. We also planted blackberries by the street, we figured they would make a good fence line. We did not check on them often, though maybe we should. The blueberry plants appeared to have buds on them as well. This was good; we might get some blueberries this year. I then hurried back inside to find out what happened at the weekly meeting.

"How did it go?" I asked in anticipation.

"Not good, they want us to double up on security at the tree road blocks. There are rumors that the guard have been going to smaller towns" Tom described.

"What for?" I asked.

"Apparently to eat their food, sleep on their mattresses, and shoot their animals" Tom said in a dead serious tone.

"What!?" I asked.

"Yeah, apparently one of the towns east of Springfield has been attacked" Terry told me.

"What did everyone decide to do? Are we supposed to shoot the guards?" I asked.

"Well, we are going to try not to, but we might have to" was Terry's very matter of fact response. I looked at all of them to see if they were serious, and unfortunately they were. I felt my adrenaline start pumping.

"Why can't they just leave us alone?" I asked in a frustrated voice. I was not really expecting an answer, it was more of a rhetorical question. But Tom felt obliged to answer, "probably because the government does not have any way to feed their soldiers, so they are stealing from the people. It's what governments have always done."

"So how many shifts will all of you have to do?" I asked. Extra guard shifts meant less time working on the land. Tom responded "at least three a week, maybe more. And there is more bad news. Word got out that you're here. Some people are ticked, so you have to do guard duty now as well, double the shifts to make up for lost time."

I was happy to hear that I could leave my own home now, and said "that's fine, I have wanted to do guard duty, because it's only fair I do my share for the town."

Tom was not convinced, I could tell. "Well, I don't think it's a good idea, because you are more likely to be recognized by the guard if they are the ones that approach the road. The whole town could be held accountable for you being here. But no one at the meeting believed me, so they insisted you do it."

"Really, I don't mind, when is my first shift?" I asked. Sam responded, "actually, you are up now, so you need to go to the west tree road block."

"Is there anything else I should know before I leave?" I asked. Terry responded "just tell us what you need done around here." I thought about it for a few minutes then determined "Rita and Charles will be back shortly with their water barrels. I set aside several glass water bottles of filtered water, you can use those to refill their drinking water. Then find a way to fill up the rest of the barrels with regular water. I also need someone to check the salt in the water softener system in the pump house, it's bound to be low by now. Oh, and then our drinking water bottles need to be refilled with filtered water, that should accumulate plenty of filter waste water for watering. So then that needs to go out to the trees and shrubs. You also need to make plans for Marshmallow, considering Rita and Charles volunteered to help... hold on..." I quickly headed to where I left the book I was reading and handed it to Terry as I said "and here is a book on how to do it." I then walked to the kitchen to pack up some jerky, and some nuts. I also filled up a water bottle, grabbed my handgun and put it in my shoulder holster, then grabbed my .308 rifle, and slung it over my shoulder.

"Do you care which bike I take?" I asked Tom.

"Nope, help yourself, and be careful okay?" Tom responded, I could tell in his eyes he really did not want me to go.

"Of course, I'll be fine, I'm just glad I'm finally able to help. Don't worry about me, I promise I'll be fine, you now I can take care of myself." I gave Tom a kiss on the lips, then headed outside and went to the garage to get a bike. With Jake staying with us, the garage was a lot more organized than I had ever seen it. I picked up the first bicycle, locked the garage, and took off to the west tree roadblock to go to my guard duty.

It was a beautiful bike ride. I had not left the property since we got here, that was when, August? Wow, I have been a prisoner of my home for seven months! The scenery along the ride was absolutely beautiful. Some trees already had leaves, and the air was crisp and clear. There were no planes in the sky, only birds. I was excited about my guard duty. As much as I love our property, getting out occasionally was a necessity.

I arrived to the tree roadblock location and at first did not see anyone. I looked around, and found a spot I could hide the bike. I moved it over, then started to look around.

"Rachel?!" I turned and saw Marty right behind me.

"Hi Marty, I was wondering who I would be standing guard with."

"So it is true, you're alive" Marty said in excitement.

"Yes, it's true, and I'm here to help guard, I was told it's my shift right now." I stated.

"Well good to see you!" Marty came up to me and gave me a hug.

"Who else is here, there are supposed to be four of us?" I asked.

"Yes, Jenny and Steven are here, do you know them? Jenny! Steven! Come on out, it's just Rachel, she's our fourth guard!" I saw two people come out from behind the bushes on the other side of tree. I did not recognize them. When they approached, I put out my hand and introduced myself.

"Hi, I'm Rachel, I don't think we've met." They brought out their hands but did not say anything. Jenny was younger, I would say late teens or early twenties. She did not look happy. Her straight black hair was well made up, and I could tell she was wearing makeup, and a lot of it. Why a person would need makeup for guard duty, beats me. Steven was older, maybe mid 40's, and had a black beard. Actually, so did Marty. Perhaps razors were not easily obtainable? Perhaps the boys at home should stop shaving to better blend in? Ooh, I did not like beards, and I did not want Tom having one. But as I looked at these men, I thought that might be a good idea.

"Aren't you wanted for murder?" Jenny's voice was snotty. I could tell she did not like me from the start. This was not good. "No, it's a different Rachel. I'm Rachel Wagner, the Rachel wanted for murder is Rachel Roberts, I just happen to look like her, and have the same first name." I did not like this. I quickly turned to Marty and said "what's the protocol here?"

"Well, Rachel Wagner." Marty had a smirk on his face. He knew better, but he was not going to say anything. However I was not sure Jenny believed me either - probably not. "We usually put two people on each side of the tree. The natural shrubs and foliage are perfect camouflage, and as you discovered it works, you did not see us. Anyway, we put two people on each end, and we watch the road from both directions"

"Why both directions?" I asked.

"In case someone broke through on the other end and we don't get radio contact first. Anyway, you can work this side with me, and Jenny and Steven can work the other end. And we wait until something happens, or our relief comes." Marty made it sound simple, or maybe it just was simple.

"Okay, should I move my bike?" I figured I should at least ask if there is a procedure for bicycles. Marty continued to answer my questions. "Oh yes, let me show you were we put those."

Marty walked me over off the side of the road, and showed me where the other bikes were. I ran over to grab my bike and moved it with the others, then found the spot in the high shrubs that was more like a tunnel. You could see the other side of the road through the shrubs. Marty explained the process to me of what to do should someone arrive. There were different protocols for people on foot and those in cars.

My four hours went by uneventfully, other than Marty talking my ear off. Two of the reliefs showed up at the same time, and replaced Jenny and Steven. I did not know them either, and decided not to show myself. The incident with Jenny was bad enough. Marty's relief was Charles. I was relieved to see someone that actually knew I was already here. Then Sam showed up to relieve me.

I rode my bike back wondering if Jenny would turn me in. She clearly did not like me, and I am positive she did not believe my story, even though I thought I was pretty convincing. When I got back, I told Tom of the situation. He did not seem happy about it either, but there was nothing we could do at this point. To my relief, all the chores were done, and Marshmallow was gone too. Apparently they had decided to just get it done and over with since pasture was still scarce, and it was easier to manage two goats than three. Tom had shot Marshmallow in the back of the head per my book, and made sure it was quick and painless. They quickly removed his head and testicles. Jake showed everyone how to save the hide, and showed everyone how to gut his way. They were successful with the gutting, did not contaminate anything, and managed to save the lungs, heart and other organs for the dogs. They were also able to save rennet from the stomach of the goat. I was kind of grossed out by the rennet. It did not look so appealing when it was in it's original form. They then hung the meat in the root cellar, making sure to cover it with plastic wrap to prevent any pests from flying into it. We would have to wait a week in order for it to age. I was kind of sad that I did not get to say bye to Marshmallow, but then I was relieved that I did not have to help with the slaughter. I was honestly attached to that sweet goat. Well, I guess that's life on the farm I thought. I hoped he had a comfortable life for the short time he was here.

I decided to volunteer to make dinner since I had worked the least today, and headed to the kitchen. I decided to make stew, and grabbed some dehydrated vegetables, along with some canned beef, and threw it in a crock pot. I then decided to speed up the process by boiling water for the crock pot. It was so nice having a real stove again. I also decided to heat up some water to make green tea. Maybe that would help me relax a little. I hung out in the kitchen thinking about Jenny, how her makeup looked so out of place to me. Perhaps it was because I had been imprisoned on my own land and had not really had contact with other people. Would that cause me to view make up as odd? I did not know. The water started boiling, so I poured it into my cup with my tea bag, then I found a jar of honey and added just a little to my tea. I wrung the tea bag with my teaspoon and thumb, and threw it in the compost bucket. I poured the rest of the hot water in the crock pot and turned it on. I added all the ingredients, and put a pot of rice on the stove.

I took my tea over to the living room and sat with the rest of the gang. Jake had started to hang out in our home for the evening news and dinner, then he would go back to the garage. I let everyone know that dinner should be ready in a couple hours, and we all sat there, exhausted as usual. "What are we going to do if someone turns in Rachel?" Jake's question was surprising, considering he once threatened to turn us in. Granted, he had never brought it up since, and we never insisted he leave again. But the subject was best left untouched. "Not sure really. If we get wind that someone turned any of us in, I guess we would get our BOBs and go" I answered. "What is a BOB and where will we go?" Terry's question was an honest one, as he and Sam were fugitives too. Tom decided to answer their question "Bug Out Bag. We have a bug out location. It has a mini wood stove, some walls, a roof, a couple of cots, and a couple of sleeping bags. Our BOBs have MREs and freeze dried food. We put a water filter up there too; just need to get water from a creek that is about a half mile away." "You have a bug out location?" Terry seemed surprised. "Well, it's nothing fancy" I answered, then added "we talked about buying a used travel trailer and putting it out there in lieu of a plywood structure. But money was not really readily available enough, so we just put some plywood pieces together, and threw some things in there."

Tom interrupted "the question is, do I go with you guys, or do I stay? No one really knows me, my picture is not out there, I have a different last name from Rachel, and I have never been finger printed."

"Well, someone has to stick around and take care of the animals and the garden." I said.

"Well I would help" Jake was quick to answer.

"So if Tom and Jake stayed here, they could get things done around here. Though it wouldn't be easy; it would be a lot more work if it's just two people." I stated.

"We could recruit Rita and Charles to help with the gardening or whatever, depending on when this would occur." Tom suggested.

"Tom, do we still have the hand held hams? We would need to keep up communication somehow" I asked.

"Yes, we still have them, we have been using them this whole time, but we can send you up with one" Tom answered.

"Maybe we should re-pack our BOB's tonight, just in case?" I suggested.

"That's a good idea. Plus we need to make a BOB for Terry and Sam anyway" Tom suggested.

"Since you're not going, can they use your BOB?" I asked before thinking.

"What if I have to bug out somewhere too?" Tom asked.

"Good point. We can use their packs and make their own" I said.

With that, we all got up and started to collect supplies for Terry and Sam. Fortunately we never used any of our MREs, and hardly any of the freeze dried foods. The MREs were strictly for emergency use only, and we always held the freeze dried food as the last thing to eat because it lasted so long. We collected two of our watertight water bottles, and suggested that Terry pack up three days worth of clothes. Tom went to the garage to find the box with extra toothbrushes, toothpaste, floss, and brought those back. Then we brought out our BOB's and unpacked them to make sure that we could set up Terry and Sam with similar gear. We did not have enough paracord, but that was okay, as I had some in my BOB and I would be going with Terry and Sam. We did manage to put together a mini first aid kit, though we already had a larger one out in our bug out location. We also found extra pocket knives, emergency candles, flashlights, and a mini water filter that could be used to pump up water from creeks. Sam came back during this time and we asked her to also pack three days worth of clothes, then showed her what was in her BOB. We then closed them up, and had Terry and Sam put them on to make sure they weren't too heavy.

"How long of a walk is it?" Sam asked.

"About half a day at a slow pace" I answered.

"That's not too bad" Sam stated, though her tone of voice did not sound too confident.

"No, it's not. We tried to be realistic." I tried to reassure her.

I felt embarrassed as I was the only one using feminine products in the house. So when they were taken out of my BOB and left out for a while, I was kind of uncomfortable. We knew Sam did not need any because she never asked for them. I wanted to get out of the room so I rushed to the kitchen to check on the stew, and it looked ready. I served up five equal portions, put spoons in the bowls, and went back to the living room with two plates at a time.

"Maybe we should watch the news, see if there's anything useful." I really wanted my mind off my feminine products. I did not know why I was so embarrassed by them.

"Good idea Rache," Tom went to turn on the TV. We had static for a short while, then the news finally came on after we settled with our bowls and began to eat.

An exciting announcement today! Due to some gang related violence, word has been received that some people are scared to leave their homes. Some people fear that the perpetrators will not be caught. This problem is to be resolved immediately, as all armed guardsman are now equipped with remote vital signs monitors. What that means, is that if a guard gets killed, and his vital signs change, the authorities are immediately notified. And with the latest RFID technology, the guard can be found within a few minutes. The technology also tracks a history of the guard's vital signs and location! That means that anyone who shoots and wounds or kills a guard member, will be found within a short time. The monitors are designed to detect any dramatic changes in vital signs, and will automatically signal for help, even if the guard is still alive. This system was also designed to include a tracking system, in an effort to help find our injured and fallen. The monitors can be detected anywhere in the world. Additional guardsmen have been hired to man the helicopters that will rush to the locations where trouble may be detected via the vitals monitors. With this added protection, you should not be afraid to leave your home because help is just around the corner.

We all looked at each other. Really, this is what it had come to? The news anchors were now talking to each other, though it was clearly still scripted.

"This is wonderful news, people should feel safer knowing that any injury to our guardsmen will result in immediate action."
"Yes, this will allow for capture of anyone who intends to injure those who protect us."
"I'm very happy about this latest technology."
"Me too."
"In other news, guard will be travelling to small towns that did not cooperate with the initial order to evacuate. The guardsmen will be making sure that any people remaining in those small towns are not in need of any supplies. Please welcome these guardsmen, and remember, if there's trouble, help will follow their vital signs monitors. We have been notified that the guardsmen also have the ability to hit a switch on their wrists that will alert for help right away, without their vital signs changing."

A commercial came on advertising the great changes the new president is bringing. Tom was clearly angry as he stated "so basically they just said that guardsmen are coming to small towns, and if you shoot them, they'll bring in a copter and shoot you."

"Yep, sounds like it" Terry responded.

"You think they really have the monitors?" Sam asked.

"Would not surprise me, remember my ID card, that had technology in it we didn't even know about" I said.

Tom was still upset. "Yeah, that's true. So now what? We just let the guards do what they want? You heard on the hams, they are destroying towns!"

Jake interrupted Tom's rant "speaking of which, we should turn on the hams after the news, there might be better info out there."

When the news came back on, they reported a story of how the monitors work, and showed images of helicopters showing up and arresting people. The images were awful and did not look real. Actually, I know it was not real; all the people were actors, and it was all too organized. If they thought that is how things are really going to look, they were mistaken.

"I wonder how much time before the helicopters arrive" Terry said.

"I was thinking the same thing" Sam added.

"Really, you could still get away with it, provided it wasn't on your property, and you had a fast getaway." Tom's response did not surprise me, always thinking ahead about how to deal with a situation.

"I was just thinking the same thing" Jake added.

"I'm really glad we repacked our BOB's, we might be using them soon" I was thinking out loud more than anything.

I got up to clean up the dishes and take them to the kitchen. As I did so, I remembered the dogs needed to be fed, so I took care of that as well. Once the dogs were happy, I went outside with them to lock up the animals. Darkness had snuck up on us. Daylight was still a little short. I realized that Marshmallow was gone, and that saddened me. Today was just not a good day for me. I tried to think of the positives, but really could not. After I counted all the chickens, and locked up all the animals, I headed toward the cold frames. Jake was already closing them, so I went back inside.

I did not sleep well again; actually, no one did. The stress level had increased significantly. We all felt like something was going to happen. I ended up getting a little shut eye, but not much.

I woke up in a bit of a better mood than yesterday. Perhaps things would not be so bad.

I thought about finding something that I could offer to Jenny so that she would not turn me in. Bribing Jake worked at first, so why not Jenny too? But what did I have that she would want? Probably nothing. And I did not even know where she lived. I could find her at barter days, or a town meeting, but that was a week away.

We still burned wood in the wood stove at night, and it was still hot this morning. So I put on a tea kettle on the stove and added a little wood. It was a chilly morning, but no where near what it was just a couple weeks ago. Spring was here and summer was on its way. That alone made me happy.

I tended to all the animals, and I was excited to see some eggs that the chickens were not sitting on. I then returned to make breakfast and feed the dogs. I was excited for omelet's, since we had them so rarely now. I found garlic, and some canned spinach, but I knew an omelet would not taste good with canned spinach. After a few minutes of thought, and after a few sips of coffee, I decided to make a quiche instead. I got out a big bowl and threw in a bunch of eggs, along with the canned spinach and garlic. I turned on the oven to preheat, and then grabbed a jar of canned goat milk. I poured in about half, then put the rest of the jar in the refrigerator. I whisked it all together, threw it in a quiche dish without a crust, and put it in the oven and set the timer for 45 minutes.

Everyone was having coffee, double cups, as everyone looked tired. Jake knocked on the door, and we let him in.
"I was going to tend to the animals this morning, but someone beat me to it" he complained.
"You can uncover the cold frames when it warms up a little" I solved his problem quickly.
"Sure, no problem." He picked up a mug, a heaping spoonful of instant coffee, and poured hot water in it. He stirred it, and sat down sipping away with everyone else.

"Will someone get the quiche out of the oven when the timer goes off? I want to get out of my pajamas" I said.

"No problem Rachel, we got it." Sam responded.

I went into the master bedroom and picked out what to wear, then went to the bathroom to brush my teeth and wash up. I got dressed and came back out just as the quiche was being taken out of the oven. Sam had cut it into five slices and put them on plates. I grabbed the forks and helped her carry them to the living room.

As we were eating, the dogs got excited and we looked out the window. John was riding up on his horse, and fast. Tom ran out to meet him, and after a short talk, he ran back inside. "Rachel, Terry, Sam, get your BOBs you have to go, now!" he yelled. I did not ask, I knew. I ran to the master bedroom, got my holster on, grabbed my gun and put it in the holster. I had already dressed for the occasion as I had a feeling something might happen. I grabbed my camo jacket, and my backpack, and started to head out to the living room, but Tom stopped me.

"Rachel, they're already here, we have to hide you guys."

"What do you mean they're already here?" I asked, worried.

"I just saw them out the window. If you run out the back door, they might see you. It's too risky" he said quickly. "The dryer!" I yelled quietly. Tom thought about it for about three seconds then said "get it ready. I'll get Sam and Terry over there shortly, duck where there are windows, better yet, crawl over there."

I got on the floor and started to crawl. I never thought I would be crawling to hide with a pack on my back in my own home. This just did not feel right. Once I got to the hallway I was able to stand up, since the only window there was covered with blinds and we never opened them. I put my pack down, and proceeded to pull the dryer out. I managed to get it out quickly, and then opened the hatch door that led to under the house. I was a little worried about unzipping the belly, as I had a flashback to when we first bought this place, and it was infested with mice. I told myself that things were different, and I stood a better chance with rodents then armed guardsmen and helicopters. I unzipped the belly and saw nothing. I grabbed my pack and gently lowered it underneath, then I lowered myself

238

down. I did not realize this at first, but Terry and Sam were right behind me. Terry came down next, and then helped Sam come down. Tom then lowered their packs, and was about to zip us up when I quickly said "get rid of the plates, there's 5 pieces of quiche out there, make it two." Tom nodded then zipped up the belly as things got dark. I heard him put the hatch down, then move the dryer into place.

I dug into my pack and got my flashlight out. I turned it on so that we could see where we were. No mice, or rats, I felt relieved. We very quietly moved over to a spot that looked more comfortable, and moved our packs next to each other. We then sat there in total silence. We heard Compass barking away. I am sure Tom would have to leash him up for this; probably Velcro as well. We heard what sounded like the front door opening, and we heard muffled voices. We really could not tell what they were saying, it was too muffled. It sounded like maybe two guards? Or three? We sat there quietly for what felt like forever. We did not dare move, we did not dare make a sound. We heard foot steps all throughout the house, back and forth several times, then more muffled voices, then silence.

We continued to wait under the house. Actually, we did not have a choice, we were locked in. There was no way to move the dryer out of the way from underneath, and there was a padlock locking the crawlspace door from the outside. Perhaps I should have thought about that before we decided to jump in. If Tom and Jake get shot or "arrested," then we would be trapped under the house. I started to have a mini panic attack but instead, I started deep breathing to calm myself down. When I heard foot steps again go through the house, I was partially relieved in hopes that it was either Jake or Tom. After a while I heard the dryer move, and then the hatch opened, and then Tom unzipped the belly and started to whisper to us.

"They are checking out the land right now, but they will be back inside, so you need to stay here for now. They are inviting themselves to stay, so I'm not sure how we're going to work that angle. Wish I could just shoot them, but if the vital signs monitor thing is true, then I can't take that chance."

"What are they looking for?" I asked.

"You. Someone turned you in." With that, he zipped up the belly, closed the hatch, and moved the dryer back in place. Damn Jenny, I knew it was her. She probably wants to use the reward credits to buy more makeup. I was furious. Why did people have to be so petty and brainwashed? Why ask useless questions? Well, we were stuck here for now, might as well make the best of it. I dug out the flashlight again, and turned it on. Then I looked in my pack for a deck of cards. I whispered to Terry and Sam "silent poker?" They nodded. I started to quietly shuffle the cards, and we played poker using hand signals for what felt like forever. I should not have been wasting my flashlight on poker, but we needed something to do to keep our minds off the situation, and this seemed to make the time pass. Plus, I had spare batteries in my BOB. Tom and I made sure we had enough batteries in our packs to last us at least seven nights, because that was the maximum amount of time we thought it would take us to get to the cabin from our city house if we had to do so on foot.

We continued to hear foot steps and muffled voices throughout the day and into the evening. We were tired, although we did not do anything but sit and play cards. The adrenaline must have worn off and we fell asleep. I do not know for how long, but the dryer moving woke us up. Tom lifted the hatch and unzipped the belly again.

"The guards are sleeping in the garage. They should be asleep by now, so we think you should be able to sneak out the back door, go through the orchard, and around the side of the house over to the Rita's place. Then go behind her place, and follow the tree line up the mountain until you hit the dense forest for cover. You should be clear to make your way from there."

I had moved to the hatch and started handing our BOB's to Tom, who took them one by one and put them in the dark hallway. I then tried to get up and out but could not. Terry crawled over and said to use his shoulders. With Terry's shoulders and Tom's help, I was able to get out. Sam was next, then we all grabbed on to Terry's hands to help him out.

"I'm not sure how much time you have so we'll make this goodbye short." Tom grabbed me, and gave me a hug, and a kiss. "I would give you Compass to take with you, but the guards might get suspicious tomorrow if they don't see him." I nodded, then asked "why are the guards in the garage?"

"They decided that they must stay here for a few days to make sure that it was a false report and that you really don't live here" he said.

"Let me guess, they are eating all our food" I whispered.

"Yep, and they sure have an appetite" he whispered back.

"Great. OK, well, we better get out of here. But, maybe you should visit Rita and Charles so they aren't surprised."

"They saw the guards here, I'm sure they know" Tom explained.

"Just in case – to prevent any accidental information..." I reiterated.

We donned our packs, and Tom opened the back door. We quietly and slowly stepped out on to the covered deck, then down the steps, and down the hill into the orchard. It was pitch black, and I knew we could not use our flashlights. It was a good thing I knew the lay of the land. We snuck away slowly since we could not really see much, and to try to make little noise. At least there was a little moonlight, which lit up the way slightly. We managed to get behind Rita's house, then on the side of her house, and started to head north. Once we made it across the road, and we were far enough away from our house, I dared to turn on a flashlight.

"Do you know how to get there?" Sam asked.

"Yeah. I have to find a specific creek, which is just north of here, up the mountain, among the dense forest. Once we find the creek, we have to follow it east a few miles until we find a specific rock formation. From there we head half a mile south of the rock formation. Don't worry, I can get us there safely" I said.

"It's just dark" Sam responded.

"I have a glow in the dark compass, so don't worry." Though I could tell from Sam's tone of voice that she was worried.

The hike took a long time, and we were tired. I had a warm coat and hat, but I was not sure about Sam or Terry. Their stuff was bought used, and most of it did not have tags to indicate the cold rating. It did not matter now, we needed to get to our destination. When we finally hit the creek, we stopped for a short while to rest and drink some water. We then picked up again to head east along the creek until we found the rock formation. I had to use my flashlight all along the creek, and I wondered if the batteries would go out. No worries though, as Sam and Terry had a flashlight readily available as well. So I would not have to worry about digging through my pack for batteries.

My pack was feeling heavy, and the Spring night cold was uncomfortable on my face, but we had to keep moving. We eventually found the rock formation that Tom and I carefully set up.

"We just have another half mile south from here, and we're there. I should warn you, it's nothing fancy, literally a bug out location" I explained.

"I'm sure it's better than the prison camps" Terry said adamantly. I looked at my compass and we started heading south. I was a little concerned about black bears as it was spring, so they were no longer hibernating. But Tom and I had done this route before, and we did not know of any bear dens. The night was peaceful, and the moon was trying to shine a little light through the trees. My flashlight all of a sudden went out and we stopped. Sam handed me hers and I turned it on.

"Guess we should not have wasted it on cards" I said.

"Well, we needed something to do" Terry replied.

We found the shelter and although dark, it looked untouched from when I last saw it. I unlocked the lock and immediately started a fire in the mini wood stove. We had set it up to be ready to light. That was a good idea to do, because it would have been hard to accomplish in the dark otherwise. Once the heat was started, I looked around for our camping light. Right where we left it. I turned it on and saw the cots were just as we left them as well.

"There might be some spiders, but otherwise, here's your crude shelter." I put my arms up as if to show off the shelter.

"We'll take it, though it looks smaller inside then on the outside, or is it just me?" Terry asked.

"Nope, it's not just you. It's double walled, there are sand bags in between the plywood, just incase we need some bullets to be slowed down. Tom wanted to do concrete, but we weren't sure the plywood would hold well enough with this design."

"You thought of everything" Terry said.

"No, but a lot. And really, this was Tom's idea, not mine. I thought he was crazy sometimes."

We organized ourselves and got out our packs. We had not eaten all day as we did not dare make noise under the house.

"CRAP!" I said.

"What's wrong?" Sam was concerned.

"Tom forgot to give me a handheld ham, we have no communication" I was disappointed.

"But Tom knows where this is at right?" Terry asked.

"Yeah, but still, that communication would have been very useful. What if the town gets taken over? We only have so much food, we need to know what's going on" I said, worriedly.

"Nothing we can do about it now." Terry seemed awfully calm.

"You're right, well, let's eat." I grabbed an empty small pot that had been saved in a plastic bag, and filled it with water from a glass water bottle that we stored there, then put the pot on the mini wood stove. It was not a cook stove, but I found a spot where I could put the small pot. Once the water began boiling, I opened a bag of freeze dried beef stew designed for four servings. I poured in the water, and mixed it with a spoon. While it was rehydrating in the hot water, I realized that we did not have bowls.

"Do you have your mugs? We will have to use those to pour the stew in for now." Terry and Sam dug out their metal mugs that we packed in their BOBs, and I got mine out. We then poured the stew and ate it slowly, as it was very hot.

After our stomachs were feeling nourished, I said "there are only two cots in here, but I think both of you might fit on one. It will be a tight squeeze, but at least you can keep each other warm."

"Yeah, we'll manage" Terry grunted. We fell asleep quickly. It had to have been early morning by the time we found the bug out location, and even later by the time we ate. I was guessing 4 am, but maybe earlier, maybe later? I did not know how to tell time well at night. It did not matter, we were here for now, and we had enough to sustain us for a about a week.

Chapter 10

Nature

We woke up to quiet, nothing. The mini wood stove had gone out. There was no sound, just silence. It was warm inside the bug out shelter. Our body heat in combination with the wood stove must have made it comfortable. Or maybe the sun warmed us up – it was not that cold out any more. Who knew what time it was. I crawled out of my sleeping bag and went to unlock the door from the inside. I stepped outside and looked at the sun, it must have been around noon.

Terry and Sam crawled out behind me and looked around. "Looks much different in daylight" said Sam. I looked around. It did look different, mainly because you could not see anything in the dark, but also because it looked different from when we set the place up. There was not as much greenery on the trees, but there was some new leaves breaking their way through, and the plywood shelter was built in a spot that Tom and I considered pretty well hidden between some conifers. The only way to find it would be to randomly run into it, though now with much less greenery around, it seemed to stand out a little more. It looked pretty sad - just painted pieces of plywood screwed together, with more plywood as a roof. The shape was odd, but we did not have a choice. The design was intended for ease of building, rather than aesthetics.

"Yeah, it does look different" I said after looking around. Then added "I'm going to run up to the creek to wash our cups from last night, and to get some water, maybe freshen up a bit. Would anyone like to join me?" I asked.

"Yes, of course" Sam replied.

"Grab your toothbrushes, and I recommend a wash cloth, the creek water is cold!" I directed.

"What do you use to bring the water in?" Terry asked. That reminded me, "oh, my BOB has a plastic foldable water container with a handle. Should fit a gallon plus. We might be making a few trips."

"Is there a way to heat the water?" Sam asked.

"Yeah, but I am not sure we want to use our fuel for bathing. We might need it for cooking. We don't know how long we'll be here, so we should probably conserve as much as we can" I responded.

We gathered our few things, and I locked the plywood with a padlock, then went on our way. We managed to get washed up, washed our cups, and then used our filter pump to draw water into our plastic carrying containers. Actually, Sam and Terry just watched me do it, as they seemed unfamiliar with these tools.

I noticed all morning that Sam did not seem her happy cheerful self. During washing up when Terry separated from us for a short while I asked "Sam, you don't seem yourself, are you alright?" Sam looked away at first, then after a long silence she responded "Yeah, I just had some bad dreams, I would rather not talk about it." I decided not to push the issue.

Once back at the shelter, we all wanted coffee, but burning the wood stove was too risky during the day due to the potential for the smoke being spotted. So instead, I got out a sterno can and heated up water that way, though it was hard holding the pot over it that whole time. We all took turns holding the pot, then had our instant coffee. I realized that we probably should have brought some folding chairs as we had no where to sit other than the cots, and we did not really want to be inside on such a beautiful day.

"So, now what?" Sam asked.

"Now we wait for the guards to leave our home, and for Tom to come tell us it's safe to return." I replied.

"I mean, what do we need to work on?" Sam clarified.

"Nothing, there's no garden here, no animals, It's just a hiding spot" I stated.

"That's going to be weird, to have nothing to do" said Terry.

"Yep, but we have at least a weeks worth of food, and if we have to, there's a cache buried here which has extra freeze dried packs and extra MRE's. We might have two weeks worth if we're careful. I suppose we could plant some seeds, but I'm not sure that's practical. I guess it can't hurt, other than maybe wasting seeds." I continued to ponder the idea after mentioning it.

Sam interrupted my thoughts. "At least it's warm enough that we don't have to run the wood stove in the daytime."

"Yeah, we wouldn't be able to anyway, someone would see the smoke, we probably shouldn't have lit it when we came in last night either, because we didn't know how late it was and if it would've burned out before daylight, but I was tired and not thinking clearly last night" I explained.

"We only brought three days worth of clothes." Sam's statement was more of a question.

"Well, we won't be working, so we should stay pretty clean. But we can always wash them in the creek, then hang them somewhere" I suggested.

"Are we reducing our food intake" Terry asked.

"We should, it will be tough, but it's just temporary. Plus we won't be active other than trips to the creek." I answered.

We seemed to have made it through our first day with out much difficulty. We decided to turn in early due to lack of daylight, and we were still tired from last night. We took turns using the shelter as a private place to clean up and change. Then we brushed our teeth, cleaned up our trash making sure not to leave anything out to attract wild animals, and turned in for the night.

I was woken up by screaming, I jumped out of my cot and reached for the

flashlight and gun. By the time I flicked the flashlight on so did Terry. I quickly realized that there was no danger and put my revolver back down on the floor. Terry was calming Sam down, she just had a bad dream. I was not sure if it was the flashlight lighting, or if it was Sam, but she looked severely distraught. I waited for Terry to get Sam back to the now, which took a bit it seemed. Once she was calm, I asked "do you want to talk about it? It might help you."

It seemed like forever, but Sam finally nodded her head and started talking. "I'm just having flashbacks of the camps." I waited for her to say more, but she was not volunteering any information, so I nudged a bit "did something happen at the camps...? Or was it just the overall experience?" I waited for Sam to make the next move, something horrible must have happened, she was clearly having a difficult time with it. Terry was just holding her close to him, I know he was not going to volunteer the information. So I tried again in a very soothing voice, "Sam, talking about it might help. You said yesterday you had nightmares the night before too. Maybe we can figure out the problem and avoid things that trigger the nightmares."

Sam finally opened up. "That's just it, running away from the guards is what I think triggered it. And then hiking it all the way here and living out in a hideout. It brought back the memories of when we first escaped." She paused for a while then continued. "There were some horrible things that happened at those camps. I felt like we were in concentration camps, except that my mind wouldn't allow me to accept that idea. Right before they tried to transfer us, they were still keeping the families together. There were some single women there, and at first I thought they were sluts because they were involved with the guards, but I realized later that they were forced to, and they had no one to protect them." She paused for a little longer, then kept going. "There was a nice couple we met there, a younger couple, your and Tom's age. Their names were Naomi and Eric. Naomi was a very pretty woman, but terribly nervous. I later found out that she was pregnant with their first child. Anyway, one of the guards had his eye on her, and she ignored him completely, I don't think she knew how to react to the situation. Well, one day, the guard seemed to act his usual pompous self, and when he saw it was just her and I talking, he came up to us and made advancements towards her, but she declined. Stated she was happily married. She was very nice about it too. Well he left, but something didn't seem right. A short while later, it was the four of us talking, and we were talking quietly because we were planning an escape, or at least trying to figure one out, when out of the blue, the guard came back, grabbed his gun, and just shot Eric right in the head, right in front of us!" At this point Sam had started to tear up, but she continued on. "Then he turned to Naomi and said… 'you're not married anymore'." At this point Sam burst into tears. I did not say anything, I did not know what to say, I knew the camps were ugly, but here was Sam, who experienced it first hand. She wiped her tears, and continued again "Naomi had kneeled next to Eric's body in tears, but the guard grabbed her, forced her to stand up, put a gun to her head, and told her he would kill her unless she followed him… Naomi just kept crying and refused… and then told him he might as well kill her, but instead… he dragged her by her hair and took her away... I felt so helpless, there was nothing we could do, he would have shot us all… And we never saw her again after that."

Sam was fully in tears and was struggling with her story. All I could say was "I'm so sorry" and I went to give her a hug. The three of us hugged for a long time, until Sam stopped crying. I was crying too. I finally decided to break the silence and said "I'm so sorry you had to experience that. I can't imagine what you're going through right now." We sat in silence, then eventually laid back down in our cots, and talked here and there about the camps some more, until we all fell back asleep.

We spent the next twelve days bored out of our minds. We played many card games, we took many trips to the creek. If Sam had any more bad dreams, she did not mention it, and we did not ask. We were cautious with our food consumption, and only ate small meals. We would literally split one MRE three ways. But we were not active, so we did not require as many calories for energy. We talked a lot, and I learned a lot about Sam and Terry; how they met, what they used to do for a living, etc. And they learned a lot about Tom and I. Terry was a plumber, but had also been an electrician apprentice, and Sam a home maker. They had known each since they were teenagers as they were both home schooled and met at a 4H event. Their children were long gone as they had moved to Panama, and they communicated only a little after that. Within a few days, we ran out of things to talk about, but we had to keep busy. We tried really hard not to allow our conversation to go to topics such as what if the guards shot Tom and Jake, or how will we know when it is safe? It was thoughts like that that caused anxiety, and we could not afford that.

249

We got used to sitting on the ground, but then Terry found some older logs that he brought over, and we used those as chairs. The weather was nice when the sun was out, but we stayed "inside" on cooler days. We did minimal bathing, mostly because of the temperature. It was not nice enough to go swimming in the creek, so we used wet washcloths to clean ourselves, and then washed the washcloths in the creek. We lost track of the days, and wondered if we should have done something to count them. But then we decided that this was really just temporary, and it did not matter how long we are here, as we could stay until we run out of food.

We used a small foldable shovel to bury our trash in, which mostly consisted of MRE and freeze dried packaging. We made do with limited cups and plates, and we learned to enjoy the walks to the creek for water, despite the mosquito's that were beginning to come out. We also buried our waste, though we used a bucket with enzymes to capture them, then we buried the bucket contents first thing in the morning, before our morning wash ups.

On the morning of what we thought was day twelve, I heard a diesel truck a short distance away. It had to be Tom. I rushed over in the direction of the running engine, and sure enough, it was Tom. As soon as he saw me, he parked and rushed over to hug me.
"You're okay!" I said as I was jumping into his arms.
"And so are you!" he said as he caught me.
"I was worried, the guards stayed that long?" I asked.
"They left two days ago, but I felt I should wait a couple days just in case. Then I learned this morning that they were seen leaving by people guarding the tree roadblocks, and then I knew it was safe to come get you. Did you have enough food?" he asked.
"Yes, we had to dig up the cache, but we had enough. Is it safe to return then?" I hoped he would answer yes.
"Yep, get your stuff" he said smiling. I ran back to the hideout and saw that Terry and Sam were already packing their packs. I did the same. I checked the mini wood stove, it was completely out. I then folded up the sleeping bags, and placed all the tools

that stayed at the hide out in plastic bags, including the cooking pot and eating utensils. When I came out, Tom had already checked the area around our hideout, and then helped us throw our packs into the back of the pick up, including our cache container since it would need to be restocked. I ran back to put the lock on our hideout, and then we all got in the truck, and Tom turned the truck around to go home. I sure was homesick.

During the drive Tom asked "did you encounter any problems on your way up?" I responded "no, we made it here just fine, though I didn't know what time it was. I lit the stove, probably shouldn't have, not sure if there was smoke the next morning." Tom quickly responded "there was, but that's how I knew you made it safely. I didn't see smoke the rest of the week, but figured what you just told me happened."
"What about you?" Terry interrupted.
"Oh, it was horrible, the guards wouldn't leave. They ate everything they felt like eating, and they kept us from tending to the animals. They were to put it nicely, assholes. They flushed toilets constantly, took super long showers, and didn't stop the water when soaping up like we do. They used the washer and dryer, they held no regard to water or energy conservation. They overloaded our septic once, but Jake and I used the outhouse to help relieve that problem."
"But they're gone now right?" I asked.
"Yeah, but if it were not for those stupid vital signs monitors on them, I would've shot them and fed them to the coyotes."
Tom had a lot of anger in his voice.
"How bad is the damage?" I was not sure I wanted to know.
"Well, they insisted we had alcohol, so they went through the whole house about 30 times. They threw our clothes out of drawers, and broke dishes too. When they found women's clothes there I had to use the excuse that my wife had died, and that I didn't have the heart to clean out all her things yet. They even took our razors. Really? Razors?" Tom was about to continue, but I interrupted "What!?" I could not believe what I was hearing. Tom continued "yeah, they weren't even apologetic, they were destructive on purpose. I wasn't able to try to use the ham radios. I didn't even take them out of hiding because I was afraid they would be taken by the guards. They

mentioned that they were under orders to confiscate any ham or CB radios because they were being used by 'domestic terrorists,' which I interpreted to mean that they were being used by the resistance movements we heard about."

I replied, "well you forgot to pack a ham radio for us you know."

Tom was quick to answer. "It wouldn't have mattered anyway. With all the trouble those guardsmen were causing us, there was no way I would've been able to try to contact you even if you had a radio with you."

"But aren't the guards here to protect us?" I asked sarcastically.

"Yeah, they sure are" Tom responded with the same sarcasm.

"What made them leave finally" Sam cut in this time.

"Yeah, so about that.... I have some bad news..." Tom hesitated for a moment.

"We're alive, you're alive, so that's good news so far, go ahead with the bad" Sam reassured him.

"Well, about three nights ago, they wouldn't let Jake or I leave the house, they wanted to chit chat and eat steak. They had Jake cook up the canned steak, and as he did that, I tried to leave to put the animals away, but they wouldn't let me. They insisted I lock up the animals when they felt like it..." I listened patiently as Tom continued. "A couple hours into the darkness, we heard a shotgun go off behind the house that got me into action. I grabbed a rifle and ran outside with Jake and the guards following..."

"and...?" I asked still patiently. Tom slowly continued, though I could tell he was getting angry. "Well, Rita happened to be helping with covering the cold frames because she knew our situation, and she saw that we hadn't tended to the animals yet. She finished covering the cold frames and was headed toward the goats when she heard one of the goats scream. So she ran to find that a mountain lion had killed one of our does. She ran back to her house, grabbed her shotgun, got Charles to grab his, ran back to the goat area, and attempted to shoot the mountain lion. But the cougar was already too far, and had taken off with a huge chunk of goat." Damn I thought, we are one pregnant doe less, and Marshmallow was gone. This was not good.

"So then what happened?" Terry urged Tom. Tom continued "well, naturally I was enraged, so I pointed my rifle at the two guards and told them that they were single handedly responsible for the death of one of our animals, and that now we wouldn't have enough of a way to sustain ourselves. I explained to them that there was nothing stopping me from shooting them because we were either going to die by starvation, or die via their helicopter buddies. And frankly, I didn't care to experience death by starvation."

"Were you really going to shoot them?" I asked.

"Heck yeah! But Jake, Rita and Charles all ran to stop me, otherwise I would have. They had to hold me back and Charles had to take my gun away from me... The guards saw it too, because they very quickly backed off and said that clearly the fugitives weren't there. Then they ran to the house to grab a bunch of jerky, then to the garage to get their stuff, and then they took off" Tom finished.

"And that was three days ago?" Terry asked.

"Yeah. I wanted to make sure they were gone. I immediately went to both the East and West tree road blocks to find out if they had left, but no one had seen them leave until this morning." We were silent for a while, then Tom added "the day after the incident, some people heard about it, and we had three groups of people stop by asking which way the cat went."

"Why? Where they worried it was headed towards them?" I asked.

Tom responded "Nope. Apparently there is no game left to hunt. All those hoping to eat from hunting haven't been able to find any game – it's all gone. That's probably why the cat came after our animals – there's no more game out in the wild for it to eat. Mountain lions usually aren't that bold. Anyway, Vince also came by, and he told me that they were surprised to hear there's still some possible wild food. Now they're all hunting for the same cat."

I wanted to tell Tom 'I told you so' but figured that wasn't a kind idea. He invested quite a bit of money on hunting equipment. I kept telling him that he could not count on being able to hunt wild game, because everyone would have the same idea. No one cared that it was not hunting season, people needed to eat. I figured the wild animal populations will be mostly wiped out that first winter. Guess they were not wiped out, there was still one cat out there.

The sight of our little mobile was such a pleasure. I did not mind camping out in the woods for almost two weeks, but the cabin was much better, even if we were a doe short. Yeah, guards for our safety? If you call that American, then I have a bridge in the desert to sell you.

Tom dropped us off right in front of the front door and said, "maybe you three should stay indoors just for a little while longer, just to be on the safe side. We'll refrain from opening the blinds too. And don't worry about your packs, I'll get them for you." We jumped out of the truck and ran inside. Compass and Velcro jumped all over us the second we opened the door. Oh, such happy moments. We managed to get the dogs down off of us, and sat down in our camping chairs. It was so nice having those again. Tom came in with our packs and directed "we should repack these immediately, we might be using them again, and we need to replenish our bug out cache too."

"I agree" I said. I then turned to Sam and Terry and asked "who's showering first?" We all stared at each other for a minute; we all longed for a hot shower. I decided to let them go first. "I need to talk with Tom a bit about the bug out location. Why don't you two go first?" Sam and Terry ran off to their room looking happy. I turned to Tom, "this was a good practice run, but we were bored out of our minds. Some books would have helped, maybe a board game, or even just our card game book so we could learn new games."

"That bad huh?" Tom said.

"Could have been worse" I replied.

"Guess there was no work to do there" Tom asked rhetorically.

"Nope, although we did plant some seeds. Not sure they'll do well with out care, but you never know, some squirrel or bunny will feel like it found gold." We both laughed about it, then Tom gave me another hug. It felt good to be back.

It did not take long to get back into routine, except that I no longer did guard duty at the tree road blocks. We decided that since I was turned in by one of the town's people, that we should let them believe that I am gone again. It worked out best that way through the winter, so we planned to do the same thing again. It was not that I did not want to put in my time for the town, it was just safer for me not to. Sam and Terry decided to continue shifts since the guard technically came after me, not them. Tom picked up extra guard duty shifts as the town was thinning out. Jake helped out a lot as well, though he decided it was time for him to go home.

Before the evening news one day, Jake stood up and said "everyone, I have an announcement to make." Terry accommodated him, "go ahead." We all stared at Jake waiting to hear what he had to say. After a long pause, he finally began. "I'm going to go home and work things out with my father, and no longer be a burden on you." Sam sympathetically responded. "Well, you're not really a burden anymore, you've been helping a lot."
"Yes, but my father has a lot more food, and I should be getting it from him and not you. But that's beside the point. What I really wanted to tell you all is: thank you for a very valuable lesson." We all stayed quiet. I was not sure what lesson we taught him, but I was not sure I wanted him leaving now either. As long as he stayed with us, I figured his dad would bring us more meat and milk. Or at least that was my assumption. And his help around the place has been valuable. Jake continued. "When the National Guard came here, and forced their way into your home, I realized what it must have felt like when I did the same to you. I realized what an awful person I was. For that, I am sorry. I can assure you that had I known then what I know now, I would have never dared to do what I did."

We all stared silently; we did not know what to say. This was not the Jake we knew before; he had changed, grown up almost. This was what his father had wanted for him. Jake continued, "I'll be leaving in a few days. I'd like to help you get some of the gardening and animal stuff worked out, and then I will head home."

After a long silence, Tom finally responded. "Jake, thank you. We accept your apology, and we will accept your help for the next few days. You too have taught us a lot, and your father will be proud." It was a very awkward, but good kind of moment. We quietly ate our dinner, and made jokes about how Jake should take the outhouse with him - just in case his dad was not so welcoming. Jake left three days later.

"Rachel, what seeds do you want me to use for the tomatoes?" came Sam's voice.

"I set all the seeds we are going to use over here." I walked to our makeshift dining room, and pointed to the seeds carefully laid out on the bins. I selected the oldest seeds, and those I saved myself. They had been refrigerated this whole time, so they should be just fine, but we really would not know for at least a week. "Plant two seeds instead of one at each spot, just in case germination is reduced" I ordered.

"Alright, so you want the tomatoes, the bell peppers, and the jalapenos all started in the sun room right?" Sam inquired.

"Yes, they can't tolerate the freezing, and we're putting the more cold tolerant stuff in the cold frames again" I clarified.

"You sure they will be okay in the sun room?" Sam asked.

"Yeah, it doesn't reach freezing temperatures there, they should be happy there" I said. Then I added "remember, we're saving the best of the best for seeds, but we'll choose those when it's time to transplant."

"What about the stuff in the cellar from last year" Terry asked.

"There's nothing left in there, but that's okay. There's still carrots in the ground from last year that we missed. I saw their tops start to grow, so those will produce seed for this year. We should be fine on carrot seed." I said that with a bit of sadness. Our food stocks were much smaller than anticipated. Between the extra mouths to feed, then the guards stealing so much of it, we were beginning to struggle again.

"Do you have the list of what goes in which cold frame?" asked Terry.

"Oh yeah, it's right here" I said as I pointed to the gardening notebook I had been keeping. It was best not to plant the same stuff in the same space every year. It should be rotated so that the harmful disease organisms and bugs do not accumulate in one area. I kept very meticulous sketches of where everything was planted last year, and where everything will go this year. Sterilizing the soil helped, as we did not have to be concerned about diseases for the starts since we killed all the insects in the soil first. But that killed the good bugs too.

The next few weeks we spent planting seedlings as I had mapped out in my gardening notebook. This year was easy, as it was the first rotation of crops. It would get tricky from here on out, especially with the crops intended for seed, as many of them required two years before they would produce seed. We also planted summer wheat, chicken forage, and grass for the goats. Since we were limited on space, we planted those over the septic field location. I learned it is safe for animals to eat food grown with our waste, but it is not safe for humans to eat food grown on human waste. We used goat and chicken waste as part of our compost. All the gardening was hard work yet again, but it felt good. Certainly better than sitting around at some hideout not knowing what was going to happen next. It was also a good feeling knowing that our work would result in an abundance of food.

Mid April we contemplated transplanting outside, the weather was certainly favorable, but we decided against it. The seedlings were not crowded yet, so there was no reason to move them, and there was still a risk of frost. We agreed to start transplanting in May, and do so slowly. Plus we had to harden off the plants in the sun room, as they were not fully exposed to the sunlight while inside.

With increased daylight, we had more energy for the solar batteries to store, which allowed us to increase our water usage. That too was a good feeling, because our seedlings needed water, and we needed water, and our neighbors needed water, the blueberry bushes and blackberries needed water, the trees needed water, and the animals needed water. Cumulatively, that is a lot of water. At least our septic seemed to be doing well; that was not something we were ready to deal with yet.

Trash was starting to become a problem however. On rainy days, we burned our trash in a burn barrel - at least the burnable stuff. We buried some things, mostly my feminine products. We did not know what else we could do with that so that it was safe and did not attract animals. So I buried them. It made me really hate that time of month. We did have all our cans washed out and sorted, and our plastic as well. Cardboard had been burned, food scraps were either given to the dogs, the chickens, or composted. Sam and Terry suggested we burn the plastic too, as that was common out in the boonies, but we disagreed with them, and argued that our health was more important, and we did not want to breathe in the toxic fumes from burning plastic.

We were also running out of toilet paper. Although we had installed bidets on our toilets, we never broke the habit of using TP. We would have to break that habit soon and switch to using bidets. Paper towels were something we were very carful using, mainly because it added more trash, and because I made them hard to find so we would not run out. I left dishcloths around everywhere instead. We had no facial tissues. Those were not a priority, so we used toilet paper or paper towels to blow our noses. We were also running low on dish soap and laundry soap. Tom and I planned for a year for two, not for five. We had more than enough toothpaste and floss for another year. We planned better for that, but our teeth were very important to us, especially with no dentist around.

Our routine was pretty much the same until summer. We continued to plant new seedlings, so that we would continue to have crops in the winter. So as we pulled up stuff from the cold frames, which were now opened for the summer, we added compost to the soil, and then re-planted with a different species of food. Our food tasted wonderful. Fresh vegetables, chicken, and our two cherry trees had a ton of flowers on them, so we hoped for lots of fresh cherries. The dehydrator was running almost daily with the greens from winter. I inspected my canner to make sure it was ready for when everything blooms. Jake had left and we had not heard from him since, but we knew he was fine.

"I don't know if I checked the days off the calendar correctly, but I think it's June 15th, or somewhere around there.

I may have forgotten to check off a day off or two" Tom explained as he looked at me worriedly.

"It happens, it's easy to lose track of time out here" I said reassuringly.

"I know, but we need to know time of year for the weather. I know it's still a little ways off, but I don't want our tomatoes to suffer from a freeze" Tom explained.

"Yeah, we're a ways off. Don't worry, as long as we are within a sort of time frame, we'll be fine. We'll just take care to protect everything early. We have a bigger problem now" I said.

"What do you mean?" Tom asked.

"There are a lot of earwigs in the garden. We need to get rid of them or they will destroy our corn, and who knows what else. Plus we have birds eying the cherry trees. And, I saw some hills, so we may have moles or gophers or some related kind of vermin. And I know there are still some wild bunnies; the dogs have been catching them for snacks." I said.

"At least we don't have to worry about dog food" Tom chuckled. "And if the dogs are eating them, then that'll keep the population down."

"I prefer the dogs eating the ones we breed, we don't know what kind of diseases the wild rabbits might have, remember the coccidian incident?" I asked. Tom must have forgotten, but I did not. One of the trips up to the cabin, the dogs caught a ground squirrel, and enjoyed it very much. Three days later, they were sick, vomiting, and refusing to eat. $400 later at the veterinarian's, we found out they had coccidian, and probably from the ground squirrel. Ever since then, I did not like the idea of the dogs eating wild animals.

"Yeah" he responded as he shrugged his shoulders. Clearly he did not want to discuss it further, but then changed his mind and added "we have some traps that Vince gave us, maybe we can trap them and get rid of them before they eat the garden?"

"Now that's an idea I like" I responded.

"What should we bait the traps with?" Tom asked.

"I don't know, but I have a rabbit book. Maybe that will offer us some info?" I suggested.

"Okay, I'll get the trap set up." He was about to leave, but I stopped him. "We still have to deal with the pests in the garden."

"Right, so what should we do?" he asked.

"We go in there and start picking them off by hand, and throwing the bugs to the chickens" I responded.

"Why don't we just let the chickens in the garden?" Tom's question seemed common sense. I thought about it, but reasoned against it. "They might destroy the crop, it's too risky."

"They're likely to eat the bugs, not the crop" Tom argued.

"It's too risky!" I said firmly. "There's nothing wrong with picking off by hand."

"In the city didn't we catch them in beer traps?" Tom kept arguing.

"We don't have any beer, so we can't use that trick" I said.

"Can we use something else?" Tom kept at it.

"I don't know, but I have a book about it somewhere, maybe I'll give you that one to read too" I said frustrated.

"Okay, okay. Sorry, you are just so full of info, I figured you would know."

"I don't know everything, you know that!" I yelled in frustration.

"I know. We'll go through the books tonight. We'll pick the bugs off with our hands today so it doesn't get out of control" he said agreeing. "I was just trying to save us time since there's so much to do" he explained.

"Thank you." I ended the conversation.

Picking bugs off of our plants was a full time job for four people, and it seemed that Charles and Rita were doing the same on their property. But it was not just the bug picking, it was seeing that the plants were not all healthy. I knew I could not expect a perfect garden, but I was hoping that problems would not arrive for a couple years. The difficulty was in diagnosing the problems. Fortunately, I had ordered some cards from an organic garden center that had pictures of problems and talked about how to deal with them. I had ordered some things that I knew I would need, like Neem oil. But overall, we were very limited on what we had to treat plant problems.

"Rachel, I think we have another problem." Tom had come up to me in the garden holding a chicken.

"What's wrong" I asked.

"I think this chicken has mites" he said. I got up from my kneeling position and inspected the chickens butt as he was holding the chicken by its feet and had it upside down, making it easy to see. I saw the black round bugs on the butt of the chicken.

"Yep, we have mites" I said.

"Will we have to dunk them in chemical treatment like we did back in the city? I'm not sure if we have any more." Tom asked.

"We have some flowers that we can use; they contain pyrethrum. We can spray the chicken area and dunk the chickens in water with the ground up flowers. Repeat it every week until we know the problem is gone, and not allow any wild birds into the chicken area, as they are a major carrier of mites. So we'll have to keep the bird netting permanently." We had set up bird netting when we discovered the birds eating our chicken feed. It was not just a few birds, it was a flock of birds we were feeding.

"Which flowers?" To asked.

"The chrysanthemums" I answered.

"Oh, I remember, you're right, that's why we have them all over the garden too. They repel other bugs don't they?" Tom asked.

"Yes. I have some in containers on the deck, we should use those for the chickens" I suggested. Tom started to ask "how do we do it?... Never mind, I know which book to look for." Tom left and I went back to picking my bugs off the plants. There were so many. The aphids, I do not know where they came from, but they had made themselves at home on the plants as well.

We managed to spray the chicken area and dunk every single chicken up to their necks. They were quite unhappy with us, but oh well. We knew we could not eat the eggs for at least a week, but that was okay, because we had plenty of them accumulating again. We actually had too many so we increased our egg intake to help keep the eggs under control. If there was only a better way to store them. We had previously tried to dehydrate them, but with no luck. Someone had even suggested freezing them first, and then dehydrating, but still no luck, the rehydrated eggs were just plain inedibly gross.

"Rachel, the doe gave birth, we have a kid!" Tom was running excited.
"Just one?" I tried not to sound disappointed, but I really hoped for twins. Tom saw my disappointment and said "well, she might not be done yet, but yeah, only one came out so far." I followed Tom out the back door making sure not to let the dogs out.
"I don't think two of those would fit inside her" he said as he pointed at the healthy looking kid. He was right, two would not have fit.
"Yay, we will have milk again!" I started to get excited.
"Well, the kid gets first dibs" Tom reminded.
"She'll produce more than he needs, so don't worry. Wait, is it a he?" I asked. Tom said "I don't know, let me check." Tom walked closer slowly, he did not want to disturb the doe's natural process. He got on all fours and started inspecting "I think it's a girl" he said. "Well, that works too, maybe we can score another male again" I said, thinking out loud.

There was something about seeing the kid, a life created, it was beautiful. This meant milk and meat. It was an exciting time. I bet Terry and Sam will be thrilled as well, but they had decided to go to the weekly meeting. Tom had decided not to go this time, the meetings were becoming useless. And while barter days were better due to the weather, we didn't really need anything just yet that we were wiling to barter for. Terry and Sam went solely to keep up with any news, but we all agreed it was really a waste of time more than anything. We hoped they would see Roy, he had not been around lately, and we figured we would go see him if he was not at barter days. We figured at least he would come by to get milk and eggs by now, but he has not, so we hoped he was okay.

We decided to leave the doe and the kid alone. Nothing was better than letting mom take care of her young. Neither of us had much veterinary skill, so we let nature take its course. Fortunately at least that occurred without any complications. We headed back to the house and sat down. This was the first time in a long time that Tom and I were alone together. It was a nice change. Although I liked my weekly mornings alone, after our hiding out incident, I really missed Tom, and was happy we were together again. Being alone together was a nice added bonus.

"You think we'll be able to get another male goat?" Tom asked.

"I think so, though it might be harder to barter something" I replied.

"We have tons of food already, and we still have stuff maturing in the gardens, we should have plenty, and we also have canned goat stew" he said.

"I meant to ask, I noticed Marshmallow wasn't in the root cellar, so I figured that you took care of him, but when?" I asked.

"After the guards left, Jake and I needed to stay busy until I knew it was safe to come get you, so Jake showed me how to make goat jerky. Actually, he ended up making it all, I just watched. He made jerky out of the pieces that were usable, and I made stew out of the pieces that would not work for jerky. The last batch of jerky was still in the dehydrator when you got back, but I didn't want to bother you with it, so we just took care of it. I'm surprised you didn't notice until now."

"We were exhausted, you would think that camping out for a week would be easy, but we had to mentally work hard to keep positive thoughts. I don't want to do that again" I explained.

Tom gave me a reassuring look and said "I'm sure you don't. I wouldn't have wanted to do it in the first place."

"I think it would have been different if you were with me, but you weren't" I said.

"Well, we're together now, that's what matters." Tom smiled at me and gave me a hug. We sat in silence for what seemed like forever, until we heard what sounded like horses coming. We looked out the living room window and saw two horses.

"John, good to see you, and Jake, I see things are working out at home?" Tom asked.

"Sure are, good to have my son on my side again" John replied.

"So what brings you two by?" I asked.

"Well, we had some discussions, and wanted to talk to you. Do you have some time right now?" Jake asked.

"Yeah, a little, come on in" I said. We let John and Jake inside and pulled out some folding chairs and all sat down.

Then Tom asked "is this something you want Sam and Terry here for?"

"Nah, you can talk to them when they get back." John responded.

"So..." I said after a brief silence.

John started "well, here's the thing, it's been almost a year since things fell apart, and, well, things are not really getting better. There are threats of gangs looting and occupying small towns, government officials are still corrupt and destructive, people are hungry, there's no fuel, things are just not getting better. Instead of re-building, it seems people are still destroying."

Tom agreed "that's true, I never hear good news on the ham radios. It's all bad, though the gangs haven't been interested in this area – yet. I think this area may not be considered prosperous enough to make it a priority; an economic camouflage if you will. But that could change as resources become scarce elsewhere."

"Or maybe it's because we're well hidden and unknown. Such people probably don't think there's much of anything out this way, so they don't bother" John added.

"Right. I'm okay with that" I said.

"Me too. Anyway, this was a tough winter, and I lost quite a few employees due to the cold. Those were good people. There are still a lot of people left in this town, but we'll lose more if we don't do something" John said sternly, with concern.

"I'm not sure what we can do about that" I replied, then added "we only have so many supplies."

"That's just it. Americans are so used to getting things from overseas that everyone has forgotten how to make their own stuff. There's no reason we can't relearn how to do so now" John said excitedly.

"So you're saying you want this town to become more self sufficient so that we don't have to depend on 'imports' – from anywhere?" Tom asked.

"Yes, exactly. And I think that we have enough skills here, when you take all of our combined knowledge, that we can figure things out and start to rebuild" John suggested.

"I agree, we have a lot of books on building and making our own things, including one called *When Technology Fails* or something like that" I said quickly.

"And I have a ton of knowledge from my grandpa that I can pass on. I know all about cattle and how to use them without using advanced technology. I even have antiques that we can start re-using, and maybe even copying and building" John said.

"You mean like your milk jugs that you brought over the milk with?" I asked.

"Yes, exactly" John responded, still excited.

"I think we can make this happen. How do you foresee this working?" Tom asked.

Jake cut in this time "I was thinking that we can turn the weekly meetings to include a lesson in something."

Tom thought for a moment, then said, "I like that idea. That way, people can still work on their land and still only take one day away from their homes."

"Exactly. So you're on board then?" John asked.

"Of course" both Tom and I answered at the same time.

"Great, because Rachel, I want you to do the first one. I know you have canning expertise, and a fancy dehydrator. But I'm sure you know how to build one too. Plus you and Tom used to do stuff like this at the community center before things fell apart." John stated.

"True, we did..." I said hesitating a bit.

"You also have the experience so that you can teach people. And since people have gardens right now, this is the best time to teach that. This way they can preserve their food for the winter" Jake added.

"They don't need electricity if they are using the sun" John reminded me.

"Then it's set. Next Sunday you'll be doing the workshop" John summarized quickly. But I was not convinced that was a good idea. "Well, I would love to, but the last time I showed my face to anyone, we almost got killed, we lost a pregnant goat, and a ton of our stored supplies were stolen" I argued.

John was quick to respond "I know, and I'm sorry that happened. The people of this town are sorry. But, if it's any consolation, Jenny left to work for the government, so she's gone."

"That doesn't mean someone else won't turn me in" I continued to argue.

"True, but if you're offering a wealth of knowledge, I think they're unlikely to turn you in. Plus you can't hide forever" Jake was trying to convince me too.

"I know, but it's still a risk" I said.

Tom interjected "It's a huge risk, I'm not sure I like this idea. Someone else can do the workshop."

There was silence for a moment, and finally John broke the silence. "Let me take care of that. I need your knowledge out there, and I'll make sure that no one turns you in."

"How are you going to do that?" Tom asked, he was as much convinced as I was, in other words, he was not at all.

John then said in a very confident tone "basically, I'm going to tell them that if anyone squeals on anyone in this town for any stupid reason, and brings authorities through our town again, then they'll be permanently cut off from my ranch."

"You think that'll work?" I asked.

"Yep, most people are depending on my cattle right now" John was to the point.

Tom argued back "but the Federal's are offering bounties of food and supplies for turning people in. That could be enough incentive to overcome the risk of being cut off from your ranch."

"Do you think they'll actually be able and willing to deliver on that?" John quipped.

"Based on how the guard acted here, probably not..." Tom admitted.

"Okay, but if I have to hide out in the woods for another two weeks, I am *not* going to be happy" I stated.

"Don't worry, it'll be fine. I'll spread the word and convince the town's people that this is the way to go. And if you need supplies for the workshop, let's talk about it. Jake and I will help you get that together" John sounded excited again.

"I'll probably need some stuff, but I need some time to prepare" I was still not convinced. Buying myself a little time might help me make a better decision on this.

"We can come by in a couple days if you want" Jake replied.

"That would be great" I stated, then added I'll also come up with a list of some of our other knowledge, like canning, bio-diesel, garden..."

"You know how to make bio-diesel??!!" John jumped out of the folding camping chair.

Tom began to explain, "well, we haven't been doing it regularly because there has not been enough vegetable oil available. But we have done it, and we have books on it. We have all of the equipment and supplies except the oil. We have a limited amount of methanol, but enough to make several batches. The main problem is, when fuel and food are both in short supply, food takes precedence, so not enough vegetable oil for fuel."

John was still excited "if I could run my diesel tractor this year, it would reduce a great deal of labor!"

"Then I guess we'll be working on that as well. But we still need oil of some sort" Tom replied.

John stood there thinking for a while. "I'll think of something. I'll keep in touch." With that, he put his hat on, then Jake put his hat on, and they started to walk out the door.

"Wait, can we ask a small favor?" I stopped them from leaving.

"Sure" John replied.

"Since you have transportation, do you think you could swing by Roy's place and check in on him, we haven't heard from him in a while." I could tell my voice had worry in it.

"Yeah, his place is on our way home, so no problem. You want me to send him over if we see him?"

"We have some eggs for him, and goat milk if he needs it" Tom blurted out.

"Eggs? We wouldn't mind some eggs ourselves" John reminded.

"Of course, how could I forget? Let me go get you a few dozen." What a relief I thought. We needed to get rid of some of our eggs, so this worked out nicely. Then if Roy comes by, then even better. I went to the kitchen and got 6 dozen eggs out of the fridge. Although we are taking a week off during the pyrethrum treatment, we are averaging almost 30 eggs a day. We had cracked and frozen a bunch, but we really needed to use or get rid of some of them. I walked back to the front door and handed them six dozen eggs.

"Four dozen for you, and two dozen for Roy. You don't mind dropping them off do you?" I asked.

"Not at all, but if he's not there?" Jake asked.

"Then keep them all, we have plenty. Let me get you a bag." I went back to the kitchen and dug out a plastic grocery bag that I had saved from the old days when you could go to the grocery store and they were available for free. I had folded and stored them all this time. Now we had a use for them. I grabbed two, and put three dozen eggs in each, then handed them back to John. They got on their horses and left.

"I hope Roy is alright" Tom said with concern.

I tried to think optimistically. "He's probably fine, though I'm sure he still hopes his kids will show."

"Yeah, it's too bad we never found them" Tom lamented.

"Like a needle in a haystack" I consoled.

I wanted to change the topic, and stated to Tom "I'm not sure I want to do this workshop. Maybe I can teach Sam everything and she can do it for me."

"I think it'll be a good way to turn people on your side" Tom argued.

"I thought you didn't like the idea?" I questioned him.

"I don't, but I thought about it, and I think that's what everyone needs - a good teacher to instruct them how to survive" Tom defended.

"Guess I better get the books out and start planning" I conceded.

Tom continued, "I like John's, it'll really help this town. I bet if we put all our skills together, we can really be successful."

"All the more reasons for the gangs to come here" I was still concerned about the potential consequences.

"That's why I listen to the hams every day, plus really, how would the gangs know that a town is successful?" Tom asked.

"Luck?" I quipped.

Now Tom was being optimistic "not so much. I think John is onto something."

We were interrupted by the dogs running to the living room window. Sam and Terry must have returned. We both got up to look, and sure enough, they were getting off their bikes. They moved the bikes into the garage, locked it, and started to come toward the house when we finally let the dogs out. The dogs were just too excited to greet them.

"Anything new?" Tom asked while walking towards them.

"Well, maybe. There's a rumor that starting next week there'll be some educational workshops" Terry replied with an excited tone.

"Oh yeah, what kind of work shops?" I asked with a sly tone in my voice.

Terry answered "well, from what we hear, the first one will be about dehydrating fruits and vegetables, and how to do it with what you've got."

Tom and I just looked at each other, John must have known I would agree.

"Interesting. Did they say who would be running the workshop?" I asked curiously.

Sam explained "not really, just that an expert would be doing so. Which is funny, because when we heard, we first thought of you. You're the only expert around here that we know."

Tom and I again just stared at each other. I did not know what to think. Either this was a sign of progress, or a sign of trouble, I hoped it was the former.

"Yeah, guess it should be interesting to see" Terry added.

"Changing topics, I think something might be wrong with the doe" Sam looked worried.

"What? what do you mean?" I asked.

"Haven't you heard it?" Sam asked.

"No, what are you talking about?" Tom answered for me. He was probably upset that he missed something going on around the property, as he prided himself on being attentive to what was going on in case any problems arise.

"The doe, she sounds like she's in agony" Sam explained.

Tom and I looked at each other again, then we immediately headed for the back door. It felt like it took a long time for us to get out to the goat area, though I am sure it took only a couple minutes. When we got to the fence, we saw that our doe was lying down, on her side, and looked in pain.

"What's wrong with her?" I asked Tom.

"I don't know, I'm not a vet!" he shot back.

"Sorry, you're right. What do you THINK is wrong with her?" I clarified.

"I don't know, I'm not a psychic" Tom added sarcastically.

"Come on, I'm asking an honest question" I pleaded.

"Well like I said, I don't know. It would be counterproductive for me to speculate at this point" he explained. "Let's go take a look at her."

We opened the gate and walked in. Her kid was off in another section of the pasture. As we got closer, I noticed that she was on the ground and shaking. Her eyes looked glazed. Her pupils were trying to go up towards the back of her head and they were shaking... no, not shaking, trembling.

"I think she might have an infection. She might be septic." Tom finally had constructive input.

"That's it? An infection?" I asked.

"Yeah" Tom replied bluntly. "We have antibiotics."

We had purchased quite a bit actually. We bought them from a veterinary supplier. Tom had researched it, and found that certain brands of animal antibiotics are made on the same production line as the ones for humans - except that the ones for animals did not require a prescription to purchase.

"Except I don't know which ones to use" Tom continued. "Normally lab technicians would take a sample, grow a culture of the bacteria, and determine which type it is and what antibiotics it is susceptible to. The best we could do would be to look at a sample under a light microscope and guess."

"Just try all of them, what can it hurt?" I suggested.

Tom gave me a dirty look. He knew I knew nothing when it came to the health field. This was one of the few times that he made me feel stupid for saying anything. That look always put me in my place, or whatever you wanted to call it.

"It's not that simple…" he tried to explain.

"Yes Tom, I know that!" I yelled. "But it doesn't matter if it's simple or not, the questions is, do you know what to do, or don't you?" I was starting to panic.

Tom responded calmly to my stress. "Not with any certainty. My training is for humans. I don't really know anything about livestock diseases."

"Then what options does that leave us?" I asked.

"If we give her everything, then we have nothing left for us." Tom made a good point.

"Then what is the most likely thing causing this, and what can we give her?" I clarified.

Tom started to brainstorm out loud. "Well, I think it's unlikely that it is rumen related, so either bacterial or birth related. Since she gave birth recently my first guess would be firth related. But that is not a guarantee."

I tried to help reason through the dilemma "how do we differentiate?"

"I don't know, let me think." Tom stared off into space for what felt like hours. I just watched our goat's eyes, it was creepy to say the least.

Tom finally reasoned out a plan. "If I take her temperature, I can at least see if she has a fever."

"There is a thermometer in the goat house just for such occasions, do you want me to get it?" I asked.

"No, I'll get it. That will give me more time to think." Tom started walking toward the goat house. I kneeled down by the doe's head and started talking to her soothingly. It was hard. If we lost her, we would lose the kid, and then we were screwed. I saw Tom jogging back.

"It shouldn't be a birthing problem. She's lean, not overweight, so that should really cut out any problems due to having a kid." Tom stuck the thermometer into her rectum without any thought. When he took it out he said "she has a fever, probably a bacterial infection. Do we have any pedialyte?"

"Yes. It's old and probably expired, but we have some" I answered.

"Can you get some?" Tom requested.

"Sure." I rushed back to the house to find the bins that had the medical supplies. I knew we bought lots of pedialyte, it just a matter of finding which bin they were in. Found it; I knew we had lots. I rushed back out to see Tom moving the goat from side to side.

"Blood circulation is really important right now" he explained. I just stared. To be honest, I had no idea what Tom was doing. This was his thing, not mine.

"Look, I need you to try to get some pedialyte down her throat. She's going to need fluids, and I'm only prepared to use IVs on people. I need to go get some antibiotics." With that, Tom rushed to the house, at which point I tried to get the doe to drink the pedialyte. That was a much harder job than anyone could imagine. For one, she wanted nothing to do with it; she kept spitting it out. And second, it was really gross when she spat it in my face. Regardless, I kept trying. I had brought down four bottles of pedialyte, and I am pretty sure the first one was all over me. That was not a good thing. I had not noticed Terry and Sam come up behind me, but they asked if they could help. I told them that if they could help me get the pedialyte down, that would be more help than anything. Sam kneeled down next to me, and went to hold the doe's head, while Terry petted the rest of her.

Tom came back holding some concoction of something. It looked pink I thought, though I was not really sure.

"It's just amoxicillin for gram positives mixed with some azithromycin for broader spectrum effect. Nothing fancy" he said as he started to bring the oral syringe full to her mouth. Sam and I held her down so that Tom could get the mix into her. "We are going to have to do this twice a day for at least 10 days" he explained.

"Okay. How do we know it's working?" I asked.

"We won't at first. But we have to make sure she stays hydrated" Tom explained.

"Keep giving her pedialyte?" I asked.

"Yes, and water too, Tom answered. "Pedialyte is nowhere near enough. Here, use this syringe." Tom handed us the oral syringe he used to give her the antibiotics.

"Anything else?" I asked.

"We need to feed the kid. I doubt he's getting healthy milk from her." Tom made another good point I had not considered.

"We have canned cow milk, that should work right?" I suggested.

"Yes, but if we have any goat milk, let's use that up first. It's more nutritionally appropriate" Tom explained.

"We should have plenty, but how far back can we use it? We don't know how long she's been sick" I pointed out.

"Anything we got this last week needs to go, so probably the canned milk will have to do" he responded.

"Is a week enough?" I wondered.

"I don't know, do we have enough to make it two?" Tom asked.

"If it's safer that way, then yes." I figured I could make it work.

"Then fine, two weeks it is" Tom agreed.

"Do we have enough antibiotics?" I asked.

Tom's answer was reassuring. "Oh yeah, I ordered quite a bit. We should be good for a while." Tom gave me the look again; I knew what the look meant. It meant he ordered more than enough, probably more than we could afford. But as with the body armor, I am glad he did so.

"We should also keep milking her so she does not dry up, we just can't use her milk" Tom recommended.

We stayed with the doe giving her pedialyte and water, though Sam took off to take care of the milk. She dumped out last two week's milk into the out house, then brought the kid canned milk and started to feed the kid.

"I think that should do it. Let's just let her be for now, and we'll give her another dose tonight. We should also put her inside tonight." As soon as Tom finished talking, we heard the sound of horses running.

"John and Jake shouldn't be back yet" I said.

"No, they shouldn't. Wonder if Roy is alright?" Tom was thinking out loud.

We ran toward the front of the house and arrived at the same time as John and Jake on their horses.

"Tom, Terry, you need to come with us. Tom, you can ride with me. Terry, ride with Jake." The looks on their faces told us not to question it. Tom and Terry complied and got on the horses with the help of John and Jake. They were off before we even realized it.

Sam turned to me "you think Roy is alright?"

"I don't know. But they wouldn't be riding like that if he was" I answered.

"This looked serious" Sam commented.

"Yes, it did. But if he was dead, then I don't think there'd be such a rush" I thought out load. We stood there in silence a while, shocked. Then I began to snap out of it. "Sam, they'll probably be exhausted when they come back. I think I'm going to cook up a big meal, and keep it warm in the oven until they come back. I'll make enough for six, no wait, seven. And I'll dig out one of the medical bins, just in case."

"Good idea. Think we should make an extra bed?" Sam asked.

"Something tells me it won't hurt for us to do so" I replied.

Sam and I proceeded to go inside. The dogs were napping and unaware that we may have additional guests again, or at least I hoped we would have additional guests.

Sam and I worked quietly. I cooked up a big pot of vegetables, mostly broccoli, cabbage, spinach, kale, and green onion. We had to harvest the cold tolerant stuff as we did not want it to bolt and go to seed with the heat coming on. We had our seed plants set aside, but still had plenty of vegetable plants. I decided for the main entrée, I would make quiche with beef of some sort, or whatever we had canned. I mixed all that up and threw it in the oven. We were completely out of rice, and we did not have any potatoes planted, as the potato's we tried to save rotted before we could get them in the ground. The corn was not quite ready yet, though I thought there were still a few cans left in storage. I checked the list, and sure enough, there were two cans left. I brought them out, but did not do anything with them. I kept them out just in case we needed a starch for any reason. While the vegetables were steaming, and the beef quiche was baking, I checked in on Sam. She had collected a ton of blankets, sheets, towels and whatever else she could find, and had put it by the front door.

She then made room in the living room and proceeded to make a bed out of all the fabric she has found.

Sam explained, "it's not too uncomfortable, so he should be okay if he ends up here."

I walked over and laid down on her jimmy rigged bed. "No, not bad at all, I could sleep on this" I said reassuringly. We continued to move stuff away from the front door, just in case they had to carry Roy in.

During this time, Compass decided that the new bed was the perfect size for him, and proceeded to move towards it. "No, no!" we both went yelling. Compass gave us a dirty look, then proceeded to go back to sleep on his dog bed. "Maybe we should block it off from the dogs?" Sam asked. Good idea I thought and nodded. We started collecting bins and chairs, and made a barrier around the bed so that the dogs could not get to it. After that, I checked on the quiche and vegetables. I was able to turn off the vegetables and put them in a casserole dish. Then I waited for the timer to go off for the quiche. Once that was done, I turned the oven down to warm, and put the vegetables in there with the quiche. At that point Sam and I went to check on the animals.

At dusk, I fed the dogs and put all the animals away. I was starting to get worried about the guys. They had been gone for quite a while. Just as I really began to worry, I heard the horses trotting. They were not going as fast this time, but they were coming back. Sam and I both hurried to the front door to meet them, to find out what was going on, and to see if they needed help. As I saw them approaching, I saw that John's horse had the trailer hooked up to it, and on the trailer was a mattress with what was probably Roy. This could not be good. I ran inside the house and locked the dogs in the master bedroom. I then cleared the area that we had set up for Roy's bed. Since he had a bed, there was no reason to keep the sheets on the floor. I cleared a spot, and the guys started to bring the mattress up to the house, but stopped at the door.

Tom spoke first. "Rache, we shouldn't touch his wounds, but we can't fit the mattress through the door with him on it. What we did to get him out of his house was to have two of us lift him, and two of us quickly move the mattress in, then move him in after the mattress. But we really should be careful about what we touch."

"I have dishwashing gloves that go up past the elbows, do you want those?" I offered.

"Yes, and some face masks. Do we still have those around?" Tom asked.

"Yes." I ran to the kitchen and searched for the bins that had those items. I knew they were next to the medical bins somewhere. It took me going through a few of them, but I finally found them, got them out, and brought them to Tom. He put on the Personal Protective Equipment, and then proceeded to grab Roy's legs, while Jake grabbed Roy's upper half. They lifted him while John and Terry turned the mattress sideways, brought it in, turned it back, and put it down. Tom and Jake then brought Roy in and lowered him down on to the mattress.

"Thanks Rache. His infection originated on his legs, that's why I wore the equipment" Tom explained.

"What's wrong with him?" I asked. You could see the abscesses and wounds; his right leg was covered in them, all the way from his knee down to his ankle. To put it mildly, it looked terrible. "Rache, do we still have any hard liquor? And I need both the ibuprofen and acetaminophen" Tom was barking orders.

"Yeah, we've never used any of it, I'll go get it." I rushed to the washer dryer area to move the dryer, Sam was right behind me to help. I moved the dryer over, and opened the hatch, then got on my belly so that I can lean in with my arms to grab the boxes of wine, which also had the bottles whiskey in them. No luck, my arms were too short. I got up and then jumped in the hole, grabbed the box, and lifted it over my head. Sam grabbed it from me, and I went for the second box, which Sam helped me get as well. She then helped me get out of the crawl space. I then tore open the plastic bags to find the box with the whiskey, while Sam got the meds from the cupboard. I handed the whiskey to Sam as soon as I found it, who took off to give everything to Tom. I closed the hatch and moved the dryer back, then put the wine boxes on top of the washer and dryer each.

I went into the medical supplies again and grabbed things I thought Tom might need. I realized we had tons of medical supplies. "Tom, we still have rubbing alcohol, do you want that? We have povidone iodine solution too!"

"Yes, bring it all – especially the iodine!" he yelled back. I yelled to Sam, "screw it, let's just take all three of these bins. We 'll hand Tom stuff as he needs it." She nodded and grabbed a bin as did I, and she followed me back to the living room. I then rushed back for the third bin. Tom started requesting items, and we would look for them and hand them to him.

Tom handed the open bottle of whiskey to Roy, who already seemed to have a diminished level of consciousness. Since we weren't able to stock up on any narcotic pain meds, we had to make due with what we had. Tom convinced Roy to take two each of the ibuprofen and acetaminophen, and then follow them with a swig of whiskey. As soon as Roy did that, Tom started irrigating Roy's wounds with an irrigation syringe. He used a mixture of 1% povidone iodine and 70% isopropyl alcohol to irrigate Roy's wounds. Roy winced as he did so, and Tom started to explain to the rest of us what he was doing. "He has a severe infection, probably staph, maybe MRSA - it's pretty serious. He probably got it because of his ischemia, he's more at risk. This irrigation solution is pretty harsh on human tissue, but he's at high risk of becoming septic, so we need to sterilize the wounds."

I looked at Tom confused, then asked "I understand how staph happens, but how did he get that gash on his leg?" Tom was busy reaching in his medical kit and did not answer. Jake answered for him. "He was shot."

"By whom?" I gasped.

"One of the guards that left here" Jake elaborated.

"What? But they left days, if not weeks ago?" I wondered.

"Yep. That's why his infection is so bad" Tom interrupted. "He has a fever, and his blood pressure is rather low. My first thought was blood loss, but Roy seemed to have done a good job of stopping the bleeding. So I suspect that he's developed sepsis or septicemia, which could explain why he's in shock right now. At least he's still breathing okay, so I don't have to use a nasopharyngeal or oropharyngeal airway on him. But I don't know how bad the damage is, or what organs may have been affected by the infection." Tom stopped working on Roy's wounds and instead started a normal saline IV in his arm.

As he did so he continued, "Rache, make sure you keep the dogs out. And anyone and everyone, strict hand washing is required, his exudate is probably contagious. Rache, we still have hand sanitizer somewhere?"

"Yes, and extra boxes of disposable gloves too. I'll leave them out so they're available to everyone." I dug through the bins that had all the medical supplies. I also checked on the pups in our master bedroom and left them there. We ran out of rawhides a long time ago, but we still had their chewy balls that seemed to be indestructible, so I gave them those to keep them pacified.

When I got back to the living room Tom continued to explain the situation.

"MRSA staph infections are resistant to most penicillins, so I normally would not bother with those. What I really need is vancomycin, teicoplanin or other glycopeptides. Unfortunately, because those drugs are IV administration only, they weren't available to purchase through the veterinary suppliers, so we don't have any of those."

"Do we have any penicillins? I asked. Or are those completely pointless?"

"We have ampicillin and amoxicillin, but those will probably not be effective if it's a MRSA infection. Even our ciprofloxacin may not be effective against that. With the limited selection of oral antibiotics we have, doxycycline is probably our best bet. I don't know if his digestive system will be able to process it, or if it will work, but it's worth a try. Anything is better than nothing at this point. Terry, the antibiotics are in their sealed packages in the fridge. Can you get the bottle that says doxycycline, and when you get back see if you can get Roy to swallow one of the 100mg capsules."

"Sure." Terry darted off to the kitchen as soon as he had responded.

Tom still had his face mask and gloves on, and went back to treating Roy's wounds. He continued to explain "It looks like

278

the bullet went in just below his knee, but it's not clear where it came out. The wounds make it look like the bullet fragmented in his leg, causing multiple wound channels. Some fragments might still be in there, but I don't know where. The bullet hit his leg in a downward direction. It shattered his tibia and the damage followed down his leg. Some of the fragments might be bone fragments. I don't know how far any of it went, or if any of these abscesses are from exit wounds." At this point Tom was feeling around with a surgical probe. Roy was out of it, but coming in and out of consciousness.

"Tom, I hate to interrupt" I said, "but I need to know what to give the doe."

"Oh, yeah, there's a bottle in the fridge, it's pre-mixed, the pink stuff, give her one syringe full and make sure she continues to get pedialyte and water." I ran to the fridge, grabbed the pink bottle, found the syringe we used earlier, and saw Sam behind me with the pedialyte. We headed out the back door to take care of the doe. We managed to medicate her, and she did much better drinking the pedialyte and water this time. Sam then ran back in for more milk to feed the kid. We struggled getting the doe into her goat house for the evening, but managed.

"Just not a good day today" I mumbled.

"No, it's not" Sam agreed.

We looked at each other sadly, then headed back inside the house. Tom was convincing Roy to keep drinking – both water and whiskey, and was telling him he had to get some fragments out. Tom managed to open up Roy's leg with a scalpel, found a bullet fragment about two thirds of the way down to his ankle, and removed it. He asked for sterile saline solution, which we did have. But in case we ever ran out, Tom taught me the recipe for it. Add eight grams of pure sodium chloride with no additives, to one liter of distilled (or boiled) water, mixed in a sterilized container.

At this point I could not handle the sight or smell of the wound anymore. It was infected terribly inside. Tom was going all out to clean it, sterilize it, whatever it took. Tom eventually said "I'm neither qualified, skilled, nor equipped enough to perform an amputation, so this is the best I can do." He then asked for a sterile suture kit. I pulled one out of the bin, but could not bare to look in that direction anymore. Sam grabbed it from me and handed it to Tom. I was getting nauseous, so I moved to the kitchen to keep from vomiting.

It felt like forever, but Tom finally gave a signal that he was done. I stayed in the kitchen, as I figured there were plenty of people in the living room left to help. Tom then said "we need to clean very thoroughly around this area where I was working. We can not afford for any of this to spread. Wear gloves and use highly concentrated bleach because I don't think we have anything else." He was right, we did not. I grabbed the bottle of bleach and poured it in the bucket, I did not bother with water. I then grabbed a fresh roll of paper towels, and double lined a plastic garbage bag. I donned gloves, and then Sam stopped me. "I know you can't look at that mess, I can tell it's making you nauseous. Let me clean it up, and don't worry." I was relieved. I handed her the supplies, and proceeded to wash my hands and sit down.

I saw Tom throw his gloves in Sam's trash, and then he proceeded to clean himself with alcohol gel, then soap and water. I could tell from his face that he did not feel hopeful, either because we did not have the right antibiotics, or because Roy's condition was so poor when they found him. That was not his fault though; we could only do what we could do. I wanted to comfort him, but he seemed pre-occupied with cleaning up. "Everyone, you need to scrub your hands real well, scrub any exposed part of your body as well." I quickly got up and grabbed another fresh roll of paper towels to hand to everyone. As I passed by Tom I knew from his eyes that Roy was not going to make it.

Three days later we buried Roy back on his property, where he would have wanted to be. It was a sad time for all of us. Roy was a good friend, and had been since we moved here. We knew all along that times would be tough, but this one hit too close to home.

Chapter 11

Hope for America

"Rache, are you ready? We need to get to town already" Tom was rushing me again.

"Yes yes, I'm hurrying" I replied. I had made a ton of notes of things I wanted to cover. John and Jake had come by a few days ago and I gave them hand drawn plans of what they could build out of wood. They promised to bring it to the presentation. "Okay, ready, just needed to get all my notes so I don't forget anything" I tried to reassure Tom I was really ready. I did not feel ready though.

"I'm sure you'll do fine, but we gotta go, bike riding takes a long time" Tom kept rushing me.

"Everyone's waited an extra week, they can wait an extra five minutes" I retorted.

Due to the death in our "family," we cancelled Sunday's event, but promised to provide it the following Sunday, which was today. It was tough dealing with Roy's death, and then his funeral, and then figuring out what to do about his place. We decided to leave it just as is, but well locked up, should his kids return. We did check for perishable and expired food, and took that. No reason to see it go to waste. Tom told me in private that he knew from the second he saw Roy that he probably was not going to make it. But Tom felt he had to try his best - there was always the chance of a miracle. We did not get that miracle, and it seemed like not many other people did this past winter either.

Our doe was fine. She was recovering and standing on her own on day four. She had better luck than Roy. We still had to keep the kid away from her so he would not be drinking her milk. She finished her course of antibiotics, so now it was just a matter of time before the kid could have her milk again. We still continued to milk her, and also continued to pour the milk into the outhouse.

The ham radios had been super active the last few days. Gang activity seemed to have increased significantly. But rumor had it that even the gangs were getting weaker, more desperate, doing stupid things. We hoped they would wipe themselves out before they discovered our little town. Maybe we would get lucky with that aspect of things as well. The TV news had turned into a voice with a picture of a person, and the voice did not even sound like it matched the person in the picture. The "news" said nothing useful really, and there were nights that the news did not even come on, apparently neither did the power during those times.

We arrived on our bikes just in time to hear John speak. I saw the dehydrators that he and Jake must have built on a table behind him. There was quite a large crowd today. I was a bit surprised, or maybe it just seemed large to me since I had not been in a crowd in over a year. John started speaking.

Welcome everyone, I'm glad to see so many of us still here, and so many of us willing to learn new skills. Before we get started, I want to say a few things. First, I want to apologize for the week long delay. As I'm sure you are aware, we lost a close friend of ours two weeks ago. We lost him because someone in this town felt it necessary to bring in the so-called "authorities." Those goons are gone now, and by the way, I don't recognize them as having any legitimate authority, since I did not get to elect any of the people currently claiming to be political leaders.

Real leaders lead by example, principles, and action, not by edict. Regardless, someone in this town brought in those goons, and those so called "authorities" took it upon themselves to steal our precious supplies, and shoot anyone that they felt like shooting.

When we found Roy, he had very little life left in him. But he told us, in his struggling gasps, that the guards had shot him over his heart medication. They told him that his medicine was not authorized, so when they found it in his bathroom, they were going to take it away. He refused to let them, and they shot him, took all his medication, and left him for dead. We found him too late unfortunately, and he developed a staph infection that had progressed too far to be curable with the antibiotics we had available here. Our friend Tom did what he

282

could with the oral antibiotics and medical supplies that he had. But without strong intravenous antibiotics, there was little hope.

Many of you knew Roy. He helped you build your deck, he moved out your old appliances, he always had a smile. He is greatly missed, by all of us. I ask that we have a moment of silence in memory of Roy....

After a long moment, John continued speaking.

My friends, my neighbor's, my employees, and, my family. This is an opportunity for us to restore our community, and our country. But we must work together. We must be willing to set aside our petty differences. We must be willing to look at facts and reality and see the truth, despite what information we're fed from elsewhere. We must not fight among ourselves, and if possible, try to watch out for one another. And I can assure you, if anyone brings any so-called "authorities" through here again, I will make sure that you will never eat from my ranch. You will be booted out of this town and never welcomed back. That was what happened with our recent deserter who tried to return when she discovered that the so called "government" only offered lies and deception in exchange for her support. To bring such callous, ruthless people into our town is a betrayal, and as you all have learned, only results in loss of life of the innocent. Roy was a good man. I had known him all my life. He did not deserve to die the way he did, and I will always hold those people accountable for their actions; just as I will hold anyone here accountable who does anything similar. The "government" personnel are not here to help, they are here to steal from you, and to kill you if they please.

With that said, I would like to now tell you how we're going to fix this town, how we're going to make it as a small community, and how we're going to restore America starting right here. From this day forward, we only follow the philosophy of the US Constitution, including individual liberty and individual sovereignty. We don't need to have an encyclopedia length set of rules to get along, nor "high priest" lawyers to interpret the "magical laws." It's not complicated. Don't aggress against others or their property. In other words, don't kill, assault or steal. And actually respect people's property rights. Honor your word or contract; do what you say you are going to do. And don't do anything stupid that will destroy the environment outside your own land – like start a fire that spreads out of control and burns down someone else's place. If you ruin your own place, well, that's your problem. Take responsibility for yourselves and your own families first and foremost, but be willing to help others if you can.

Any so-called "laws" set forth outside of this town and outside of common sense and outside of Constitutional principles, which have not been voted for by all of us directly, are not recognized by this town, and shall be ignored. Circumstances have forced us to rebuild our society from the ground up, so let's do the best job we can, based on sound principles.

From this day forward, we are a community. We should work together, we should teach each other, we should learn from each other. But we should do so not because we are coerced or compelled to do so, but because we freely choose to do so, because it is in our own best interests. Step by step we will learn to recreate skills, abilities, and technologies, locally, and make them better as we can. As a community, we should help take care of those that can't help themselves. Not with handouts, but by teaching them skills that they can use to provide for themselves and survive. We will restore what we once had, but better. This will not happen over night, but it will happen over time. You will see improvement daily, in all of us, and we will keep moving forward.

So, with all that said, I would like to introduce Rachel. Rachel has been preserving food for who knows how long. I actually don't know, but I know she makes some mean jerky, and that's coming from me. Let me assure you I'm no stranger to making jerky, but hers is very good. Today she will teach you different methods to preserve your food, with what supplies are available to you, so that you can have a winter that is full of food in your cupboards, and you are not hungry.

284

Oh, one more thing before I bring Rachel out here. I have a little contest. My son Jake came up with the idea actually, and I thought it was a good one. The contest winner will be voted on by everyone based on merit. So here it is. Right here behind me is a simple dehydrator you can build yourself with minimal supplies. It's one that Rachel told me about that she felt was simple enough. Now, Jake and I put this thing together, and yes, it was not difficult. It uses the sun's energy to dehydrate your food, and it just takes a little effort on your part. But here it is, here is the contest: after you learn what Rachel has to teach today, for any one person, or any group of people, that builds a better solar dehydrator, that is simpler than this, or more practical, or I don't know, better in some significant way, 1st prize will win a butchered side of beef from me, ready for dehydrating, and I mean ready, sliced and all. 2nd and 3rd prize will win smaller sections of butchered meat, also ready for the dehydrator. Just add marinade. The idea is, to create incentive, to start people thinking about creating better ways we can all do things. Better technology. That is one of the keys, along with sound principles, that will allow us to rebuild our society, and begin to advance humanity again.

So... the judging will be held two weeks from today, after the workshop we hold in two weeks. We will need some type of voting system, but we'll figure all that out later. Anyway, for what you've all been waiting for, here is Rachel!

I hurried through the crowd to get to the podium. I was surprised to hear clapping instead of booing. I suppose I should not be so cynical, that was quite a speech that John gave; it sure made me feel safer coming up in front of everyone. I did not waste any time, I got straight to business. "How many of you have a car that you can't drive because it's out of gas?" Just about everyone raised their hand. "Guess what? You already have a solar dehydrator. Sure, your car will smell like beef jerky, but it's something that you already have, and can use immediately, though it won't win you a cow." Everyone laughed. This was going better than I expected. The rest of the lesson went just as smoothly, and with the help of my note cards I covered all the details: what you can use for trays, how long to dehydrate, how to preserve with water canning, how to check if the food was done, everything.

It was a good thing I did a lot of public speaking throughout college and in previous jobs, as I was o't nervous one bit - even though I was "wanted" for "murder." I saw the eyes in the crowd, everyone wanted to learn. Everyone wanted to know how to save their garden and survive through winters. This was good. This was the way to rebuilding our community. Everyone shares a bit of their knowledge. True, some have more knowledge than others, but that did not matter. That person who had no knowledge could help spread the knowledge that they gained, and perhaps perform more labor in the process.

By the next winter the townspeople had acquired an amazing amount of skills. Which wild plants were safe to eat, how to trap various animals, how to skin, butcher and cook various animals, how to milk a goat or cow, how to breed animals, how to make methanol, ethanol and bio-diesel, how to make things from leather, how to repair and in some cases make clothes, and how to substitute or improvise for tools we could not make ourselves, how to grow grains, how to grow a vegetable garden, how to root plants and trees, how to build your own water pump that does not require electricity, how to build cold frames, hoop houses, and greenhouses, how to save seed for replanting, how to use a ham radio, how to recycle garbage, how to cut wood manually, how to purify water, how to handle medical emergencies, how to build animal housing, how to improvise women's toiletries, how to make soap, how to best use firearms, how to use bows; the lessons went on and on. It was amazing the amount of knowledge we held collectively.

Our town was lucky. We never got hit by the gangs. Eventually the television news stopped completely. The one hour periods of electricity stopped as well. The "government" as we knew it seemed to have disappeared altogether, at least from our corner of the world. Jake slowly took responsibility for the operations of his father's ranch. John continued to coordinate various people to teach the town various topics. Sam and Terry continued to reside with us for that next year, until we were able to start making some of our own building materials. They repaired their home, and built a brick fire place in the center of it. Little by little we recreated what we used to know, except as John pointed out, we made it better. Other than the communication we had with the outside world via ham radio, our town felt like it was the only place left in tact. And perhaps, we were.

Made in the USA
Lexington, KY
03 October 2012